3 A.M. PREMIUM

(HENRY BINS BOOKS 1 - 5)

NICK PIROG

Copyright © 2018 by Nick Pirog

www.nickthriller.com

3:00 A.M.

:01

One hour. Sixty minutes. Three thousand six hundred seconds. That's how long I get each day. How long I'm awake. I won't bore you with the science of it all; I'd rather get to the story. And what a story it is. And I only have an hour to tell it. But just know that I have seen every doctor and taken every medication in the book and nothing helps. I wake up at 3:00 a.m. each morning and fall asleep an hour later. Then I sleep for twenty-three hours. Then repeat. It isn't much of a life, but it is the only one I know.

I'm thirty-six.

By my age, most people have been awake for over two hundred thousand hours. I've been awake for less than fourteen thousand. According to the doctors, there have only been three people in existence to ever have the condition. Condition, that's what they call it. Not a disease, not an illness, a condition. A young girl in Taiwan has it. And another guy in Iceland. But it's named after me. I had it first. Henry Bins. That's what they call it. I'm Henry Bins and I have Henry Bins.

Anyhow, you might be wondering how I can string two sentences together if I've been awake fewer hours than a normal three-year-old. Well, what can I say? I'm a prodigy. And maybe because God gave me Henry Bins – I'm Henry Bins and I have Henry Bins – He found it only fair to compensate with a brilliant mind.

It's now 3:02. I'd better get started.

...

I open my eyes with a jolt.

It's April 18th. I know this because yesterday was April 17th. And the big electronic clock on my dresser tells me so. The glowing green embers also tell me it is 3:01 a.m.

One minute gone.

I rip the covers off and jump out of bed. I am fully clothed. I'm wearing gray sweatpants, a maroon hooded sweatshirt, and lime green Asics. Next stop, the kitchen. My laptop is sitting on the kitchen table. I hit the mouse pad and the black screen vanishes, replaced by the frozen picture of a castle. I've been watching *Game of Thrones* in ten-minute intervals. I hit the spacebar and the show resumes. Keeping an eye on the screen, I open the fridge and remove a sandwich—roast beef, heavy on the mustard—and a peanut butter protein shake. Both have been premade by Isabel, a Mexican woman who cooks, cleans, and does countless other things I don't have time for.

I pick up my cell phone. No calls. Three text messages. All from my father. Two are pictures of his dog. I message him back that he needs to find a woman and sit down to the computer. I devour the sandwich and the smoothie as I open a separate window and log into my E-Trade account. It's all about multitasking. I can't help but glance at the clock in the bottom right corner.

3:04.

Four minutes gone.

I check my stocks, which look good—I've made roughly eight thousand in the last twenty-four hours—then make some minor tweaks on the parameters I have in place for buys and sells, then close the window. I log onto OkCupid, a dating site, and go through the various messages. Nothing worthwhile. My screen name, NIGHTOWL3AM only attracts the crazies. As you might think, meeting a woman has proven difficult. For many years I would try twenty-four-hour bookstores, coffee shops, or diners, but after three trips to the emergency room and one woman calling her brother to dispose of my dead body, I gave up.

I close the window and devote three minutes of my undivided attention to *Game of Thrones*. I love Tyrion.

At 3:10, I hit pause, grab my iPhone and earbuds and sprint out the door.

It's the beginning of spring and the Alexandria air is cold. I wish I'd worn a beanie, but I don't dare waste the time going to grab one. The streets are silent. Three in the morning must be the quietest time of the day. Even the nocturnal night people have turned in and the crazy, morning folk are still tucked away. But then again, I don't have anything to compare it to. I just know the half hour I spend in the world, it might as well be on mute. I run under the streetlights, the closest thing I know to sunlight, and concentrate on every sensation. The burn in my thighs, the cold air as it travels through my nostrils and down into my lungs.

I force myself to stay in the moment. I don't have time for the past or the future. My life is the present. For many years, I played the *what if* game. What if I had a normal life? Where would I be? Would I be married? Would I have kids? But then twenty or thirty minutes would be gone. Wasted. Thinking about things that I can't change. That are unchangeable.

I listen to three songs by The Lumineers, my new favorite band, then five minutes of Feed the Pig, an investment podcast. It is two miles to the Potomac, a highway of water separating Virginia from Maryland, and I spend a perfect minute watching a trawler sucked downstream by the sweeping black current. I used to wonder what it would look like during the light of day, how the water would look under a burning sun and puffy white clouds, but day doesn't exist in my world. Only night. Only darkness.

As I head back, I see a car turn onto the side street. This is the first car I've seen in six days. It is a Ford Focus. A new one. The Ford stock closed at 13.02. Just saying.

I do the four miles in just under twenty-eight minutes and when I reach my condo steps it is 3:38 a.m.

Twenty-two minutes left.

I do push-ups and sit-ups for three minutes.

I take a four minute shower.

When I pull on a clean set of nearly the same outfit and head back to the kitchen, it is 3:48.

Twelve minutes.

I pull a salad from the fridge: greens, carrots, tomatoes, quinoa, and chicken. Healthy stuff. I grab an apple, two chocolate chips cookies, and a big glass of milk. I sit down at the table and click on my Kindle. I'm reading *Lone Survivor*, about a Navy SEAL who survives a shootout against the Taliban in the Afghanistan mountains. Amazing stuff.

I eat slowly, soak up each word.

I take the last bite of my second chocolate chip cookie at 3:58.

I turn the Kindle off, stand up, and walk toward the bedroom.

I sit down on my bed at 3:59 a.m.

That's when I hear the woman's scream.

I stand up and run to the window. Directly across from my condo is a ranch style house with a gate. The Ford Focus I saw earlier is parked on the street directly in front. I have no idea who lives there. I've never seen them. That could be said for all my neighbors.

I know I should go back to my bed, that I am going to fall over any moment. But I can't. I'm glued to the window. I might as well be stuck between the two panes. I tick off seconds.

The gate opens and a man walks briskly through.

As he opens the door to the Ford Focus, he walks directly under the streetlight. As if sensing my gaze, he turns and looks up. We lock eyes. Then he gets in the car and drives off.

My last thought as my eyes close and I start falling is the chiseled features and piercing stare of the man.

The President of the United States.

:02

By the time I get to my feet, the first minute of my day has already come and gone. My neck is stiff, a consequence of sleeping in such an awkward position, but I count myself lucky. I hadn't hit my head on anything. No blood. No concussion.

I rub my neck as I peer out the window. An echo of the President's face plays over my eyes and I shake my head, eliciting a shooting pain through my sternocleidomastoid—the long muscle running from the clavicle to just below the ear. Could that really have been him? But it was. There wasn't a shadow of a doubt that the man I'd seen was Connor Sullivan. The 44th President of the United States.

I walk to the kitchen and sit down in front of the laptop. After a short couple seconds I have pulled up the bio of Connor Sullivan on Wikipedia. The once three-term Governor of Virginia has dark brown hair parted on the left and gray-green eyes that aren't unlike my own. But that's where the similarities end. Sullivan is the tallest president, dwarfing Lincoln by three inches and Madison by nearly fifteen. He is a head taller than me, which would put me eye-level with the most famous chin dimple in the free world. It only adds to his allure that he was an All-American small forward at Dayton.

I thought about adding a quick update to his long and tedious Wikipedia page: April 18th – murders woman in Alexandria, VA.

On this note, I search the local news outlets for an attack or murder, but come up empty.

My cell phone chirps and I quickly respond to my father's "are-you-still-alive?" texts and know that he will finally be able to sleep knowing his baby boy is alive and well. My mother left when I was six, unable to cope with my disease, leaving my father to care for me. He worked two jobs, sixteen hour days, but he was there every night when I woke up at 3 a.m. He tried to make my life as normal as possible. When I was young, I had twenty minutes of school each morning with Professor Bins. Math, science, spelling – he covered everything. My father was adamant that I develop social skills and would pay parents, literally pay them, to get their kids to come play video games or tag or ping-pong with me for a half hour. (I actually still keep in touch with a couple of them on Facebook.) My dad would call in favors or shell out grand sums of money for establishments to make special arrangements for me. On my tenth birthday I woke up at an amusement park. For an hour the two of us had the whole park to ourselves. When I was eighteen he set up a prom for me. The girl was the daughter of a woman he worked with, and she wasn't all that cute, but it had been exciting nonetheless and I did get a quick kiss out of it. He administered my SATs to me over the course of ten nights, standing over me with a stopwatch (I got a 1420 by the way). On my twenty-first birthday I woke up and my dad had turned the house into a bar and it was full of coeds. I later found out he paid a University of Virginia sorority a couple thousand dollars to pack the place.

I contemplate calling him and telling him about his favorite president, but my father would bury me in a thousand questions and my hour would dissolve like sugar in water.

I grab a sandwich from the fridge and try to shake last night from my mind. Last night was the past. I don't deal in the past. I deal in the present. And presently, I'd wasted eighteen minutes of my day.

I grab my phone, slip on my Asics, remember to grab a beanie, and run out the door.

It is 3:26 a.m.

I will have to cut my run short. I do a seven-minute mile out, then a six-minute mile back. By the time I stand beneath the streetlight, the same streetlight Connor Sullivan parked his car under a day earlier, it is 3:39.

Twenty-one minutes.

I turn and face the house. It is silent, as if the wrought iron gate surrounding it protects it from all threats, even sound. I pull my hand into my shirt sleeve and fiddle with the lock atop the gate. It unlatches and the gate swings open with a soft creak. I know what I'm about to do is wrong, both ethically and legally, but what if there is a woman in the house that needs help? It had been nearly twenty-four hours since the scream; she could feasibly still be alive. Right? Either way, you might be asking yourself, why wasn't I calling the police to come check it out?

Simple.

This was the most exciting thing to happen in my 14,000 hours of being awake.

I slide through the opening in the gate, then tiptoe up the steps. There are two narrow panes of glass running vertically along the door and I lean forward and peer into the house. My eyes are still pinging with the light from the streetlamp and I can't make out a single shape. I lift my hand, still covered by my sleeve – I have no plans of leaving any fingerprints – and push down on the wrought iron handle. It gives and the door pushes inward.

I wiggle my foot in the space and push inward until I can fully slip my body through. The door eases shut behind me. I pull out my cell phone and click on the flashlight app. The room brightens.

Breaking and entering. Check and check.

From the shape of the house, I know the garage is left and the kitchen, living room, and bedrooms are to the right. I take a deep breath and whisper, "Hello."

No one answers.

I begin moving slowly through the house. It is bigger than it appears from the outside, stretching back nearly double what I would have predicted. The house smells clean and tidy and it is. The kitchen is spotless, save for two dishes in the sink, which I deduce once held grilled cheese and tomato soup. The refrigerator is full. Some healthy items. Some not so. There is a large sectional in the living room adjacent to a flat screen TV that I assume, by the 3D glasses next to the remote, is one of the newer models. There are two small bedrooms and one master. The master is the only one that appears lived in. Trinkets, mostly of elephants, fill every imaginable surface.

The bed is made. The pillows perfectly plump and arranged.

My phone vibrates and I realize it is the alarm I set. Knowing full well there was a good chance I might end up inside the house across the street, I'd set the alarm to go off at 3:50.

I start back toward the front door and pull it open. Giving the foyer one last survey, I decide that if Connor Sullivan had in fact hurt the woman – who might or might not be the owner of the house –then she wasn't here. So, he'd either come back to clean up his mess or there had never been a mess to start with, ergo, the woman wasn't hurt. Regardless if it was A, B, C, or otherwise, she wasn't here.

A shadow.

I flick my head around, which sends a bolt of lightning through my neck. The two Advil and the Icy Hot I applied had markedly alleviated the pain, but the wrenching of my neck has overpowered the drugs.

I groan at the cat.

He is tan and black, and his eyes are orange against the light from my cell phone. He comes forward and rubs against my leg.

"Hey, cat."

He doesn't respond.

I reach down to pet him, but before I touch him, he darts away and slinks down the hallway. I shine my light after him. He meows at a door. I walk toward him and pull the door open.

The smell is overpowering.

I can smell it in my eyes.

I can hear the smell.

The woman is on the hood of the car. She's wearing a blue tank top and plaid pajama bottoms. The woman's neck is swollen and is a tie-dye of red, purple, and blue. Icy Hot and Advil will not help this woman.

The cat bounces up and begins meowing at the woman. Below the neck, the woman's body is drained of color, a pastel white. The cat curls up on the woman's chest and lies down.

I take a couple steps forward. By my best guess the woman is in her early twenties. Blond hair and petite. Eyes that were once electric blue are dull and rimmed in blood. She's still attractive in death and I wonder how many necks she'd turned in life.

There is a chiming and I look down at my phone. I've been standing over the woman's body for seven minutes.

Shit.

As I turn to leave, I realize the sound isn't coming from my phone. It is coming from another phone. Possibly the woman's. The phone rings a third time. It is under the car. I get down on my hands and knees. I drop to my belly. I army crawl until my torso is halfway beneath the low hanging Audi. My fingers touch the outside of the phone's pink casing. I groan, edge forward, try and flip the phone back over on itself. It takes me seven tries. I grab the phone, push myself painfully from beneath the car, and get to my feet.

I am huffing and puffing.

I look down at the phone. It is a white Samsung Galaxy S4 in a pink case. The call has expired. The time is 3:59.

I sprint out of the garage and to the front door. Can I get home in time? It's a hundred yards then up three flights of stairs. What if I fall over in the middle of the road? What if I only make it to the front yard? What if someone finds me, then comes and finds the woman's body?

I will wake up in jail.

I decide there's no way I can make it.

I have to hide.

I run to one of the small bedrooms, open the closet, and lie down. I'm still looking for a way to extend my legs when I fall asleep.

:03

He's on my stomach. The cat.

"Yo."

Cat lifts his head, stares at me with his orange eyes, then rests his head back down on my chest. The events of the past night come flooding back. The woman's body. The phone under the car. The fact that I am hiding in a closet with a cat on my chest.

I push myself up on my haunches, sending Cat fleeing to places unknown. This time it isn't my neck, it's my back. It is screaming. I run my hand over my lower oblique and feel a quarter-inch depression that is sore to the touch. Gentle moonlight cascades through an open window, softly illuminating the plastic hanger I have slept on.

Ugh.

Once on my feet, I find my phone.

It is 3:02 a.m.

I feel around in my opposite pocket and find the other phone. The pink Samsung. A picture, a narrow white obelisk, the Washington Monument, fills the screen. The woman has been dead for going on forty-eight hours and I expect to see a barrage of texts, but there is only the missed call from the night before. Did this woman have any friends? Co-workers? Did anyone even know she was missing? I want to see what the number is that called, but the four boxes centering the phone screen lead me to believe the phone is locked. It is. I try 1234, but surprisingly it doesn't work. I make a mental note to put the Samsung back under the car for the police to find. I wipe any prints I might have left on the phone with my sleeve and put it in the pocket of my sweatpants.

As for the police, obviously they hadn't come in the last day, or if they had, they were a shoddy bunch. I'd been asleep in an open closet. Surely, they would have stumbled upon me and I would have awoken in jail, possibly already having undergone my first round of sodomy. So I'm altogether surprised to find the woman in the same place I'd last seen her. As for the state of her, that is an entirely different story. The condition of the body is a far cry from what I'd seen just a day earlier. Beneath a steady swarm of insects, the woman's body is decomposing. It smells of sulfur and it is intolerable. The smell twenty-four hours earlier was of fresh linen comparatively.

I gag and retreat back into the main house.

It is 3:04.

I make my way into the kitchen and once again slink my hand into my sweatshirt and open the refrigerator. Grabbing two string cheeses, I open one and slowly begin checking drawers. I am looking for mail. Or something with the woman's name on it. But there are no electric bills, no catalogs, not a single trace of her identity. No wallet, no White House press pass, no steamy letters from Connor Sullivan.

I spend another five minutes poking around, then decide I've already pushed my luck and head for the front door. Thinking better of it, I make my way through the living room and to a sliding glass door that leads to a small back patio. Sliding the door closed, I give one last glance behind me.

Cat is staring at me through the glass door.

Meow.

"What?"

Meow.

"Sorry, I'm more of dog guy."

Meow.

"I don't know, go drink out of the toilet."

Meow.

"There's plenty of string cheese in the fridge."

Meow.

"Fine."

I quickly open the door and Cat jumps into my arms.

It is 3:13 when we get back to my place.

I am just as thirsty as Cat and I drink three glasses of

water. I grab a sandwich and shake for me and open a can of tuna for Cat. He takes another couple laps of water from the bowl I set down then makes his way to the food and starts lick-eating it, like they do. I lean down and check his neck, but he doesn't have a collar.

"Well, I can't be calling you Cat, now can I?"

I think back to how he'd directed me to the garage door and say, "Just like when Timmy fell in the well."

Lassie.

He looks up and nods, almost if to say, "Works for me."

"Well, Lassie, I hate to tell you this because I know you are a staunch, right-wing conservative, but your mom was killed by the President of the United States. This is what happens when we elect Republicans."

He licks himself in response.

I toss my clothes on the couch and take a two-minute shower. After rubbing Icy Hot into my lower back, I throw on some fresh sweats, a fresh hoodie, wrangle my cell out of the pocket of my sweatpants on the couch, and look at the time.

3:22 a.m.

I have a lot to accomplish in thirty-eight minutes.

Fifteen minutes later, I am holding the pay phone in my hand. It is the only pay phone I know of and it happens to be at Summer Park. I'm not overly concerned with anyone seeing me, but I pull the beanie down and flip up the hood of my sweatshirt, which I'm guessing makes me look all that more suspicious. The 911 call is simple and short: there is a dead woman at 1561 Sycamore.

There is a squad car parked in front of the house when I return and I take the back entrance to my condo.

Peeking through the curtains, Lassie on my lap, busily licking his hind paws, I watch as three more squad cars arrive, followed fittingly by a van with Alexandria Crime Scene Unit inscribed on the side.

With one minute left, I give one last glance out the window at the dancing red and blue lights, then lie down on my pillow. Lassie snuggles up next to me.

After sleeping on the ground two nights in a row, I'm quite happy to have made it back to my bed, but as I close my eyes, I can't shake the feeling I've forgotten something.

Something important.

...

I'm surprised to find Lassie still curled up next to me twenty-three hours later. He bats his eyes at me and he still looks tired. I think he would happily have slept for another twenty-three. But I don't have a litter box and I'm guessing he has to take care of business.

I open the door to a small third-story balcony. I have a long dead plant and I rip it from the planter and scatter the remaining dirt in a heaping mound.

Lassie is still on the bed and I tell him, "Go pee and poop on that mound of dirt."

To my absolute amazement, he does.

Holy shit.

"Good dog."

I head to the opposite window and peer out. There are still two police cars parked in front of the house. Crime scene tape has been strung around the perimeter of the wrought iron fence.

I plop down in front of my laptop and pull up the local news.

Young Woman Slain.

Being that Alexandria is only fifteen minutes from the White House and is home to a huge percentage of bigwigs, I expect a bigger story, but the report is just the basics. No name. No age. Simply that a woman was found strangled in the garage of her home in Alexandria. No suspects.

Once Lassie and I have eaten, I call my dad. Knowing he is coming two nights later to play cards, we only chat for a couple minutes. I wait for him to ask about the murder, but he doesn't. I will tell him in person in two days. His face will be priceless.

As for the murder, I wonder if the police have connected the woman to the most powerful man in the world yet. Was she one of Connor Sullivan's aides? An intern?

And what about the President? Who should I tell? Should I write an anonymous email and send it to the Alexandria police? I'm not so naive that I think I can accuse the President of the United States of murder and not face some sort of repercussions. No matter how sure I am that it was him—and I am unwaveringly positive—there would be backlash. Not to mention how unbelievable the idea was. First, where was the President's Secret Service? Did they know? Had they arranged the tryst? Did the President somehow sneak from the White House unknown? Could it happen? I wasn't sure. What I did know was that when the President should have been asleep in his bedroom at the White House, he was in the house across the street from me strangling a woman to death.

I'm about to start crafting said email when I notice a small rectangular card near my front door.

"Grab that card," I tell Lassie.

He jumps off my lap, licks the card, but comes short of retrieving it.

I shake my head at him and grab it.

Ingrid Ray, Alexandria Homicide.

The police had probably spent the better part of yesterday canvassing the neighborhood to see if there were any witnesses. Knocking on my door and not getting an answer, she'd slipped her card under my door. I pull out my cell phone and dial. She would no doubt be asleep, but I plan on leaving a message that I'd heard about the murder but I hadn't seen anything.

Surprisingly, she answers.

"Ray, Alexandria Homicide."

"Oh, hi, um, my name is Henry Bins. You slipped your card under my door?"

"Where do you live?"

I tell her.

"I'll be there in five." She hangs up.

I look at Lassie and say, "Well, that didn't go according to plan."

...

She shows up seven minutes later.

It is 3:33 a.m.

She has auburn hair held pack in a ponytail. She is clad in jeans and a Washington Redskins hoodie. She doesn't have a trace of makeup on. She doesn't need any. High cheek bones. Brown eyes. Too attractive to be a cop, which probably accounted for her no-nonsense demeanor.

"So, you always up at this time?" she asks, taking a seat at my kitchen table and running her hand over Lassie's arched spine.

I decide for the short answer. "Yep."

"You some sort of weird writer or something?"

"Nope. Day trader."

"It's night. Wouldn't that make you a night trader?"

I smile. "It's day somewhere."

"Right, right. What markets do you trade in? London? Tokyo?"

"Uh, yeah," I manage.

"So, are you up for the day or finishing for the night?"

"Up for the day." Not a total lie. Only my day has fifteen minutes left. "Early bird and all that."

She forces a smile, then after a deep breath, asks, "You hear about the girl that got killed across the street? You know, between all that trading that you do?"

"Yeah, I heard about it."

"Where?"

"Where what?"

"Where did you hear about it?"

"On the internet."

"Right, you're always on that thing. With all that trading in Tokyo you do."

I force a smile.

It is 3:49.

I have to wrap this up before I pass out in front of this lady or at least before any more of my stupid lies – which I wasn't even sure why I was telling – start to pile any higher.

"You see anything, anybody walking around or anything?"

I shake my head. "I was pretty busy two nights ago, didn't even look out the window."

"Who said anything about two nights ago?" Her eyebrows furrow.

"Oh, I thought I read that she was killed two nights ago? Was she not?" I stammer. "Was she killed last night?"

She stares at me for a couple seconds. "Not sure. The coroner is still trying to figure that one out."

"Well, I didn't see anything last night either."

"What about three nights ago? You see anything suspicious three nights ago?"

I shake my head.

"You know her?"

"Who?"

"The girl from across the street. You know her? Ever meet her? Ever take her out for coffee?"

"No. Never met her."

She nods. Stands. "Well, if you hear anything, or remember anything, give me a call."

"I will."

My phone rings. Change that, a phone rings. Not mine. My cell phone is set to the standard BA-RING. This ring is set to chimes.

"You gonna get that?" she asks, nodding toward the couch where my sweatpants and hoodie from the previous night are strewn.

"Naw, probably not important."

"You get a lot of unimportant calls at four in the morning?"

Remember how I'd had a feeling I'd forgotten something? Something important? Well, I had. I try to keep a straight face as I realize the phone ringing is the dead woman's. I'd forgotten to put it back under the car because I'd been overcome by the smell. And doubly stupid, I'd left the phone in the pocket of my sweatpants.

"Tons," I reply to her question.

"How many cell phones do you have?"

"Just the one."

She opens the door, then pulls her cell phone from her pocket and hits a couple buttons. My cell phone, the one in my pocket, BA-RING, BA-RINGs.

She ends the call with a grin. "I'll be in touch, Mr. Bins."

And then she's gone.

I look down at Lassie.

"What just happened?"

He doesn't know either.

:04

I wake up on the couch with the cell phone in my hand. The last thing I remember is pulling the phone from the pocket of my sweatpants and seeing that it is 4:00. I'd attempted to find a decent sleeping position but had failed. Miserably. I'd slept with my feet up on the sofa and everything else corkscrewing onto the floor.

I can feel the pattern of the carpet on my cheek and know I look like someone has branded my face with a cheese grater. I'm not sure where Lassie slept, but as I roll over onto my back, he appears on my chest and begins licking my forehead.

"Hey, cut that out," I say, although I kind of enjoy it.

Pushing Lassie off, I stagger to my feet and realize just how angry my spine is (which I'm pretty sure is now shaped like a double helix).

After a five-minute shower – a minute longer than I ever allow – I can stand up relatively straight. Opening the fridge, I decide I can't stomach another sandwich and grab a yogurt and a piece of banana bread. Lassie splits both with me.

I pick up my phone to text my dad and see I have three missed calls. All are from the same number. Detective Ray.

Based on my performance from the night before, I'm guessing while I might not be a suspect in the woman's murder, I am at least a person of interest.

I look at the pink Samsung on the counter. How could I have been so stupid? How had I forgotten to put the phone back under the car? But to my credit, had I stayed in the garage a single moment longer, I would have left some very acidic chunks of Henry Bins behind.

I'm not sure what course of action I'm willing to take with the detective. I can't give her the phone without her knowing that I had been inside the house. And without the phone, they may never be able to connect the woman to Connor Sullivan.

Conundrum. Check.

I decide my best bet is to write an anonymous letter and mail it, along with the cell phone, to the Alexandria Police Department.

But first, I need to go for a run.

The time is 3:22 a.m.

Lassie is pawing at the front door as I pull the beanie down over my ears.

"What do you want, buddy? You want to go outside?"

Meow.

"Promise to come back."

Meow.

I open the door and he darts out.

The corpse of the woman continuously creeps into my thoughts as I run, but each time I am able to ward it off with a tight squeeze of my eyes and a gaze up at the starry sky. This is my time. Not hers.

After two miles, the muscles in my back start to relax and it no longer hurts each time I inhale. As I head back, a shadow darts out from behind a tree and into my path.

"Ahhh!" I scream.

Under the streetlight I can see him smiling.

Once I get my heart rate back under 200, I say, "Have you been waiting there all this time just to jump out and scare me?"

Meow.

I make a scary face and claw the air at him.

He claws back.

Best friends.

"Come on, let's go."

I start running and he falls in next to me, gliding along silently.

As we take the steps up to my third-story condo, I'm startled to see two people walking away from my door. Detective Ray is wearing a brown jacket and her hair is down. It is longer than I would have thought, cascading down well past her shoulders. She reminds me of Rene Russo from the Thomas Crown Affair. (It is my dad's favorite movie and one of just twelve I've seen. I'd watched the original and the remake over the course of a month. I prefer the original but I also prefer to see Rene Russo naked.) The gentleman with Ray is twice her age and three times her size. His head is shaved bald and he has a perfectly trimmed goatee circumventing nearly invisible lips. He is more muscle than fat, but barely, and he wears his Men's Warehouse attire smartly.

"He always go running with you?" asks Ray, bending down on her haunches to pet the approaching Lassie.

"Sometimes."

She nods her head upward and says, "This is my partner, Cal."

I nod my acknowledgement and step past them.

"We have some questions for you," barks Cal, the words aimed at my back.

"Then I shall answer them," I say, bending down to untie the key from my shoelaces. "I could do something later this week."

"How about right now?"

I look down at my cell phone. It is 3:48.

"Why are you always checking the time?"

I glance up at Ray with raised eyebrows.

"Last night, I must have seen you check the time on your phone eight, nine times."

Was she counting? I squint at her, but say nothing.

"What's one minute to the next at three in the morning?"

Those minutes are my life, I nearly scream. Those minutes that you take so much for granted because you get a thousand of them each day are priceless to me. Your life is measured by title, wealth, and status. My life is measured in grains of sand, trickling from one teardrop to the other.

My nostrils flare when I'm angry and I wonder if Ray feels a small gust of wind. Taking a calming breath, I ponder telling her that I'm Henry Bins and I have Henry Bins. I don't.

"I've always just been a little OCD like that. We all have our quirks, am I right? What's yours, Cal?" I'm guessing it's his goatee. It is too perfect. Rulers, levels, and protractors have been consulted in its creation.

He isn't amused.

I put the key in the lock, twist and pull. I ease the door open four inches and Lassie darts through. With a puff of my cheeks, I say, "I can't really do this right now. How about tomorrow? Say 3:15?"

I don't wait for a response, though I'm fearing if there is one, it will be, "We have a warrant."

A response does eventually come.

"Callie Freig."

I'm dazed. Not because the name means anything to me — it's just a name, a woman's name, indistinguishable among any of the seven billion on this planet — but because she has been humanized. As in birth, a fat, crying, pink baby becomes Jake or Molly, the woman in death has become Callie.

The two detectives use my second of stunned silence to move past me. I sidestep them, and knowing they are too far in to forcibly remove them, I retreat two steps.

The phone—Callie Freig's phone—is on the table, next to the laptop.

"Hey, can you guys take your shoes off?"

Not an unreasonable request and both lean down to comply. The kitchen table is ten carpeted steps away, but it would look odd if I didn't also remove my shoes.

"Just set them outside."

Slightly more unreasonable, but my only chance.

In the split second it takes for both to toss their shoes outside, I flick the beanie. It flips end over end, hits my laptop, then falls.

"What?" Ray asks, cutting her eyes at me. "What's so funny?"

"Nothing." I'm just an amazing beanie tosser is all.

Flipping my shoes next to the door, I say, "So, who is Callie Freig?"

:05

"Callie Freig is the girl you've been watching out your window for the past three months," Cal bellows.

I shake my head. "Sorry, buddy, but I've never seen her before." I had, just not while she was alive.

"You've never seen a woman who has lived across the street from you for three months?" asks Ray.

"She's only lived there three months?"

Both Ray and Cal look confused by my question and I can't blame them. The woman could have lived there for the past six years and I might never have seen her.

"I never saw her," I repeat.

"What about the Clemens?" asks Cal. "Have you seen them?"

"Who are the Clemens?"

"The people who own the house. The people who have lived there for the last ten years."

"Oh, the Clemens—" I pause, "nope, not ringing any bells."

"How long have you lived here?" asks Ray.

"What did it say on my lease?"

She glares at me. "Seven years."

"That's correct."

"And you've never seen the people that live in the house directly across from your window?" barks Cal.

"I'm not awake during the day very often. I'm sort of a night owl. If you haven't realized, we are having this conversation at four in the morning." Well, 3:54. If it was 4:00, he would be having a conversation with the linoleum.

The two detectives take this in and I ask, "So who is Callie Freig?"

Cal squints his distaste at the role reversal. Ray takes a deep breath and says, "Twenty-four-year-old female. Has been renting the house from the Clemens – who spend half the year in Florida – for the past three months. Craigslist post. Fifteen hundred bucks a month. Steep, but they gave her a good deal. No Facebook. No Instagram. Very little credit history. No next of kin. Parents unknown."

I'm left trying to synthesize all this information, pondering how and when she met the President of the United States, when Ray asks me for a glass of water.

I nod at the kitchen and say, "Help yourself."

A cupboard opens and shuts and she asks, "Where?"

I walk into the kitchen.

"Funny thing," Cal says behind me. "We never did find Callie Freig's cell phone. And even funnier thing, last night, my partner said she heard two phones ringing, after you — and this is the funniest part — after you said you only had the one."

I pull a glass from the cupboard, fill it with water, and hand it to Ray.

"And you think I stole her phone," I say, trying to buy myself some time.

Cal grins.

"I'll be right back." I head to the bedroom.

It is 3:57 when I exit the bedroom. I have three minutes to get them out. Three minutes to convince them that I didn't kill Callie Freig.

I hold out my hand to Ray. "I still use it as an alarm. Check it."

She takes the original iPhone from me and clicks on the alarm clock. It is set to 3:55 a.m. She hits it and chimes play. It isn't exactly the same as the ring on Callie's phone, but it is a close enough approximation.

"Why do you have an alarm set for 3:55 a.m.?" scoffs Cal.

"Tokyo markets close at 4:00 a.m. I set the alarm so I can remember to get my last trades in." I have no idea what time the Tokyo markets close, but as Tokyo is on the other side of the globe, it seems rational.

"Why not use the alarm clock on your new phone?" asks Ray.

"Uh—" I stall. "I made a lot of money while I had that phone. Good luck charm, I guess."

It is 3:58.

"Speaking of, I have to make a last minute trade. Thanks for stopping by."

The two reluctantly head toward the door.

"Oh, another thing," remarks Ray. "We found a bunch of cat food across the street, but, well, no cat."

I look at Lassie sitting on one of the chairs at the table, curled in a ball.

"And, while I was looking at that lease of yours, I happened to notice there was no mention of a pet."

"Just trying to save fifty bucks a month," I say with a smile.

"Really," says Cal. "With all that money you made with that lucky phone, you're worried about fifty bucks?"

I glare at him. Take a deep breath.

"Lassie."

He jumps off the chair and sits at my feet.

I take a deep breath. Please work. Please work.

"Lie down."

He lies down on his belly and wags his tail.

"Roll over."

He rolls onto his back.

"Play dead."

He extends his legs, closes his eyes, and I swear he sticks his tongue out the side of his mouth.

"Do a backflip," I say, knowing I'm pushing my luck.

Lassie doesn't do anything, and I look up at the two detectives – Cal whose eyebrows are scrunched and Ray whose mouth is slightly agape – and say, "We're still working on that one."

I open the door and the two detectives grab their shoes and leave.

It is only when Lassie and I are lying in bed, when I realize my mistake and jump up.

The glass Detective Ray was drinking out of.

It's gone.

And my fingerprints with it.

:06

I expect to wake up in jail. I don't.

And when I still haven't heard a knock on the door at 3:25 a.m., I decide that one of three things has occurred: 1) it takes longer than twenty-four hours to match up fingerprints, 2) I hadn't left any fingerprints (which is a possibility as I had been very conscious of this and had tucked my hands into my sleeves), or 3) there had been a break in the case and even though they had matched my prints to those found at the scene, it didn't matter, because now they had their eyes set on the most powerful man in the world.

But according to the internet, the President was meeting with last year's NFL Champions, the Denver Broncos, at the White House. He wasn't being accused of murder. So that left 1) or 2).

"Shall we go for a run, buddy?"

Meow.

Lassie scampers behind me for about a mile, then disappears. I'm just starting to loosen up when a car turns onto the street. I haven't seen a car on the road since the Ford Focus, the one driven by the Connor Sullivan en route to strangle Callie Freig.

The car is a Crown Vic.

It pulls to the side of the road ten feet in front of me.

I pull out my ear buds and stop.

Ray steps from the passenger side and says, "We need you to come with us."

Cal clambers from the driver's side and pulls open the back door. "NOW," he says.

I climb into the back seat.

They both get back in and we drive away.

It is 3:33 a.m.

...

"Did you ever go into the house across the street?"

I'm sitting across from Cal. Ray is leaning against the wall parallel with the steel table.

"No." I'm guessing that they're bluffing. If they had my prints, I would have been arrested. Instead, I am in Interview Room B having a voluntary—which doesn't feel very voluntary—chat.

"So you never went inside the house?"

"Never."

"Not once?"

"No."

"Never were invited in, never had a sandwich, never opened the refrigerator?"

My stomach tightens. "No. Never."

"What time is it?" I ask. Cell phones aren't allowed in "voluntary" interviews. I would get it back, I was reassured by the lady who took it. It had been 3:43 when I'd signed the form and handed it over. That had been more than five minutes ago.

The door opens and a cop walks in. Hands Ray a piece of paper, who in turn hands it to Cal. Cal's goatee stretches wide. "Well, well, well."

I lean forward.

They had been bluffing. They hadn't gotten the results back yet. Apparently, it takes exactly twenty-four hours to match fingerprints.

"Guess whose prints are all over that house?"

Shit.

"A partial on the hood of the car. A partial on the tire of the car. A partial on the handle of the refrigerator. A full on the closet door in the guest bedroom. A full on the sliding glass door."

"How did you get my prints?"

"Were you not listening? They were all over the house."

"Yes, I was listening," I grunt. "How did you get my

prints, the ones you matched those to? I've never been arrested. I have nothing on file." I glance at Ray. "If, by chance, you took my prints off a cup that you illegally stole from my house, you'd better believe that won't hold up in court."

"Of course that wouldn't hold up in court," Cal laughs. "We got your prints off your cell phone. You know that form you signed that you didn't read?"

Crap.

"So I'm gonna ask again. Have you ever been inside the house before?"

"Yes."

"Were you in the house three nights ago?"

"Yes. But she wasn't murdered three nights ago. She was murdered four nights ago."

"How do you know?"

"Because I heard her scream."

...

"Connor Sullivan?" scoffs Cal. "As in the President of the United States?"

I nod.

He looks at Ray. She shakes her head.

"I swear, I heard a loud scream and then a minute later a man walked out the front door and directly underneath the streetlamp. It was Connor Sullivan."

"Getting into, what did you say, a Ford Focus?" Ray says chuckling.

I nod.

"Where's his Secret Service? How would he get out of the White House?"

"I don't know. Ask him."

"Why did you kill her?" asks Cal.

"What?"

"Why – did – you – kill – Callie Freig?"

"I didn't. I'd never seen her before, until I went over there that night. Seriously."

"Yeah, you said that before. And guess what, I didn't believe you the first time. Your window looks out on her house. You never go to check the weather and see her walking to her car. Bullshit. You were in love with her. Watched her every chance you got. Then one night you go over there and strangle the shit out of her."

"I have Henry Bins."

"What?"

"You are Henry Bins," quips Ray.

"Yes and I have Henry Bins. It's a sleeping disorder. I'm only awake for an hour a night. From 3 a.m. to 4 a.m."

Both shake their heads like Parkinson's patients. And here I was, the one with the condition.

"Google it." I look up at Ray. "Seriously, Google it. Or you can just wait and watch what happens to me in what I'm guessing is probably four minutes."

"And what happens in four minutes, asshole?" asks Cal.

"My body will crumple like JFK and I will basically be in a coma for twenty-three hours. Then I will wake up at 3 a.m., be awake for an hour, then repeat."

He pushes back from the table, his laughter riotous. "Well, if that isn't the biggest load of shit I've ever heard. Are you getting this, Ingrid? Are you listening to this shit?"

I stand up. "That's why my prints are on the closet in the guest bedroom. I had to find somewhere to sleep. I got stuck under the car trying to get her phone out and I didn't have time to make it back across the street."

"You mean the cell phone you threw in a dumpster three blocks away?"

"What?"

"Yeah, idiot, you busted it up, but it still logged its last known GPS. Took two hours going through some trash, but we found it."

My brain is whirring.

I lean against the wall.

Ray has been quiet for the last minute and I see her fiddling with her phone. "Um, Cal, you might want to come read this. I think this Henry Bins thing might actually be—"

:07

My head is pounding.

I lift my right arm up and touch it to my scalp. I can feel a clump of hair missing and a patch of gauze in its place. I lift my left arm to assist in the damage assessment, but am met with the clink of restraint. I open my eyes. My left arm is handcuffed to the hospital bed.

"What did you do?" asks a familiar voice. "Did you rob a twenty-four-hour bank?"

Sara is Japanese-American, a nurse at Alexandria Municipal Hospital, and an ex-girlfriend.

We'd started dating after my third concussion. She worked the 6 p.m. to 3 a.m. shift, so she would just scoot over after work and hang out until my hour was up. It was fun and casual for six months, but like the others before her, she realized seeing me for half an hour three days a week just wasn't enough. After four failed relationships, I realized the only thing worse than having Henry Bins, was falling in love with Henry Bins. Luckily, we'd been able to remain friends.

"Nope. Murder."

She laughs and says, "Well, the good news is no concussion. The bad news is thirteen stitches."

"That puts me over a hundred. Is my next set free?"

"I'll see what I can do," she laughs, then as if I'd hit the refresh button, her smile fades and she says, "I have to alert the officers that you're awake."

I nod.

She squeezes my calf and disappears behind the curtain.

Ray and Cal walk through.

I pull my arm up, clinking the cuffs, and say, "Does this mean I'm under arrest?"

Cal doesn't hesitate and Mirandizes me. When he's done, I say, "Let me get this straight, you obviously read up on Henry Bins, you watched me fall at exactly four and crack my skull open, and I'm sure you've checked with the nurses here and know that I'm no stranger to the emergency room."

Ray nods.

"So you believe I have this condition and yet you also believe that in this slim window I get, this hour, that I killed Callie Freig."

"Doesn't change the fact that the window of opportunity is still there, you easily could have killed her within that one hour," says Ray. "Your prints are all over the place, including the car that her body is found on, not to mention that every single thing you've said, except for this stupid sleeping disorder, has been lies."

My mind is racing.

"I need to make a call."

"Lawyering up already," snorts Cal.

"Actually, my dad probably thinks I'm dead, so I'd like to call him."

Ray hands me her phone. I raise my eyebrows and both the detectives leave. My dad is frantic when he answers. It was our card night and finding that I wasn't there, he called my phone. When I hadn't answered, he'd started toward the hospital.

"Turn around and go back to my house."

I tell him what to do once he gets there.

Before I hang up, I ask if he saw a cat prowling around outside my apartment.

He hadn't.

...

The nurse – not Sara, though she'd come to say goodbye when her shift ended – is changing the dressings on my head when my dad shows up.

The best word to describe my father is frumpy. He wears

slacks too short and too high on his waist, sweaters that should have been given to the Salvation Army decades earlier, glasses that could fry a caterpillar in seconds. He has a full head of curly gray hair and three days' worth of stubble on his chin.

I introduce him to Cal and Ray, both of whom have taken seats, waiting for what I've told them is concrete proof of my innocence.

"Do you have it?" I ask.

He reaches into his coat pocket and pulls out the pink Samsung.

I take it from him. It's dead, the battery having run out.

"What's that?" asks Ray.

Holding the phone up with my right hand, I say, "It's the phone I found under the car, the phone I can assure you I was not lying about."

"But we found Callie Freig's phone," spits Cal.

"Maybe she had two," Ray says with a shrug.

I lower it out of his reach and say, "It's not Callie's phone."

"Then whose is it?" asks Ray.

"It's the President's."

...

"The President? As in the President of the United States?" asks my father.

"Yep."

Cal is laughing. Doubled over. He composes himself and says, "That's your proof."

I hand the phone to Ray. "It's his."

"Is the President even allowed to have a cell phone?" she asks, taking it.

"Of course not," Cal manages.

"Actually, he can, and he does."

Both Cal and Ray stare at my father. He continues, "Obama was so adamant that he be able to keep his Blackberry that they made a special stipulation that he could keep it."

"Really?" I found myself asking. I'd hoped this was the case, but I was still surprised.

"Of course they had to make some considerations for national security, added encryption and disabled the GPS so no one could track him. But he was able to keep it and Connor Sullivan was allowed to keep his."

"But it's pink," shouted Cal. "And why are we even having this conversation? This is not the President of the United States' cell phone."

"The phone is white, the casing is pink," I say. "And it's not just any pink casing. Look closer."

Ray turns the phone over in her hand. "It's got a ribbon embossed on the back. It's a Susan B. Komen casing."

"The First Lady," remarks my dad.

The First Lady had been diagnosed with breast cancer two years earlier. They caught it early and it'd gone into remission.

Cal was silent.

Ray hits the button for the nurse and when one comes a moment later, Ray asks, "Does anyone have a Samsung charger here?"

"Deb would," the nurse responds and returns a moment later with Deb's charger.

Ray plugs it in and it takes ten seconds for the phone to come alive.

"It's locked," she says, showing everyone.

"The Washington Monument," remarks my father.

"What?" asks Cal.

"The lock screen. The picture in the background, it's the Washington Monument."

The monument is only six miles from my house and I'd assumed that Callie had loved it and taken a picture of it. Now I was hoping that it had a special place in Connor Sullivan's heart.

I look at my dad. He shakes his head. He knows plenty about the President, but the monument doesn't trigger any tidings.

"What use is it to us if it's locked?" says Cal. "Let's get it down to the precinct and get one of our resident nerds to crack it open. The faster we get it open, the faster we find out this phone isn't the fucking President's."

"How many numbers?" asks my dad.

"Four," responds Ray.

My father mulls. When he mulls his lips move back and forth. Mull. Mull. Mull.

"Try thirteen, forty-four."

Ray punches them in and my dad explains, "Thirteen was his number when he played basketball at Dayton. Forty-four because he's the forty-fourth president."

Ray shakes her head.

"Switch 'em," I say.

"What?"

"Forty-four, thirteen."

"Four-four-one-three," she says aloud. Pause. "Holy shit."

Cal rips the phone from her hand, looks at the screen, and then hands it back to her silently. She shows it to both me and my father. The Washington Monument has dissolved into the home screen. The picture is of the President spread eagle on the eagle carpet that centers the oval office. A picture that would have been infamous had it ever been leaked.

"Look at this," Ray says, reading through his contact list. "The Vice President, the Treasurer, Supreme Court Justice Billings, the head of the CIA." Ray shoves the phone in Cal's face and says, "Look at this picture. It's the President taking a selfie . . . and here's one of his dog . . . holy shit." She looks at me. "You were telling the truth."

I nod.

"Now will you get these cuffs off me so I can go home?"

Cal nods at Ray and she unlocks the cuffs.

"What time is it?" I ask.

:08

Lassie is licking my face.

Only it isn't Lassie.

It's my dad's one-hundred-and-sixty-pound English mastiff.

Murdock.

Not only has Murdock been licking my face for God knows how long, he'd slept on my legs, and I am paralyzed from the waist down.

Can't I go just one night without waking up feeling like I've been tackled by Ray Lewis?

By the time I get Murdock off me, get my legs to work, clean my face, change the dressing on my stitches, and join my dad at the kitchen table, it is 3:06 a.m.

"Why are you walking like that?" he asks.

"Your dumb dog slept on my legs."

He laughs.

Murdock comes trotting in and buries his face in my dad's lap. "You're not dumb," my dad tells him.

He's not dumb. To be dumb, he would have to be much smarter.

I open the fridge and see that Isabel has made a fresh round of sandwiches. Reubens. My favorite. I grab two and a strawberry protein shake and set them on the table where my dad is shuffling the cards. I grab a can of tuna, open it, and set it outside the door.

Just in case.

I dive into the sandwiches and flip up my laptop.

My dad deals the cards.

"Nothing in the news about the President being arrested, if that's what you're wondering," he says.

I close the laptop and set it on the ground.

"How much do you know?"

"After you fell asleep, the lady detective told me most everything." He smiles. "She's not bad looking."

I laugh. "No, she is not."

He's waiting for me to discard, but I also know he wants to hear my version of the story. I oblige him with a six of clubs and an animated narrative.

"And you took the cat?" he says with belly laugh. "You hate cats."

"I couldn't leave him there. And he thinks he's a dog, so he's not too bad."

I give my dad a hug at 3:58 and let Murdock lick my face goodbye.

I have my first peaceful sleep in a week.

...

It's 3:08 a.m. when I pick up the phone and dial Ray.

She answers, then says, "He says that he lost the phone two days earlier."

"And you believe him?" I shout into the phone.

"There is an official report filed," responds Ray. "I have a friend in the White House who faxed it to me."

"Could it have been doctored?"

"I don't see why not. But proving it would be hell."

"Well, did you at least get the President's fingerprints off the phone?"

"Nope, he must have wiped it. And we didn't find his fingerprints in the house."

I blew out a long exhale.

"What about the car? Did you check the stoplight cams or ATM cams for the Ford Focus?"

"Yep. Nothing."

"So where does that leave us?"

"Us?"

"*You.* Where does that leave you?"

"Well, we can't do anything without rock solid evidence and the phone isn't enough. In fact, the Secret Service already came by and got it."

"Seriously?"

"Yep."

"And they had a quick conversation with my captain, who then tore me a new asshole for using my back channel at the White House and warned me the only way we would ever go after the President is if there were a video of him strangling the girl and even then we probably wouldn't do shit."

"What about Cal? He didn't back you?"

"No."

I wait for her to expand on this. She doesn't.

"So he just gets away with it?"

"The only thing tying him to the scene is you and the phone, but the phone is no longer in our possession."

"There has to be a connection somewhere. You sure Callie Freig never worked at the White House?"

"She graduated from Ohio State in the winter, then moved out here four months ago. She might have met the President in Ohio somewhere, but we'd never be able to prove it."

"What about friends and family? Ask them."

"No family to speak of. As far as friends, we can't locate any."

"But you have her cell phone records."

"Sure do. She called and received calls from all of one number. And that number is now disconnected."

"That's odd."

"Very. This could easily be how she communicated with the President, but the cell company couldn't get a report on the number. We'd need a warrant to dig any deeper and since my ass is still stinging, I'm not doing anything that could come back on me."

"So it's done. The President gets away with murder."

"For now." She pauses. "Yes."

I hang up.

Three minutes later, my feet are pounding the cold Alexandria asphalt.

I dig a moat around my mind, fill it with alligators, and place a thousand archers on the turrets of my cerebrum, but I am unable to defend my thoughts. They are dominated by Connor Sullivan, Callie Freig, and the white noise of injustice.

I do not have a temper. I don't have time for anger. But my insides are engulfed in blue flames.

The car pulls to the curb. Doors open. Men jump out.

I cut left into an alley.

I think about what Ray said, that the only thing tying him to the scene is you and the phone, but the phone is no longer in our possession.

I am the only connection.

If I'm dead, no connection.

My pursuers are ten strides behind me. I run a quarter mile, knock over two trashcans and exit the alley. Headlights flash at me. I cut right and sprint three blocks, then take a left onto a side street that leads to the Potomac. I can feel the headlights on my back, singeing as they grow closer and closer. I can hear the river. I hit the concrete embankment and turn. Both cars have skidded to a halt. The doors fly open and four men leap out. I gaze down at the moving water twenty feet below.

I jump.

The water is cold, but I'm not in it. I am in a large drainage pipe that opens into the Potomac.

Gross, I know.

The pipe is impossible to see from the high embankment and I only know it's there because I'd jumped in the river once on a self-dare and crawled out just below it. It is roughly four feet high and I crouch down and wait.

I check my phone.

3:46 a.m.

Two minutes later, I hear wheels squeal on the asphalt.

I wait another minute, then climb out and scale the embankment. My pursuers are gone.

I have dual concerns as I start sprinting back: can I make the two-and-a-half-mile trek in time, and are those dickheads still out there looking for me?

The constant head-turning and the many times I stop to hide decimate my time. With a mile left, I have four minutes. And since I'm not Usain Bolt, I'm screwed.

The hunt begins.

Where can I sleep for twenty-three hours without being discovered?

There is only one logical answer.

I shine my cell phone into the dumpster behind the Italian restaurant. It is two-thirds full and I'm hoping this means the pick-up is still a couple days off. I climb inside, dig myself down into the slimy refuse, cover myself in as many bags as I can, and close my eyes.

:09

Every once in a great while, I will wake up a couple minutes early. 2:59. 2:58. Once, even 2:57.

It's like Christmas, each minute a beautifully wrapped gift just waiting to be opened. Should I allow myself an extra minute in the shower? Could I read three more pages of my book? Run another quarter mile? Watch a YouTube video? Watch the swimming pool scene from Wild Things, twice?

Today, I wake up at 2:58 a.m.

Two extra minutes.

It requires one of these minutes to pull myself from the now three-quarters full dumpster. And it necessitates another minute to rid my hair and body of the potpourri of spaghetti, breadcrumbs, day-old lasagna, and maggots. As unpleasant as maggots are—and they are unpleasant, trust me on this—I try to look on the bright side: I wasn't killed by those pesky guys trying to kill me, and I wasn't discovered by an underpaid busser who called 911, and I wasn't at a landfill. All things considered, I called myself lucky. And quite honestly, I'd slept well. Day-old lasagna is like memory foam.

I take the back way to my condo, which adds two blocks, but I don't want to risk discovery by the goons patrolling the street in front of my condo, and when I walk through the door, it is 3:06.

I check the blinds, but don't see any suspicious cars on the street. As for the goons, I'm not sure if they were a hit squad, the Secret Service, or some angry congressmen, but I know I hadn't seen the last of them. I latch the security lock on my door, throw my clothes in a garbage bag, and shower. When I sit down to the computer, it is 3:17 a.m.

There is no breaking news about the President being arrested and I concede that he's gotten away with murder. And that I should let him if I want to remain alive.

I check my stocks, which have been crippled over the last couple days – I'd lost about 40k – and I decide to ride out the storm with a couple of them and sell off the remainder.

I try to watch *Game of Thrones*, but I can't remember what has happened in the previous episodes and I feel lost. What happened to the Kingslayer's hand? Although it has been nearly twenty-four hours since my harrowing chase and physically my body has recovered from the fight or flight-endorphin release, my brain has not. I feel sluggish, my synapses delayed and unresponsive.

At 3:42, I give up and lie down on my bed.

For the first time I can ever remember, I fall asleep on my own.

...

The next few days pass in relative monotony. I have made a couple small tweaks, as I have decided never to venture outside again, and I run on my new treadmill that I'd had overnighted and delivered (the days of leaving my door unlocked are in the past and I had Isabel meet the delivery people and let them in). Anyhow, the treadmill is the latest and greatest, and there is a screen that shows where you are running. You can run the Appalachian Trail, the streets of Boston, the beaches of San Diego, or even the nearby Potomac.

I mean, who needs to go outside, am I right?

It's my fifth day on the treadmill, and I opt for a little run down the streets of DC. The White House looms in the background and I flip it off.

I've run 2.43 miles when I hear a noise.

I jerk my head toward the door, my eyes scanning to see if the regular security lock, and the Ideal Security Heavy Duty lock I'd had installed are both latched. They are.

I continue running.

At 2.51 miles, I hear it again.

I jump off the treadmill and tiptoe to the door and gaze through the peephole. Nothing.

Was I hearing things?

Two steps back toward the treadmill and I hear it again. I again press my eye to the peephole. Again, nothing.

I unlatch both locks and gently ease the door open.

Meow.

"LASSSSSSSSSSSSSSIE!"

He jumps into my arms.

I hold him up high, my cheeks cramping I'm smiling so hard. "BUDDDY! . . . WHERE DID YOU G—DUDE! WHAT HAPPENED TO YOU?"

Lassie is a bloody mess. He has a huge cut on his belly, a bite out of his ear, and one of his eyes is swollen shut. I swear he is smirking as if to say, "You should see the other five guys."

I set him on the table and go to work on him with a warm cloth. He winces as I touch him, but altogether he's a pretty good sport.

I'd been so happy to see him and so overwhelmed by his many cuts that I'd failed to notice he smelled something awful.

"Dude, did you pick a fight with a skunk?"

Meow.

"What are these?" I pull out two spines from his butt. Porcupine spikes.

"Dude, did you pick a fight with a skunk and a porcupine?"

Meow.

I am laughing uncontrollably and hug him tight.

He winces.

"Sorry, buddy."

I feed him a can of tuna, then I give him a bath in the sink. I gently rinse all the dried blood off him. He is having trouble keeping his eyes open. "I've been there, buddy. Trust me."

I carry him to bed and rub his little body until he falls asleep.

...

"Lassie . . . Lassie!"

His eyes flutter, but he doesn't move.

It's 3:03 a.m.

I gingerly roll him over. The cut on his belly is red and swollen. I touch it with my finger and he yelps.

Shit.

"Dude? Are you okay?"

He's not.

My heart starts racing.

"I'm sorry, buddy. We'll get you fixed."

Meow.

My eyes are filling with tears and I wipe them away. He's just a stupid cat, I tell myself. I grab my phone and am about to search for an emergency vet when I stop. I've actually seen the emergency vet before. It's adjacent to the park about a mile and a half away.

I don't have a driver's license, but I do have a little Vespa that I use every so often.

I grab Lassie and a backpack, then bolt out the front door.

It's the first time I have left the sanctity of my apartment since *the chase.* I scan the street. It's all clear.

I open the backpack and put Lassie inside.

"Ten minutes, buddy," I tell him.

I make it in seven.

Lassie clings to my shoulder as I walk through the sliding glass doors of the Alexandria VCA Emergency Animal Hospital.

There is no one else there and after filling out some paperwork, we see the doctor.

It is 3:20.

"So, what seems to be the problem?" the vet asks in an Australian accent. He has reddish blond hair, glasses, and tells me to call him James, or as he says it, Jahms.

"He was gone for about a week, came back all beat-up last night. I think he picked a fight with a skunk and a porcupine."

"Is that right?" He laughs. "Well, let's have a look-see, shall we?"

Lassie looks at me over his shoulder as the doctor begins his examination and I reassure him, "It's okay, buddy."

The doctor flips him over and looks at the cut on his belly. "Somebody really got you there, didn't they?" He gazes up at me and says, "Looks like he got pretty lucky, actually. The skin on the belly is pretty soft. A little deeper and he could have done some real damage."

He presses on Lassie's belly and I expect him to wince, but he doesn't. But when the doctor touches a little higher on his ribs, he lets out a painful wail.

My stomach tightens. I wait for the doctor to tell me that he is bleeding internally and will surely die. But, after another minute of prodding, the doctor diagnoses some bruised ribs—nothing major. He prescribes some pain meds and gives me a couple ointments to put on his cuts.

I blow a sigh of relief.

"Hear that, buddy? Just some bruised ribs."

Meow.

"He should be back in action in a couple days."

"Thanks, Doc." I remember something from a week earlier when I'd been petting Lassie and ask, "Actually, while we're here . . . did you happen to feel that lump on his shoulder?"

He shakes his head and I guide his hand to a little lump behind Lassie's right shoulder.

I wait for the doctor to tell me it is obviously cancer.

"Microchip."

"What?"

"That's his microchip. Sometimes they put it in behind the shoulder."

He sees my confusion and asks, "You didn't have the microchip put in?"

"No. I found him on the street about a month ago. No tags."

"Well, whoever owned the cat had a microchip put in. Costs like fifty bucks, some places do it for free."

My mind is racing.

"Could you find out who he belongs to?" I ask. "I mean, I should at least try and track them down, right?"

"Sure thing."

He opens a drawer, unwinds a little scanner, and plugs it into his computer. A moment later, he runs the scanner over Lassie's shoulder, like he is produce at the grocery store. He writes the name, phone number, and address on the back of one of his business cards and hands it to me.

I read the name and try to keep a straight face.

...

It is 3:46 when we get back.

I put two of the tiny little pain pills inside a blueberry and feed it to Lassie. Then I spread ointment on all his cuts and then carry him and my laptop to bed.

I pull out the card the vet gave me.

Jessica Renoix.

A Richmond address.

I Google "Jessica Renoix and Connor Sullivan."

There are several hits. I click on images.

Bingo.

There is a picture of Jessica Renoix and the then Governor of Virginia, Connor Sullivan.

Jessica Renoix is Callie Freig.

:10

It'd been a double homicide. Twelve nights ago, Callie Freig had been murdered. But so had Jessica Renoix.

It is 3:07 a.m.

Lassie and I are back in my bed. I'd given him another round of pain medicine and he is on his back snoring. The cut on his belly has improved dramatically and he'd told me in face licks that he was feeling a little better.

I've been staring at the picture of Connor Sullivan and Jessica Renoix for the past couple minutes. Under the picture of the two, a caption reads, "Campaign volunteer Jessica Renoix gets an armful of incumbent candidate, Governor Connor Sullivan."

The photo must have been taken six years earlier during his final reelection campaign as Governor of Virginia.

In the photo, there are fifteen people clad in white T-shirts with the slogan "The Man With the Plan." Sullivan had been quoted ad nauseum on television saying, "I've got a plan . . ." During his bid for governor it had always been "I have a plan for this great state" which quickly became "I have a plan for this great nation" during his bid for president. To his credit, he'd had a plan, and he was delivering on all fronts. The economy was the strongest it'd been in eight years, unemployment the lowest in a decade, and every troop had been pulled from the Middle East.

Jessica Renoix and the President are front and center. Jessica is petite and of medium height. Though she must have been barely out of high school, her confident eyes and wry smile speak to a girl who is not naive about the realities of the world. The President is wearing a crisp blue shirt under a black blazer. He towers over her, his right arm draped over her shoulder. There is nothing overtly sexual about the pose, and if anything, the contact appears fatherly. I surmise that any of the other fifteen volunteers could just have easily been in Jessica's place.

I spend the rest of my forty-five minutes in bed, scouring the internet for more information on Jessica Renoix.

I find very little.

...

It's ten minutes into my day when I scroll down to Ray's telephone number and nearly hit the Call button, then decide against it. I want to know more about Jessica Renoix before I talk to the detective.

I log onto the internet and find a company that does background checks. I fill in all the information I have on Jessica Renoix—a six-year-old address and a long out-of-service telephone number—then pay the nearly $200 for the rush job.

"Well, now I guess we just wait," I say to Lassie, who is lick-eating his breakfast. In forty-eight hours, he has made a near full recovery.

Meow.

"You would think you would care more. This is your mother we're talking about."

Meow.

"Yes, living with me is awesome, but still."

Meow.

"Candy? What kind of candy?"

Meow.

"Dude, Twix is a cookie."

We argue about this for another minute, then I open the door to the balcony and he goes to his mound and takes care of business. The fresh air feels wonderful and I decide I am going running outside.

Goons be damned.

There is a brown box on the kitchen table with an Amazon sticker. It had come two days earlier, but I'd yet to open it.

A minute later, I'm holding the strongest Taser on the market.

I shake it at Lassie. "Next time you go pee-pee on the carpet, zap. Four thousand volts, buddy."

He laughs.

I pull on my beanie, slip on my running shoes, and open the front door. Lassie sticks his head out, surveys the hall, then slinks back in. If I'd gotten over my little scare, Lassie was yet to get over his.

"I guess we'll have to get you a Taser too."

Meow.

"No, I'm not getting you a knife."

Meow.

"We'll discuss this when I get back."

After running on the treadmill for close to week, I forget how amazing the air tastes. I decide to take a different route and head north toward Summer Park. I've already thought of escape routes, should the need arise. The stun gun is in my right hand, cranked on high.

I sweep the perimeter as I run. No signs of life. I try to remain on alert, but my mind continually drifts. I try to move past her, but she keeps popping back into my thoughts. Not Callie Freig. Not Jessica Renoix. Detective Ray. Her auburn hair, her crooked smile, how she would stare at me when she thought I was a murderer. I try to configure what her body is shaped like beneath those jeans and bulky sweatshirts. What sounds she might make. How her nipples would respond to my teasing tongue.

Bright lights.

Two sets.

Escape Route D.

I dart across the street. There is a ditch and I jump down into the water, then crawl up the embankment and enter Summer Park.

I head for the darkened tennis courts to my left. I crash through the chain-link gate, hurdle the net, then start on the eighteen-foot fence enclosing the two courts. I turn and look over my shoulder. Three guys have entered the court. They are all wearing black. They have guns. I wonder why they don't shoot. As I sweep my leg over the top of the chain-link, all three hit the fence and shake it for all it's worth. Somehow I'm able to hold on, then hop down the last ten feet.

I look through the fence at them. They could be Navy SEALs for all I know.

"Hey, guys."

They don't respond.

They go to work on the fence and I wait until all three near the top.

"Sorry about this."

I taser the chain-link fence.

Three screams, then three thuds as they fall to the green court floor.

I turn and run.

"Don't move."

I'm staring into the barrel of a gun.

"Drop the Taser."

I drop the stun gun.

"You guys okay?" he calls to his buddies.

"That motherfucker electrocuted us."

He picks up the stun gun from the ground and looks at it. Then he pushes it into my chest and I scream.

...

I'm in a car.

"You okay?"

My vision is blurred. "What time is it?" I ask.

"3:35 a.m."

I squint at the voice.

"Don't worry, we'll get you back before your 4 a.m. curfew."

I recognize the voice, but the face still swims in front of me.

"Henry Bins," he says. It isn't a question.

My vision is starting to clear. I'm in the back seat of a car. My chest is burning.

I try to speak, but only a cough comes out.

He hands me a Perrier and I take a small sip. A chill courses down my arms.

"Mr. President."

...

The car light above illuminates Connor Sullivan's face in roughly the same shadow as the streetlamp had two weeks earlier. He is wearing jeans and a University of Dayton sweatshirt. He could be any other guy out for a drive. But he's not. He's the President of the United States.

"Sorry about my guys," he says. "No harm was supposed to come to you."

I bring my hand to my chest where I was shocked and know a ruby red burn is in the making.

I nod.

"I know time is of the essence, that for you time is always of the essence, so I will get right to the point. I knew the moment I saw your face in that window that you were going to pose a problem."

We lock eyes, relive that moment in time.

I think about his words: *that you were going to pose a problem.* Callie Freig had also posed a problem. And she was dead. So why wasn't I?

"I didn't kill that girl," he says.

I would have been more apt to believe if he told me he could turn off gravity. That if I dropped the Perrier in my hand, it would float to the ceiling.

I scoff.

"I don't blame you," he says with a shake of his head. "If I had the information you have, I would have no doubt that I killed that woman. Let's see, you heard a scream, you saw me leaving, you found my cell phone, and you made the connection between me and Jessica Renoix."

I try not to blink. I wonder if my house is bugged. Or if they know everything I've searched on the internet. Or both.

He takes a breath and says, "I met Jessica six years ago when she volunteered for my reelection campaign." He whistles. "Still remember the day she walked in. Every male from eighteen to fifty literally stopped and stared. She had that effect."

"How long did it take for you to start sleeping with her?"

"Not long. A month into the campaign, the lot of us were staying at a hotel. She snuck into my room and, well, I didn't turn her down."

"I didn't take you for much of a philanderer." In fact, he reeked of the consummate family man.

"Nothing I'm proud of," he offers with an upward glance. I'm not sure if he was repenting or checking the roof of the car for tears.

"And you've kept this up for six years?"

"No. It only happened the one time."

I am confused and must look it.

"She videotaped it. Came to me the next day and demanded a hundred thousand dollars."

My eyebrows rise.

"I paid her. She disappeared the next day."

"You paid her?"

"If that video got out I would have been ruined. Paid her a hundred thousand dollars cash and she took it with a smile and disappeared. Didn't hear a peep from her for six years. Then I got an email a month ago. She was back and she wanted more money."

"Did you give it to her?"

"I did. Two weeks ago."

I study his face. I find myself believing him. But that he was being blackmailed by Callie/Jessica didn't mean that he didn't kill her. In fact, it gave him motive.

"I know what you're thinking, even a better reason to kill her. And don't think it didn't cross my mind. But she'd gone away for six years the first time I paid her. I had little doubt she would disappear for another six, whereby if she ever came back to the well, I would have served out my presidency and I could deal with the fallout if the tape came out."

"Okay, so say I believe you. What happened that night? And start from the beginning, like how you got out of the White House and into a Ford Focus."

"You know that was the first time I'd driven in nearly three years. Man, it felt good!" He laughs.

I don't react. I'm still sitting next to a killer. And I don't give a shit when the last time he drove a car was.

He straightens.

"I told my guys I wanted to go for a drive and that I didn't want any record of it. Red, the guy that tased you, heads up my detail. He made it happen, but he insisted he come with me. Snuck me out, got me into that car, and we drove.

We went five miles, then I pulled over and told him to get out. Some SS might not have gotten out of the car, but Red and I go back to college. We'd played ball together for two years. Like brothers. He got out. I told him I'd pick him up in an hour. Drove down to the address that Jessica – I had no idea she was calling herself Callie now – had given me, and went inside.

"I gave her the money, two hundred grand this time, and she took it. She tried to kiss me and I pushed her away. That's when she started screaming. I covered her mouth and told her to shut up, then I ran out."

"What about your phone?"

He shakes his head. "I had this great plan to record the exchange so I would have proof she was blackmailing me if it ever came to that, but Jessica is smart. She patted me down, found the phone, and said she was keeping it. It was her insurance if I ever tried to prove she was blackmailing me."

"And what, you just left and then someone came and strangled her?"

"Yep and they took the two hundred thousand dollars with them."

...

The President drops me off five blocks from my house at 3:50 a.m.

I open the door and ask, "So if you didn't kill her, then who did?"

He had no idea.

:11

I have no idea if the Clemens moved back. If they have, I will know in the next thirty seconds.

I pick up a rock from a nearby garden and weigh it in my hand. It has some heft, maybe three pounds. It will work.

My plan is to smash the lock on the sliding glass door and hope it opens. I raise the rock above my head.

Meow.

I look down.

I decided to bring Lassie along for my B & E encore, hoping he might be able to sniff out something the cops had missed.

"I know it's a stupid idea, but how else are we going to get in?"

Meow.

"Really?"

Meow.

"Well, why didn't you say something earlier?"

He shrugs, then leads me to a flower pot at the back edge of the porch. The flowers are long dead, having not been watered in two weeks, and the soil is filled with small crusty leaves. I dig my hand in the soil and feel around, then hit pay dirt. I pull out a key.

"Good job, Watson."

Meow.

"No, I'm Sherlock."

Ten seconds later, we are inside.

It is 3:10 a.m.

The TV remote is in the same place I last saw it, and I decide the Clemens are still tanning their hides in the Florida sun. I wonder what their plans are for the estate. And I also wonder if they believe in ghosts. Ten to one, the house would be on the market within the year. Virginia real estate prices were on the rise, some were even throwing out words like "seller's market," but I'd be surprised if the Clemens get sixty percent of their asking price.

As for the cops, if they'd moved stuff around, they'd put it back in relatively the same fashion as they'd found it.

I head into the kitchen and I grab myself a couple string cheeses from the fridge. Lassie springs onto the counter and begins clawing at one of the cabinets. I open it and find some little treats. I feed him a couple. He gobbles them down.

"Dude, you didn't even chew it."

Meow.

"You're gonna spoil your appetite."

Meow.

"If you find us a clue to who killed your mom, I'll give you a couple more."

Meow.

"Seven? How bout three?"

Meow.

"Four, but no more."

Meow.

"Fine, five."

He jumps off the counter and zips out of the kitchen.

After my unlikely chat with the POTUS, I was far from convinced that Jessica Renoix had not died at the hands of Connor Sullivan. But he had put a couple chinks in the armor, enough that I was looking for a connection between Jessica and a third party. If this was a ménage à trois, then someone knew the President was coming over to Jessica's house with a big bag of cash. I was hoping to uncover some clue as to who that person could be.

I spend five minutes in the living room looking through a bunch of pictures on the walls. The Clemens appear to be in their late sixties, but that could have been exacerbated by UVA and UVB rays. There is a son and a daughter. Four grandchildren by the looks of the framed school pictures.

Finding nothing that speaks to the murder of Jessica Renoix, I make my way into the master bedroom. I hit the flashlight on my phone, illuminating the many elephant trinkets scattered about the room. I wonder if Jessica or Mrs. Clemens was the elephant nut. I guess the latter. In fact, everything in the room, the entire house, appears to belong to the Clemens. Had they known Jessica well enough to let her around all their valuables without a care in the world? Detective Ray had said the Clemens told her Callie/Jessica had contacted them through Craigslist, so Jessica wasn't an old family friend. Ray also mentioned they'd given her a great deal on the rent. Did she charm them, much like she'd charmed the President?

Jessica had been living in the house for going on three months, yet there was no sign of her.

The closet was full of the Clemens' clothes. The dresser as well. Well, at least most of the dresser. Unless, Mrs. Clemens was wearing thongs and a size two, which I highly doubted, the bottom three drawers belonged to Jessica. I rifle through her bra and panties, then her shirts and tops, then her jeans. I stick my hand into the pocket of each pair of jeans. On the fifth pair, I find a small slip of paper. A receipt.

I unfold it.

Best Cash Pawn Shop.

She sold something to them for $1,200.

Meow.

I look down at Lassie.

"Too late, buddy. I already found it."

Meow.

"Okay, okay."

I give him two more treats.

Meow.

"You're welcome."

Five minutes later we are home.

...

"It's up here on the left."

"That neon sign?" asks my dad.

Best Cash Pawn Shop is in one of the sketchier parts of town, just on the outskirts of DC. The drive had taken nearly 35 minutes and I'd eaten my breakfast in the car.

I turn around and look at Murdock and Lassie in the back seat. They hadn't gotten off to a great start. According to my father — who had driven to my house around midnight — when he and Murdock had entered my apartment, Lassie had come out from the bedroom to investigate. Murdock — big, sweet, dumb, Murdock — had never seen a cat before and went berserk, barking his head off and chasing the cat all over the condo to the point where the couch was overturned and the downstairs neighbors were banging on the walls. My dad was trying to harangue the giant pooch when Murdock suddenly stopped barking. My dad looked down and couldn't believe his eyes. Lassie had somehow found the bag of treats I'd brought home the night before, opened it, and had dropped a treat at the feet of the enraged canine. Murdock ate the treat and Lassie set another peace offering at his feet.

When I woke up a couple hours later and walked into the living room, the two were asleep next to one another, Murdock's huge paw cradled around the small cat.

"Don't forget who feeds you," I tell Lassie, who is lying on Murdock's back, gently rocking with each of the mastiff's breaths.

Meow.

"You can't have two BFFs."

"Are you okay?" my dad asks.

I ignore him and point to a place across the street and tell him to park.

"You sure this place is open?" he asks.

"It said it was open twenty-four hours."

There is a group of unsavory characters standing just outside the entrance and my dad says, "You want me to come with you?"

"No, better you stay with the car."

I hop out and walk past three leering gangsters, trying not to look like I'm carrying five thousand in cash in my right front pocket. I push through the barred door and the chiming of bells alerts someone to my presence.

The man behind the counter is a white guy with a ponytail. He is wearing a jean jacket and fingerless gloves. He looks like what a guy who is working at a pawnshop at three in the morning is supposed to look like.

"What can I do for ya?" he inquires as I approach.

I pull the receipt from my pocket and hand it to him. "My girlfriend sold this and I'd like to buy it back."

He scrunches his face at me, then pulls up glasses attached to a chain around his neck and peers down at the receipt. There is a code on the receipt that reads 2F49. It could be anything, a TV, a coat, art, jewelry. I'm hoping whatever it is will somehow connect Jessica to whoever killed her. Killed her and took $200,000.

"Let's see here," he says. He walks down the counter, bends down, and says, "You're in luck. Number forty-nine is still hanging around."

He pulls out a watch and lays it on the counter.

It is silver with a black leather band. The second hand sweeps effortlessly across the numerals. It is a beautiful piece of craftsmanship.

"Nice watch," he says.

I nod.

"This what you're looking for?"

"That's it," I say, hoping it is. "You remember the girl who sold you this?"

"I wasn't here, but Chip, one of the other guys was, and he told me about some hot little number who came in wanting ten thousand for some watch." He pauses, "That sound like your lady?"

I nod, but I'm thinking about Jessica. She wanted ten grand, but took twelve hundred. She must have been desperate.

"How much for it back?" I ask.

"How much you willing to pay?"

"Three grand."

He laughs and says that it is worth three times that.

"Thirty-five hundred," I counter.

Laughs again.

"Four."

Less laughing.

"Forty-five."

Almost a nod.

"Five."

"Deal."

I fork over all five grand. He polishes the watch for me, then hands it over, and I realize I have just spent five grand on a watch that most likely belongs to Mr. Clemens. I put it in my pocket and walk quickly across the street and get back into the car.

"You get it?" my dad asks.

"Yeah." I turn and look at Lassie and say, "I really could have used you in there, buddy. Guy cleaned me out."

Meow.

"You would not have gotten it for fifty dollars."

He laughs.

"Let's see it," my dad says.

The clock on the dash reads 3:53 a.m.

The gangsters are staring at us from across the way and I say, "Let's get out of this neighborhood first."

We drive for five minutes, then pull into a neighborhood with fences.

"Now that is a nice watch," my dad says, though I hardly hear him. I am too busy trying to make out the inscription on the back. I read it out loud, "To Risky, may all your dreams come true. Mom and Dad."

My dad's eyebrows jump.

"What?" I ask.

"I think I know whose watch that is."

I stare at him.

He explains how he is openly referred to as Risky.

My dad says the name. "Ricky Sullivan."

The President's son.

:12

Years ago, my dad tried to drag my lifeless body from his car up to my condo, but it hadn't ended well. It'd taken him over twenty minutes, he'd slipped two discs in the process, and my neighbor down the hall, thinking my dad was disposing of my body, had called the cops. Since then, anytime I fell asleep in the car, he'd recline the seat, put a pillow under my head, lay a blanket over me, and crack a couple windows. And although he wouldn't admit it, I know he checked on me every couple hours throughout the day.

At 3:00 a.m., I wake up, crawl from the car, and make my way up to the apartment where my dad, Murdock, and Lassie are all spooning on the bed. Lassie and Murdock both jump off, run forward, and lick me clean.

"Hey guys, did you have fun playing?"

"They sure did," my dad says, pushing himself up. "Long lost brothers, you'd think those two are."

I laugh.

The four of us move to the living room.

"You gonna stick around?" I ask my dad.

"No, I think we're gonna head out. Got some things to do tomorrow."

"Cards on Wednesday?"

"Always."

"What are you gonna do about the watch?" he asks.

"I'm not sure. I have to do some research. But if the President's son is involved, I'm going to find out."

In the couple of minutes before I'd fallen asleep last night, my dad had told me everything he knew about Ricky Sullivan. The President's only child made the Bush twins seem tame by comparison. He'd gotten into his fair share of trouble when Sullivan was governor — though he was never officially arrested for anything — and his father's rise to the presidency did little to quell "Risky's" insatiable appetite for fast cars and fast women. He had been likened to Prince Harry on several occasions and the two were actually close friends. In the past year, he'd kept a low profile and was said to be buckling down for his second year at Georgetown Law.

"I thought of something else," my dad says, "about the President's son."

I nod.

"I guess he has a bit of a gambling problem. His bookie was busted a couple years back for cocaine possession. He thought rolling over on the President's son's gambling habits would lighten his sentence. It didn't. But the story did leak to the press; Risky was into him for about eighty grand at the time."

As if I hadn't put it together, my dad adds, "The two hundred grand that was stolen."

"You might be on to something," I tell him.

He shrugs and says that he'd better get going. He starts toward the door. Murdock appears to have no intention of leaving his sidekick and lowers to the ground next to Lassie.

"Say goodbye to your friend," I tell Lassie, picking him up and making my way toward the open door.

Meow.

"No, he can't stay over."

Meow.

"Because you guys are gonna stay up all night drinking soda and playing video games, that's why."

Meow.

"He's coming back over in a couple days and you guys can stay up as long as you want."

Meow.

"*Grand Theft Auto VI*? Is that even out yet?"

Meow.

"I'll see what I can do."

Murdock jumps up on my chest and gives Lassie a big kiss goodbye, then my dad yanks him by the collar and shuts the door. I can hear him whining in the hallway as my dad wrestles the beast away from the door.

...

Lassie and I are just sitting down to eat when there is a knock at the door.

It is 3:11 a.m.

I look through the peephole, expecting to see my father, thinking he'd left something at my condo. It's not.

I pull the door open.

"What the fuck, Bins?"

"And a hello to you, Detective Ray."

She storms in. She is wearing a black top and tight jeans. Her hair is up. Her arms are also up. As is her apparent temper. "You didn't have to go to the FBI!"

"FBI?"

She cuts her eyes at me.

"What are you talking about?"

Her eyebrows rise, then slide together. "You don't know?"

I shake my head.

"Tomorrow morning." She pauses. "They're going to arrest the President for murder."

...

"What?"

"Callie Freig isn't really Callie Freig."

I put on my best surprise face. Big eyes. Open mouth. A loss for words. It works.

"The FBI got an anonymous tip. Before she changed her identity, Callie Freig was actually a young girl named Jessica Renoix. She worked for Sullivan's governor campaign in Virginia. The tip also said that they saw the President leave the woman's house the night of the murder."

She looks at me skeptically.

"It wasn't me," I assure her, then add, "Still that's not a lot to go on. The Secret Service came and got the phone, so they couldn't use that. You would think the FBI would have more."

"They do."

She takes a deep breath.

"President Sullivan underwent a battery of tests when he became President, one of which was a DNA workup. His DNA wouldn't show up in a routine search of the national DNA database, but the FBI has it on file somewhere. They ran his DNA against a couple of hairs found in her bed and it was a match."

I didn't have to fake my surprise face this time.

"They made a courtesy call to my Captain, because the homicide is technically our jurisdiction, but yeah, they are arresting him at the White House tomorrow morning."

"What did your Captain say?"

"What could he say? He let the biggest arrest in the history of the United States slip through his fingers. He smelled like he'd drank a fifth of scotch by the time he called me and Cal into his office and told us what was going on."

I thought of Cal, who had been so adamant that I'd killed her. "It would have been nice to see Cal's face."

"He still thinks it's bullshit," she scoffs. "Thinks it's some big left-wing conspiracy to get the President out of office and get a democrat back in."

"Asshole."

She nods and both of us go quiet. I wonder if she is playing the same simulation in her head, the one of the President being arrested, and the media atomic bomb that is going to explode tomorrow. This will, without a doubt, be the biggest story since 9/11.

"I talked with him."

She cuts her eyes at me. "Who?"

"The President."

"Yeah, right. You talked with Connor Sullivan."

"I did. Two nights ago."

It takes her three seconds to realize I'm not joking. She takes two steps toward me. We are a foot apart.

"Tell me."

I start at the beginning. The very beginning. "So, Lassie isn't my cat. I mean, he is now, but he was Jessica's."

She looks at Lassie who is sitting on the top of the couch. Hearing his name he meows.

It takes ten minutes for me to bring her up to date: the vet, the microchip, Jessica Renoix, the goons, the tasing, the back seat chat with the most powerful man in the world.

I leave out the part of my breaking back into the house, the pawn receipt, and the watch.

"She was blackmailing him?"

"That's what he said."

"And this tape, it never came out?"

"I think even the people of Jupiter would know if a video of the President banging an eighteen-year-old campaign volunteer leaked out."

"Okay, so then what? He admits to being there that night, bringing the blackmail cash, and then leaving. Then someone else comes and kills her and takes the money. Who?"

Well, his son for one. He'd obviously been in contact with Jessica at some point. Maybe he knew about his dad's affair. Maybe she'd told him everything. Maybe he needed the money to pay off his gambling debts. Maybe Jessica and Risky were supposed to split the money, but he got greedy and killed her. Lots of maybes.

"I don't know," I reply. "Odds are it's a bunch of bullshit and Sullivan did it."

"Is that what you think? You think it's bullshit? You think he was lying?"

I run the clip back in my head. His clenched jaw. His commanding gaze as he said, "I didn't kill her."

"No." I say, "I think he was telling the truth."

She exhales.

I reach out and touch her arm. I'm not sure why, but I do. It is an automatic response, as unconscious as my next breath.

She looks at my hand on her shoulder, then looks up at me. I don't know what is going on behind her soft brown eyes. But I want to know.

"You want to stay for some coffee?" I ask.

"It's three-thirty in the morning," she says with a laugh. "I've got to get to bed. Tomorrow is going to be a circus."

Lassie jumps off the couch and rubs up against her leg as she starts for the door. She leans down and pets him, then stands and pulls the door open.

"Did you vote for him?" I ask.

She turns. Stares for a second. A flash of her crooked smile.

"Rain check on the coffee," she says.

:13

Within ten seconds of waking up, I am on the internet.
PRESIDENT ARRESTED!
PRESIDENT ARRESTED FOR MURDER!
PRESIDENT SULLIVAN A MURDERER!?!
PRESIDENTIAL MURDER!
MURDERGATE!
Those are just a few of the headlines.

I click on a video and watch as the President is escorted by his Secret Service detail and no fewer than fifteen FBI agents down the White House steps. The Director of the FBI is one of Sullivan's strongest opponents. He is making a statement. No one is above the law. Even the President.

There are other videos: Wolf Blitzer, Anderson Cooper, Bill O'Reilly, all chomping at the bit. This is the biggest scandal since Cain and Abel went to the old fishing hole and only Cain came back. I don't spend too much time on the videos, but do watch a couple flashes of press conferences: the head of the FBI, the White House Press Secretary, even one where Charles Barkley weighs in ("That guy an idiot"). Bottom line, the President was arrested for the murder of Jessica Renoix. The Senate and House are calling for an impeachment and the wheels are in motion. For the moment, Connor Sullivan is still the most powerful man in the world, but that could change any moment.

"What do you think, buddy? Should they impeach him?"
Lassie cocks his head to the side, thinking.
Meow.
"Stone him?"

Meow.

"Cut off his hands?"

Meow.

"Okay, no more *Game of Thrones* for you, buddy."

We get out of bed, get some grub, and sit down to the breakfast table. I search "Ricky Sullivan."

I read a couple tidbits about him, corroborating most of what my dad had already told me. The latest hit was from twelve hours earlier. Some website called TMZ. "Risky's Wild Spring Break."

I read the small blurb, then call my dad.

He answers.

"Get the car. We're going to Vegas."

...

The drive time from Alexandria to Las Vegas is approximately thirty-four hours.

When I wake up, we are in Colorado.

"Good morning," my dad says.

"Morning."

I turn around.

"Hey, guys."

Lassie is chewing on Murdock's ear. He stops long enough to give me a quick kiss then goes back to the business at hand. Murdock seems to be enjoying it thoroughly.

"You mind driving for an hour?" asks my dad.

"Not at all."

We pull over and switch spots. My dad is asleep within three miles.

I pull out my phone and log onto the internet. It takes me a couple moments to find what I'm looking for. I click play.

Connor Sullivan is standing behind a lectern on the White House steps. At the time of the press conference, he is still the POTUS.

"My fellow Americans," he begins, "I come before you not as the President, but as your fellow man. A man wrongly and unjustly accused of a crime I did not commit. I have every faith in the United States judicial system and that I will be found unequivocally innocent of this heinous crime. I am not disenchanted but proud that we live in a democratic state where its highest powers are not above the law, and hold no ill will toward the FBI or any other institution. The truth will come out. God bless this great nation."

Not bad.

I wonder how long he actually spent in a jail cell before they rushed him into a courtroom and posted bail.

Doesn't matter.

What matters is in the background. His wife is there. His son isn't.

I put the phone down and force myself to the road. I've seen mountains before, but nothing as majestic as the snow-capped Rockies that loom under the full moon.

At 3:58, I pull the car over into a small dirt enclave and I nudge my father. We switch seats.

When I wake up, it will be the bright lights of Vegas.

:14

There are 122 casinos, 874 clubs, over 2,000 restaurants, and more than 50 strip clubs in Las Vegas. Nearly everything is open until four in the morning, if they close at all. And Ricky Sullivan could be in any one of them. That is, if the paparazzi and his father's arrest hasn't sent him underground. It takes my dad six hours and five greased palms, but he finally tracks the President's son and his buddies to the XS Nightclub.

At 3:06, my dad pulls up to the massive Wynn hotel and I jump out. After a twenty-minute wait in line, and a fifty-dollar cover charge, I enter.

House music blares. Purple, orange, and green strobe lights threaten to give me a seizure. The air is sticky, a million tiny post-it notes. I feel like I've walked into a beehive. It's madness.

I push my way through the swarming bodies. A young woman wearing six square inches of fabric grabs my crotch and whispers something unintelligible in my ear.

She grabs my hand and yanks me toward the dance floor.

I shake her hand off. I measure women in minutes and she is worth about thirty seconds. Detective Ray flashes across my mind. I give her all sixty.

When I finally get to the bar, it is 3:34 a.m.

"Where's Ricky Sullivan?" I scream at the closest bartender.

He feigns ignorance. I am not the first person to ask him this question tonight. I wave a hundred dollar bill at him. He walks over and snags it, cocks his head to the right, then moves on to the next customer.

It takes me four minutes to push my way through the crowd and to the VIP tables. Two bouncers guard a thick rope that cordons off ten plush circular tables that currently hold three NBA stars, two rappers, a restaurateur, a comedian, an actress, a supermodel, a late-night host, and the President's son.

Ricky Sullivan is with two other guys and eight scantily clad women. They are sitting on a plush purple sofa. At least a thousand dollars' worth of bottle service litters the table next to them. Three men in black suits stand close by— Ricky's Secret Service detail.

They look especially alert and I'm guessing the past forty-eight hours have been a deluge of reporters and paparazzi trying to get a snapshot or a comment.

The bouncers appraise me as I approach.

They are checking my wrist for the bright green band that all the "visitors" to the VIP section are wearing.

I have one.

I bought it from a girl on the dance floor for $200. She wiggled it off and I was able to wiggle it on.

What can I say? I have dainty hands.

They let me through and I pick my way past four of the tables. When I am within six feet of Ricky Sullivan and his posse, two of the Secret Service goons jump forward and block my path.

"Hey, guys."

They don't respond.

"I just need a quick second with Ricky."

They look at one another.

"Get lost," says one.

"Ricky!" I yell. He doesn't turn around.

The Secret Service guys start pushing me back.

I pull the watch from my pocket and toss it underhand. It lands on the lap of a girl next to Ricky.

Before my arms are wrenched behind my back, I catch Ricky's eyes as he sees the watch.

"He's good."

The force that is about to break my wrist lessens slightly.

"I said he's good! LET HIM THROUGH!"

I dust myself off, give the two SS a little nod, and walk past. Ricky has already ushered all the girls and his two buddies from the table. It's just him and the watch.

I sit down a couple feet from him.

I grab the Ciroc vodka and pour myself a vodka cranberry.

"Where did you get this?"

I look up.

Ricky Sullivan has his mother's brown, doe eyes and soft features. He has his father's weight, but on a foot shorter frame. He's lost twenty pounds in the past few years but he's still a chubbo.

"I got it from the pawn shop that Jessica sold it to."

He inhales.

"When did she take it?"

He pours himself a stiff drink, takes a long swallow, and says, "About two months ago."

"Did you know?"

"Yeah, I knew. But I didn't care. Just figured she needed money and was too proud to ask. It wasn't the only thing she took."

"Where did you meet her?"

"A coffee shop on campus. She said she had a class with me, but I could tell she was lying. But who cares?" He shrugs. "She was the sexiest girl I'd ever seen."

He asks who I am. I ignore him.

"Did you kill her?"

He is a deer in headlights. His doe eyes start to leak. He is crying. It takes him thirty seconds to compose himself.

"NO!" He sniffs. "She was the first girl I ever really cared about. Ever."

"Did you know about her connection to your father?"

He shakes his head. "No, she never talked about her past. She just wanted to, well, screw mostly. At least, at first. At the beginning, I think she just wanted to fuck the President's son. But then, I think, she kinda started to like me." He smiles sheepishly, like the idea of a girl actually liking him for himself is preposterous.

"Did you ever go to her house?"

"No. I didn't even know where she lived. Dave and Jerry," he nods toward the two Secret Service guys who had manhandled me, "would sneak her up to my apartment."

"How long were you two involved?"

"Three months."

"Did you know her as Callie or Jessica?"

"At first it was Callie, but after six weeks, we were in bed, and she told me to call her Jessie."

Jessie?

"And she never told you about her past, how she worked for your father's campaign?"

"Nope, never."

"What would you talk about?"

"I don't know. Movies, books, she wanted to go to vet school someday, to travel. She liked sports, especially the Ravens. She loved to play cards. We'd play cards for hours."

"Did she ask about your dad?"

"At first. She wanted to know what sort of dad he was. Was he around? Stuff like that. But she abhorred politics. My dad didn't come up very often after the first couple weeks."

"How did you find out she was killed?"

"Jerry came in and took my cell phone. Told me that Callie had been murdered. Brought me a new phone a couple hours later with a new phone number."

That would explain the phone number that had been untraceable. It hadn't been the President's. It was Ricky's.

"What's the spread on the Laker's game tomorrow?"

He scoffs. "I haven't gambled in six months. I learned my lesson."

I nod.

"What do you think 'Jessie' needed the money from the watch for?"

"I don't know. She didn't have a job. She had to pay rent somehow."

"And you didn't care that she stole a ten thousand dollar watch from you?"

"I know I should have. But I didn't."

"You loved her."

He is quiet.

He did.

"Do you think your dad killed her?"

His lips quiver.

I've heard enough. And I'm out of time. I chug the rest of my drink, pat him on the shoulder and leave.

...

I drive my one hour, this time in Tennessee.

The next time I wake up, I am in my father's car parked

outside my condo. There is an unmarked car parked down the street and I feel the occupant's stare as I get out and enter my building.

My dad and Murdock leave, and Lassie and I sit down to the computer.

I log onto the internet.

The email from the company I'd paid to do a background check on Jessica Renoix is waiting for me in my inbox. I click on it and am not surprised to find very little information. There is a credit card, a phone, and an Oregon address. All are for show. Just like they'd been for Callie Freig.

That's why Jessica needed the money from the watch. She wanted to change her identity. She had done it before.

Twice.

I'd known four Jessicas in my life. Some went by Jess. None went by Jessie. It was a totally different name. Like a Matthew going by Mark. Didn't happen.

I go to the Virginia Missing Person's Database and search "Jessie."

No hits.

Maybe I'm wrong.

I think back to what Ricky had said. She liked sports. Especially the Ravens.

The Baltimore Ravens.

I log onto the Maryland Missing Person's database and try again.

Two hits.

One is a twelve-year-old boy.

The other is a sixteen-year-old girl.

Jessie Kallomatix.

She is younger, but there is no mistaking it.

It's her.

Jessie Kallomatix is Jessica Renoix is Callie Freig.

Two Google searches later and I have it all figured out.

What had Ricky said? "She'd ask what kind of dad he was. Was he around a lot?"

Connor Sullivan had lied.

She'd been blackmailing him all right, but not because he'd slept with her.

She'd been blackmailing him because Connor Sullivan was her father.

:15

It takes three days – well, three hours – for it all to come together. Three hours of planning, phone calls, and favors.

I pull open the curtains.

The car is still there.

Still watching.

It is 3:03 a.m.

At 3:04, I hear the sirens.

"Here they come."

Meow.

"Sorry, buddy. I have to do this one alone."

Meow.

"Yes, it's going to be dangerous."

Meow.

"Danger isn't your middle name."

Meow.

"Because I didn't think to give you one."

Meow.

"Pistol? I don't think so."

Meow.

"No. I don't care if he is a triple threat. How bout Roger?"

Meow.

"Well, Lassie Timberlake Bins sounds stupid too."

Meow.

"Well, I don't care what Murdock says."

Meow.

"Fine, your middle name can be Danger."

Meow.

The ambulance pulls up in front of the condo.

"All right, Lassie Danger Bins, it's go time."

Three minutes later, I am in the ambulance and we are flying down the street.

"Hey," Sara says from the passenger seat.

"Thanks again."

Her boyfriend, Clay, and his buddy, Jake, who had taken me out on the stretcher both nod. Clay says, "It was a slow night."

"Did they follow?" I ask.

"Yep," Sara says with a nod. "They're probably two lights behind us."

A minute later, the ambulance pulls up to Summer Park and I jump out.

"Good luck."

I nod and take off running.

...

I bang on the window and she jumps.

"Shit, you scared me," she says, climbing out of her Crown Vic.

"How long have you been here?"

"I got here right at three, just like you said." She pauses. "You gonna tell me what this is all about?"

I scan the side street for approaching headlights. "Not yet. Not till he gets here."

"Who?"

I ignore her.

Ten seconds later, lights turn onto the street and grow brighter as the car pulls into the lot and parks next to us.

The door opens and he says, "Get in."

Ray's eyebrows jump five inches off her forehead. "Is that the President?"

I nod.

The two of us climb in the back of the town car.

Connor is wearing the same outfit as last time: jeans and a gray sweatshirt.

"This is Detective Ingrid Ray from the Alexandria PD," I say.

He takes her hand.

"Pleasure to meet you, Mr. President."

"Likewise." Then turning to me, he asks, "So what is this about?"

I hadn't told him anything. In fact, I'd simply called the private number he'd given me the day we'd first met and left a message telling him to meet me at Summer Park at 3:15 a.m. That it was important.

I hand a piece of paper to him and say, "Tell your driver to go to this address."

He looks down at the paper, if the address means anything to him, he doesn't show it. He pushes a button and the divider slides down and he passes the paper through to his driver.

"Hey, Red," I say.

He nods.

The divider goes back up and the car begins to move.

I can feel four eyes on me.

"You lied to me."

The President doesn't flinch.

"There was no video."

Sullivan's face is marble.

"You never slept with her. She never seduced you."

I wait for Sullivan to scoff, to tell me that I'm full of shit, to get out of his car.

He doesn't.

"She was your daughter."

Ray pinches my leg. A "what the hell are you doing?" pinch.

"Yes, she is."

"What?" Ray shouts. "Jessica is your daughter?"

He nods.

"Wait, what, how . . ." Ray bumbles.

"I'll explain in a second," I tell her.

"How did you find out?" Sullivan asks.

"Your son."

He sighs.

"She told him to call her Jessie."

"Jessie? I thought her name was Jessica?" Ray shouts, trying to piece things together.

"She changed her identity twice," I tell Ray. "Her real name was Jessie." I explain about the pawn receipt and my chat with Ricky Sullivan in Vegas, how I'd found Jessie on the missing person's database on the internet, and how after searching her name, I'd put the pieces together. Then I turn to the President and say, "He thinks you killed her, you know."

"Better than the alternative," he says, leaning his head back. "Better than him knowing he's been fucking his half-sister for the past three months."

"Wait!" shouts Ray. "Will one of you tell me what is going on?"

I nod toward the President. "Why don't you start at the beginning? And no lies this time."

"All right, but first tell me where we're going."

"You don't recognize the address?"

"Just that it is in Maryland. Should I know?"

"Yeah, you married the woman who lives there."

...

It was a story that was said to have won Connor Sullivan the presidency. A story that could have been told in any bar in the world. It made you see him as a guy, any guy, who accidentally married the wrong woman.

Kimberly A. Bells was born in Nevada. She went to college at a small school in Ohio, Dayton University, where she met and fell in love with one of the stars of the basketball team. After graduating, Kimberly moved to Virginia with her new love, married him, spawned him one child, and eventually became the First Lady of the United States of America.

Kimberly S. Bells grew up in Virginia, met Paul Kallomatix when she was 22, and had a daughter. The couple would move to Maryland years later, stay happily married for sixteen years, then divorce bitterly.

Both marriages took place at the same church in northern Virginia. Kimberly A. Bells to Connor Sullivan on the Saturday. Kimberly S. Bells to Paul Kallomatix on the Sunday.

To this day, it still isn't known how it happened, if it was the clerk at the courthouse, the minister, or a third party, but the documents were mixed up and Connor Sullivan ended up married to Kimberly S. Bells and vice versa.

You would think one little initial wouldn't have been such a troublesome problem and it wasn't, at least, not until it came time to pay taxes. It took Connor Sullivan two weeks to figure out why he owed so much money to the United States government. It was because he wasn't married to a third grade teacher as his wife had been for the past three years, but to a marketing executive who made nearly three times her salary.

He finally realized the small faux pas and after a couple of phone calls, rectified the matter.

"I wanted to meet her, meet the woman I was married to," the President says with a laugh. "But not just her, I wanted to meet him too."

I glance at Ray and wonder what is going on in her head.

"The address on file for her was only a half hour away and one day I found myself in the neighborhood and decided to pop by." He shakes his head. "The second she opened the door, I knew I was in trouble."

I'd seen a couple pictures of her on the internet. When the story had come out during Sullivan's initial run for governor, some journalists had tracked her down and taken some photos. She was of medium height, brown eyes, high cheekbones, full lips.

"Did the affair start that day?"

"No. We just talked for an hour. Laughed over the whole thing. Promised to get our spouses together and have dinner some night."

"But that never happened?"

He shakes his head. "In fact, I didn't see her for another three years. Then I was up in Maryland for a meeting and I ran into her. She and her husband had moved up there a couple years earlier. We had coffee and well, you could tell she was unhappy. The marriage was on the rocks. She never saw him. He worked constantly. After that, we'd see each other a couple times a month."

"When did the affair start?"

"In December of that year. Kim, my wife, was out of town for the week. The other Kim called and said she'd be down in Virginia for a couple days visiting her folks. She came over and, well—"

"How long did it last?"

"Six months. I stopped when my wife told me she was pregnant."

"Was the other Kim okay with it?"

"I guess so. I never heard from her again."

"Then how did Jessie come into the picture?"

"Well, she'd already changed her name when I met her. If she'd come to work for my campaign and said her name was Jessie Kallomatix, I don't know if I would have let her work for me. So, when I met her, her name was Jessica Renoix. She worked hard for me for three months, then one day she comes into my office, tells me point-blank who she is, that her mother had gotten drunk one night and told her about her affair with me. Then she shows me a little baggy and a piece of paper. The baggy has a lock of my hair in it, says that she cut it off my head one night when I was asleep on my desk. The piece of paper is a DNA test. She says that I'm her father and that she wants a hundred thousand dollars."

"And you gave it to her?"

"I did. And she disappeared the next day. I didn't hear from her until three months ago."

"What did she say?"

"It was an email. I have the same private email I had back then. It was a picture of her and my son."

"That must have gotten your attention."

"Sure did."

"And this time she asked for two hundred grand?"

"Yep."

"To stop dating your son?"

He nods.

"And then you went over there that night to give her the money."

"But she didn't want it."

"What?"

"She didn't want the money. She said she really liked my son, that she'd fallen in love with him."

"And that's when you killed her?"

"NO."

I didn't think he had, but I wanted to see his reaction.

"Why did she scream?"

"I pushed her up against the wall and slapped her. Told her what she was doing was sick, that if she didn't stop seeing my son I was going to make her disappear. I dropped the bag of money and left."

The car slows. I look out the window. We are in front of a small row house.

It is 3:34 a.m.

Twenty-six minutes.

Twenty-six minutes to get a confession.

:16

"Does this place look familiar?" I ask the President.

He shakes his head.

I'd doubted Kim Bells lived in the same house she lived in over twenty years ago, but you never know.

We get out. I tell Red to park a couple blocks down the road and he peels away. The four of us walk up the small stone steps. I am in front, then Detective Ray, then the towering Sullivan in the rear.

"You really think she had something to do with Jessie's murder?" asks Sullivan. "That she would kill her own daughter?"

I shrug. "Only one way to find out."

I ring the doorbell.

Nothing happens for a long minute.

I ring the doorbell again.

Lights come on. The padding of feet. The door opens.

"Uh, yeah?" The twenty or so years have not been kind to Kim Bells. The thirty pounds she's put on since the photo drip from beneath a pink tank top and the skin under her eyes is a heavy black. She is wearing gray sweatpants. She is twice the size of her daughter. It would have been easy for her. Easy to strangle her daughter to death.

I pull Ray to the side.

Kim's eyes widen. "Connor?"

"Kim," he says with a nod.

"Can we come in?" I ask, checking the street for activity.

"I, um, guess so." She takes a step backward and the four of us walk past.

I find the living room and the others follow.

I introduce myself and she shakes my hand limply. Ray shows her badge and I can see every muscle in Kim's body tense.

"What's this about?" she asks with a hitch in her throat.

"It's about Jessie," answers Sullivan.

The air in the room drops a thousand degrees.

"Jessie?"

I try to read her emotions. Her labored breathing. The double blink of her eyes. The smack of her lips. Could be guilt. Could be indigestion.

"I haven't seen her in eight years," she spats.

The three of us look at one another.

Sullivan doesn't buy it. Maybe it's a wrinkle around her mouth, a flicker of the eyes. It's something. A crack in the veneer. She's lying.

"Bullshit," he scoffs.

She doesn't respond.

Sullivan sees blood. This is the woman who framed him for murder. He has every right to be furious. He has every right to want to physically harm her, which he looks as though he might do any second. I step between them.

"How could you do it?" he screams. "How could you kill your own daughter?"

"Kill? Who? Jessie?"

"You murdered Jessie and framed me for it!"

Kim's head whips left, then right. "She's . . . Jessie's dead?"

Sullivan looks at me. Back to Kim. Stares at her. Through her.

"Are you saying that you didn't kill her?"

"NO! I didn't even . . . No . . . I would never . . . I mean she was a terrible person . . . psychotic . . . but I would never hurt her. Never . . . Oh, my God, she's dead . . . how? WHEN?"

I knew that she didn't kill her, but I find it hard to believe she didn't know her daughter was dead.

"You really didn't know she was dead?" I ask.

"No."

"Really?" asks Ray, her first words in over twenty minutes. "Did you know about the President's arrest?"

"Uh, yeah, I guess I heard about that." She looks at Sullivan. "But I didn't want to believe it. I started reading an article about it in the paper a few days ago, but I had to stop."

I could see it in her eyes, still to this day. I'm not sure how Sullivan had felt about her, but she had loved him.

"But you'd seen her since she was sixteen." I say. It isn't a question.

"Yeah, once," she admits reluctantly. "She came by about two years ago asking for money. No 'Hi', no 'Sorry I ran away without telling you three years ago', just 'Got any money?'"

"Did you give her any?"

She shakes her head. "That girl ruined my life. Started doing meth when she was twelve, having sex by thirteen. Cost me my marriage and hundreds of thousands of dollars in rehab. They foreclosed on my house. I lost everything. I didn't give that lying slut a dime. Best thing that ever happened to me was her leaving that day."

"Why didn't you call and get her removed from the Missing Persons database?"

She shrugs. "Never thought to, I guess."

"You could have told me," interjects Sullivan.

"Told you what?"

"That Jessie was mine."

"Yours?"

"My daughter."

"Jessie's not your daughter."

"According to the DNA test she showed me, I am."

Kim scoffs. "Jessie was a pathological liar. Pathological. She started making her own fake report cards on the computer when she was seven. They were perfect. Her teacher couldn't even tell the difference. She forged a sixty thousand dollar check when she was eleven. She made fake IDs for everybody at the high school when she was fourteen."

That would account for all her fake identities. I'm sure she'd had help along the way, but if she had one foot in the world, it would have been far more accessible.

"But I called the company who did the test. They wouldn't give me much information, but I wiggled out of one of the receptionists that Jessie Kallomatix was in their files."

"That was probably from when I had her tested when she was young, to make sure Paul was her father and not you."

"And he was?"

"Yep."

"Shit."

Sullivan had a right to be pissed. He'd paid out over $300,000 based on Jessie being his daughter. But he didn't look pissed. In fact, he was smiling.

I could tell he was thinking about Ricky. Glad his son hadn't been sleeping with his half-sister. That must have been giving the President nightmares.

"That's why she sent you the picture of your son the second time," I say to the President. "Because if she would have blackmailed you for being your daughter, you would have checked more thoroughly this time. You would have had Red or one of your other guys get to the bottom of it. So she started hooking up with your son. She knew you would keep that to yourself."

Sullivan nods.

"Hooking up with your son?" asks Kim.

Sullivan spends the next ten minutes explaining everything. From how he'd first met Jessie, to her blackmail, to the picture she sent of her and his son, to him going over to her house and dropping off the money, to her being found strangled to death.

I look down at my cell phone.

It's 3:50.

Ten minutes.

Sullivan gazes at me. "So then, another dead end."

Lights turn onto the street.

Get brighter. Brighter. Brighter. Then disappear.

All six eyes are trained on me.

I put my finger up to my lips.

Ten seconds later, there is a knock.

"Bins," comes a voice. "Bins, it's me. I'm here."

I pull the door open.

:17

Paul Kallomatix is wearing the same suit he'd been wearing when I'd first met him. His forehead is heavily creased over furrowed brows. His goatee is perfectly groomed around his gaping mouth.

"Hey, Paul," I say.

"What the fuck is going on here, Bins?" he says, ignoring my jest. He sweeps his eyes over his ex-wife, his partner, and the President of the United States. "Kim? Ray? What the fuck is this?"

"You tell me, Cal. Why don't you tell me about Jessie?" spits Ray.

When the President had been telling his story about the marriage mix-up, he'd said the name Paul Kallomatix and Ray had gone silent. I could almost see her trying to put the pieces together in her head. Cal? A murderer?

Cal looks over his shoulder. Thinks about running. Thinks better. His goatee smirks and he takes two steps in and closes the door.

"Are the guys you had following me still at the hospital?" I ask.

"I don't know what you're talking about."

"Sure you do. The off-duty cops that you had watching me the last week. Watching to see if I was going to take a drive up to Maryland to see your ex wife." Luckily, she lived in a different house. One he obviously didn't know about if he'd driven up here to meet me in this one.

"Again. No fuckin' clue what you're talking about."

"You're late by the way." I'd texted him this address right before I'd knocked on Ray's window. Told him to meet me here at 3:45. And to be alone.

"Why'd you do it, Cal?" asks Ray.

"Do what?"

"Why'd you kill her?"

"You? They got to you?" he scoffs. "Come on, Ray, I didn't even know it was Jessie until they showed that picture of her with him," he nods toward Sullivan. "And what difference would it have made? He killed her."

He glares at the President.

"If you aren't gonna tell them how it went down, I will," I say.

"I didn't do anything to that girl."

Not his little girl. That girl.

I look down at my phone.

3:54 a.m.

Six minutes.

"What happened when Jessie accused you of raping her?"

There had been an article about it on the internet. It was one of the things that came up when I searched 'Jessie Kallomatix.' When she was twelve she accused her father, a Maryland cop, of raping her. The case was later thrown out, but it made big news.

"What other lies did she make up about you?"

His face is turning red.

"How much of your hard earned money did you spend sending her to rehab and therapy?"

I can hear his teeth grinding together.

"I'm sorry."

He looks at the President.

"I'm sorry," Sullivan repeats.

Cal snorts. Snorts again.

"It all started with you!" he screams. "You sticking your little dick where it didn't belong."

He scans the room. Locks eyes with each of us. I can feel it. Feel the dam breaking.

"THAT LITTLE CUNT RUINED MY LIFE!"

Spittle shoots from Cal's lips.

"If I could strangle her again, I would."

The four of us don't dare move. Don't dare derail the train.

He shakes his head back and forth as he walks in a tight circle.

"Do you know that when she was fourteen she told me that if I didn't buy her a Range Rover when she turned sixteen that she was going to tell everyone that I got her pregnant and forced her to have an abortion? That little bitch got me kicked off the force. No one in Maryland or DC would touch me, even after the judge ruled that I never touched my daughter. My wife," he points at Kim, "thought I was a sick bastard who raped our little girl and divorced me. Then I had to file for bankruptcy because I spent my life savings putting my psycho fucking daughter through rehab three times.

"Then two months ago, I get called to a strip club. One of the strippers is going bat-shit on a customer, and low and behold it's my own flesh and blood. She's coked out of her mind, and I take her home, and she tells me a funny story about who her real dad is. Turns out this crazy fucking girl who ruined my life isn't even mine. Says that she has his hair in the freezer if I want proof. She passes out and I start looking through her place. Her email is open on her computer, and I see a message to the President. She's blackmailing him. He's supposed to drop off two hundred grand in two days.

"I didn't plan on killing her. I was just going to take the money. I deserved it, damn right I did, after all the shit she put me through. But when I broke in and saw her holding the President's fucking cell phone, I decided it was too good of an opportunity to pass up. I dragged her to the garage, wrapped my hands around her larynx—the same one that told a judge that I'd raped her—and squeezed the life out of her. Left the President's cell phone under the car, sprinkled some of his hair on the bed, grabbed everything of Jessie's I could find, then tossed the cell phone and wallet in the dumpster two blocks away."

"You're the one," Ray says, shaking her head at Cal. "You're the one that gave the FBI the anonymous tip."

"Well, our captain turned out to be too big of a pussy."

"But you said yourself, Cal, that you didn't think it was Sullivan."

"Well, no shit, Ingrid. What the fuck was I gonna say? I know that's his fucking hair because I put it there?"

"She's yours," Kim says.

Cal looks at his ex-wife, who continues talking.

"Jessie was lying. She was always lying. Connor wasn't her dad. You were. I had her tested when she was a baby."

The color drains from his face.

He staggers.

I lean over to brace him.

"No . . . no . . . NO!" he yells.

He is behind me before I can react. I can feel the gun sticking to my ribs.

"Move over there!" he shouts, directing the others to the front of the living room, their backs to the window.

"Settle down," says Ray. Her fingers inch toward her gun.

"Don't even think about it!" Cal shouts into my ear.

She drops her hand.

"You don't have to do this," I find myself saying.

It is 3:58 a.m.

In two minutes I am going to fall over and he's going to think I'm trying to get away and he's going to shoot me.

"You!" he screams in my ear. "If you would have just minded your own fucking business, then everything would have gone just fine."

"My bad," I say, though I don't think he hears. He is too busy thinking. Formulating an escape plan. He breathes heavily in my ear for twenty seconds. Thirty.

It is 3:59 a.m.

I have to do something.

Now.

I lift up my hand.

I do the peace sign.

At least that's what I'm hoping Cal thinks it is.

"Don't fucking move."

I flash the peace sign again.

Two.

I drop a finger.

Ray glares at me curiously.

One.

I drop the second finger.

Now.

I whip my head to the side.

The sound of bursting glass fills the room.

When I look down, I see Cal on the floor, a bullet hole just over the bridge of his nose.

The last thing I remember is Red crashing through the door, the sniper rifle held at his side.

...

POLICE OFFICER FRAMED PRESIDENT!
PRESIDENT INNOCENT!
SULLIVAN DIDN'T DO IT!
INNOCENT-GATE!

Those are the headlines.

The FBI interviewed each of us — mine was done over the phone — but the main evidence was the tape of Cal's admission that Red had been recording through the microphone in the President's sweatshirt. Lucky for us, he'd been listening and knew that Cal had taken me hostage. I'd noticed a glimmer off Red's scope through the window, something Cal had evidently missed.

I'd woken up the next night in my bed and had later found out that the President himself had carried me up the three flights, though I'm sure Red helped. There had been a card next to me. An orange Monopoly card. A Get Out of Jail Free card. I think it was the President's way of saying that he owed me one.

That had been four days ago.

Lassie and I were still trying to decide what we should use the card for.

"What do you think, buddy? Should we cash this baby in for a ride on Air Force One?"

Meow.

"The Taj Mahal? Is that even a thing?"

Meow.

"What it is with you and Justin Timberlake?"

Meow.

"A bag of mice? Now that's a little too practical."

Meow.

"That's what I'm talking about. Jet packs."

Meow.

"I think Jessica Alba's husband might have something to say about that."

Meow.
"Pretty sure you can only do that in Mexico."
Meow.
"I'm gonna act like you didn't say that."
Meow.
"Thanks. Now I'm thinking about midgets."
Meow.
"He's the President, not the Wizard of Oz."
Meow.
"Twenty Murdock clones? Seriously?"

I'm pretty sure this would have gone on forever, or at least for the forty-seven more minutes left in my day, had a stunning, and very naked woman not walked in with two bowls of cereal.

"Breakfast in bed."

Ingrid plops down next to me.

She feeds me a big spoonful of Cinnamon Toast Crunch and says, "I think the Justin Timberlake thing sounds pretty good."

"I bet," I say, sending us both into a fit of laughter.

At 3:55, she looks up at me, panting and says, "You got time for one more?"

"I guess we'll see," I say, grinning.

3:10 A.M.

:01

"Rise and shine."

Lassie opens one eye. He has some gunk in the corner near his nose and I wipe it away with my thumb. He shakes his head, then rests it down on my chest.

"Come on, buddy, we have stuff to do."

Meow.

"Ten more minutes? We've been asleep for twenty-three hours." Well, I had. I couldn't speak for Lassie; though I was nearly certain he was curled up on my chest the entire time.

I brush the cat off and stand up. The clock on the dresser screams that one minute of my day has already elapsed.

I pick up my phone off the bedside table and read Ingrid's text. She won't be able to stop by. She just wrapped up a homicide-suicide investigation and needs to catch up on some sleep. But she will see me tomorrow for sure. Smiley face.

Tomorrow is October 7th, Ingrid's and my sixth-month anniversary.

Though I saw her two days earlier, it feels like I haven't seen her in weeks. I am toying with the idea of asking her to move in with me. I made her a key a couple months back—which is one of the few things accomplishable at three in the morning—and she uses it when she stops over once or twice a week.

But two hours a week isn't enough. I wanted her for all seven.

I pad to the kitchen and pull out the bowl of cereal Isabel prepared for me. I peel off the Saran Wrap and pour in the measured glass of milk. Not only does Isabel cook and clean, she also finds small ways to save me time: my toothbrush laid out with toothpaste on it, the microwave preset for three minutes and thirty seconds (the exact time needed to heat her famous enchiladas), Lassie's food bowl filled and covered in the refrigerator, headphones and running shoes laid out next to the door, the NASDAQ and DOW closing numbers written on a sticky note next to the computer. The seconds she buys me would mean nothing to the average person, but to me, each second is the Mona Lisa.

I eat the cereal, a banana, and a peanut butter protein shake and watch four minutes of *Game of Thrones*. My dad turned me on to the series eight months earlier, and I was up to episode four of season two.

At 3:07 a.m., I check my stocks on E-Trade. I dump a couple thousand shares of a floundering pharmaceutical company and pick up an equal amount of corn futures—which is a huge gamble but has big upside potential.

There is a soft chime and I answer my father's call on Skype.

My father is as frumpy as ever. Big glasses sliding down his nose. Receding gray hair running as fast as possible away from a big shiny forehead. A white mock turtleneck, possibly the last in existence, holding up a sagging Adam's apple.

"Hey, Sonny boy," he mutters.

"Hey, Pops. How's your back?"

"Sore as shit. In fact, I think I'm gonna have to sit out of our game tonight."

My dad's back had been acting up for the past couple weeks, and we'd been forced to play our weekly poker game online. He cleaned me out the previous Wednesday and I was looking forward to some payback.

"Just pop a couple Advil, old man."

"That's just it. The over-the-counter stuff doesn't help and if I take the pills the doctor prescribed, I'm out in five minutes."

I can tell from my father's grimace that he is truly in pain. I can't help but feel partly responsible. My dad's back was fine until a few years ago when he tried to carry me from his car to my third-story condo. Long story short, he slipped two disks and my neighbor called the cops thinking my dad was lugging around a dead body.

"Go pop those pills, then we'll chat for another minute or two."

He nods and disappears from the screen.

A large brown head takes my father's place. The head belongs to my dad's one-hundred-and-sixty-pound English mastiff.

"Hey Murdo—"

Lassie is on my lap before I finish the second syllable. It's been three weeks since the two have seen each other and big stupid Murdock doesn't understand that Lassie isn't actually on the table in my dad's house. Murdock smashes the computer with his giant paw and the feed disappears. My dad calls my phone a moment later and tells me that Murdock shattered his laptop and that he's going to bed.

It is 3:09 a.m.

I'd allocated the rest of my day to playing cards and contemplate what I want to do with my remaining fifty-one minutes. Wednesdays are the only day I don't exercise and I ponder going for a quick run. I lift the curtain and stare out on the glistening asphalt. It'd been a wet October thus far in Alexandria and the asphalt shimmers under the streetlight. I gaze at the house across the street. It's been over six months since I heard Jessie Kallomatix's scream, the impetus that set in motion one man being framed for murder and another taking a bullet between the eyes.

The latter, Jessie's father, like most people who get shot in the face, died. The former, well, he returned to his day job, aka the leader of the free world.

Nearly two months after Conner Sullivan was exonerated from Jessie's murder, my phone rang. It was 3:33 a.m. It was President Sullivan. He couldn't sleep and needed someone to talk to. I was the only person he knew *for certain* was awake. For ten minutes we made small talk about the weather, his beloved Redskins, and how long I let myself sit on the pot. A month later he called again. And two weeks after that he showed up on my doorstep with a six-pack of beer. He knew I played poker with my dad each Wednesday and wanted to know if he could crash our game.

So my dad, me, the President, and Red (the head of the President's Secret Service detail) played poker for forty-nine minutes.

But I hadn't heard from him in three months.

Blasted Ukraine.

I decide to watch fifteen more minutes of *Game of Thrones*, then go for a short walk with Lassie.

I am set to hit the play button when an alert comes in that I have a new email.

It is 3:10 a.m.

IhaveHenryBins@gmail.com doesn't get much action, mostly from Amazon or the online trading podcast I subscribe to, and I've only received a handful of emails while I was awake.

The email is from AST. Advanced Surveillance and Tracking.

The email is only three words.

We found her.

I take a deep breath.

They found my mother.

:02

The last memory I have of my mother is on my sixth birthday. I remember being excited because she missed the previous two. The moment I woke up, I searched the room for her, but it was only my dad standing over me.

"Where's mom?"

"She's . . ."

This sentence always ended the same.

". . . *working.*"

My mom had the most boring job in the world. Or at least, when I was little, I remember thinking a *geologist* was the most boring job in the world. But that was because I viewed her job — rocks — as competition. Why was sandstone more important than me? What did quartzite have that I didn't? It wasn't until I grew up, learned that my mother wasn't spending those three-week to three-month long stretches looking for rocks, that I understood. She was looking for oil. Companies paid her a lot of money to do this, which allowed my dad to stay home, earn a modest living as a technical writer, and care after me.

". . . right there," he'd finished.

My mother came into the room holding a birthday cake. The cake was of Snoopy and it had a big blue number six candle on it.

I can still see the look on my mother's face. Her sharp and angular features — nearly the opposite of my father's — were a billboard of her Czech heritage. She had piercing green eyes — little pieces of jade, she'd called them — that must be what mood rings were made of.

Today, they were somber.

I wonder if she knew then that she was leaving. Leaving us.

After I blew out the candles and ate nearly half the cake, my parents brought in my birthday present. Or should I say, wheeled it in.

A bright red Huffy.

I couldn't have been happier.

"Dad, can you teach me *now*?"

I just assumed my dad would teach me how to ride a bike. He was the one who spent twenty minutes a day reading history to me, or quizzing me on spelling, or making me practice my cursive or long division, then another twenty minutes teaching me how to throw a baseball, swing a golf club, do a handstand, cook an omelet, play gin rummy, and every other life lesson.

"You know, your mom is the bike riding expert in this family. Maybe she'll teach you."

My dad must have already known.

If she hadn't already sat him down and said, "Richard, I can't do this anymore. I can't handle seeing my son only awake for an hour a day. This isn't what I signed up for. I'm leaving," then he'd read it in those jade eyes of hers.

"I do ride a mean bike," my mother said with a smile.

My mom spent the next thirty minutes teaching me how to ride a bike under the streetlights of the small cul-de-sac where my dad still lives today.

I didn't realize it then, but when my mother let go of the seat of my red Huffy, let me balance all on my own, it wasn't just the bike she was letting go of.

When I did a loop back around, it wasn't my mother, but my father waiting for me.

"Where's mom?"

"She had to take a call."

I would never see my mother again.

...

Over the years, I asked my dad about my mother from time to time, but nothing ever came of it.

"She's gone. Don't waste your time thinking about her" is all he would ever say. And he was right, because if I did start thinking about her, I would be lost in a black hole, only to snap out of it and my day, my *hour*, would be gone. If I were normal, I could have spent hours, days, months, even years, pondering why my mother walked out on us. But I wasn't normal. I had sixty minutes a day and I wasn't going to let anyone dictate how I spent those minutes. So I built up a wall. A wall that would make The Wall seem meek by comparison. A wall my mother could never scale.

Or so I thought.

Five years ago, I was trading online. I was looking into buying some oil futures and I came across a stock.

GGU.

Whenever I asked my mother who she worked for, she would always say Global Geologist Unlimited. I did some routine background on them. The company was *started* in 1987.

My mother walked out on us in 1984.

After calling and emailing Global Geologist, I firmly established Sally Bins was never associated with them.

Next, I contacted George Mason University, where my mother attended under her maiden name, Sally Petrikova, and received her degree in Earth Science.

They had no record of her.

My mother's father was deceased, but her mother still lived in Czechoslovakia. There were two Deniza Petrikova's. Neither had a daughter.

That's when I first contacted AST and began shelling out the five thousand a month for them to find Sally Bins.

The first report, looking into both my father and mother's financials, marriage, birth certificates, and credit reports, was jaw dropping.

Sally Bins never existed.

...

My dad met my mother at a coffee shop. Apparently, this is cliché, though I wouldn't know. The only women I've met were either on Match.com—NIGHTOWL3AM—or in Ingrid's case, a homicide detective questioning me for murder.

The coffee shop was called the Mighty Bean. The place was three miles from my dad's apartment in Arlington, just on the west side of the Potomac. He would frequent the establishment, sitting in the corner, working on his latest project while sipping on cup after cup of the house brew. Being so close to DC, much of his work had to do with the alphabet soup of government agencies.

I imagine my father hasn't changed much in the past forty years. I suppose he might have had a bit more hair, a little less forehead, and maybe even a collared shirt on, but I can't imagine he would have made even a blip on the radar of the brunette sitting at the table nearby. And equally so, I imagine my father was so immersed in government jargon that he was unaware the woman next to him was staring at him quizzically.

"What are you working so hard on?"

According to my mother, my father didn't react the first time, and she had to repeat the question.

When he did look up, his large glasses fell down his nose and he squinted at her through dark eyes under heavy brows. Pushing his glasses back up, his eyes opened wide and he said, "Holy moly."

My mother was well aware of the power she held over the opposite sex and hadn't worn an ounce of makeup since she was in her early teens. With her hair in a tight bun, a business suit designed to square off her naturally curvy frame, and glasses — equal in thickness to my father's — magnifying those green eyes into two small planets, my mother was caught off-guard by my father's candid reaction.

Never having blushed a day in her life, my mother's cheeks grew warm.

"Well, holy moly to you too."

They spent the next six hours chatting.

They were married three months later.

And a year after that, I arrived.

Babies sleep a lot, so neither of my parents were overly concerned when I was only awake for an hour that first night. In fact, for the first day, my parents were convinced they gave birth to the easiest baby on the planet. I slept until 3:00 a.m., woke up crying, my mother nursed me, I gooed and gaa-ed for a little while, and then boom, 4:00 a.m. hit, and I was out like a light. When my parents couldn't get me to wake up the next morning, they rushed me to the emergency room.

They ran a bunch of tests on me, and then at 3:00 a.m., I woke up with a loud cry and everyone celebrated. At least for an hour.

I stayed at the hospital for the next four months until every test was run. I was fed intravenously during the day, then nursed by my mother for the hour I was awake. Finally, when I reached fourteen pounds and I was deemed as healthy as any baby in existence, save for my peculiar sleeping schedule, my parents took me home. They continued to feed me intravenously and my mother continued to nurse me each night for the hour I was awake. I can only imagine the stress and worry I caused them.

They waited and waited, hoped and prayed, that one day I would wake up like a normal baby, but it never happened.

My father took me to see twenty specialists in six different states and three different countries. No matter what time zone I was in, I woke up at 3:00 a.m. and fell asleep at 4:00 a.m. After twelve years of tests and more tests, no one could ever determine why I was only awake for this specified time. What they did discover was that I had an excess of melatonin in my bloodstream. Melatonin is the hormone that regulates the body's sleep-wake cycle. My pineal gland, found in the center of the brain and responsible for melatonin secretion and regulation, was three times the normal size.

When I was fourteen, I had brain surgery and the gland was removed.

Nothing changed.

The condition was thusly named Henry Bins.

...

There is a file attached to the email and I click on it.

A PDF downloads.

It is the full report.

I read the small blurb prepared by the co-founder of AST, Mike Lang.

Mr. Bins,
I am sorry to tell you that we matched the fingerprints you provided us to a Jane Doe pulled from the Potomac

River on Monday, October 4th, 2014, in Alexandria, Virginia.

I want to be sad, but I'm not. I hardly knew my mother. I had a basket full of dusty memories, and everything else I knew was secondhand from my father. But it was a subject he'd shied away from for the last thirty years. It'd been ten years since I uttered the word "Mom" in his presence. I can't remember exactly what I said, or asked, but I do remember my father shrugging. And that's exactly what he'd done: he'd shrugged her off long ago. Just like she'd shrugged us off.

For a quick moment, I feel a rush of—I don't want to say justice, that's a bit macabre—but more like a karmic subpoena. Maybe falling into the Potomac River and drowning was, if not deserved, then an unintended consequence of a decision made three decades earlier.

I imagine her standing near one of the hundreds of guardrails, bridges, or platforms that escorted the river through DC, Virginia, and onward. Maybe a tear runs down her cheek as she thinks of all those lost years with her baby boy. Maybe her breath catches while she ponders what happened to him. Did he grow into a man? Did his one-hour-a-day constraint hold him back from living a normal life? From happiness? Was he still asleep in the same room where she'd last seen him?

She jumps.

The report lists the contact information for the morgue where my mother's body is being held. Then Lang goes on to say our contract has been fulfilled, he sends his deepest regrets, and he will reimburse me a prorated amount for the month of October. Signed, Mike Lang.

The next page is a screenshot of the fingerprint database. The print I lifted off a vase in my parent's bedroom many years earlier is on the left. The print from the Jane Doe is on the right. There are a bunch of numbers and words, but the only ones that matter are near the bottom.

Positive match.

The next page takes me by surprise. AST must have deep connections to have obtained the autopsy report this quickly.

I scan the document for cause of death, already penciling in the word "drowning" in my mind. Or maybe she jumped from a bridge and hit the water and broke her neck. Either way it will be judged an accidental death or a suicide.

But it's not.

It's a homicide.

My mother didn't kill herself.

She was murdered.

:03

Meow.

Lassie stares at me with his yellow eyes.

"I'm not gonna call her."

Meow.

"Yes, I know my mother was found in Alexandria and that my girlfriend works for the Alexandria Police Department."

Meow.

"Yes, I know she's a homicide detective, you moron."

Meow.

"Yes, thank you for pointing out that homicide detectives investigate murders and that my mother was murdered. What did you do at your last home, just sit around and watch *Law and Order*?"

Meow.

"SVU?"

Meow.

"You love iced tea?"

Meow.

"Oh, *Ice T.*"

Meow.

"Dude, I told you, I'm not gonna call her. She's sleeping. I'll see her tomorrow."

I look at the clock.

It's 3:23 a.m.

I'd spent the last seven minutes searching the internet for any information regarding my mother's murder, but there was no mention of a woman's body pulled from the Potomac River with a bullet hole in the back of her head. That being said, Alexandria is only a short fifteen minutes from Washington, DC, so if it wasn't a politician with the hole in their head, then it wasn't newsworthy.

Meow.

"Fine."

I pick up the phone and dial.

Ingrid picks up on the third ring.

"Hi, honey." The words come out like cold molasses.

"Sorry to wake you."

"It's okay. How was your morning?"

Ingrid called the first twenty minutes of my day the *morning*, the second twenty the *afternoon*, and the third the *night*.

"I've had better."

I can almost feel her eyes open slightly.

"Did something happen?"

I'd never mentioned my mother to her and I spend the next four minutes bringing her up to speed: my mother walking out, searching up Global Geologist Unlimited, paying AST to find her, and her fingerprints matching the Jane Doe.

I can hear the sheets of Ingrid's bed rustle as she sits upright.

"I'm sorry, honey."

"It's okay. I hardly knew her." And everything I did know about her was *a lie.*

"Still, she's your mother."

I'm not ready to be sad and ignore her. "She was found in Alexandria. Did you hear about the case?"

"No. With my own caseload and Robby, I haven't had time to talk shop with anybody."

Ingrid's last partner, Cal, was the aforementioned gentleman who had taken a bullet between the eyes, and her new partner, Robby, was a green second-year detective.

Without my having to ask, Ingrid says, "Let me make some calls, and I'll find out everything I can."

"You're amazing."

"I know."

We hang up.

It's 3:31 a.m.

...

Lassie strains the full ten feet of his leash. I yank him back from the tree he wants to climb.

"Dude, I don't have time to patch you up tonight."

Lassie had a history of getting into fights with other mammals — fights he rarely won — leaving me spending the rest of my minutes cleaning his wounds from the raccoon he was chasing, pulling out the quills from the porcupine he snuck up on, or washing the stink off him from the skunk he was trying to copulate with.

He retreats to the sidewalk and we continue east.

I have a windbreaker and a beanie guarding me from the light sprinkle, but Lassie is half-soaked, his tan and black fur slick and shiny.

We cross the street, Lassie darting toward a puddle and nearly submerging his entire body before I'm able to yank him back.

Meow.

"I'm no fun? Well, you're no fun when I wake up with your stinky puddle body asleep on my chest."

I know how much Lassie loves a good puddle, and I usually get a kick out of him slapping at the water with his little paws, but I'm in a hurry.

We cross three more blocks in a half-run.

A minute later, we reach a small platform with metal guardrails.

The Potomac River sweeps past. A quarter mile south, the river runs under a long stone bridge. Three cars zoom over the bridge in quick succession. I wonder if the car that transported my mother's body passed over that bridge. Or did they park on it, pull her body from the trunk, and toss her overboard? Or just as easily, they could have killed her where I stood this very moment. Shot her in the back of the head, then pushed her over the guardrail. Or was she killed miles from here? Who knows how far the mighty Potomac carried her body? The autopsy report said she died twenty-four to forty-eight hours before she was found. She was found Monday morning. So that means she was murdered, *executed*, sometime over the weekend.

Lassie and I walk north along the sidewalk. I instinctively stop above a huge drainage pipe that flows into the Potomac. The six-foot-high pipe is only visible if you lean over the railing and look backward toward the shore. A stream of water, which were millions of separate raindrops minutes earlier, flows into the mighty river.

Six months ago, I spent twenty minutes hiding in the pipeline while a carload of gentlemen — the sort that would have done to me what someone did to my mother — searched for me. I wonder if my mother was as frightened before her death as I was then. Did she know she was being hunted? Was there a chase? I didn't know much about my mother — it appeared as though I knew almost nothing — but I did remember those eyes of hers. You can't fake the intensity or intelligence that lived there. My mother would not have been easy prey.

The cell phone in my pocket buzzes.

It's Ingrid.

I put the phone to my ear and head back toward home.

It is 3:46 a.m.

...

"Walker pulled the case."

Charley Walker was a fat blob, who was third cousin to somebody important, or else he would still be writing traffic tickets. At least that was according to Ingrid's last rant. He had an affinity for stretching the truth and was known around the precinct as "Walker, Texas Liar."

"He wasn't thrilled to chat at three in the morning, but I reminded him he had an upcoming IAB investigation into making illegal bets and that he should talk more quietly next time he put two hundred and fifty dollars on the Redskins to cover. That got him in the mood to talk."

I nod along, dragging Lassie behind me as I speed walk through the drizzle.

"Thing is, he didn't have the case for long. When he showed up on the scene, he was lead for thirty minutes before he got shoulder-tapped by some suit."

"The FBI?"

"Nope, Homeland Security."

I stop walking, Lassie continuing until he is yanked backward by the leash.

"The Department of Homeland Security?"

"Yep. Suit told Walker to pack up and leave. Walker said he was back in bed thirty minutes later."

My brain is whirring. Lassie gazes backward at me. He's sitting on his hind legs shivering.

"Homeland Security," I utter again.

"I've worked with DHS a couple times and they are a tight-lipped bunch. They don't play well with others. Luckily, I've been keeping a favor in my pocket from a guy whose son I helped wiggle out of a DUI, and I called it in."

For a moment, I think of the card I have in the drawer of my condo. Blank, save for the single word, *anything*, scribbled in black ink. And the three initials, *CRS*. The President of the United States gave me a Get Out of Jail Free card. One favor, for anything, redeemable at a moment's notice.

"So, I woke another guy up," Ingrid continues. "I asked him about the woman pulled from the Potomac on Monday morning. He said he hadn't heard about it. I leaned on him. Told him that his kid was still on probation and the Dean of UVA was a close family friend."

"Really? The Dean?"

"No, but I looked it up online. Either way, he bought it and started talking. He called me back a couple minutes later on what I guess was an encrypted line. Told me how on Monday morning a Red Four came in."

"A Red Four?"

"An interagency alert. Four being highest priority. Red being—"

I know the word that is coming, but it still hurts.

"—terrorist."

:04

I hang up the phone.

Lassie yanks on the leash.

"Dude, gimme a second."

Meow.

I ignore him.

My brain has never felt so incapable. Like trying to run a marathon having never run a day in your life.

A terrorist.

My mother was a *terrorist*?

I think back to 9/11. Waking up at 3:00 a.m., going through my routine, having no clue that eighteen hours earlier, two planes crashed into the Twin Towers. Had it been any other week, my father would have texted me about the attacks, but he was on vacation in the Bahamas and without cell phone service. He would later tell me what a nightmare traveling back to the States had been the day following the worst terrorist attack in US history. He'd camped out at the Bahamian airport for three days, finally chartering a flight to Miami, then renting a car and driving home to Virginia.

I found out about the attacks not through the news—I don't have time for news—but when I logged into my E-Trade account. I'd lost nearly $200,000 the previous day as the stock market plummeted.

I spent the rest of my day and the rest of each of my next four days watching the 9/11 saga unfold. I once asked Ingrid how much coverage of the attacks she'd watched and she said it was more than fifty hours that first week. Can you imagine that? Fifty of my days watching reruns of two towers collapsing. Now I'm not judging; it was compulsive and entertaining coverage causing me to sleep with my laptop on my chest. But after that fourth day, I washed my hands of it. I couldn't give any more of my time to sadness and anger.

But now.

My mother was a terrorist.

My mother was one of these assholes.

Meow.

Meow.

Meow.

"Dude, what?"

Meow.

I look down at my watch.

It's 3:57 a.m.

I look at Lassie.

"Run!"

We take off in a sprint.

I'm a quarter mile from my condo. The fastest mile I've run is right around seven minutes. I will have to run the tail end of a six-minute mile if I don't want to sleep in the street.

My feet pound against the pavement.

I glance down at the phone.

3:58 a.m.

I turn onto my street, Lassie scampering parallel with me. I don't have to look down to know his tiny teeth are gritted in concentration.

We pass a coffee shop and a dry cleaner.

I see my condo a block and a half away.

I ponder calling Ingrid back and alerting her that I might not make it home, that she should drive down my street to look for a guy on a bus bench with a cat on his chest. I glance down at the phone.

The numbers turn from :58 to :59.

I still have time.

I can make it.

I have forty-five seconds to run a hundred yards, go up three flights of stairs, and unlock my door.

Twenty seconds later, Lassie and I dart up the front entrance of the condo and into the stairwell. I start looking for places to lie down. The last thing I want is to end up in the hospital.

Again.

When the nurses at the local ER send you Christmas cards, you know something is wrong. Six concussions, what seems like a zillion stitches, two broken arms, a broken collarbone, two broken ribs, and a collapsed lung. And that was just in the last eight years.

We hit the hallway.

We're gonna make it.

The key is already in my hand.

I put the key in the door and turn the handle.

...

It would have been better if the door hadn't opened. If it had stayed closed, I would have crumpled to the carpeted floor of the hallway. But the door did open, and I fell forward into the condo, going down sideways onto the wood floor, which would account for the dull throb in my shoulder.

At least, that's how I recreated it in my mind.

But I didn't wake up on the wood. I woke up on the carpet in the living room, a pillow tucked under my head, a blanket pulled up to my shoulders, and a glass of water and three Advil sitting on the coffee table next to me.

I throw back the three Advil and pick up the yellow legal pad sitting near the water glass.

Hey Sleepyhead,

I came to drop off some leftovers and I found you on the floor. I'm guessing after we hung up last night, you started thinking about your mom and time got away from you. Then you had to book it home and you didn't make it in time. From the position of your body, I guess you conked out right as you pushed the door in.

Sometimes I forget she's a detective. I keep reading.

I gave you a thorough examination, and everything appeared to be in working order.

*Your left shoulder was starting to swell, and
I think it took the brunt of the fall. Get some
ice on it when you wake up. (You're lucky
you didn't break your nose. Well, I guess I'm
lucky. I'm the one that would have to listen
to you snore. Haahahaa.) I apologize if you
have any rug burns on your back. I dragged
you by your legs and your shirt kept riding
up.*

I reach my arm behind my back and feel at the top of my
hips where I do indeed have a big raspberry.

*As for your mom, I didn't find out a whole lot
more. I spent most of the day making calls,
and no one is talking. I tried the morgue, but
they said the body was moved to the federal
freezer in McLean. When I tried calling them,
they gave me the runaround. But I'll keep at
it. I have a B-I-G meeting bright and early,
so I couldn't stay over and play with you (sad
face). Should be interesting. I'll tell you all
about it tomorrow.*

Kisses,
Grid

*P.S. Lassie got into the leftovers while I was
dealing with you and he ate a bunch of Thai.
Just want to warn you in case he's super gas-
sy (happy face).*

P.P.S.S. HAPPY SIX MONTH ANNIVERSARY!

My smile fades with her words and the lightning in my
shoulder returns. I look around for Lassie, thinking he will
be asleep on the arm of the brown sofa, but he's not. I push
myself up with a grunt, holding my left arm to my sternum,
and walk into the bedroom. Lassie is sleeping in the center
of the king bed.

The clock on the dresser reads 3:03 a.m.

"Hey!"

Lassie bats his eyes and wrinkles his nose.

"Glad to see you were worried about me."

Meow.

"I don't know, *maybe* sleep on the floor next to me."

Meow.

"Yes, I know you aren't a dog."

Meow.

"How would it not be fair to the bed?"

Meow.

"Dude, forget it."

I turn around and head for the kitchen. The Advil aren't sitting well on my empty stomach and I stand in front of the open fridge chugging a smoothie and devouring a sandwich in four bites.

Lassie looks up at me.

I shake my head at him.

"Dude, you don't get any breakfast."

Meow.

"Because you ate a shitload of Thai food that Ingrid brought for me."

Meow.

"You're telling me that if I smell your breath right now, I won't smell curry?"

I lean down and he runs away.

"That's what I thought."

I ponder making an ice pack, but I don't have time.

I sit down to the computer.

It is 3:06 a.m.

I hit the Skype button to call my dad, then remember Murdock shattered his laptop. I find my cell phone where Ingrid has it charging in the kitchen and dial my father.

He answers on the third ring.

"Sonny boy."

"Hey, Pops."

"Listen, sorry about last night."

"Don't worry about it. Is Murdock still in the doghouse?"

"Naw, he feels bad. Don't you, boy?"

I can hear the dripping kisses through the phone.

Lassie hears them as well and jumps up on my lap. He claws at the phone. I shake my head at him.

After a couple more kisses, my dad asks, "So, how was your yesterday?"

"Mom is dead."

"What?"

I spend the next three minutes speed-talking. Once I finish, there is only silence. "Dad?"

"I'm here."

"Did you know?"

"No."

"But that would explain everything: her weird schedule, the extended trips, her walking out on us. Do you think it's true? Do you think mom could have been a terrorist?"

He is silent. I imagine him scanning nine years of marriage, looking for red flags.

A silence follows.

Three seconds become eight.

Eight become eleven.

Lassie glances up at me.

My nostrils flare.

"Lassie!" I push him off. "Dude, take that outside."

It smells like three-week-old curry.

"What did Lassie do?" my dad asks.

I transition into the end of my yesterday. My falling, Ingrid taking care of me, Lassie eating the leftovers and his insides turning rotten.

"She's a good one, that Ingrid. You keep hold of her."

I wonder if my father's words have anything to do with my mother. Did he plan to hold onto her but couldn't? And what about me? What if I found out Ingrid had secrets? Deep dark secrets. Would I be able to look past them?

"I plan to," I say, then quickly add, "You never answered my question. Do you think mom could have been a terrorist?"

"No, your mom could not have been a terrorist."

The conviction in his voice surprises me.

"And what makes you so sure of that. How would you know?"

"Because your mother worked for the CIA." He pauses. "She was a spy."

:05

I wait for my father to start laughing. To tell me that he got me good. That he's pulling my leg.

But he's not.

"Mom was a spy?"

"Yes."

"Wait, if you knew this, then why didn't you ever tell me?"

"I promised her I wouldn't."

"So what? That was thirty years ago. You could have told me. You *should* have told me."

"Sorry, son, but there is no statute of limitations on a promise."

If there is one thing I have never questioned about my father, it is his integrity. But that he chose my mother over me pisses me off. I push the phone hard against the side of my face, a Samsung Galaxy sized impression on my cheek.

"I can't believe you didn't tell me," I say, my voice heating. "This whole time I thought she left us because of me. If she worked for the CIA, then it's different. Maybe she left because she had to go do, well, spy stuff, and not because her son was this sad little rent-a-kid."

"It doesn't matter what her job was, geologist, spy, astronaut. She chose it over you. She still walked out on us. She should have *chosen* you."

I ease the pressure of the phone off my ear.

That's why he didn't tell me. He wanted me to be upset. If he'd told me my mother worked for the CIA, I might have let her off the hook. Possibly even been proud of her. *Yeah, my mom walked out on me, but she's out there saving the world, so it's okay.*

But my dad was right. It wasn't okay.

I change directions. "How did you find out? Did she tell you?"

"You were two years old," he says after a long second. "She'd just returned from a trip. I, of course, thought she was on assignment with Global Geologist somewhere in Northern Africa."

I ask, "Did she call you when she went away on these trips?"

"You need to understand, this was the early eighties, and it wasn't like people had cell phones. Her projects were always in some rural, hard-to-reach place. She would call whenever she could, which was about once a week. Usually just a quick hello. Give Henry a kiss for me. Can't wait to see you."

The thought of my mother sending me a kiss over the phone thirty-odd years ago is a mental sour-patch kid. Sweet then sour.

"Keep going," I say.

"She'd just gotten back. You were up, crawling around the place like a crazy man. She and I were on the couch. You somehow got into her purse and started pulling everything out. And I mean everything: wallet, lipstick, compact, change purse, hairbrush, *passport*."

"Your mom's passport picture was hilarious," he says with a mini-laugh. "She looked stoned, eyes half open, hair a mess, and I loved teasing her about it. I flipped it open and stopped cold. At first, I thought she was so sick of me making fun of her picture that she got a new picture taken without telling me. But then I looked at the name. I still remember it to this day: Rebecca Hulgev."

I write the name down on the top of the legal pad and ask, "How did she explain that?"

"She didn't. She told me straight off that she worked for the CIA."

"And you believed her?"

"I didn't know what to believe. Then she showed me a small safe she had hidden in the basement. It was just like in the movies. Five different passports. A bunch of money from different countries. And a gun."

"Holy shit."

"Yep."

"Did she tell you anything else?"

"That's it. She said she couldn't tell me anything else. Made me promise never to tell anyone, not even you. She said she would tell you when the time was right."

"And you were okay with this?"

"What was I going to do? It was her job."

"But she lied to you. All that time."

"I know. But, son, when you love someone, you look past that. When she was here, with us, she was Sally and she was great. When she walked out the door, she went to work. If she had to be somebody else, I was okay with that."

"Then she walked out on us. Chose Rebecca over Sally."

"Right. And that is unforgivable."

Unforgivable.

I want to spend the next five hours talking to my dad, but I can't. For one of the few times in years, I'm pissed off that I have Henry Bins.

"I need to go but I'm gonna call you tomorrow, and you are gonna tell me everything you know about mom."

He agrees, though I have a feeling he just did.

It is 3:23 a.m.

I jump on the internet and type "Rebecca Hulgev." There are a bunch of Hulgevs, a bunch of Rebeccas, but no Rebecca Hulgev.

Lassie jumps back on my lap.

I sniff.

He smells fine.

I scratch behind his ears while I think.

My mother wasn't a terrorist. She was a spy.

She would have been in her mid-sixties now. She couldn't possibly have still been a spy, could she?

I imagine my mother's dark brown hair laced with gray. The sharp angles of her face slightly more relaxed, crow's feet adhering to the edges of her blistering green eyes. Surely, she was retired by now, living out her days on her pension, drinking piña coladas somewhere tropical.

But she hadn't.

And now she was dead.

My brain fills with question marks.

How did my mother end up on the Department of Homeland Security's radar? If she was a spy, why was she flagged a Red Four? What if my mother turned? What if she flipped sides? I wasn't sure where she was from, but my mom wasn't from the United States. She had an accent. Didn't she? Eastern European? You can't fake that. Or could you? Was she recruited into the CIA during the Cold War? Was she a sleeper agent this whole time? Was she Russian? Ukrainian?

President Sullivan had mentioned the problems in the Ukraine. Could my mother's death be related?

I shake my head, trying to exit fantasyland and get back to reality.

I look at the clock.

3:37 a.m.

Lassie looks up at me.

I know the look.

"Fine."

I go to the fridge and uncover his bowl of cat food and put it on the ground. I grab a premade Cobb salad and sit down to the computer.

I ponder calling the federal morgue in McLean where, according to Ingrid, my mother's body was moved. But if they gave her the runaround, then I have little chance.

I imagine them asking me what her name was and my reply. *Um, it could be Sally Bins, Rebecca Hulgev, or ten others.*

No, that wouldn't work.

I pull up the report sent by AST and reread it. For the first time, I notice that although it says my mother was killed twenty-four to forty-eight hours before she was found, the coroner lists a more specific time of death — 3:30 a.m., Saturday, October 2nd.

I find it ironic that, of all the hours in the day, my mother was killed during the one I'm awake. I think back to what I was doing while a bullet was ripping through the back of my mother's skull. Saturday wasn't much different from any other day. Wake, eat, GOT, stocks, read, run. Nothing exciting.

Except.

When I left to go on my run, I opened the door and there was a package.

This in itself wasn't odd. I ordered a bunch of stuff from

Amazon. But I rarely saw the packages. Isabel would open the packages for me and have whatever it was—clothes, dumbbells, yo-yo, cat sweater, or fish tank — assembled and ready for use.

But Isabel didn't come on Fridays or Saturdays. Those were her two days off. So if anything was delivered on either of those two days, I would have to put it together myself. Which is why I ordered stuff on Sundays, and with two-day shipping it always arrived before Friday.

Odder yet, I didn't remember ordering the DVD that was delivered.

I just assumed my dad ordered it for me, which he'd done in the past. I repeatedly told him I could stream the movies online, but my dad was old school and he liked buying DVDs. When I asked him about the movie that came on Saturday, he said he didn't buy it for me. His exact words were: *That stupid alien movie? I would never buy you that crap.*

I figured he was joking.

He pulled the same thing with *Bridesmaids.*

It's just a stupid chick flick. I would never send that to you.

Liar.

I was a bit backlogged on my viewing. I still had two and a half more seasons of *Game of Thrones* to watch before I could even think about watching anything else, and I still hadn't watched the last two movies my father sent: *The Shawshank Redemption* and *Midnight Express.*

Five days earlier, I'd added the "stupid alien movie" to the pile and forgotten about it.

But what if he didn't send it?

What if someone else did?

What if it came from my mother?

...

I thought of one more scenario in which my mother would have been flagged as a Red Four.

Intel.

She knew something. Or stole something.

Had my mother stolen national security secrets and that's why Homeland was involved?

What did Ingrid call the DHS guy who had shown up at the scene?

A *suit.*

A man in black.

I run to the pile of three DVDs stacked neatly on a bookshelf in the living room. *Men in Black* is at the bottom and I slip it out.

I open the case and look for any writing. There is none. I set the DVD down on the computer then run to the trash can hoping to find the Amazon packaging, but the trash has been emptied.

I imagine what could have been written on the inside of the brown cardboard.

For the first time, I wonder if the coroner's time of death was right on the money. How easy would it be to fake the Amazon packaging, especially for a lifelong spy, then leave the package on my doorstep?

My mother was found less than six miles from my house. Could it be a coincidence? Or was it because she'd just left my condo?

I sit back down to the computer and slip the DVD in.

It is 3:49 a.m.

I wait for the plans for a nuclear warhead to start streaming. Or a list of all the spies in Russia. Or a picture of the President with his pants down.

What I don't want to start playing is exactly what starts playing.

The movie.

:06

For the first time in months, I wake up early.

The clock reads 2:58 a.m.

Two extra minutes.

Time is currency to me and I start shopping. (I once tried to explain this to my father and I told him two extra minutes was the equivalent of him waking up and finding two thousand dollars cash on the bedside table. He would immediately start thinking of ways to spend it. It was no different with me.) Should I use the two minutes all at once or should I break it up? Take an extra minute shower? An extra thirty seconds on the pot? Do sixty sit-ups? Run a couple extra blocks?

I think about asking Lassie for his feedback, but he's still out cold. Anyhow, he'll probably want me to spend it rubbing his belly.

I decide to spend the time on the phone with my dad. Getting two more minutes of insight into my mother.

"You're up early."

I glance up.

Ingrid is standing in my doorway.

Naked.

My eyes soak up her perfect breasts, toned stomach, and the beautiful curvature of her buttocks.

I know how I will spend my extra time.

She jumps on the bed and we attack each other.

Nine minutes later, we lie panting.

"That was awesome," I mutter.

Eyes closed, she holds up her hand.

We high five.

Lassie appears from wherever he hid and licks Ingrid's nipple.

"Dude!"

He gives two more licks, then jumps away before I can smack him.

I spend a couple minutes in the bathroom then head to the kitchen. My dad has texted twice, and I text him back that I'm fine and Ingrid is over and I will call him tomorrow.

He sends back a happy face.

If only he knew.

I uncover Lassie's bowl and put it down. "Here you go, you little perv."

Meow.

"Yeah, I probably *would have* done the same thing."

I microwave some lasagna Isabel made and run back into the bedroom.

Ingrid has pushed herself up at the back of the bed. I hand her a plate of lasagna, a fork, and a glass of milk.

"Guess what?" I say.

She shoves a huge bite of lasagna in her mouth and shrugs.

"My mom wasn't a terrorist."

Her eyebrows rise.

"She was a spy."

She coughs, reaches for the milk, and washes down the bite. "What are you talking about?"

I give her the rundown.

"I can't believe your dad never told you."

"He didn't want me to forgive her."

After a long second, she says, "I guess I can understand that."

I tell her about my theory that my mother stole or knew some CIA secrets and that's why DHS was involved in her murder.

"That would make sense."

I expand on my theory.

"You think your mom sent you the movie?"

"Who else would send it? It wasn't my dad."

I look at her.

She shakes her head. "I didn't send it to you."

"Well, someone did and it just happened to be delivered the day my mother was murdered." I tell her about the autopsy report and how my mother's body was found less than six miles from my condo.

"Walker told me where the body was found. But it doesn't mean that's where her body was tossed into the river. She could have been thrown into the Potomac fifty miles upstream."

"Well, it's a big coincidence they found her so close to my place."

"True, but in the six years I've been doing this, there's one thing I've learned: there are a lot more coincidences than people think."

I nod, but I'm not convinced.

"What movie?" she asks after a lengthy pause.

"*Men in Black.*"

She smiles. She's seen it. "And the DVD is actually the movie?"

"So far."

Last night, I watched nine minutes of *Men in Black* before heading to bed. The opening scene was a black guy chasing a thief. The thief jumps off a ten-story building, revealing he isn't human at all. He's an alien. Then a white guy in a black suit comes in and makes the black cop stare at a red light which makes him forget everything he just saw.

"What about the box the movie came in?" she asks.

"Isabel threw it away."

She puffs her cheeks.

"Yeah, I know. I keep thinking she wrote something on the inside."

She shrugs, as if to say, *well you can't do anything about it now*, then says, "Let's go. Movie time."

I grab the laptop and flip it open.

"Do you have any popcorn?"

I laugh and say, "I think I might."

The Redenbacher in my cabinet is a month past its expiration date and I yell to the bedroom, "It's expired."

"Who cares?" she yells back. "I want popcorn!"

I throw it in the microwave then move to the couch where Ingrid has disposed of her clothes. I gingerly fold them and place them on the coffee table. Her cell phone is half out of her purse and I snag it. Her home screen is a picture of me asleep with Lassie on my chest, and it always makes me laugh. Her phone flashes on. She has a missed text, and I quickly read the one sentence.

I don't hear the microwave buzzer until the third chime.

I replace the phone, snag the popcorn, and climb into bed.

Lassie snuggles up on my chest and Ingrid makes a little pile of popcorn on my belly that Lassie quickly devours.

It is 3:19 a.m.

"Okay, so run me through what's happened so far."

I shake the text from thought and give her a minute long recap.

We spend the next forty minutes watching the movie.

At 3:59 a.m., I flip the laptop closed and Ingrid rests her head on my shoulder.

I stroke her head and say, "Goodnight."

"Goodnight, Sleepyhead."

"Oh, wait, you were gonna tell me about the meeting you had this morning."

I feel her head squirm in my arm. "Oh, it turned out not to be anything. Actually, it was canceled, and I got to sleep in."

I think back to the text on her phone.

Thanks for coming this morning.

But it wasn't the words that were unsettling.

It was the phone number.

It was the same number I had written on my Get Out of Jail Free card.

Ingrid's meeting had been with the President of the United States.

...

I spend the next two days finishing off the movie and talking to my dad. He compiled a list of everything he knew about my mother: her upbringing, her parents, her schooling, the car she drove, her friends. Everything he tells me I either already know or was researched by AST and proved a falsity.

As for the movie, it had its moments. What it didn't have was a secret. In fact, I was starting to have serious doubts my mother was responsible for the DVD showing up on my doorstep.

That is, until ten minutes ago, when I called Amazon's twenty-four-hour customer service line. After giving the representative my shipping address and the date the movie was received, she was able to trace the purchase to a credit card listed under the name, get this, Jane Doe.

I'm still reeling from this revelation when the phone in my hand vibrates.

It's a text from Ingrid.

DIDN'T HEAR FROM YOU YESTERDAY. HOW DID THE MOVIE END UP? I'M GUESSING YOU DIDN'T FIND ANY CLUES.

I don't know how I want to respond. Or *if* I even want to respond. I'm still miffed she lied to me about her meeting with President Sullivan. The meeting itself didn't overly concern me. After all, Ingrid had been in charge of the murder investigation in which Sullivan was the primary suspect. The sit-down could easily be a routine follow-up. But then why lie and say the meeting was canceled?

From the text message, *Thanks for coming this morning*, it sounded as though Sullivan was the one to request the meeting. I'd come to like the guy, but liking someone and trusting them are two different stories. Ingrid and I had been dating for six months, but this translated to roughly sixty or seventy hours of face time. I wasn't exactly sure where our relationship stood. How could I be certain I was meeting all her emotional and, let's be honest, *physical* needs?

I text back: MOVIE WAS OKAY. NO CLUES.

BUMMER....GOT A NEW CASE...SERIAL KILLER....CALLS HIMSELF THE POPE...MIGHT NOT SEE YOU FOR A WHILE.

OK.

YOU ALRIGHT?

YEP. JUST BUSY.

OK. I'LL KEEP MY EAR TO THE GROUND ABOUT YOUR MOM.

THANKS.

DON'T GET SUCKED INTO MEN IN BLACK 2. NEVER SAW IT, BUT IT GOT TERRIBLE REVIEWS.

I WON'T. SEE YOU LATER.

I'm tempted to text her to tell President Sullivan hi for me, but I set the phone down before I do something stupid.

It's 3:37 a.m.

"Let's go!" I yell.

Lassie jumps off the back of the couch. I reach for his leash, then think better of it. It's been three days since he was outside. His nerves are just as shot as mine.

One minute later and I'm sprinting down the side street, Lassie nipping at my heels.

The only way not to think about Ingrid is to think about my mother. Still, it takes a mile until I rid Ingrid from my thoughts. I'm tempted to text her goodnight, to tell her I'm so glad she came into my life. That I don't care if she lied to me about meeting the President. That I trust her. That I love her.

I shake off the thought and tap Ingrid out and tap my mother in.

Initially, I thought my mother recreated an Amazon package and left it on my doorstep, but that wasn't the case. She'd ordered the package from Amazon, therefore, the packaging didn't have any clues written inside, not unless the person who packed and shipped the DVD colluded with her. This meant the DVD wasn't doctored either. So then why go through all the trouble of sending it?

Unless the name of the movie itself meant something.

Men in Black.

CIA, right?

That was obvious. But was there more to it? Did it have something to do with one of the actors?

I'd done a quick background on both the lead actors, Will Smith and Tommy Lee Jones, but found nothing from either actor's past that leapt out at me.

I didn't know much about pop culture. Was there a clue somewhere I just didn't get? Was *The Fresh Prince of Bel Air* supposed to mean something to me? Maybe I didn't have the worldly experience to connect the dots.

I stop and look at my cell phone.

It's 3:48 a.m.

I turn around and head back home.

It's 3:56 a.m. when I return to the condo.

Lassie is nowhere to be found, but I have faith he'll make his way home. I leave the door open for him. I drink water until my stomach hurts, then head to the bedroom. I don't have time for a shower, but I don't want to sleep in my sweaty clothes and strip down naked.

Lying in bed, I reopen Ingrid and my text thread.

I'm about to start typing, to tell her that I miss her and that I can't wait to see her again, when it hits me.

Her last text.

DON'T GET SUCKED INTO MEN IN BLACK 2. NEVER SAW IT, BUT IT GOT TERRIBLE REVIEWS.

That was it.

Reviews.

I jump out of bed and run to the computer.

I log into Amazon and search *Men in Black*. There are 517 reviews. I scroll down to the bottom. The second to last review was written on October 2nd.

The day my mother was killed.

And it was written by me.

:07

The last time I fell asleep in the chair at the kitchen table was four years earlier, the night before General Motors' post-government bailout IPO. I was waffling back and forth, deciding whether or not I wanted to buy shares. At 3:58 a.m., I decided not to buy and stood up to go to bed, but then at the last second I changed my mind and rushed back to the computer. I was unable to get the purchase scheduled in time — five thousand shares — and I woke up twenty-three hours later with a QWERTY impression on my forehead.

In regards to the stock, I lucked out. Though the IPO was the biggest in history, the stock fell thirty-five percent the first year and I would have lost my ass. That being said, I would have gladly taken the loss if it meant I made it to my bed that night, as I spent nearly the equivalent of that amount on a physical therapist and chiropractor who both charged me exorbitant amounts to make 3:00 a.m. house calls.

I take three deep breaths and try to lift my head off the kitchen table. I can't. Every muscle in my body is frozen solid. I try to wiggle my toes but I can't even feel them.

This is bad.

I feel a light touch of my forehead and open my eyes.

"Hey, buddy," I whisper.

Lassie gives my eyes a couple licks, then takes a step back. He is smiling ear to ear.

"Looks like somebody got lucky."

Meow.

"A fox? Or the cat was a fox?"

Meow.

"An actual fox. Wow, good for you. I didn't even know that was possible." I want to smile, to laugh, but even the slightest movement sends a bolt of lightning down my spine. I exhale deeply.

Meow.

"No, I'm *not* okay."

Meow.

"Yes, the bed would have been more comfortable."

Meow.

"I *need* my phone."

I can see my left arm on the table in front of me. Though I can't feel my right arm, I think it is dangling by my side.

I try to remember where I left my phone. Is it on the kitchen counter? The couch?

Lassie jumps over my head. I feel scraping. A moment later, he comes back into view. He is pushing my phone toward my hand with his nose.

It's too soon to get excited. The phone hasn't been charged in over a day. It had a full charge when I last used it, and it wasn't like I made any calls or used any data in the last twenty-three hours. There was a chance it still had some juice left.

I slowly start trying to move my fingers.

Nothing happens for a long minute.

Finally, I get my index finger to twitch. Three minutes later and all my fingers are slowly beginning to wake. Lassie nudges the phone under my hand. I hit the bottom button. It flashes on.

Thank God.

I hit the button on the side for voice command and ponder calling 911. I don't. I bark, "Call Ingrid."

The phone rings.

Goes straight to voicemail.

"End call."

My phone beeps. I've never heard the sound before and I'm guessing it means the battery is almost dead.

"Call Pops."

The phone rings.

He picks up on the second ring.

"Hey Sonny B—"

"Listen," I interrupt. "My battery is about to die. I need

you to come over. Bring your back pills. Hurr—"
The phone dies.

...

My dad lives twenty minutes away. Plus, he has a bad back himself, so I don't even know if he can get out of bed. But it only takes fifteen minutes until I hear heavy clomping in the hallway, then a loud thud as my front door bangs open.

I forgot I left the door cracked open for Lassie. Speaking of whom, he jumps off the table and runs to greet his bestie. I hear the two thumping around in the living room wrestling.

If you Googled "Bromance," a video of these two idiots might pop up.

"Settle down, you morons."

They don't.

Ten seconds later, my dad enters.

I don't need to see him to know he's biting his tongue. I try to imagine what he saw when he walked through the door, his only son sitting in a chair at the table, naked as the day he was born.

Unable to squelch it any longer, he erupts in violent laughter. "Do I even want to ask, Son?"

In the fifteen minutes since I called him, I'd made some headway and I'm able to lift my head slightly. I can see him wiping tears from his eyes out of my periphery.

Murdock and Lassie tumble off the couch loudly, no doubt waking my downstairs neighbors from a pleasant slumber.

"Be quiet, you two," my dad yells.

To their credit, they stop.

I feel my dad's hand on my shoulder. He is still chuckling, but he also knows what an ordeal it was the last time this happened to me. I easily could have done irrevocable harm to my spine and there could be nerve damage in my arms, hands, legs, and feet.

Murdock appears next to my father and begins licking my face with his foot-long tongue.

"Hey, you big lug."

Lassie is standing on his back, riding him.

Meow.

"Yes, like a horse," I agree.

"Move it," my dad says, pushing the beast out of the way. "Now let's get you to the couch."

I'd given this some thought and decided the best bet was for my dad to slide my chair to the couch, then roll me over the back.

It isn't easy, but by 3:27 a.m., I am on the sofa. My dad pulled some boxers on for me, which wasn't the highpoint of my life, but he didn't bat an eye.

What a champ.

"You want a couple of those pills?"

It's all I want, but I also want my wits about me for the next ten minutes.

"Not yet," I groan, the vibration of the words causing an aftershock in my neck. I change my mind. "Pills. Now."

He brings me some water and I wash down the two pills.

"Can you feed Lassie and grab me a shake out of the fridge?"

He does both.

He sits down on the couch next to me and holds the shake while I drink.

"So, you gonna tell me what happened?"

"Grab the laptop."

He does.

The screensaver, a picture of Ingrid, is on-screen, and I say, "Refresh it."

He is apprehensive.

"It's not porn, dad. I just happened to be naked."

"I don't judge."

I spend the next minute telling him about *Men in Black*, how I think the woman who walked out on us thirty years ago sent it to me, and how I'm pretty sure she sent me a hidden message through a review written for the movie.

"I don't see the review," he says.

He shows me the screen. The pills have taken hold and the screen swims. I squint. The review is gone.

"It was right there. It was written by me." There is one from September 8th and another from October 7th, but the one from October 2nd is gone. "They erased it."

"Who?"

I don't know yet.

"Check the printer," I mumble.

I remember printing the review. At least I think I did.

My brain has stopped working. My eyes close.

4:00 a.m. comes early.

...

I wake up in my bed.

A page from my yellow legal pad is sitting on the bed-side table, filled with my father's neat all-caps. It is a run-down of everything he'd done, and *had* done to me, the past twenty-three hours.

A chiropractor came by to adjust my spine. A massage therapist spent two hours kneading my destroyed muscles. Sara, a young woman I'd come to know through my several stays at the ER, stopped by to give me an IV. My dad picked up meatball subs from his favorite deli, and mine was in the fridge. He called his doc for some extra back pills, but he also picked up some Aleve just in case I didn't want to spend my one hour hallucinating. He took Lassie and Mur-dock to the park and bought them hot dogs. And he fixed the drain in my shower.

He left around midnight.

I look over at Lassie.

He is dead to the world. Playing with Murdock has wiped him out. He has some yellow junk on his whiskers, and I inspect it closer.

Mustard, from the hotdog.

I laugh.

I push myself up, which hurts, but is ecstasy compared to the last time I attempted movement. I pick up my phone and text him.

THANKS, POPS. YOU DA BEST.

FEELING BETTER?

YEAH, I CAN TURN MY HEAD TO THE SIDE WITHOUT CRYING.

GOOD...MICROWAVE THE MB SUB FOR 43 SECS.

ROGER THAT.

IM BEAT...OFF TO BED...DIDN'T THINK YOU WOULD BE

UP FOR POKER SO I HEADED HOME.

I can't believe it's already been a week since I received the email from AST.

I text back: THAT'S OKAY.

IT'S A DATE.

WHAT IS?

THE REVIEW. THE ANNIVERSARY. I THINK IT'S A DATE.

I notice a second piece of paper on the table. It is the review. I printed it after all. I read it earlier, but I can't remember a single word. I reread it, my smile threatening to leap off my face.

I text back: I THINK YOU'RE RIGHT.

LET ME KNOW WHAT YOU FIND OUT. NIGHT.

WILL DO...THANKS AGAIN...NIGHT.

I push myself out of bed. My body is still a knotted mess. I hobble to the bathroom and send 400ccs of IV into the toilet.

I microwave the sub, grab my laptop, and head back to the bed.

It is 3:12 a.m.

My phone has two more texts. Both are from Ingrid. She still hasn't wrapped up her new case. She won't be able to come over tonight. She misses me.

I text that I miss her too.

I take a giant bite of the delicious sub and reread the review once more:

THIS MOVIE ROCKS!

My wife and I saw this movie on our first date eight years ago. (It was love at first site.) We watch the movie every year on our anniversary, August 5th. Smith and Jones are amazing together and Heghil did a great job directing. My nine-year-old, April, loves the movie too. She gives it twelve stars.

Published 10/2/2014 by Henry B.

My dad thinks that *August 5th* and *eight years ago* is a date.

I agree.

I flip open the laptop and Google the date.

The top result is from Wikipedia, and I start skimming. August 5, 2006 was a Saturday. George Bush, Jr. was President. The Orioles and the Dodgers played sixteen innings. SARS was back in the news.

There are a couple of other highlights, but only one that interests me. Only one that makes sense. Two high-ranking Al-Qaeda operatives were killed in an explosion in northern Iraq.

If my assumptions are correct, then my mother wanted me to read this exact sentence. But why? What did the death of two terrorists mean to me?

I continue reading.

The two men, Abdul Al-Rahmin and Hammad Sheik-Al-zar, were rumored to have been in a basement in northern Iraq when there was an explosion. One of the bombs they were building detonated and the basement caved in on them.

Two dead terrorists? Is this why my mom was flagged as a Red Four?

There had to be something I was missing.

I reread the Amazon review.

Again.

Again.

Again.

Then it hits me.

There wasn't one date, there were two.

His nine-year-old. April. Twelve stars.

April 9, 2012.

I Google the date.

Nothing related to terrorism in the least.

I switch out the numbers.

April 12, 2009.

Skim the results.

My brows furrow.

Two Al-Qaedas killed in an explosion. This time in Afghanistan. Nearly the same fashion. Building a bomb. Cave-in.

I go back and reread both snippets.

Two explosions, two cave-ins. I could only imagine what

condition the men's bodies were in. They must have been torn to pieces. How did they even identify the victims?

But, then, that was it. Someone didn't want the bodies to be identifiable.

I was still missing something.

I reread the review.

Love at first site.

Not sight.

Site.

There had to be a link to a website.

But there were millions of websites. How was I supposed to find the right one?

I Google "terrorist website."

There are thousands of hits.

I scroll through ten pages.

On the eleventh page, there is a match for both "terrorist" and "site."

But it isn't a website.

Men in Black didn't have anything to do with the CIA.

It wasn't the *men* that mattered.

It was the *black*.

A black site.

A CIA secret prison.

:08

I spend the next twenty minutes doing research on black sites. A black site is a clandestine facility operated by the CIA outside US jurisdiction to detain alleged unlawful enemy combatants.

Otherwise known as a *secret prison*.

In 2006, President Bush acknowledged the existence of these secret prisons, more than twenty in both Iraq and Afghanistan, plus others in Poland, Romania, and several other countries. In the years following, many reports came out about the treatment and abuse of these prisoners, or what many people refer to as the t-word.

Torture.

I was all for a little waterboarding if it prevented another 9/11, but I couldn't support anything beyond that. Lines need to be drawn.

After all of these allegations, reports, and investigations were launched into what the United States calls its Extraordinary Rendition Program — which I admit, sounds better than underground torture facility — the shit hit the fan.

On October 7, 2007, the CIA admitted to destroying videotape recordings of CIA interrogations of terrorist suspects. These tapes were alleged to document harsh interrogation techniques, including waterboarding, hypothermia, electrocution, and even instances of dogs used to scare the sand out of these guys. But one can only assume far worse acts were performed on these men.

In 2009, President Obama gave an executive order to shut down all black sites and have the prisoners moved to Guantanamo Bay.

After beating out Obama for the presidency in 2012, Conner Sullivan continued this crusade against the unlawful treatment of detainees.

But according to an article written just this February, more than twenty of the detainees held at these secret prisons were still missing. From what my mother sent me—the four terrorists who were allegedly killed but their bodies never recovered—I now guessed these men were four of the missing. Or were of a different assortment of prisoners who were *presumed* dead. And the limitations of abuse on a dead man are far less than those on a man whom someone might come looking for.

That my mother was executed could mean only one thing.

These prisons still existed.

And my mother knew of their locations.

I read the review one last time, then hobble out of the bed and into the kitchen.

I pull the card from the drawer and dial.

It is 3:46 a.m.

I'm doubtful he's awake, but he answers on the third ring.

"I'm calling in my favor," I tell the President.

...

Twenty-three hours and twenty-nine minutes later, I flip up the hood of my sweatshirt and hunker behind a large tree at the edge of the parking lot. Summer Park is asleep, the tennis and basketball courts dark and silent. I wonder how many people have hit tennis balls or shot hoops since the last time I was here? How many aces had scorched past their opponent? How many three-pointers had rattled the chain nets?

Six months ago, the President and Red picked me up from this exact parking lot. Over the next hour, I led the three of us and Ingrid down a rabbit hole that ended with a man getting his head blown off and the President being cleared of Jessie Kallomatix's murder.

Which is why I know the President will show.

He owes me.

Big time.

At 3:15 a.m., lights appear on the side street and thirty seconds later, a black town car eases into the lot. Another thirty seconds later, a black SUV follows suit.

I wait for the man in the SUV to join the man in the town car. I step out from behind the tree and make my way toward the lone man outside the car.

I nod.

Red nods back.

I extend my hand and we shake. "I still can't believe you pulled that flush out on the river card."

"Nine of diamonds," he says with a smirk. He's a solid two hundred and fifty pounds and stands six-four. If he weren't in the Secret Service, he could make a living playing one on TV. He slaps me on the shoulder and says, "Hey, you could have folded."

"Fold three Kings? No way."

He nods his agreement.

"Any problem getting out?" I ask.

I wasn't exactly sure how the President and Red routinely came and went from the most protected fifty-two acres in the United States, but they did. I once asked Sullivan if he used Lincoln's Tunnel and he'd laughed and said, "Yep, and I used Biden's skateboard." On one phone conversation, he confided that if the public knew how easy it was to slip away from the White House undetected they would be astounded.

"Too easy," he says, shaking his head and pulling open the back door.

I lean down and peer inside.

Two men are sitting across from one another in the spacious back seat. I shake hands with Sullivan who is wearing jeans and a gray Washington Redskins sweatshirt, looking more like an unemployed screenwriter than the leader of the free world.

He introduces me to the man across from him.

John LeHigh.

The Director of the CIA.

...

"You better have a damn good reason for dragging me out here," is what I expect the man in the suit and tie to bark, but he simply shakes my hand and says, "The President speaks highly of you."

John LeHigh is on the right side of sixty. His gray hair is cut short, almost to a whitewall, and the top has long ago been washed down the shower drain. His eyes mimic his navy blue tie. His face is fleshy, a result of the wine, spirit, or beer he'd consumed in the last few hours.

"Yeah, well, don't tell him that I voted for Obama," I say, eliciting some loose chuckles from my audience. I add, "He speaks highly of you as well."

And he did. When I told the President what I was cashing in my card for, that I wanted a sit-down with the Director of the CIA, he only had good things to say about the top brass at the Central Intelligence Agency.

LeHigh spent twenty-five years with the CIA as an analyst before becoming Deputy Director of the newly created Terrorist Threat Integration Center in 2003. Six years later, he was nominated as Homeland Security Advisor to the Obama administration, and in 2012 was nominated by President Sullivan to be Director of the CIA.

LeHigh nods, but says nothing.

"So you want to tell us why we're here?" Sullivan asks, running his hand through his famous presidential salt and pepper waves.

I didn't tell Sullivan anything last night, only that I was cashing in my favor, that I needed ten minutes with Director LeHigh. And I needed those ten minutes face-to-face.

"My mom," I say.

Both men glare at me.

"Elena Janev."

After I'd hung up with the President, I'd sent Ingrid a text. I needed her to lean on her contact at DHS one more time. I needed my mom's name. Her *real* name.

Maybe Ingrid felt bad about having not come over for nearly a week. No matter, when I woke up twenty minutes ago, my mother's name had been waiting for me.

Both men stare at me blankly. If my mother's name means anything to either of them, they don't show it.

"She worked for the CIA," I say.

The President cuts his eyes at LeHigh, but the Director is impossible to read.

A statue.

"You didn't know her?" I prod.

"No," he says with a soft shake of his head.

To expect Director Lehigh to know all the people who work at the Central Intelligence Agency is to expect the CEO of Coca-Cola to know Jim who stocks the local Coca-Cola machines in Telluride, Colorado. But my mother wasn't a paper-pusher at Langley. She was a Red Four.

Big difference.

"Thousands of people work at the CIA," interjects President Sullivan.

"And how many of those people were murdered ten days ago?"

The President straightens. "What are you talking about?"

"A woman's body was pulled from the Potomac River last Monday. She was shot in the back of the head. The woman's name was Elena Janev. She was my mother."

"How do you know about this?" asks the Director, with a hint of annoyance.

"I've been paying a surveillance firm to look for my mother for the past five years. I received an email Wednesday morning that the prints of a Jane Doe pulled from the Potomac matched the fingerprints I sent them."

This was a big leap to knowing my mother's real name and that she worked at the CIA, but LeHigh doesn't ask how I made the connection.

"I'm sorry," offers Sullivan.

I nod. "I didn't know her very well. She left when I was six."

"Still."

I know. She was my mother.

I stare at the Director. I wonder if he is always so tight-lipped. Is this a trait he was born with or one cultivated over three decades of espionage?

"I'm sorry to hear about your mother," he says. "But I'm confused where I come in."

"The Department of Homeland Security flagged her as a Red Four."

This doesn't mean anything to the President, but with everything on his plate, he can't be expected to know every code from every agency that reported to him. But LeHigh had been Homeland Security Advisor to President Obama and he knew damn well what it meant.

"What's a Red Four?" asks Sullivan.

We both watch LeHigh. After a moment, he replies, "A Red Four is a high priority terrorist."

"Wait, I thought you said your mom worked for the CIA."

"She did."

"Then why was she flagged as a Red Four?"

He stares at me and then it dawns on him. "Right. That's what you want to know. That's why you asked to meet with the Director."

We both turn and stare at the Director.

"I'm not sure how you stumbled on all of this information, and whoever leaked it will probably not have a job come tomorrow," says LeHigh, "but it still means nothing to me. I don't know, nor have I ever known any Elena Janev."

These might be the words he says, but his eyes say something different. His eyes are telling me that I am sticking my nose where it doesn't belong. That I am barking up a tree that I shouldn't be. There isn't a squirrel in this tree. There's a Bengal tiger.

"Why didn't you go to the police?" asks Sullivan.

"The police got shoulder-tapped by DHS."

"How did you kno—" He pauses. "Ingrid."

I nod.

The text the President sent Ingrid flashes across my mind.

I shake it off.

"I have some contacts at Homeland," chimes the Director. "I can look into it for you if you like."

He smiles smugly.

He knows my mother and he knows why she was killed.

I ask, "Do the words "black site" mean anything to either of you?"

LeHigh can't hold his eyebrows down.

"What does that have to do with anything?" asks Sullivan.

"You know all those black sites Obama shut down?"

The President nods.

"What if I told you that they weren't *all* shut down?"

"That's absurd," barks LeHigh.

I pull a folded piece of paper out of my sweatshirt pocket and hand it to the President. It is the *Huffington Post* article from February detailing the more than twenty detainees still missing.

The President pulls a pair of glasses from within a small compartment between the seats. The glasses have two small reading lights on the sides, illuminating the printed text.

"Twenty detainees were never transferred to Guantanamo Bay," I say. "Twenty detainees are still locked away somewhere. And those are only the detainees on record."

"What do you mean *on record?*" the President asks, looking up from the article.

"On August 5th, 2006, two high-ranking Al-Qaeda operatives were killed when a bomb they were building detonated in a basement. The same exact scenario played out on April 9th, 2012. All four of these men's bodies were eviscerated beyond identification."

"And what, you think someone faked these explosions and the men are being held somewhere illegally?"

"Not someone, the *CIA*. And not being held, being *tortured*."

"I've heard enough," the Director says, shaking his head. "I don't know what conspiracy theory website you went to or what kind of crazy dreams you had last night, or what you think your mother was, but these black sites do not exist. Obama made an executive order to close every one of these facilities, and that's what we did. Do I think it was the right decision? Fuck no, it wasn't. We are at war with these terrorists. They don't play by the rules, but we have to. It's like playing soccer without a goalie. It's only a matter of time before one of their shots goes in the net. But it isn't a goal; it's two thousand dead Americans.

"But when an executive order comes down, it is followed. Fifty-two black sites were closed within six days, the detainees moved to Guantanamo Bay or to other similar facilities. The article you read about the twenty terrorists that are missing is bullshit. They are all accounted for, every last one. Did you ever think that some of them cooperated with us? That they work for us in some capacity? That they were given new identities and released? That some escaped and we don't want to alarm the public? That some killed themselves?

"Everybody wants to know everything these days, right up until they don't. We live in a time of transparency, a time when secrets aren't allowed. But guess what? When information falls into the wrong hands, people die."

I swallow his last words: *when information falls into the wrong hands, people die.*

Like my mother.

But it wasn't that the Director just as much admitted my mother was killed for this very reason. He wanted me to know that if I continued pressing, I was going to wind up at the bottom of the Potomac as well.

Unfortunately for the Director, I'm on a strict schedule and I don't have time for threats.

"My mother was killed because she knew the locations of these black sites," I say, leaning forward. "I'm not sure how she got her hands on the intel—if she stole it, or if she was personally involved in their operation—but she did. Maybe she threatened to go public, maybe she was trying to force the CIA's hand into actually closing them like they were ordered to do. Maybe she saw things, unthinkable acts that shouldn't be done to mice, let alone human beings, and she couldn't sleep at night."

"Are you accusing the CIA of killing your mother?" asks the President.

My mother passed along one more piece of information in her review. I didn't catch it until the last time I read it, right before I called the President. The third sentence: *Smith and Jones are amazing together and Heghil did a great job directing.*

I thought to search up Will Smith and Tommy Lee Jones, but for some reason I didn't think to search up the director.

Turns out the movie was directed by a guy named Barry Sonnenfeld. Not by anyone named Heghil.

Then why put that name?

It took me awhile. Well, three minutes. But, then again, I *had* just done an internet search on the CIA.

Heghil is an anagram of LeHigh.

"I'm not accusing the CIA," I say, then point at the director. "Him. *He* killed my mother."

...

The President and I watch the SUV speed away.

"What are you thinking?" screams Sullivan. "Accusing the Director of the CIA of murdering your mother. Are you insane?"

LeHigh didn't so much as blink when I accused him of killing my mother. He simply looked at the President as if to say, "You stole me away from my bottle of wine for this?" and proceeded to open the door and leave.

I wish I could say his reaction helped dissolve any residual doubts I had about his innocence, but it didn't. It made me question his guilt. And in line with the President's last three words, question my sanity.

"Tell me you have proof and you aren't just shooting from the hip here. I went to high school with LeHigh's son. I've known the man for more than half of my life, which is why I personally appointed him as the Director of the CIA two years ago."

"I have proof," I say with little conviction.

"What?"

I don't dare tell the President that my proof is a review written for *Men in Black.* He would give Red an executive order to clobber me in the face with one of his giant ham hands.

"Trust me," is all that I can say.

"Get out," he says.

I want to object, but I have nothing to say.

"We're even," he says.

I nod and pull open the door. I'm not sure why I do it, maybe because I think this is the last time I'll ever speak to him, maybe because I want to stay in the fight even though I can't lift my arms above my waist. I get out, then turn and lean down on the door and say, "Do me a favor and stay away from Ingrid."

He leans backward.

"Yeah, I know all about your little meeting the other day."

He shakes his head softly from side to side, and I know for the second time in one night I have taken a giant leap of faith and landed in a giant stinking pile of shit.

"Oh, you do?" He pauses. "Then you know we were meeting to discuss a little ceremony I planned for you, to give you a key to the city. You know, for helping me out and all."

I gulp loud enough that a bird flies from a nearby tree.

"But you can forget all about that," he says, then pulls the door shut.

:09

"I can't believe you thought I would cheat on you with the President."

Even over the phone, I can see the disappointment in her face. "Yeah, I know. Stupid."

"If I was going to cheat on you, it would be with that hunky senator from Mississippi." She whistles a catcall.

I know she's trying to bring some levity to the situation, that this is her way of saying that she accepts my apology, but the smile she's trying to elicit never comes. I don't feel deserving of her or her kindness.

I've spent the last ten minutes telling Ingrid every last detail. The review, figuring out the clues, the black site, calling the President and demanding a face-to-face with the Director, then my ambush and falling into a vat of shit.

"I should have told you about the meeting," she says.

"No, you shouldn't have. It was supposed to be a surprise. I shouldn't have been snooping in your phone."

"Yeah, *creepy.*" She says the word in a high-pitched twang.

"Okay, I get it. I'm sorry."

"You don't have time to be sorry. Just trust me a little bit more, okay?"

"Okay."

"So, no key to the city ceremony?"

"I think not."

"That's okay. Who wants a key to DC anyways? And what are you going to do at 3:00 a.m? Go to the all-night diner?"

"I'm not sure that's how a key to the city works."

"Yeah, he didn't really talk much about the actual perks, just that he wanted to give you one and have a little ceremony for you at the White House."

"Would have been cool," I say.

"Don't worry, I'll give you a key to my city."

I laugh.

"What are the perks?"

She explains the perks. They are mouthwatering.

"Alright, I have to get back to looking at this house with binoculars, and you need to get to bed," she announces.

I look down at my phone.

It's 3:56 a.m.

This is the first time Ingrid and I have spoken in over a week, and it feels so good to hear her voice. I don't want to hang up. Ever.

"Hopefully, this thing wraps up in the next couple of days and we can have our key ceremony," she says.

"Yes, please."

"Goodnight, Sleepyhead."

"Goodnight."

I open the door and step inside. I have everything to be upset about. I made a fool out of myself in front of two of the most powerful men in the free world. I accused one man of killing my mother, which seems more and more ridiculous each second that passes, and accused another of putting the moves on my girlfriend.

But I can't help but smile.

...

"Dude!"

Lassie is clawing at my face.

"Dude, what's wrong?"

I push myself up. Lassie is wailing.

"Are you sick?"

I flip on the light and look at him. His hair is matted; he looks like he's been sweating for twenty hours. His yellow eyes are rimmed in red.

"Shit."

I jump up.

"What is it? Your stomach?"

I feel his stomach. He winces.

"What did you eat?"

I jump out of bed and run into the kitchen. After getting off the phone with Ingrid last night, I'd come inside, scooped Lassie off the back of the couch, and we'd gone to bed. I'd rubbed his belly for a long minute before I'd fallen asleep. He'd been fine.

I look for anything that he might have gotten into. Could he have gotten into some Windex? Isabel kept all her cleaning supplies in a closet, but it was closed. But then again, that's not to say he couldn't have gotten into something earlier. He was unsupervised for twenty-three hours a day; anything could have happened. He could have jumped off the couch and landed wrong. Smacked his belly on something and now he was bleeding internally.

I'd taken Lassie to the emergency vet once before after he was slashed by a raccoon, and luckily, the twenty-four-hour vet was only a mile and a half away.

I run back into the bedroom, grab a backpack out of the closet, and snatch Lassie off the bed. "It's gonna be alright. We're gonna get you fixed."

I'm having déjà vu.

I snag the Vespa keys off the key ring, sprint down the stairs, and find the small scooter parked between two cars on the street.

I gingerly put Lassie in the backpack.

"Ten minutes. Hold on, buddy."

I put on the backpack and zoom onto the side street.

Two blocks later, the backpack starts thrashing wildly.

I pull the Vespa over to the side of the road. The backpack feels like there is a miniature bucking bronco trying to free itself. I unzip the backpack and Lassie stops.

He is panting wildly.

"It's gonna be okay. Just another couple of minutes."

Meow.

"What?"

Meow.

"You aren't sick?"

Meow.

"You were faking it? Why would yo—"

Meow.

"You needed to get me out of the house? Why?"

Meow.

"Two men came in?"

Meow.

"Seriously?"

Lassie explains how he was sleeping last night when the front door opened. He thought it was Ingrid or my dad, but it wasn't. It was two men he didn't recognize. He went up to them, but they swatted him away. Lassie hid for the next twenty minutes until the men left.

"They bugged my condo," I say to myself, more than to Lassie. "Holy shit, they bugged my fucking condo."

I should be pissed, but I'm not. I'm relieved. Because the only logical assumption I can make is that my house was bugged by the CIA. And if so, then Director LeHigh is to blame. And innocent men didn't bug houses.

He was spooked.

That means I was on the right track.

Everything my mother sent me was true.

Meow.

I straighten.

"Really?"

Meow.

"Which car?"

Meow.

Someone is following us.

I put Lassie back into the backpack and start back onto the road. If my house was bugged, then whoever did it had either video or audio, or both, of my thinking Lassie was sick. And now they were following me.

Five minutes later, I pull up to the emergency vet.

It is 3:13 a.m.

I sign in on the iPad near the receptionist. There are two people ahead of me. I take a seat on one of the plastic chairs. There is a fiftyish man with a white Pomeranian. It barks at me.

I pull out Lassie and put him on my lap. He is playing the part of sickly cat well.

I pull out my cell phone.

I have two missed text messages from Ingrid.

Ingrid's first text is: I MISS U. The second one is: COULD YOUR MOM HAVE SENT YOU ANYTHING ELSE?

I send back: LASSIE IS SICK. AT THE VET. GONNA FORGET ABOUT MY MOM JUST LIKE SHE FORGOT ABOUT ME.

The phone vibrates almost instantly.

OK. I SUPPORT YOU EITHER WAY. HOPE LASSIE IS OKAY.

HE WILL BE. TALK TO YOU TOMORROW.

She sends: XOXO

But the cyber hugs and kisses aren't my main concern, it's what she said about my mother. *Sending me something else.*

What if my mother sent me something before the DVD? She had to know there was a bounty on her head. That her time was limited. Did she try to get something to me before, but I was too wrapped up in my regimen to notice?

I try to think if Isabel ever opened any packages that I didn't order myself. Would my mother have stuck with Amazon? She had to send the message anonymously, or it never would have made it. Even the review she posted was taken down right after I checked it.

Which means.

They knew I checked it.

Did they already bug my computer? Were they just waiting for my mother to get in contact with me this whole time? What other ways might she have tried to get in contact with me?

No, she did it out of desperation. I visualize her writing the review on her phone as she hid from her pursuers. It was a last minute Hail Mary. There had to be one more clue somewhere in the review. Something about the locations. Some sort of proof.

I remember the review word for word and recite it under my breath.

My wife and I saw this movie on our first date eight years ago. It was love at first site. We watch the movie every year on our anniversary, August 5th. Smith and Jones are amazing together and Heghil did a great job directing. My nine-year-old, April, loves the movie too. She gives it twelve stars.

Five sentences.

I repeat it twice more, but I have squeezed the words dry. They have nothing left to give.

Was that it? Did I get the review right? I think so.

But I feel like I'm missing something.

The title of the review.

I think back.

There was a title? Right?

It takes a long minute.

This Movie Rocks!

How did it take me this long?

Rocks.

The guys who bugged my house easily could have bugged my cell phone, and I don't want to use it to search up anything on the internet. I stand up and grab the iPad off the stand just in front of the receptionist. I exit the vet homepage and search *Global Geologist Unlimited.*

The company's web page is the first hit, but this isn't what I want. My mother wouldn't be able to manipulate the code of their website.

But Wikipedia on the other hand.

I load the Wiki page for GGU.

I've visited the page before and scroll down to the bottom where they list the locations and coordinates of their drill sites.

There are twenty-five entries.

Last time I'd checked, there were twenty-four.

There is a small number next to the twenty-fifth entry — the reference number.

I scroll to the bottom and read the reference: "SB."

Sally Bins.

It had to be.

I look down at Lassie and say, "Greenland?"

I'm not all that good with geography, but I'm pretty sure Greenland is up near the Arctic, east of Canada. It would be uninhabitable conditions, though if you were hiding a secret prison this might be a perfect spot.

"Mr. Bins, that iPad is for signing in only."

I ignore her.

If you are the CIA and you have a secret underground prison where you keep and torture enemy combatants, well, I can't think of a better place.

What I don't understand is this: if the location were Romania, then there was a possibility I could do something. Stir things up. Make some noise. Since I was at the vet, I was thinking in terms of a puppy. Imagine if there were a puppy lost somewhere in Romania and I knew the puppy's coordinates. I had enough money that I could probably get the puppy found and flown home in twenty-four hours. But if said puppy was lost in Greenland, well, three million dollars might not bring the puppy's bones back.

And if this was all happening in Greenland, what did my mom expect me to do with the information, and why was the Department of Homeland Security involved?

I scroll back up to the locations.

I read the coordinates of the Greenland drill site: 38.94445718138941 N, 77.70492553710938 W.

My eyebrows scrunch together.

Greenland was almost into the Arctic. It was much higher than forty degrees north of the equator.

My heart rate quickens.

I search and find a GPS coordinate website and cut and paste in the coordinates.

Not Greenland.

Virginia.

:10

My dad opens the door. He is wearing boxers and a white T-shirt. His eyes are half open.

"What are you do—"

I push past him.

It's 3:41 a.m.

Murdock rushes forward and starts pawing at the backpack. He can hear or smell Lassie inside. My dad tries to pull him away, but he is too strong. He springs forward, knocks me down, snatches the backpack and begins tearing at it. Seconds later, Lassie wiggles his way through the hole in the fabric.

Prison break complete.

Murdock bathes Lassie in kisses, then the two disappear through a sliding glass door that leads to my father's neatly kept backyard.

"Say goodbye to all your flowers."

"I said goodbye to those a long time ago."

For the first time, I realize it's been over nine years since I stepped foot in the house where I grew up.

For many years, my dad would drive to see me fifty-two Wednesdays a year, plus Thanksgiving and Christmas and birthdays. Sure, my one hour was precious, but I still should have made the pilgrimage back before now.

"What are you doing here, Son?" my dad says, pulling the door closed. "And what's with the car parked across the street?"

Lassie and I left the vet without being seen by the doctor. Back on the scooter, I'd headed home, zoomed past my condo, taken a hard right, and then merged onto the northbound freeway. Within five minutes, a black car caught up with us. Throwing all pretense to the wind, it stayed close on my tail as I exited ten miles later, then weaved through the neighborhood tentacles before pulling up to the house where I spent the better part of twenty-seven years.

"The guys in the car are CIA. They are following me. And I'm here because they bugged my house."

His eyebrows rise.

"They what?"

I tell him.

"Why would they do that?"

I tell him about the clues, the meeting with the President and Director LeHigh. "He killed her, Dad. He so much as admitted it."

"Why?"

"Because mom knew of a secret black site here in the States."

"They were torturing terrorists here?"

"Yep. Can you imagine what would happen if that ever leaked?"

"They would probably shut down the CIA for good."

"Exactly. Which is why they couldn't allow that information to get out. And why mom was found with a bullet hole in the back of her head."

This is too much for my dad, and he takes a seat on the couch in his living room.

I look down at my cell phone.

3:44 a.m.

I have sixteen minutes.

I have a lot to accomplish in sixteen minutes.

"You still have that GPS?"

My father had a brief stint with an activity called geocaching. People would hide things all over the US, then post their coordinates on a national website, then people would try to track these things down and win whatever prize was inside or simply add a notch to their geocaching belt.

My father hunted down a couple of these caches, even getting a five-dollar bill out of one of them. But my dad was the ultimate hobby slut, and within a couple months he moved on to his newest phase, air-controlled helicopters or water-coloring or whatever.

"I think so. Somewhere in the basement. Why? You're not thinking about going to this place, are you?"

"It's here in Virginia."

"Langley?"

"No, about thirty miles west of CIA headquarters. Out in the boonies."

"I'll drive you."

"No, you're gonna stay right here."

I tell him my plan.

I'm guessing his reaction wouldn't have been much different if I told him I wanted to go base jumping. He pushes his glasses up his nose and asks, "Are you sure about this?"

I nod.

"Okay, then," he says. "Let's go get that GPS."

I follow him downstairs.

Though you wouldn't know it from the tidy first and second floors of my father's 2,200-square-foot suburban home, my father is a hoarder.

Mostly it's where his hobbies go to die.

A third of the way down the stairs he pulls a chain, and a solitary bulb illuminates the beginnings of the hobby cemetery.

"I forgot about the kites," I say, shaking my head.

We continue down. We reach the bottom and my dad pulls on another chain.

There are huge piles of parts, accessories, and other various implements of his many *distractions*, between which my father has somehow carved a foot-wide walkway.

"That whole ship inside the glass thing never really panned out."

"It's on the backburner." He pauses. "For now."

Right.

"You don't use that Nordic Track anymore?" AKA, the slim-down phase.

"Oh, every once in a while."

"That thing has not been used since I left here nine years ago."

"Once my back is better, I'm gonna use that thing every day."

I laugh.

We snake through the pottery phase, the piano phase, the inventor phase, and the magic phase.

"That 'cut-the-girl-in-half box' was a really good purchase."

"I was going to perform at birthday parties."

"Just find me the GPS, Copperfield."

He pushes a couple boxes out of the way, takes a quick peek inside one, and says, "Here we go."

He pulls out the small black device and hands it to me. It's twice the size of the ones that you can buy today, but considering it was only used a handful of times, I'm optimistic it works.

I hit the power button, but nothing happens.

"Don't worry, I've got batteries around here somewhere."

He moves past me and heads back toward the inventor phase.

I'm near the far wall. In the corner I notice a blue tarp. I was thinking I could use the tarp to help me elude the guys across the street. Drape it over their windshield and make a run for it. I lift a corner of the tarp and see three small black boxes. They are arranged too neatly to be my father's.

I pull one of the boxes out and flip open the top.

"Found 'em."

I turn.

Whatever is in those boxes will have to wait for another day.

A minute later, I'm back upstairs with the coordinates programmed into the GPS.

It is 3:50 a.m.

...

My room is how I left it. Half boyhood memorabilia, half grown-up CPA. Only having an hour a day means that you are forced to prioritize. Even when it came to cartoons, sports stars, bands, girls, I was forced to pick. And not one of each. One, *period.* Cartoons were too juvenile, sports were too long, and girls were out of my reach. But music was easy. I could listen to a couple songs a day, and I could have the music on in the background while I traded stocks, did push-ups, or daydreamed about girls.

I chose Prince.

He was mysterious, odd, and about as different as it got. Maybe I felt in some way he would understand what it was like to be me. To be and have Henry Bins. But mostly, I loved him because he could sing his ass off.

Intermixed with the Prince posters were a mass of whiteboards. When I first started trading stocks in the early 2000s, I remember telling my dad that I needed a bunch of whiteboards. Then each day for ten minutes, I would wake up, check stocks and graph them. Of course, all this information was available on the internet, but I liked drawing them out myself—it made me feel more connected to whatever I might be buying. Not just a mere spectator, but an active participant in the stocks' triumphs and failures. And in those first five years, I lost a lot of money, my father even having to take out a second mortgage on the house to invest in his son playing Wall Street. But eventually, I picked the right stocks. Maybe I just got lucky. Or maybe because my time was so constrained I was forced at times to simply go by my gut, but I always felt it was something about holding that red dry erase marker, graphing the company's past, present, and future, that led to my eventual success.

Three years after my dad took out the second mortgage, I paid off both the first and second mortgages, and I told him that if I ever caught him hovering over a government manual again, I would break both his arms. So I can be blamed for my father's licentious hobbying. I enabled him. But there was no amount of money that could repay what that great man did for me. For every hour that I was awake, he put eight hours into planning out every minute of my day so I would turn into the man I am.

But Prince and walking down memory lane isn't what brought me upstairs to my neatly kept room. It was a shoe box hidden in the back of my closet.

I sit on the queen bed, the brown and green striped comforter pulled taut, and lift the lid. I smile and remember the day my dad handed me the shoebox twenty years earlier.

"Every kid should have one of these," he'd said smiling. "A shoebox full of fireworks."

...

"Lassie! Murdock! Pay attention!"
I look down at my cell phone.

3:53 a.m.

Seven minutes.

I wipe off one of the whiteboards with my forearm, the steep rise in Oracle coloring my arm pink, and pick up one of the aged markers resting in the tray at the bottom.

My father is sitting with his legs draped off the bed. Murdock is standing next to him. Lassie is sitting on Murdock's back. But Lassie isn't watching me; he is chewing on Murdock's ear. And Murdock is chewing on Lassie's tail.

"Guys!"

They both snap to attention.

"We only have one shot at this."

"This is our house." I draw on the whiteboard. "And this is the car across the street."

Meow.

"Where are *you*? You are here in the house."

Meow.

"Draw you? Fine, here." I draw a cat face with whiskers.

Meow.

"Murdock? Gaaa. Fine." I draw a little stick figure dog. "And here you are, dad, and this is me."

Meow.

"Why am I so big? Because I'm in charge, you stupid cat."

I exhale.

"Okay, once I open the garage, Lassie, you and Murdock run here." I draw a line from the house to the car. I make two X's. "Box them in. They won't move if they think they'll hit you. Can you do that? Lassie?"

Meow.

"Good. Murdock?"

Murdock lets out a huge fart.

"I'll take that as a yes."

I draw another line. "Dad, this is you."

"Got it."

I look down.

3:55 a.m.

"Alright. Garage opens in two minutes."

...

I push the button for the garage.

When it is halfway open, Lassie and Murdock both scamper underneath. When it is fully open, Lassie is five feet behind the car and Murdock five feet in front.

I light the longest fuse on the fireworks — though I'll be surprised if fireworks bought during the first Gulf War will still work — and close the lid on the shoebox. Then I place it on the skateboard I found in my closet and give it a roll with my foot. The skateboard glides down the driveway, into the street, and underneath the black sedan. I hit the button and the door begins to close.

There is a door on the side of the garage, and I run out and peek around the side of the house.

The windows are heavily tinted on the car and I can't see the men's faces. The passenger side door opens, and a man steps out. I expect him to look under the car, but it appears they were too distracted by the one-hundred-and-sixty-pound dog now sitting on their bumper.

The man approaches Murdock.

"Get off the car!"

Murdock doesn't budge.

The man walks up to Murdock and shoves him. Murdock remains passive. Zen. He isn't going anywhere.

A screaming echoes from beneath the car. That would be the fountain I lit. The Howler.

The man turns and drops to the ground.

The entire shoebox is aflame. A half second later, Armageddon erupts. A second and third Howler begin screaming. Twenty bottle rockets zip out in twenty different directions. Black Cats pop off in one hundred round successions. Spinners shoot out and begin zipping all over the street in neon sparks. Smoke bombs begin hissing out their colored clouds.

It's a light show Prince would be proud of.

My dad dashes from the front of the house. He is wearing the clothes I wore earlier as well as a motorcycle helmet. If the two men looked closely, they might realize he isn't me. But they are a bit preoccupied celebrating July 4th with their new pets.

My dad jumps on the scooter parked on the street, hits the engine, and takes off. He gets a ten second head start before the man dives back into the passenger seat and the black sedan revs its engine and Murdock gallops away.

I dart back into the garage and jump into my father's Lincoln.

It is 3:58 a.m.

I hit the garage door opener, check if the coast is clear, and then zip out of the neighborhood. I take a left, then a right, then another left, then pull over on the side of the street.

I have less than a minute.

I jump out, grab the tarp I took from the basement, and throw it over the car. I only have three-quarters of the car covered when the alarm on the watch I borrowed from my dad goes off and I crawl under the tarp and dive into the back seat.

:11

I half expect to wake up in an underground dungeon, chained to a wall, rats having eaten off both my big toes.

But it appears the CIA took the bait.

I directed my dad to drive just fast enough so they would be able to see him and to lead them out of the neighborhood. I didn't want to risk them losing sight of him, then doubling back and searching the neighborhood, then seeing a car with a blue tarp over it and growing suspicious enough to check its plates. Whereby they come back to a Richard Bins, and then I'm in a dungeon with my toes eaten off.

Whether the CIA boys followed my father to a motel ten miles south, it didn't matter. They would still find him.

He had my cell phone.

They would have traced the GPS to the Motel 6 just on the outskirts of Alexandria and settled in for another night of watching.

I'd thought about keeping my dad's cell phone, but I didn't want to underestimate the CIA. They might figure out my dad was simply a diversion and trace my father's cell phone thinking I might have it. No, it was better to be off the grid.

Plus, I doubted how long my dad would be able to play possum. He needed to buy me a full twenty-four hours before he could return. But an hour from now, I would be sixty miles away and he could safely return home.

As for Lassie and Murdock, I can only imagine what the two unsupervised teenagers were up to the last twenty-three hours. Murdock would do just about anything Lassie asked him or dared him to do. I am tempted to go see if my father's house is still standing. If after the two snuck back into the house through the sliding glass door, they burned the place to the ground. Or if they'd eaten all my dad's pickles.

But I don't have time.

I jump out of the back seat, rip the blue tarp off the Lincoln and toss it to the ground. Then I hop in the driver's seat and speed out of the neighborhood.

There is a quarter tank of gas, plenty to get me where I'm going.

I pull out the GPS and turn it on.

My destination is one hour and seventeen minutes away.

I merge onto the highway and drive five miles over the speed limit. It's going to take me two days to get there, but I'm hoping to cover considerable ground today, so I will have as much of my hour tomorrow to locate the black site and take pictures with my father's expensive Nikon.

Pictures I will then show to President Sullivan and say, "Told you so."

Possibly with my tongue out.

The Lincoln eats forty miles of the interstate before the GPS directs me to get off on the next exit.

It is 3:35 a.m.

There is a large gas station — a truck depot — and I pull into the lot. I dash in, use the restroom, then grab two bottles of water, a premade sandwich, three protein bars, some Peanut M&M's, and a large bag of beef jerky.

The cashier asks, "Where you headed?"

It is the same question he asked the guy in front of me and the same question he will ask the guy behind me.

"Taking a load to Ohio."

He nods and hands me my change.

Back in the car, I zoom out of the truck stop. A half mile later, I enter the town of McLean, home to Langley. CIA headquarters.

I wonder how much time the goons sitting outside my father's hotel room spent at the sprawling campus. Is that where they were trained, where they cultivated their espionage skills, where they were taught how to deal with enemy combatants? Did anything in the thick manuals they'd read or the hours of hands-on training they'd endured instruct them how to deal with an English mastiff sitting on the hood of their car?

I take a left and continue in the opposite direction. I spend the next twenty minutes on a one-lane highway shoving processed food into my gullet, swigging down the water, and staring at the three-quarter moon brightening the rolling hills and greenery that litter the beautiful Virginia countryside.

I glance at the passenger seat. I picture Ingrid sitting there, her head craned to the side, her blue eyes gazing upward into the night sky.

I so badly want her to be in the seat next to me.

I haven't spoken with her since Lassie and I were at the vet. Did she wrap up her case? Is she worried about me? Is she staring at the moon at this exact second as well? Or is she fast asleep, Henry Bins the furthest thing from her mind?

Granted I was only awake for an hour a day, but it seemed like only a couple minutes could go by before something reminded me of her and she did a cannonball into my thoughts.

But how often did she think about me? Once an hour? Once every five? Her day was so diluted by time that even if I popped into her head a dozen times, it still couldn't match the percentage of time I was thinking of her. But is it even fair to think like that?

The alarm on my dad's watch breaks my reverie.

I don't have time to search for a good hiding spot. I pull the car over on the side of the road, flip off the lights, and crawl into the back.

I look at the GPS.

Six miles to go.

...

A green Prius drives along the road under the afternoon sun. The car passes the white Lincoln, then slows, then begins to reverse. The driver wonders what such a nice car is doing abandoned on the lonely country road. Where is the owner? Did something happen? Car trouble? Something worse?

The car parks in front of the Lincoln and a man steps out. Not a woman. A woman wouldn't stop and get out of her car in the middle of nowhere. At least a smart one. Prius is forty. Upper middle class. Successful. Church going. Out for a drive. Nowhere pressing to be.

He walks up to the Lincoln. Checks the front tire. Gazes into the front seat. Sees a bunch of discarded wrappers on the passenger seat. Sees the man in the back seat.

Your average guy might head back to his car, but Prius isn't your average guy. He recycles, he holds the door open for people, he buys fifteen boxes of Girl Scout cookies every year. He assumes the man in the back seat is taking a nap. That he got tired and pulled over to catch a couple winks. But why go through the trouble of getting into the back seat? Unless the man spent the night in the car. Which would be odd, but surely not unprecedented. But it was *odd* to still be asleep at four in the afternoon. Surely the guy should be up and continuing his journey.

Prius gives a little rap on the window. Best to see if the man is okay. But the man is nonresponsive. Prius knocks harder. Still no movement.

That's when the cell phone comes out.

It takes the sheriff ten minutes to show up.

This is where it gets strange.

The sheriff pulls a hose from his car and inserts it in to the muffler of the Lincoln. The car starts to fill with red Jell-O.

The Jell-O, which isn't your average Jell-O, dissolves the car and everything around it. Except me.

Now it's the sheriff, Prius, and then me in this red cocoon.

Then another man joins. Then a woman. Soon I am surrounded by men, women, children, dogs, even a couple horses. And then everyone starts eating the Jell-O. They are devouring it, getting closer and closer to me in the middle.

The six foot radius of red is soon just two feet, then two inches. They are about to be out of Jell-O and then they are going to start eating me.

That's when I wake up.

I jolt upright and peer out the back window. The car hasn't moved. I shake off the dream, which may have gotten slightly *unrealistic* at the end, but easily could have happened. Someone could have stopped. Could have peeked in the back seat. Could have called the cops. Sure, the road was off the beaten path, but over the course of the past twenty-three hours, a hundred cars sped past the Lincoln. Maybe a dozen gave the car a single thought, half dozen even contemplating where the owner of the automobile might be. And one even considered stopping. But lucky for me, that one continued on his merry way.

I jump out, do my business on the side of the road, and then hop into the driver's seat. I put the car in drive and chug the remaining water bottle, eat half a bag of beef jerky, and then finish off a second pack of Peanut M&M's.

I cover five miles in five minutes.

At 3:06 a.m., the GPS tells me to take a right onto a dirt road.

I keep the Lincoln around forty miles per hour up and over a large rolling hill, down the backside, then up his brother. Two more hills. I take a left. Drive for a quarter mile and the road stops. There is a gate. Private Property.

NO TRESPASSING.

There is a good chance that by driving this far up the road, I have already tripped an alarm. That if I hop over the gate and continue forth, that some commandos are going to jump out of the brush and tackle me. Or put a bullet in me. Or worse.

My only hope is my mother.

That she wouldn't send her son on a death mission.

I grab my dad's Nikon and a flashlight.

Two minutes later, I am over the gate and running up the dirt hill.

It is 3:14 a.m.

...

The GPS tells me I am one thousand feet from my destination. But the road is gone. I am surrounded by thick brush. If there is a trail that leads to the black site, I can't find it. I take five steps into the thick woods, the disrupted fallen branches, leaves, and rubble cutting loudly through the still night air.

I imagine the two men from the first article I read, Abdul Al-Rahmin and Hammad Sheik-Alzar, being led through these same trees. How long did it take the CIA to sneak the men to this location? How hard was it to get two *presumed* dead men out of Iraq and to the Virginia backcountry? How many people were involved? Was the process compartmentalized so the group that got them onto the airplane in Iraq didn't know where they would end up? Or was it a small group that saw it through to the end? Were the men who snatched Abdul and Hammad the same men that led them to their fate through these trees? Did they know what would happen to them when their little hike ended? That they would be subjected to horrific acts? That they might never again see the light of day?

I push forward.

Slowly I follow the arrow on the GPS, moving stealthily through the trees, until I am standing on the exact two-foot radius that marks the coordinates.

I'd looked at pictures of black sites on the internet and there were various kinds. Some looked like small houses, others looking more industrial, and even others looking like government offices.

But there is no black site here.

Only trees.

Did my mother send me on a wild goose chase? Where did she get the coordinates from? Was her source reliable?

I look down at the watch.

It is 3:22 a.m.

I need to leave myself time to hike back to the car and then drive back to the highway. I figure I need a solid twenty minutes, and set the alarm to go off at 3:40 a.m.

I scan the flashlight in every direction, but there is no small building, cabin, or outpost hidden within the veil of trees.

"Fuck."

The word echoes through the cold air, but I'm no longer worried that someone might hear. There is no one to hear. Probably no one within miles.

But then why the NO TRESPASSING sign?

These woods belong to someone.

I return to the exact spot of the coordinates and notice that unlike its immediate surroundings, the two-foot area is flat. I clear the fallen leaves from the ground, then fall to my knees. I move an inch of dirt and hit a hard surface. Squatting, I pick up the flashlight and shine it downward.

Plywood.

It takes me a long minute to uncover the four-foot section of plywood and lift it, revealing a bronze plate. The plate is the width of a doorway and three feet high. There is a giant padlock locking the plate to its cement foundation.

Bingo.

I pull my dad's camera from around my neck and snap three pictures in quick succession. But the plate alone isn't enough proof. If I show the President a picture of an underground door in the middle of the Virginia woods, he might shrug and say, "So you found some nutjob's bomb shelter. Big whoop."

I kick at the rotund lock with my foot and am surprised when the locking arm slips from the sheath.

I toss the lock to the side.

From the amount of leaves that had fallen, it'd been months, probably years, since the tomb was uncovered. Whatever lay beneath the bronze plate, be it a doomsday bunker, black site, or otherwise, is empty.

But then again, if it were a black site and the location was compromised, aka my mother, then it would only make sense the CIA shut it down. But what I didn't understand is why they didn't erase all evidence of its existence. But again, I was getting ahead of myself. I could easily lift the steel plate and reveal a concrete slab.

I lift the steel plate with a grunt and shove it backward.

No concrete.

Just stairs leading down into a dark abyss.

I look at my watch.

3:28 a.m.

I take two quick photos then start down.

...

Six stairs. Ten. Twelve.

I splay the flashlight in every direction. The concrete chamber is triple the size of my father's basement, maybe a thousand square feet.

But unlike my father's, this chamber is void of nearly

anything. The flashlight illuminates the chamber in a soft glow. I walk toward a set of three pop-up banquet tables and five folding chairs.

I imagine Abdul sitting in one of the folding chairs, a bag over his head, his arms and legs tied to the chair, the other chairs occupied by men who only cared about one thing: preventing the next 9/11 and willing to go to great lengths to do so.

I snap several pictures, then continue along the perimeter.

In the far corner there is a smaller table. A metal tub directly behind it, knocked on its side. Five dry, brittle rags littered about. A droplet of water drips from a water spigot in the wall.

The waterboarding station.

I imagine Abdul on his back, the rag over his head, a CIA man pouring a jug of water over his face as he coughs and sputters and prays to Allah for strength.

I snap three shots.

I check my watch.

I've been down here nine minutes already.

Directly above the table are two chains hanging from thick bolts in the concrete ceiling eight feet above. I push one of the heavy steel manacles and watch as it sweeps back and forth, crashing into its twin restraint, their echo ringing through the chamber. To strap someone up like that you have to hate them. There is no other way. I thought back to that day when the towers fell down. I hated that it happened. I even hated those men who did it. But it was a generalized hate. Of course, all of those guys died in the respective crashes, but what if they survived? Would I have been okay with the CIA chaining them up and doing only God knows what to them?

I didn't know.

I run the flashlight over the dark stains on the concrete.

"There's no drain."

I snap my head, my last breath caught somewhere in my throat.

I shine the flashlight on a man striding toward me.

"When we built this place, they said they wouldn't be able to put in any plumbing in the floors, which means no drain. So when the prisoners bleed — and they do bleed, trust me on that — the blood just has to dry."

"You're sick," I say.

Director LeHigh shrugs.

"I prefer results-driven."

"You killed my mother," I say.

"I didn't pull the trigger, but yes, I had your mother killed."

"Who was it?"

He shrugs. "It could have been any number of our more advanced operatives."

"Assassins?"

"Call them what you like."

For the first time I notice the bulge on LeHigh's hip. I scan the room. He is standing in the middle, directly in my path to the stairs.

I pull up the camera and take a couple pictures of him. If I had my phone, I could have bluffed that I was uploading them online, but I would be surprised if there is cell service.

I flip off the flashlight, sending the two of us into icy blackness.

Thirty seconds of silence go by. I wait for LeHigh to turn on a flashlight of his own.

He doesn't.

I take three silent steps to my right.

He says, "The chains were your mother's idea."

I wonder if he can hear me gulp.

"That's right. Your mother helped build this place. Hell, it's named after her. *Mother's Bunker*." He pauses. "I suppose you would need a little background to understand. Your mother was born in Macedonia, where Mother Teresa is, *was*, from. Your mother was so nice to the prisoners, well, when she wasn't waterboarding them or electrocuting them or pulling out their fingernails, and one day someone called her Mother Teresa and it stuck."

I know that he is goading me, trying to get me to give away my location. And I almost break. I almost scream, "My mother did not torture these men, she couldn't have! The warm, loving woman I knew would never harm a soul!" But I hold back. If I learned anything the previous two weeks, it was that I didn't know a single thing about my mother.

"Your mother was the one who trained me. But then again, she trained just about everyone," states LeHigh. He is still at the center of the room, now to my almost immediate left.

I take three quick steps toward where I think the entrance is located.

"Your mother wrote the book on torture. Literally, she wrote a book, *The Pain Game*. There are only a handful of surviving copies, but for a while, at least during the Reagan administration, it was mandatory reading for all recruits. Did you know the Honduran government paid your mother nearly a hundred thousand dollars to train them how to torture their prisoners? A hundred thousand dollars. And this was 1986. That's how good your mother was."

The Director's voice is moving toward the entrance. He knows what I'm up to and wants to head me off.

If I'm gonna get out of here alive, I have to do something, and now.

I try to think like him. He thinks that I will make a break for the entrance. And that was Plan A. But LeHigh is twice my size and he has a gun. And I have no doubt he knows exactly how many steps away from the entrance he is at all times. And what's to say that he didn't pull the door shut and lock it behind him or that there aren't three agents waiting just outside the entrance?

My only hope is to get the gun away from him.

The camera is no use to me at this point, and I set it on the ground. I'm not far from the pop-up tables and the folding chairs. I put the flashlight in the waist of my pants and move slowly, my hands outstretched. I take two steps. My foot hits the chair. The scraping is soft, but in the chamber it is a full New York Symphony.

"What are you doing over there?" barks the Director.

He is fifteen feet from the entrance.

I pick up the chair by the legs and I throw it in his general direction.

It clangs to the ground.

"Temper, temper, Mr. Bins," he says, obviously unfazed by my assault.

I pick up another chair and toss it wildly in his direction, then a third, then I turn and run back toward the chains.

I pull the flashlight from my waist and flip it on just long enough to get my bearings and to see if any of my chairs connected with LeHigh. They didn't. The Director is on his feet, gun in hand, his arm coming up from his hip.

I flip the flashlight off, grab the chains, and swing them hard against the ceiling. They make two hollow thuds, then come together in a series of violent chimes.

Under the umbrella of echoes I make an improvised play, then I find the far wall. I follow it for a hundred silent feet until I come to the corner nearest the entrance.

My chest is heaving, and I pull my shirt up over my mouth to mask my breathing.

I know LeHigh is close, less than twenty feet from me.

I don't imagine that after thirty years as a spy he is easily rattled, but his breathing is heavier than mine.

"It doesn't have to be this way. We can both walk out of here," he says, his voice swirling as he whips his head from side to side. "I just need you to sign some paperwork stating that you will never talk about this place, and then we can go our separate ways."

Bullshit.

I take one more breath.

Any second.

Another breath.

Any second.

The alarm on the watch goes off.

Only it isn't on my wrist.

After I smashed the chains together, I'd slid the watch across the ground toward the tables and chairs.

I can hear the Director move his feet, turning toward the sound.

I'm already on the move.

I flip the flashlight on.

The Director is turning back around but it's too late. I smash the flashlight against the side of his head. He turns his head just enough to avoid the full impact, but I still land a solid blow, one that ripples through the room.

LeHigh somehow gets an arm out and sends me reeling to the ground. My knee hits the concrete and explodes in pain, but it is the furthest thing from my mind. All I care about is the gun. Did he drop it? I don't remember hearing it clatter to the ground. My plan was to hit his right arm with the flashlight, hopefully sending the gun flying, but I changed strategy at the last minute, hoping to knock him out cold with one blow to his head.

I push myself up.

The flashlight is somehow still working, sending a beam across the floor ten feet from my right. Within its golden grip, it holds a black gun.

I dive for it.

As my hand grasps the butt, a large shoe presses down on my fingers. And I feel the other shoe moving toward my face.

And then the lights go out.

:12

"Henry."

I open my eyes.

"Henry."

The Director is standing over me, his face brightened by the flashlight close by. Blood is smeared on what little hair he has left on his head.

"Who did you tell?"

"No one." As I say the words, I realize I am lying on a table.

"Don't lie to me. Your mother told you where it is." A damp rag is placed over my eyes, nose, and mouth. "Who else knows?"

"About this place? Just me," I sputter, but the water is already being poured over my face.

It doesn't seem like it would be that terrifying. To have a towel over your face and water poured over it, but it is. You feel like you're drowning. That you can't get air. That each breath will be your last.

The water stops.

The rag comes off.

I am gasping for air.

The flashlight is cascading off the back wall, sending light up and into the corners of the bunker. I bat the water out of my eyes and squint upward.

Another round of water. A long minute of terror.

"Who did you tell about the other black site?"

"Other black site? I don't know what you're talking about. Please." I'm begging. I don't want another round of water. I'll do anything to never have to endure that again. "These were the only coordinates she gave me. I swear. Please, you have to believe me."

"You know what? Those are the exact words your mother's last prisoner said to her. Kept repeating them, over and over again. *You have to believe me,*" he mocks. "I'll admit, he wasn't more than a kid, maybe fifteen, but his brother blew up nine people. Your mother knew this kid knew where his brother and his crew were making these bombs. And she was going to get the intel out of him come hell or high water."

My right arm is pulled upward. There is a snap. Left arm. Snap. The table beneath me is kicked away and all one hundred and fifty pounds of me is suspended by my wrists.

My wrists scream for the three seconds it takes me to find my feet.

"Five days. Five days of this and the kid still wouldn't crack. I remember telling her that the kid didn't know, but she wouldn't listen. She kept at it. Pulled the kid's fingernails, electrocuted the shit out of him. Sleep deprivation, and of course, something you know about very well, sleep *amplification.*"

"What are you saying?" I blurt.

"How do you think you turned out like you did? Why you are only awake for an hour a day? You don't really think it's some medical disorder, do you? No, it's classical conditioning."

"Are you saying that my mom did this stuff to me when I was a kid? And that's why I'm the way I am?"

He punches me in the stomach.

"You were her first test subject."

I vomit. Whether it is from the blow to my solar plexus or from what LeHigh has just told me, I can't be sure.

"The kid never broke. Even after being only awake for an hour a day for over a month, he stuck to his story. But then his heart gave out. Four days later, we bring in another kid. He knows where the bombs are being made. But he also knows the brother — the one your mother killed — didn't know anything. Knows he hadn't seen his brother in years. Just like he'd said over and over again."

I can't think. My brain is imploding.

"Your mother was never the same," he says. "She got spooked."

He punches me in the face, my head whipped to the side so violently, I see the Little Dipper.

"She said she was going to go to Obama, tell him that we were still operating illegal black sites. That we had one right under his nose in Virginia. That for the last seven years a group of highly trained CIA operatives were faking the deaths of enemy combatants and sneaking them into the US"

Another punch in the stomach.

"You don't blow the whistle on your own," he says. "She knew what would happen, so she ran. But we couldn't risk her opening her mouth. So we shut this place down. It took us fifteen months to set up a new facility, to get the Vatican up and running."

"Did you say Vatican?" I mutter with what strength I have left.

He nods.

"Let me guess, if they call my mom Mother Teresa, that makes you—"

"The Pope."

I think back to Ingrid's text message.

JUST GOT A NEW CASE...A SERIAL KILLER...CALLS HIM-SELF THE POPE.

I run everything that happened the last two weeks over in my head.

How could I have been so blind?

But I do see a sliver of hope.

I'm not dead yet.

"How do you even know my mom knows about this place?" I ask.

"One of the other members of our team. We think your mother got to him. That he told her where the Vatican was located before we could, well, quiet him."

"Maybe she didn't know. And if she did, she didn't tell me."

He stares at me.

"You're telling the truth."

I nod.

"Holy shit, she didn't tell you."

I shake my head.

"Where is it?"

He glares at me.

"Is Abdul Al-Rahmin there?"

"Look at you, doing your homework. No, sadly Abdul didn't make the transfer."

"Dead."

He nods.

"But ten of his friends are there. And the intel they supplied helped us infiltrate three Al-Qaeda training camps and put a stop to a possible bombing in downtown Minneapolis."

"Is the Vatican underground, like this one?"

He looks around. Pulls the gun from his hip. I wonder if he's going to tell me before or after he pulls the trigger.

"Sure is."

He wants to tell me. Wants to tell someone.

"Here in Virginia?"

He shakes his head. "Nope, our friends to the west."

"West Virginia?" I say loudly.

He nods.

I expect them to come crashing through the door. They don't. They need more specifics.

I rack my brain. Underground. West Virginia.

"Let me guess, an abandoned coal mine?"

He smiles.

"Walton, West Virginia. Bought the mine outright. Transfer the prisoners in the back of a covered beat-up truck. No one even bats an eye. And if they did, we could just set off a couple sticks of dynamite and blow the thing to bits."

I let out an exhale.

"Okay, you guys can come in now," I yell.

He looks confused.

"What are you talking about?"

I nod at a corner of the bunker, the tiny video camera in the faint shadows of the flashlight's outer beam. The one I saw while I was being waterboarded.

"You're on TV, you fucking idiot."

Three seconds later, there is a clamoring of footsteps.

I don't need to see the group rushing forward to know that one of them is the President. And another is Ingrid.

The room fills with bright light.

"Drop the gun! Hands up!" someone yells.

LeHigh does both.

"Henry, oh my God." Ingrid pulls my wrists from the manacles and I crumple to the ground. "I wanted to come in sooner, but they wouldn't let me," she pleads. Tears are streaming down her cheeks in floods. "They wouldn't go until he gave up the second site."

Someone helps me to my feet. It's the President. "I'm so sorry about this," he says. "I never thought it would go this far. You did a great service to your country today. And I will never forget it."

"What time it is?" I whisper.

"3:57 a.m.," Ingrid says, rubbing my back.

I'm still dazed.

I look over my shoulder. Three men in black camouflage have their guns trained on Director LeHigh. I nod at them. "Hey, guys. What's up?"

I'm delirious.

The President turns to LeHigh. "When I appointed you Director of the CIA, I told you there would be zero tolerance for any of this off-the-books bullshit, and then I find out that you have a black site up and running in my own back-yard."

"You have no idea what it takes to protect this country," LeHigh scoffs. "You have no idea what we're up against. You sit there in your little office signing orders that will end up killing innocent Americans. You might as well put the bullets in their heads yourself. "

The Director continues his rambling, but all I can do is stare at Ingrid.

I thought I could never feel what I felt the day I realized my mom was never coming back.

That betrayal.

"You have to lie down, Henry."

I can't hear her words.

I would rather be waterboarded again than feel what I feel this second.

A tear falls from each of my eyes just before they close.

:13

The phone buzzes.

"It's her again," I tell Lassie.

Meow.

"No, I'm not going to answer it."

Meow.

"I don't care if you miss her."

Meow.

"Okay, I don't care if *I* miss her. Dude, she lied to me. And she got me chained up."

Meow.

"Dude, have you not seen my wrists?" I turn my wrists toward him. They are still a ghastly purple and black. "And she let me get waterboarded."

Meow.

"Big deal? Yeah, it is a *big deal.* Come here, I'm gonna show you what it feels like."

I grab him before he can get away and carry him over to the sink. I turn on the faucet and flip him over. I put his head under the water for five seconds then pull him out.

He is smiling.

Meow.

"Fun?"

Meow.

He wants me to do it again.

I put his head back under.

He makes me do it three more times.

I dry him off and give him a kiss on the head. "You are so weird."

The phone buzzes again.

And again.

It's been almost a week since I was, well, tortured. Both Ingrid and the President had called me nonstop. Ingrid had tried to come by twice, but I changed the locks.

The doorbell rings.

I limp toward the door, my right knee screaming each step, and say, "Go away."

The doorbell rings again.

"Go away."

I hear rustling in the lock. She is trying her key.

"Not gonna work."

Two seconds later, the door opens.

"What the—"

It's Red and the President. Red puts his key pick back in his pocket and says, "Sorry."

"You aren't returning my calls," barks Sullivan, once again clad in jeans and a Redskins hoodie.

"I don't really want to hear what you have to say."

"Well, I have to tell you some things. They don't make what I did okay, but they might help you understand why they had to be done."

Lassie runs up to the President and rubs against his leg.

"Don't," I say running up and grabbing him.

Meow.

"Because he's the one who got me waterboarded."

Meow.

"No, he can't do it to you right now." I put him down. "Go sit on the bed."

He does.

"You talk to your cat?" the President says with a raised eyebrows.

I ignore him. "You have five minutes."

I look down at my phone.

3:16 a.m.

The President clears his throat. "Remember when I came to play poker?"

I nod.

"Well a couple days before that, Red broke into your apartment with his little gadget there."

"Why?"

"Standard safety check," Red chimes. "He *is* the President of the United States."

"Right."

"Routine stuff we do everywhere the President visits."

"Like what?"

"Check for bugs, guns, surveillance."

"Right, I don't have any of that stuff."

"Wrong."

"What?"

"Your house was bugged?"

"I know, a couple weeks ago."

"No," the President says, shaking his head. "We're talking *months* ago."

"Are you sure?"

"Yes," says Red. "But they weren't your average Radio Shack job. These were top of the line. Spook stuff."

"Okay."

"We ran the prints on them, hoping this would give us some information, and well, they came back belonging to a person of interest."

I sigh. "My mother."

"Elena Janev," he says with a nod. "Apparently, she kept an eye on you over the years."

For some reason my mom bugging my house makes me almost smile.

"Turns out the CIA put a kill order out on your mom six years ago."

I nod. "LeHigh put it out on her. He had her killed."

Red and the President look at each other.

"Not exactly," says Sullivan.

"What do you mean?"

"I'll get to that." He takes a deep breath. "After we ran the prints and found out who your mother was, Red did some more investigating. He came across your emails to Advanced Surveillance and Tracking."

"So you knew I was looking for her?"

"Right. And like you said, you weren't the only one. A year ago, President Obama came to me. He said that he stumbled on something that slipped through the cracks while he was still in office. It was a letter. A letter from your mother that cataloged the CIA's *still* operational Extraordinary Rendition Program. There was a black site being run right under our noses, right here in Virginia. If this went public, I could have been impeached, never mind running for reelection. A torture site on American soil? The Democrats would ride me out of office in less than a week."

"Why didn't you confront LeHigh about it?"

"In the letter, your mom said there was more than one. I knew that if I blew the whistle on him, the second site would never be found."

I nod.

"So when we found out that your mother was this very woman, well, we had to act. It didn't come together overnight. It took months of planning. I had to bring in people from a number of different agencies, Homeland Security, CIA..."

"Ingrid," I say.

I think back to the meeting the President had with Ingrid. The meeting she lied to me about. The meeting the President lied to me about.

"We planted a body," he says, side-stepping Ingrid. "A woman who met your mother's overall description who died of a brain aneurism a couple days earlier. Red here had the unfortunate task of putting a bullet in the back of the woman's head."

I look at Red. He balks. Looks away. Not proud of what he'd done.

I can't blame him.

"Then he threw her in the Potomac. Then we just let things play out. I had my guy at Homeland Security flag your mother a Red Four, take over the case, and make a false match to your mother's fingerprints. Of course, AST got wind of the match and they sent you an email."

"And from there, I became your little puppet."

"More or less, yes."

"Whose idea was it to use Amazon?"

The President cocks his head at Red.

"It seemed about as innocuous a way to pass information and just cryptic enough to seem reasonable."

"*Men in Black*?"

The President smiles. "My idea."

I want to slug him.

"And then, let me guess, you call in Ingrid. You need somebody close to me to give me a couple nudges in the right direction."

I think back to the text Ingrid sent: *DONT WATCH MEN IN BLACK 2, IT GOT TERRIBLE REVIEWS.*

Had she not sent that text, I never would have thought to check the reviews on Amazon. Never in a million years.

"And your man at Homeland Security. How did you know Ingrid would call him?"

"That was our litmus test to see if our little charade would work. When Ingrid called her contact at Homeland and he told her about the Red Four flag, that's when we knew the information leaked to the right people. Then I met with Ingrid the next morning and we fed her everything she needed to know."

"A key to the city?" I ask.

"It was all I could think of."

And of course, after he told me why he met with Ingrid, he called her and made sure their stories aligned. And then she'd lied to me again.

I wonder if the President can see the steam rising from my scalp.

"How did you know I would follow your cookie crumbs?"

"I didn't. But you did."

"How did you know I was going to make the connection between *this movie rocks* and Global Geologist Unlimited?"

"Your correspondence with Advanced Surveillance. In your initial email you mention GGU frequently." He adds, "This isn't something we put together overnight."

"Tell me about Ingrid."

"She didn't want to be involved. But I asked her to do it for her country."

This doesn't quench the betrayal that has burned in my chest for going on a week.

"She followed LeHigh for over a week."

I'd figured that out already. The moment LeHigh said that they called him the Pope, it hit me.

"What about the two guys who bugged my house?"

"Those were LeHigh's guys."

"And the meeting with LeHigh in the car?"

"Sorry about that. I was playing my part. Just like you played yours."

"You didn't get waterboarded."

"Again, I'm sorry it came to that," he says, which appears genuine. He adds, "And by the way, I know damn well what a Red Four is."

"Yeah, I was wondering about that."

He smirks.

I ask, "When did you guys set up the video cameras?"

"Six weeks ago." He nods at Red.

"You did a nice job making it look like no one had been there for years."

Red says, "Yeah, I spent about three hours arranging the leaves just so."

"A true artist."

He laughs. He's not the one I'm pissed at.

"How did you know the Director would show up?" I ask Sullivan.

"They didn't just bug your house."

"I didn't have my phone on me."

He shakes his head.

I point at myself.

"Me? They bugged me?"

"Check the bottom of your foot," says Red.

I sit down on the chair. I pull off my sock and lift up my foot. On the arch is a small translucent circle the size of a pencil eraser.

"This is a tracking device?"

"Latest and greatest."

I peel it off and toss it in the trash.

"So what now?"

"Well, we can't exactly prosecute LeHigh in open court. I don't want the public to know that for the past seven years we've been torturing enemy combatants on American soil."

"So, what, he just gets to go free?"

"Not exactly."

"What does that mean?"

"The Vatican."

"Let me guess, there was a cave-in."

Hc nods.

"And LeHigh was there?"

Again he nods.

"What about all the prisoners?"

"We couldn't risk them talking."

"So you killed them?"

"To everyone else they were already dead."

"You are no better than LeHigh."

"Say what you want about LeHigh, but the man got results. He saved us from at least two separate attacks while I was in office, and those black sites were probably the reason. But in this new era of diplomacy, there are lines that can't be crossed. If the public found out about the black sites, the CIA would have been condemned, possibly shut down, and we need them. They are the front lines in our war on terror."

"And you would never be reelected."

"There is that too," he says with his prize winning smile.

"And Ingrid?"

"Just so you know, she refused to help, even when I asked her to do it for her country. She said she wouldn't lie to the man she loved."

The breath is pulled out of me.

Loved?

"The only reason she did it is because I told her that if she did, I would give you this."

The President pulls a red folder from the back of his pants and hands it to me.

"This is your mother's file."

I stare at the folder in my hand.

"Before you open that, I have to warn you there are things in that file that you can't unsee."

He and Red open the door and leave.

I stare at the folder.

I think back to what the Director said, to what I'd been thinking about nonstop for the last week. *How do you think you turned out like you did? Why you are only awake for an hour a day? You don't really think it's some medical disorder, do you? No, it's classical conditioning. You were her first test subject.*

And not only that.

If the woman they pulled from the Potomac wasn't my mother.

Then she is still alive.

3:21 A.M.

:01

June 18th
Alexandria, Virginia

It had become part of my routine. Sometimes it was only a glance, other times I would pick it up, walk around the room with it, spend a couple minutes toying with the notion of opening it. But when you are only awake for sixty minutes a day, those couple minutes are a precious commodity. Those are two minutes I'm not kissing Ingrid or rubbing Lassie's belly or playing cards with my father or making trades or running or showering. Two minutes I'm not living my life.

But I could never bear to open it. I could only postulate the words and images that lived inside the red folder.

"Honey, we need to go. It's a twenty-minute drive to the airport!" Ingrid shouts from the living room.

I gaze down at my cell phone.

3:32 a.m.

The Potomac Airfield is located ten miles away, on the other side of the river. It would be much easier for everyone if we arrived before 4 a.m., though I am certain Ingrid made arrangements for a wheelchair to be waiting.

Just in case.

"I'm coming!" I yell, my eyes still locked on the folder lying on the middle shelf of the four-foot tall safe in my closet.

It had been eight months since the President of the United States handed me the red folder. When he handed it to me, he said, "I have to warn you, there are things in there you can't unsee."

He read it.

He knew.

Knew what my mother had done to me.

But it wasn't my mother who concerned me.

It was my father.

If what Director LeHigh had said was true — that my mother was an acclaimed CIA torture specialist and the reason I was only awake from 3 a.m. to 4 a.m. each night wasn't because I had some one-in-a-trillion sleep disorder named after me (*I'm Henry Bins and I have Henry Bins*) but because she had conditioned me through *sleep amplification* — then where was my father when this was all happening?

Yes, my mother might be alive, but I hadn't seen her in thirty years and I had no intention of ever seeing her again. But my dad was my rock. He taught me everything I knew, made me into the man I am today. What if he allowed her to do these horrible things to me? What if he'd been lying to me for thirty years?

"Don't bring it."

I turn around.

Ingrid stands in the doorway of the large walk-in closet. She looks good for having been awake for going on twenty-seven straight hours. She wears a typical outfit for summer on the east coast: dark blue jeans, a gray University of Maryland T-shirt, and white and purple Nikes. After helping me pack last night, she headed into work early, then spent the next twenty hours trying to wrap up two open cases and all the paperwork that accompanies a week-long vacation as a homicide detective.

"This is supposed to be our time together," she says.

I nod.

She's right.

Although we'd lived together for going on seven months now, we only saw each other three or four hours a week. She couldn't control when or how long she would be away working her next case, and sometimes three days would go by without the two of us seeing each other. The unique circumstances of our relationship seemed less challenging on paper than they proved to be in reality. And with everything that transpired in the fifteen months we'd been dating —

Jessie Kallomatix's murder, not to mention Ingrid colluding with the President to help me expose a CIA secret prison on American soil (and getting me tortured in the process) — it seemed like there was always someone else in the room.

I shut the door to the safe and give the dial a quick spin.

"You're right."

She smiles, then shouts, "Viva la Mexico!"

"We're going to Alaska."

"Viva la *Alaska*."

I laugh and pull her into my arms and give her a long kiss.

"Come on," she says, giving my butt a slap. "I don't want to have to drag your ass onto that plane."

I nod and we exit the closet.

"Where's Lassie?" I ask.

"He's sulking. I don't think he wants to go. I think he'd rather go to your dad's and hang out with Murdock."

Lassie is indeed sulking. He is on the kitchen table, his black and tan body liquefied. His tawny eyes are half open.

"Dude, what's your problem?"

Meow.

"I told you. Murdock is sick. He isn't going to be any fun." Actually, Murdock isn't sick. He'd become increasingly aggressive with some of the neighborhood dogs and the vet attributed this to the vast amount of testosterone in the one-hundred-and-sixty-pound English mastiff's softball-sized testicles. He was getting neutered tomorrow and my dad didn't want him chasing around Lassie while he recovered.

Meow.

"I don't know, the flu or something. You can stay over at my dad's for a month when we get back."

He glares at me.

"Alaska is going to be great."

Meow.

"No, we aren't staying in an igloo. It's summer there too. It's supposed to be really nice."

Meow.

"Can you ride a moose? Well, if we see one, I'm not gonna stop you, though I'm not sure if they have them in Fairbanks."

He sighs.

"But what they do have . . ." I flip open the laptop and scroll through the pictures I'd downloaded. For the past month, I'd spent a couple minutes each day reading up on, and looking at, pictures from Alaska, aka *The Last Frontier*. I click on one of the pictures, then turn the laptop toward Lassie, ". . . is arctic foxes."

Lassie's eyes open wide.

"Now, go pack."

Ten seconds later, he has his favorite jingle ball in his mouth and paws at the front door.

...

"Alaska is going to be so much fun in a body bag."

Ingrid gazes at me with pursed lips, which eventually turn into a smile. She slows down but still manages to get us to the Potomac Airfield with three minutes to spare.

A man in a golf cart waits for us, and we load our bags into the back. We're only half in when he zooms toward the jet sitting on the tarmac two football fields away.

It is 3:58 a.m.

The chartered flight plus a week's rental at one of Fairbank's most luxurious cabins wasn't cheap, but my last trade — loading up on corn futures — paid for the trip.

I can see the wheelchair waiting for me outside the small thirty-passenger jet.

I won't need it.

At exactly 3:59 a.m., the golf cart pulls up to the plane. The man says he will take care of our luggage and the three of us jump out and clamber up the wheeled steps of the plane. The pilot nods his cap at me and gives Lassie a quick rub on the head.

We hurry down the aisle and fold into two of the large reclining seats.

Lassie settles in on my lap and Ingrid gives me a quick kiss before I fade into blackness.

When I wake up, I will be in Alaska.

And at 3:07 a.m., I will see the sun for the first time.

:02

June 19th
Sunrise 3:07 a.m.
Fairbanks, Alaska

Fairbanks, Alaska, is 200 miles south of the Arctic Circle, the imaginary line that extends in an arc across the upper third of Alaska. The Arctic Circle marks the southern limit of the area where the sun does not rise on the winter solstice or set on the summer solstice. While there is no Polar Day — twenty-four hours of sunlight — in Fairbanks, the sun is still scheduled for a heavy workload at over twenty-two hours.

I push myself up with a gasp.

My heart races. I am covered in sweat.

Snippets of the nightmare swirl around me.

A white room.

A doctor in blue scrubs.

An IV in my arm.

Where is it?

I don't know.

Where is it?

Where is what?

The flash drive.

What flash drive?

A syringe of pink liquid.

I squirm.

He injects the syringe in my IV.

I scream.

And that's when I wake up.

It takes me a long minute to calm my breathing. It doesn't help that I am in a strange bed, in a strange bedroom. I'd seen pictures of the room where I would wake up, but it is still a shock to the system. The master bedroom — one of three bedrooms in the expansive cabin — holds a king-size bed resting in a frame of shiny logs. Across from the bed is an oak dresser, with a wide mirror. Heavy champagne blinds guard guests from the blistering sun that will rise in mere minutes. To have made it here means everything went seamlessly: the eleven-hour flight, being transported by wheelchair to the waiting van, the twenty-minute drive to the cabin on the bank of the Chena River, and being dumped onto the aforementioned Sleep Number.

I jump out of bed and throw on the jeans and gray sweatshirt Ingrid has laid out for me. After slipping on my shoes, I spend a long minute in the bathroom, wiping the sweat from my brow and ear-marking a soak in the Jacuzzi tub with Ingrid in the coming days.

I exit the bathroom and follow the smell of sizzling bacon.

"Hey, Sleepyhead," Ingrid calls from an exquisite kitchen of oak and marble.

"Good morning," I say.

"Are you okay?" she asks, her head cocked to the side.

"Yeah, I'm fine."

I don't want to tell her that I had another nightmare. That I'd been having them ever since I was waterboarded. Ever since I was strung up by my wrists and beaten. I didn't want to tell her that the nightmares were getting worse. That last night's was the worst yet.

Lassie sits on the marble island eating a plate of bacon and eggs Ingrid has prepared. I give him a scratch behind the ears, then pull Ingrid into my arms. She appraises me for a long second, making sure I'm not lying, then hands me a plate and says, "Hurry up and eat."

I toss a piece of bacon in my mouth and survey the rest of the cabin. It is wide and spacious, logs running the length of the twenty-five-foot ceiling. It is filled with all the amenities and luxuries one would expect for the $4,000-a-week price tag: giant flat screen television; suede couches; antiques, picture frames, and vases that were surely haggled over at auction houses all over the world. Four windows have been cut from the ceiling, revealing the dark denim that is the sky.

Four minutes until sunrise.

Lassie has already finished his breakfast and stares at me with sad eyes. I crack a piece of bacon in half and feed it to him.

"What have you two been up to?" I ask.

Ingrid gives me a quick rundown of how we landed at Fairbanks International Airport at 11:30 a.m. — it was an eleven-hour flight, but we gained four hours going west — and then arrived at the cabin forty minutes later. Once I was situated, she and Lassie headed to downtown Fairbanks — which was only a short mile upriver — to buy groceries and hit the shops. She did some cooking and then went to sleep around 9:30 p.m. She woke up an hour ago.

"What's on the menu?" I ask.

She shakes her head. "It's a surprise."

I hunt for the refrigerator, but all I see is oak in every direction. Ingrid pulls one of the oak panels open, unveiling a fully stocked refrigerator. She removes a smoothie and hands it to me.

I take it from her as though it is made of Uranium. "Why is it green?"

"I added a little kale to Isabel's recipe."

Isabel is my housekeeper/executive assistant/personal shopper/cook. She not only prepares smoothies for me but also every meal I eat. She finds small ways to save me precious seconds throughout my "day" — from having my toothbrush pre-pasted to writing down the closing numbers of some of my more important stocks to ordering the bug spray that I would need for this trip.

I take a drink and cringe.

"What is your definition of a little?"

"Okay, a lot. But it's good for you."

The last month or so, Ingrid had grown increasingly curious about my condition — *I'm Henry Bins and I have Henry Bins* — and in turn, decided to take a more vested interest in my health. Being asleep for twenty-three hours a day, she couldn't believe I drank enough water and consumed enough nutrients to get me through each night's *hibernation*. Whenever I woke up, there was now a bottle of Smartwater, an organic energy bar, and a packet of vitamins sitting on the bedside table.

I told her I would eat whatever she wanted me to eat if it would make her feel better.

That was before *now*.

Before Kalemageddon.

"Just drink it," she says, looking at her watch. "We have to go."

I chug it down, wipe my forearm across my mouth, leaving a trail of green sludge, and set the cup in the sink.

"Follow me!" she shouts.

It is 3:05 a.m.

I follow her to a utility room.

"Eyes closed," she barks, then sprays me with a can of Extra Strength OFF. Many of the snippets I read about summertime in Alaska warned of the giant murderous mosquitos.

After returning the favor, I follow Ingrid through the living room, out a sliding glass door, and onto the back deck.

I stop, transfixed.

The deck is nestled up to the languid Chena River, which is two-hundred-feet wide. Across from the river are thousands of evergreen trees, giving way to halos of red and orange.

I am unable to speak.

A long minute passes in silence.

"Here it comes," Ingrid whispers, wrapping her hands around my back.

And then, there it is.

Just the slightest edge of radiant white.

The sun.

"I never thought I would see it," I utter, my voice barely audible.

For the next twenty minutes, I watch the sun inch above the horizon. The reds, pinks, and oranges are slowly gobbled up by the advancing blue as the sun moves above the tree line and inches across the rippling water. As it crawls to the near shore and up the small embankment, I reach out my hand and plunge it into the light. I can feel the rays in my palm. They are made of granite.

"Here, come sit."

I didn't realize Ingrid had disappeared and I turn around. Behind her I notice two chaise lounges and two plates of filet mignon.

If she notices the tears in my eyes, she doesn't comment on them.

Ingrid made a small plate for Lassie, and the three of us eat in silence.

At 3:58 a.m., the dive watch Ingrid gave to me for Christmas beeps three times.

"You should go lie down," she says.

"I'm gonna sleep out here," I tell her. "Under the sun."

:03

June 20th
Sunrise 3:07 a.m.

"Ouch!" I scream, wincing.

"Oh, stop, you big baby," Ingrid says, applying another layer of Aloe Vera to my face and neck.

"You aren't the one who has third-degree burns."

"I can't believe you didn't put any sunscreen on."

"I can't believe you let me sit out in the sun for six hours before you realized I was turning into a tomato."

"I fell asleep. And I didn't know it was going to be eighty-five degrees. This is *Alaska*."

"I told you it was going to be hot." I checked the weather the day before we left. The ten-day forecast called for sunny skies and temperatures in the high eighties.

"I thought hot in Alaska meant, like, fifty degrees."

"Wait," I say, "if you fell asleep outside, then why aren't you sunburned?"

"I put sunscreen on," she says, trying to turtle her head into her body.

I scoff.

I own a pair of UV lights that I hook up to my computer twice a week to ward off seasonal depression — or in my case, four-seasonal depression — and I do have slightly darker skin than most Caucasian males, but it was foolish of me not to have lathered myself in SPF 1000.

"I'm gonna get you a cold washcloth," Ingrid says, then disappears.

A moment later, Lassie bounds onto the bathroom vanity.

He reels back and hisses at me.

"Dude, it's just a sunburn."

Meow.

"No, it's not Ebola."

Meow.

"Because I haven't been in Liberia lately."

Meow.

"A sunburn. I was *burned* by the *sun*."

Meow.

"Well, that's because you are covered in hair."

Meow.

"Because the smarter a species is, the less hair they have."

Meow.

"You're not the one who looks like *who*?"

Meow.

"Who is Freddie Krueger?"

"Come on!" Ingrid shouts from somewhere. "Food is ready."

Lassie jumps off the vanity and zips from the bathroom.

I grab my phone and text my dad that everything went smoothly, that the sun is more magnificent than I ever could have imagined, and that I hope Murdock is feeling okay.

A moment later, he sends me a picture of Murdock lying on the couch with a giant cone around his neck, his enormous mouth drooping onto a pillow, his eyes staring daggers at the photographer.

Underneath the picture my dad has written.

He knows.

I contemplate showing the picture to Lassie but think better of it.

I give myself one last glance in the mirror — my brown eyes framed by a crimson face glistening in goopy translucent green — and walk to the back deck.

Ingrid has prepared a big plate of sandwiches, another green smoothie, some lemonade, and a bag of caramel corn. She has everything set up on a stunning picnic table with an attached umbrella. Three citronella candles keep the mosquitos at bay.

"You should probably try and stay out of the sun," she says, draping a cold rag around the back of my neck. She adds, "Lobster boy."

We both laugh and I ask, "Who is Freddie Krueger?"

"Why?"

"Lassie said I look like Freddie Krueger."

"Oh, did he?" she says, sneaking a quick peek at where Lassie is taking a post-breakfast nap on one of the chaise lounges. "Freddie Krueger is the bad guy in a bunch of horror movies. His face is all burned up and he has this razor glove he wears on his hand. He haunts your dreams and if he kills you in your dream, he kills you in real life."

"So nobody ever wants to go to sleep."

She nods.

"Sounds like my life."

"Freddie Krueger never got laid by the hot detective."

"Right," I say with a laugh.

She gives me a long kiss, then we hold hands and watch the sunrise.

...

Fifteen minutes later, three canoers and two kayakers float down the river. They all wave as they move past and Ingrid and I wave back.

"We should do that tomorrow," she says. "Rent a canoe."

"I already checked into it," I say with a smile. "There are three or four different places all along the river. They call it 'Floating the Chena.' It doesn't get this hot too often, so when it does, everyone heads for the water. The whole trip is twelve miles, takes about four hours, but I figure we could do the last couple miles."

"I'll pack the sunscreen," she says, slapping me on the leg. "Freddie."

We laugh and kiss, which leads to some more kissing and some light funny business.

At 3:55 a.m., I remember I packed a little surprise.

"I'll be right back," I say, giving her forehead a gentle kiss. "I have dessert."

My dad gave me an expensive bottle of scotch to take on the trip. I rummage through my suitcase and pull out a bottle of forty-year-old Macallan. I snag two tumblers from the kitchen and head back outside.

My dad and I would occasionally drink a beer or a glass of scotch when we played cards each Wednesday, but I didn't do a whole lot of drinking. Mainly because I didn't have time.

I pour two fingers of scotch into both glasses and hand one to Ingrid.

I lift my tumbler to clink glasses.

Ingrid stares at hers on the table.

My watch beeps.

Two-minute warning.

"What?" I ask. "You don't like scotch?"

She fingers the glass.

I say, "You don't have to drink it if you don't want to."

She shakes her head.

When she gazes up at me, her navy eyes have melted and drip softly down her cheeks.

"Henry," she says, softly, "I'm pregnant."

:04

June 21st
Sunrise 3:07 a.m.

It's 3:02 a.m. when I walk into the kitchen. Ingrid sits at the kitchen table, her hands wrapped around a cup of steaming coffee. She gazes at me. Waiting for me to speak.

"You said you were on birth control."

"I am," she says with a nod.

"And you were taking it?"

"Almost every day."

"*Almost?*"

"Sometimes with work it slips my mind."

"How long? How long have you known?"

"A month."

"*A month?*"

"I wanted to be sure."

"And you are?"

She sniffs and nods.

I take a deep breath. "I told you that I don't want kids. I told you we had to be super careful." It isn't that I didn't want kids. I loved kids or at least *the idea* of kids. It's that I didn't want to be a rent-a-dad. How could I be expected to raise a child, be a father, when I only had an hour a day? "I'm only awake an hour a day!" I shout. "What don't you understand about that? Sixty minutes is all I get, and now you want me to take care of a *baby*?"

I turn. I don't want to look at her. I don't want to see what my words have done to her. I walk into the bedroom and strip off my jeans. I pull on gray sweatpants and a matching gray hoodie, then lace up my running shoes.

Lassie is asleep and I give him a nudge with my hand.
"Come on, let's go."

He does a quick stretch, then hops off the bed.

A minute later, when the sun does rise, Lassie and I are
wending our way through the trees, headed toward downtown Fairbanks.

...

The trail spits us out onto a side street two blocks from
downtown. My feet pound the pavement. Lassie glides on
the sidewalk next to me.

My face burns hot. From the anger. And the lasting sunburn.

I can't remember a time when I was so angry.

How could she do this to me?

How could she be so irresponsible? So reckless?

How could she get pregnant?

Was I supposed to spend my one measly hour a day
changing diapers?

We follow the Chena River toward downtown, which is
less impressive than the pictures had depicted. The outskirts of Fairbanks are bland and industrial. A saltine as far
as cities go. The tallest building we pass is a sixty-foot rectangle of gray. There is a large gold banner with a polar bear
and six multicolored rings.

Each summer in Fairbanks, they hold the Olympics.

The World Eskimo-Indian Olympics.

The Olympics draw a couple thousand spectators each
year and kick off tomorrow at sunrise. The events are somewhat odd: the Seal Hop, the Ear Pull, the Two-Foot High
Kick, the Indian Stick Pull, the Blanket Toss, among others.
I had bought tickets for the second day and had hoped Ingrid and I could catch one of the sunrise events.

There are about sixty people milling outside the building setting up booths for the following day.

Two blocks later, we come to the Cushman Street Bridge.
The river is twice as wide as it was outside our cabin and the
two-lane bridge is a quarter-mile long. It's the first bridge
I've seen since I'd run to the Potomac River after learning
my mother's body was pulled from the river. That day, I

remember staring at the concrete bridge straddling the Potomac and visualized her throwing herself into the water. I imagined her with this huge rock of guilt from abandoning me, from running out on her freak-show son, and how she couldn't live with herself anymore. I remember back to something my father said a couple years after she walked out on us.

"It's her loss, not yours."

Was my current situation any different? Sure, my kid was the size of my fingernail right now, but it was still my child cooking in there. In thirty years, would it be Ingrid telling our child, "It's his loss, not yours"?

Of course, it wasn't my mother who was pulled from the river. No, she was still alive. And it turns out, she may have done far worse things than simply abandoning me. But this wasn't about my mom. This was about Ingrid and me. And our baby.

Lassie and I make our way onto the bridge, run to the halfway point, and then stop.

The heart of Fairbanks is much more flavorful. The bridge is lined with slim silver poles with small yellow flags commemorating the Olympics. Each flag has a picture of a different event. The one closest to me has a picture of two men, their heads a foot apart, a large rubber band stretched around both men's ears.

I guess this is the infamous Ear Pull.

Flower pots packed with screaming purple flowers hang from the guardrails. A Key Bank, Radisson Hotel, another competing hotel, and two other businesses huddle on the corner of the intersection up ahead. The parking lots are overrun with cars, and I suspect it has to do with the Olympics being held down the street.

Across the river, the sun is two inches above the tree line, reflecting off the small ripples of movement on the water.

Lassie lies down on the concrete next to me.

He knows to leave me alone, to let me stew.

All I can think about is Ingrid, how she was back at the cabin, alone, scared, and yes, abandoned.

I lean my head back.

"I'm such a dick," I say to the soft blue sky. I want to teleport back to the cabin. I want to tell Ingrid how sorry I am.

I peer down at my watch,

It's 3:21 a.m.

"Let's go," I say to Lassie.

He shakes his head. He's exhausted.

I lean down and pick him up.

There is a tremor under my feet, and I turn and look over my shoulder. I expect to see a line of semi-trucks pulling onto the bridge, but there isn't a single car in sight.

There is another tremor, one strong enough to send me flailing to the guardrail.

"What the fuck?" I say, holding onto Lassie with one hand, the guardrail with another.

Meow.

"I'm not sure."

The bridge lurches and I drop to my knees. The flower pot in front of me falls into the water twenty feet below. I backpedal to the center of the road. The bridge shakes sending the many flags into a frenzy.

"Holy shit, it's an earthquake!"

When researching the trip, I stumbled across a statistic that Alaska was home to over fifty percent of all the earthquakes in the United States. However, because Alaska was so remote, there was usually little damage or injury.

Off to my left, the Radisson Hotel sways back and forth. If it falls, there will be lots of damage. Lots of injury. Lots of death.

The bridge lurches, sending me back to my knees. I hold Lassie by the collar, bracing myself with one hand. Under the railing, I see a series of trees on the river's edge uproot and fall into the water.

I attempt to stand but it is like trying to balance on a bucking bronco. There is an explosion as a huge section of the bridge fifty yards behind me collapses into the river. I stare at the thirty-foot gap in the street.

I push myself up.

I need to get us off the bridge.

A flag pole crashes down right in front of me. I roll to my side, sending Lassie flying. He scurries back and jumps onto my back, his claws digging into my sweatshirt. Another pole falls. The bridge is crumbling to pieces.

An atom bomb of dust explodes downtown. The first building has fallen. I can only imagine how many people were just crushed, who lay dead or dying in the giant cloud of rubble.

I stumble toward the dust. A section of the bridge in front of me falls away and I backpedal on hands and knees. I push myself up and grab the guardrail. I am on a one-hundred-foot concrete island.

Directly below, the small ripples on the river have doubled in size.

The shaking stops.

I take a deep breath.

"Lassie!"

Meow.

He is between my legs.

Shaking.

I pick him up.

Keeping one hand on the guardrail, I gaze in every direction. Fifty yards behind me, there is a thirty foot gap where the street has collapsed into the river. Thirty yards ahead of me there is a smaller piece of the bridge missing. Of the twenty flags that line the bridge, only two poles remain attached. Neither carries their flag. Behind the cloud of dust, both hotels have been flattened. So have the bank and two other buildings. One remains standing. The sole survivor. I wonder how many other buildings have fallen. How many other hotels?

The death toll could be staggering.

All I can think about is Ingrid.

Is our cabin still standing?

Was she far enough from the epicenter to escape the worst of it?

If the cabin did fall, is she buried? Is she trapped and helpless, screaming out my name?

I look down at my watch.

3:23 a.m.

The quake lasted over two minutes.

I run south to the edge of the island. My concrete glacier. I peer down at the jagged edge of road and the three-inch thick rebar that bends downward toward the thirty-foot section of road that lies in the river. I had hoped we could drop down to it, but the river has intensified and it rushes past in waves of brown.

I run to the north end. The gap is half as big, but the story is the same.

Meow.

"I can't jump it."

Meow.

"Well, I'm not *Carl Lewis.*"

I gaze down at the river. I don't know if the earthquake broke a levy, or a dam, or if it simply pushed a huge excess of water forward — a river tsunami, if such a thing exists — but it has morphed into raging brown rapids. A sweeping sludge of angry water. The rising water rides high on the banks and continues to rip trees from their roots and sweep them away. Those trees begin hammering at the support of my concrete island. A cabin, or what is left of a cabin, swirls around a bend in the river, and moments later, smashes into the pillar beneath our feet.

The island rocks and a huge chunk falls away.

Our glacier is crumbling.

I line myself up over the support pillar. This is where I am going to wait it out. Wait until help arrives.

I check my watch.

3:28 a.m.

Where are the fire trucks? Where are the choppers?

The bridge lurches.

I gaze down.

The debris could no longer fit under the bridge. Trees upon trees, sections of docks, a boat, cabin decks, a car. It is a stew of casualties from the monster quake. I can feel the bridge creaking. It can't hold out much longer.

I run to the opposite side of the bridge. There isn't much debris in the water, it is all piled up on the opposite side. I can feel the weight of it pushing on the bridge. An elephant leaning on a picket fence.

Meow.

"We have to."

Meow.

"Otherwise we are going to die when this thing crumbles."

Meo—
The bridge rumbles.
Aftershock.
I grab Lassie by the collar and without thinking, I jump.

...

I'm in a washing machine of freezing water. I try to calm myself down. *You jumped into the river,* I tell myself. *Stay calm, you will come to the surface.* I can't stay calm. I need to breathe. Now.

I twist and turn. I paddle with my right hand toward what a reptilian part of my brain senses is the surface. My head breaks free of the cold water and I gasp for air.

My left hand is tight around Lassie's collar. I lift him out of the water. His yellow eyes bulge as he chokes for air.

I take four or five breaths, the landscape of the river flashing by in a haze of green. The river feels like it is going sixty miles an hour.

Behind us, I see what is left of the bridge.

Nothing.

I have no idea how long my body can stay functional in forty-five degree water, though I figure it's only a few minutes. It doesn't matter, because if I don't get us to shore before the sludge of death overtakes us, we are toast.

Holding Lassie to my left shoulder, I start angling toward shore. After ten long seconds I realize we will never make it. We are at the mercy of the raging river. I have no control over where the river takes us, which right now is to our death.

I submerge underwater, then fight my way back to the surface.

It is nearly impossible to tread water with Lassie's body tucked to my shoulder.

Then I see it.

On the banks of the river, lined up behind a small structure, lying vertical on the flat of the bank, are a fleet of canoes and kayaks of all makes and sizes. It is Canoe City or Kayakville or one of the two other rental places. The river laps at the bottom of the boats. I can't be certain how many kayaks and canoes the river has already swept into its clutches, if any, but I know all their fates are sealed.

I watch as a green canoe slinks down into the brown water and is carried away.

I turn as we fly past, trying to keep the boats in view.

My muscles are already starting to cramp. My clothes are heavy.

The river pulls me under.

It takes the last of my energy to kick to the surface.

Lassie chokes for breath.

This is it.

Game over.

Something brown whips past.

It is already twenty yards ahead of me when I realize it is a canoe.

I turn around.

Another canoe zips past.

The freezing water whips at my face.

Two kayaks are headed downstream. Both blue. They pass by fifty feet to my left.

Another kayak. Red. Upside down. Headed right for us.

I reach my hand out and grab for it, but my fingers are frozen and my hand slides off. I might as well be trying to pick up a toothpick with boxing gloves.

I watch as the red kayak races ahead, around a bend, and out of sight.

Shit.

I turn around and my eyes open wide.

The mother lode. The rest of the fleet is a hundred yards away and coming fast. The whole section of riverbank must have collapsed into the water.

I reach for a blue kayak. I get my arm over. The kayak flips, throwing me off. I roll in the white water.

I kick back to the surface.

Eight more float by, none within ten feet.

Then they are gone. All of them.

No.

No.

No.

My right leg starts to cramp. I can barely keep us above water.

Meow.

I look over my shoulder.

A lone canoe.

Green.

Headed right for us.

Put on the river, just for us.

Our *salvation*.

I grit my teeth.

Fifty feet.

Forty.

Thirty.

Twenty.

Ten.

Five.

Two.

I kick hard, and lunge for the side. I get my right arm over, then my left. I drop Lassie inside. The canoe rocks under my weight. I try and pull myself up. I can't. My body is frozen.

My left arm slips off.

If I let go with my right arm, I'm dead.

I think of Ingrid.

I think of the baby growing in her womb.

I throw my left arm back over. The canoe rocks under my full weight and I rock with it, then with the momentum headed in the opposite direction, I grit my teeth and push myself up with a grunt. I get my stomach up on the side. Lean forward. Then flop inside the boat.

I crawl to Lassie and wrap my hand around his collar.

I lay there gasping for several minutes.

I pull my watch to my face.

The digits swim in front of me.

I squint.

3:37 a.m.

It's been sixteen minutes since the quake.

It takes everything I have left to push myself to my knees. If I stay down I will die from hypothermia. I need to keep moving. I need to get us to shore in the next twenty-three minutes. I need to get us off the river.

Halfway to my feet, I crumble.

I have nothing left.

:05

June 22nd
Sunrise 3:07 a.m.
Somewhere in Alaska

I wake up gasping. I am underwater again. Drowning. Fighting for breath. It takes a long minute to calm my breathing, then another long minute for reality to hit. The earthquake. The bridge. The river. The canoe.

Every muscle, every tendon, every fiber in my body aches.

What I can't understand is how I am alive. How did I not succumb to hypothermia? I suppose the only explanation is the intense heat wave. Was this enough to thaw me out after spending nearly six minutes in forty-five degree water?

I roll over on my side, then push myself up into a sitting position. The sky is the purplish-yellow of a vanishing bruise.

The canoe floats silently on a glass of water. The river is wide, twice as wide as I remember. The water is guarded by sandbars, then thick grass and rolling forested hills.

I look down at the canoe.

It is fifteen feet long, two and a half feet deep, three feet wide. There are two spots to sit, though you could fit three people if you tried.

"Lassie?"

I push myself up and sit on one of two wooden dividers which act as footrests.

"Lassie?"

I crawl up and down the boat.

He's gone.

My stomach tightens, then begins to spasm. It takes everything I have to hold down whatever food is left in my stomach.

What did I expect? For him to be sitting on my chest when I woke up? He weighed five pounds. There is no doubt in my mind he froze to death. That we hit some rapids and he was thrown from the boat.

I want to tell myself he was just a cat.

I take a long, deep breath.

My eyes begin to water.

"Dammit."

Maybe he made it. Maybe the canoe came close to shore and he jumped out.

I want to believe that, but if Lassie's body were in the same condition as mine, then he wouldn't have been able to move. Then again, it had been twenty-three hours. The hot sun could have thawed him, then he made a leap for it.

In my heart, I know.

As hard as Lassie's death hurts, the thought of Ingrid buried somewhere in the rubble of the cabin with our unborn child in her belly hurts more.

I need to get back to them.

I need to find her.

Save her.

I do some quick math. If it took four hours to float twelve miles on the Chena, then we went about three miles per hour. After the quake, the river flowed twice as fast, perhaps three times as fast, but at some point downstream it would have found its equilibrium and slowed back down. Who knows how many miles, or how many hours that took? Here and now, it moves at a crawl, two miles per hour, maybe less. I decide to use four miles per hour as an average. The canoe could have gotten stuck at some point, possibly for hours at a time, but I have to assume the worst, I have to assume I floated for twenty-three hours straight. At four miles per hour, that was almost a hundred miles.

"A hundred miles," I say to the river.

If I had all day to traverse the distance, I could do it in

a week. I ran eight miles an hour on a treadmill, but I'd be lucky to cover four miles an hour in this terrain. It would take me a day to recover each hour I'd been on the river.

Twenty-three days.

I check my watch.

It is 3:04 a.m.

The sun will be rising in the next few minutes, and I realize I am freezing.

Hopefully, it will be another hot one.

...

The river is waist-high. I bite my lip and wade through the freezing water, holding the canoe with my right hand. The water recedes to my thighs, then my knees. I trudge to the sand and pull off my still half-soaked sweatshirt and my fully-soaked sweatpants, shoes, and socks and throw them on the coarse sand. I am shivering, nearly convulsing, and I force myself to do two hundred jumping jacks. By the time I'm done, the sun has poked its head out from behind the rolling mountains.

I catch my breath and start to think.

What are my chances of rescue?

I'm sure the skies were full of airplanes and helicopters the past day — from the Red Cross to FEMA, even the National Guard — as they delivered medical equipment, supplies, soldiers, food, and water to the disaster site. Local and national news choppers would be hovering over the wreckage twenty-four hours a day. The chances of one of these planes or helicopters flying over me — from the lightening sky and the flow of the river, I guess I am a hundred miles *west* of Fairbanks — is slim to none.

As for rescue by water, I give myself a slightly better chance. Summer is the peak season on the water, and a boat, kayak, or canoe could float past at any moment. Most of these tourists, or enthusiasts, would stay, or live, in Fairbanks, and they were either dead, grieving, helping, or had caught the first plane back to Tampa. I also needed to factor in that the river might be impassable. There had to be mountains of debris all over the place, making it difficult, if not impossible, to navigate.

The only person looking for me would be Ingrid. And even if Ingrid did survive, if she didn't find me in the next hour, she would lose all hope. I imagine her frantically explaining to rescue workers that I could be asleep anywhere. "What's Henry Bins?" they would utter incredulously. "Never heard of it," they would say. And she would have to explain her boyfriend's mysterious condition where he was only awake for one hour a day and that they had traveled three thousand miles so he could see the sun.

Right.

It had been nearly twenty-four hours since the first buildings fell. Come tomorrow it would be forty-eight. Starting tomorrow, I wouldn't be missing. I would be dead.

I will have to save myself.

...

The sound of my stomach rumbling breaks my reverie. The last thing I ate was the sandwich and smoothie forty-eight hours earlier.

My body is acclimated to long periods without food or water, but I am suddenly aware of how thirsty and hungry I am. I can go another week without food, but I need water.

I gaze down at the river. The shallow water has taken on the color of the rock and silt directly below. I cup my hands together and scoop the water to my face. It smells faintly musky. It is as clear as the water from my faucet in Virginia, which doesn't mean it isn't crawling with deadly microbes, bacteria, or intestinal parasites.

I open my hands and let the water fall back to the river.

I check my watch.

3:13 a.m.

My eyes move to the canoe resting high up on the sandbar. What if I continued down the river? Pushed the canoe back into the flow and rode it until I lucked upon a small river community? In any other state this might be an option, but in Alaska, where heartbeats were separated by thousands of miles, this would be a huge gamble.

There are three large rocks near where the brush begins, and I wring out my clothes and drape them over two of them. Standing on the third rock, wearing only my boxer briefs — which thankfully are nylon and nearly dry — I survey my surroundings. Rolling green mountains and yellow valleys in every direction.

"I am in the middle of fucking nowhere," I say, laughing at the absurdity of it all.

I can't go far without my shoes, so I stick to the sandbar. I find a stick and I begin trying to sharpen it on one of the rocks.

I've seen sixteen movies in my life and one of them is *Castaway.*

It was the closest thing I'd ever seen to a horror movie.

In fact, I couldn't finish watching it. When he lost Wilson, I turned the movie off. But not before I learned a thing or two.

"You can do this," I tell myself. "You are in good shape. You can go long stretches without food or water. You are made for this."

I spend the next twenty minutes moving up and down the sandbar, using my stick to etch HELP ME in elephant sized letters.

At 3:50 a.m., I check on my clothes. My sweatshirt is nearly dry and I pull it on. Everything else is still soaked, but the rocks have started to absorb the sun's heat and they will be dry when I wake up tomorrow.

My heart races.

Dehydration is setting in.

My body can't go another day without water. Drinking the water might make me sick. Not drinking the water will kill me. I cup my hands in the river and drink heartily. It tastes like water you drink from a cup that was used for milk the day before. I drink ten handfuls, splash my face, then retreat back to the sand.

At 3:54 a.m., I drag the canoe up toward the third rock.

I can't spend twenty-three hours in the sun, so I plan on flipping the canoe over and propping one side up on the rock. A makeshift hutch.

I flip the canoe over on its side and pick up the front end.

Something falls out.

There is a hollow space in the nose of the boat. I figure it must be warm. That's why he went there.

I drop the canoe and fall to my knees.

"Lassie!"

His eyes flitter and open halfway.

I carry him to the edge of the river and hand drip water into his mouth, his little tongue licking up each drop.

A minute later, I slide under the canoe and hug Lassie to my chest.

He is back asleep before I am.

:06

June 23rd
Sunrise 3:08 a.m.

I wake up to the sound of my stomach growling. At least, I hope it's my stomach. In the Alaskan wilderness, if something is growling, you *want* it to be your stomach.

But it isn't my hunger that worries me.

It's my legs.

I roll out from beneath the canoe and gaze down.

"Oh, shit."

I am covered in a thousand mosquito bites. There isn't an inch of flesh that isn't an angry raised boil of red.

I claw at my legs with my fingernails, momentarily quelling the insane itching.

How could I have been so stupid?

No matter how wet my clothes were, I should have covered up every inch of skin.

Meow.

I turn around.

Lassie is still huddled underneath the canoe.

"No, I don't have leprosy," I say, giving my legs another violent itch. "I got bitten by a thousand mosquitos."

Meow.

"My *face*? What's wrong with my face?"

I feel my face with my hands. I feel something flaky on my forehead and pull at it. I look at my hand. It looks like a jagged piece of wax paper.

Skin.

I peel a piece off my nose twice the size.

Meow.

"No, I'm not going to eat it."

Meow.

"No, you are not going to eat it."

We were not resorting to cannibalism.

Yet.

Meow.

"Me too, buddy." What I wouldn't do for a smoothie right now. Even a green one.

Meow.

"No, I don't have any Fancy Feast. Why don't you go catch us some breakfast?"

Meow.

"Your leg? What did you do to your leg?"

For the first time, I notice how Lassie is sitting. Back on his haunches, his front right leg curled inward.

I lean down and touch it gingerly.

He whimpers.

"What happened?"

Meow.

"I did it? How did *I* do it?"

Meow.

"I *did not* dunk you into the canoe like I was LeBron James."

Meow.

"Well, I didn't do it on purpose. Can you move it?"

He wiggles his foot and whines. If it isn't broken, it's badly sprained. Either way, he won't be catching us dinner any time soon.

After raking my nails over my legs for a long thirty seconds, I retrieve my sweatpants from where they are draped over one of the black rocks. They are dry. I pull them on, hoping they will bring itch relief. They don't. I pull on my socks and shoes, then hobble back to the canoe.

I pick up Lassie.

"We have two options," I say. "We can hike back to Fairbanks, but I figure we are over a hundred miles away. I can cover four miles a day, five if we can hug the sandbars. So we are looking at close to a month. Or we can hop into Mr. Canoe over there and take our chances on the river. I figure we can travel about the same distance each day. It will be easier, but we will be headed even deeper into the wilderness and we might not come across anything for a thousand miles."

Meow.

"It's summer. There are no igloo people."

Meow.

"I'm not sure, huts or something."

"We need to get moving," I say. "What do you think? Land or water?"

On land, I knew what to expect. If we follow the river upstream — east, toward the sunrise — it would eventually lead us back to Fairbanks. Plus, there is always a chance we would run into some "hut people" or a river community en route. Heading downstream — west, in the canoe — there were no guarantees. There could be rapids. The river could be blocked. We would be at the mercy of the water.

Meow.

"Sorry, I vote land."

Meow.

"Can you walk? Can you steer the canoe?"

Meow.

"Well, then your vote *doesn't* count."

I spend the next five minutes scribbling a message in the sand near the canoe.

Stranded. Headed upstream toward Fairbanks. June 23rd. Henry Bins.

Meow.

"Fine."

...And Lassie the cat.

I take stock of my assets. One sweatshirt. One pair of sweatpants. One T-shirt. One pair of boxers. Two socks. Two shoes. One stick. One watch. One cat.

"All right," I say, leaning down and picking up Lassie. "Let's go."

...

The water is low and the sandbar is dried out by the high temperatures of late, making for a leisurely jog along the riverbank. If the coarse sand and small pebbles escorted the river for all one hundred miles upstream, we might have made the journey in two weeks. It doesn't. Every half mile or so, the sand disappears into the river and I am forced to wade through waist-high grass and a slalom of birch, fir, and pine trees. Each step is scheduled and planned. It is slow and worsened by the swarming insects that bite at my hands, neck, and face.

Lassie is tucked in the nook of my left arm. I slap at my neck with my right hand and inspect my palm in the soft daylight.

The insect is the size of a hummingbird.

Meow.

"No, it's not a bat," I say laughing, then add, "Just be glad you're covered in that mangy fur."

Meow.

"I know, I was kidding. Now, Murdock on the other hand."

Meow.

"Probably just lying on the couch resting."

Meow.

"*Cats can't get the flu?* Do you have any research to back that up?"

He doesn't.

After a long minute, I tell Lassie, "I have a confession."

Meow.

"I lied. Murdock didn't have the flu."

Meow.

"He got neutered."

Meow.

"It means he got his balls chopped off."

Lassie swipes at my face with his good paw.

I squeeze him until he calms down.

"It wasn't my decision."

Meow.

"Because he nearly humped the neighbor's poodle to death."

Meow.

"Yes, Mitzy."

Meow.

"No, he will be exactly the same, he'll just be a couple pounds lighter."

Meow.

"I don't know what they do with them. I doubt they are in my dad's freezer." I take a breath and add, "Anyhow, I just wanted to tell you."

Just in case we didn't make it. Just in case this was our last day together.

This started me thinking about what I would tell Ingrid right now if I knew things were going south.

I look down at my watch.

3:32 a.m.

What would I tell her if I only had twenty-eight more minutes with her?

I would tell her I love her. How I never thought I could love anything as much as I love her. How she made me furious I only have sixty minutes a day, but also profoundly lucky that I was able to spend some of those precious minutes with her. I would tell her how sorry I was. That no matter if I didn't want a child, I should have supported her. That no matter how hard it would be for me to give my precious minutes to a baby, I would do it. I would try not to be selfish. Try not to see the baby as a small clock gobbling up my minutes. Try not to think about what would happen when the kid grew older, making him wake up at 3:00 a.m. so he could spend some quality time with his old man. Try not to think about all of his or her life events, successes, and failures I would miss out on. How I would constantly be trying to play catch-up. A bicycle trying to catch an airplane. All because she couldn't remember to take her birth control.

I shake my head.

How did my thoughts end up there? How could I be so selfish? What is wrong with my brain?

My thoughts are interrupted by a beautiful sight. The sandbar has returned.

I take off in a jog and we cover another mile and a half.

At 3:55 a.m., we stop. By my estimate, we've covered close to five miles.

I set Lassie next to the river and we both drink our fill.

Lassie tries to take a step on his front paw, then pulls it back in agony.

"Don't," I tell him. "I don't mind carrying you." After three days without food, he can't weigh more than four pounds.

Meow.

I nod. *I'm hungry too, buddy.*

I hunt for another stick — I had to ditch the first one in order to swat at mosquitos — and find a perfect specimen on the riverbank. It already has the beginnings of a sharp edge and I spend three minutes shaving it on a rock to a finer point, at least sharp enough to spear a fish.

I take off my shoes and socks, roll up my sweats, and wade into a pool of shallow water. The cold water soothes the stinging mosquito bites. A multicolored fish shoots through the shallow pool of clear water and I jab at the river with the stick.

Not even close.

:07

June 24th
Sunrise 3:09 a.m.

I was starving when I fell asleep. There is no word to describe how hungry I am when I wake up.

Lassie is curled into my body, lying on a thick bed of pine needles. I stroke his back, noting how my hand grates against his rib cage. I was a hundred and sixty pounds and my body is used to long durations without food. I am a genetic camel. Lassie, on the other hand, is a genetic tapeworm, and without food, his body is wasting away.

I push myself up, dust the fallen pine needles from my lap, and stretch out my arms. My legs, hands, and neck itch uncontrollably. I bite my tongue, take deep breaths, and fight off the urge to cheese-grate my body with my fingernails.

I last three breaths.

After a long minute — my hands racked in red slashes from my fingernails — I straighten.

There are a couple of pine needles on my shoulder and I pick them off and put them in my mouth. I chew them down, gag on the needles as they move down my throat, and somehow swallow.

Lassie stares up at me and I ask, "You want to try a couple?"

Meow.

"No, they do not taste anything like a Honey Baked Ham."

Meow.

"No, I don't have any Honey Baked Ham."

Meow.

"No, I don't think there is a Honey Baked Ham close by."

I pick him up and we do our daily ritual at the river's edge. I notice my heart beating faster than usual and that someone turned off the autofocus on my eyes.

How long has it been since I ate?

The last thing I ate was the sandwich, smoothie, and caramel corn four days earlier. Or was it five? Or three? Or six? My normally Bruce Lee-like brain has become a slovenly sumo wrestler.

I lick my lips and bat my eyes at the lightening sky.

"Four days," I say, nodding. "It's been four days."

I pick Lassie up and we continue up the river.

...

The fish are both a foot long. One is silver. One is red. They swim in a tight circle in a shallow pool of water. I stand on a three-foot rock, my stick — now shaved to a sharp point — cocked over my right shoulder. Lassie is on the bank, thirty feet of river away. He is curled next to my shoes, socks, and sweatpants, which I'd peeled off for the short trudge to the rock and the shallow pool. Even from this distance, I can see his yellow eyes pleading with me catch a fish. To give him something to eat.

I watch the two fish dart within the shallow pool. I try to visualize a pattern to their movement. Patterns are my bread and butter; they are how I make my living. So-and-so stock did this for ten years. How will this pattern in this entirely different market affect so-and-so stock two years in the future? It was all about forecasting tomorrow. But if Silver or Red have any method to their madness, I don't have the cognitive dexterity to discern it.

"Okay, fish," I whisper. "One of you is going to be dinner."

I take two more breaths, cock my spear back a foot, and tomahawk it down into the water.

I pull it out.

"HOLY SHIT!" I scream.

Silver flaps wildly at the end of the spear.

"I GOT 'EM!"

The last thing I want is for the fish to wiggle his way off the spear and back into the river. I slowly raise the stick. The spear has gone through the meat of his belly and pokes out three inches on the opposite site.

I turn around and proudly showcase my catch to Lassie. He stands up on his back paws.

The fish isn't as big as he appeared underwater, but he is still close to eight inches and weighs a pound or more. He will be a fine meal.

Meow.

"I'm coming, I'm coming, settle down." I still have to get off the rock and trudge through thirty feet of knee-high river. I gingerly ease myself down to my nylon boxers, half sitting on the rock.

I smile at Lassie. He is so excited he's hobbled to the edge of the river.

Meow.

"What's amoose? Is that the type of fish?"

Meow.

"Amoose, I know, I get it, you know your fish names. Good for you." I slide my feet into the water.

Meow.

"A *moose?*"

Meow.

I turn.

Twenty feet behind me, half submerged in the river, is a giant fucking moose.

He is massive, a thousand pounds of Alaskan bull. His antlers are five-foot clamshells with spikes. He is staring directly at me.

I splash into the water, trudge three feet, then ten.

I am halfway to the bank when I turn and peek over my shoulder.

The entire moose's torso is now above water. He is fifteen feet behind me. And gaining. There is no way I will make it to the sandbar. He is going to impale me on his giant antlers, then flip me around like pizza dough.

I trip.

I feel myself falling and then I am underwater. My left elbow sinks into the soft silt of the river bottom. The water is only a foot deep and I bear crawl forward using my left hand, the stick and fish still held firmly in my right.

It isn't the moose, but the shadow of his giant antlers moving over me and onto the sandbar that hint I only have seconds remaining.

His antlers slide under my right knee, then lift me up, sending me reeling forward. I tumble twice, then land flat on my back. I lift my head. The moose is stopped six feet short of me. He is standing over my stick.

Silver flaps back and forth. He is eaten in one quick bite.

The moose glares at me, then gallops into the trees.

...

"Sorry about the fish."

Meow.

"Yeah, but it would have been nice to eat *something*."

Meow.

"What? How am I looking at you?"

Meow.

"I am not looking at you like you are meatloaf."

Meow.

"If anything, I have to worry about you eating me. I'm the one who sleeps for twenty-three hours. I'm gonna wake up with two less toes."

He is silent.

"Don't even think about it."

Meow.

"Pinky swear we won't eat each other?"

He touches his paw to my pinky.

"I couldn't help but notice that you made no attempt at riding the moose."

Meow.

"Right. *Next* time."

A minute later I am asleep.

I don't know if I will wake up.

:08

June 25th
Sunrise 3:11 a.m.

I pull the shirt off my face and squint. My eyes won't focus. They zoom in and out. I shake my head and stare at my hand. In the soft twilight, I can see every line on my palm one second and a blur of pink the next.

I push myself up. Lassie and I are sleeping on the sand. I'd draped my T-shirt over my face so I wouldn't get sunburned. I pick up the shirt and wipe the sand off the back of my head.

I reach down and feel my left leg. There is a surface cut and a deep bruise. It could have been far worse. The moose had been gentle on me. He just wanted my fish.

I walk to the river and take a long pee.

"Captain's Log," I say. *"Today is June 25th. Day four in the Alaskan outback. Day five without food. We've traveled ten miles. Lassie still can't walk. I was almost killed by a moose. Mosquitos devour me each night. Itching is unbearable. Saw an eagle..."*

I continue to ramble and when I finally look at my watch, it is 3:06 a.m.

I turn around and walk back to where Lassie is still asleep.

I stop.

Squint.

"What in the hell?"

Five feet above where Lassie and I slept is a large pile of black pebbles. I lean down and inspect the perfect pile. They aren't pebbles. They are berries.

I shake Lassie. He opens his eyes.

"Where did you get these?"

Meow.

"These. Where did you get these? And how? I thought you couldn't walk."

Meow.

"Well, I didn't get them."

Did the river sweep them up? Did they fall from a tree and roll down the bank?

No, they are in a perfect pile.

A hundred of them.

I don't really care where they came from, only that they might be food.

Meow.

"You try one."

Meow.

"Sometimes I wish you *were* a guinea pig."

Meow.

"Black is not the color of death."

"Okay," I say. "We'll go at the same time."

I give him one.

Meow.

"Why do I have to eat more than one?"

Meow.

"Fine, I'll eat twenty so we *can die together.*"

I grab a handful, then take a deep breath.

"One . . . two . . . three."

I toss them back.

They are sweet and earthy. Unlike any berry I'd ever tasted. Which doesn't answer whether or not they are poisonous.

Lassie and I stare at each other, waiting for the other to grab at their throat and begin frothing at the mouth.

A minute later, we deem the berries safe. It's amazing what a few calories can do for a glucose-starved brain. My eyes slowly begin to refocus.

Now that my brain is once again firing on a few cylinders, the big question arises: where did the berries come from?

I push myself up.

The sun has stolen the darkness from the sky, and I walk to the top of the sandbar and to the edge of the thick grass.

Here lies the answer.

Literally.

Curled in a ball, lying in the soft grass, is a small boy.

A little Eskimo.

...

He wears a yellow T-shirt and I can see the back half of the polar bear and the first two rings of the Olympics logo. For all I know he is an Indian and not an Eskimo, though I wasn't clear on the distinction, and since we were in Alaska, I preferred to think of him as a little Eskimo boy.

I tiptoe back to where Lassie sits on the sandbar and report, "There is a little boy asleep in the grass. He's wearing a T-shirt from the Indian-Eskimo Olympics, so I'm guessing he was swept into the river in Fairbanks."

Meow.

"They compete in a bunch of weird contests. It was supposed to start the day after the earthquake."

Meow.

"Yeah, I think he did. I mean, who else would have left the berries for us?"

Meow.

"I am not gonna check his pockets for more." I start back up the bank. "Wait here, I'm gonna go see if I can wake him up."

I look at my watch.

Forty-one minutes left in my day.

I ease my way into the tall grass. I half expect the kid to be gone. He is still there, his hands tucked between his knees, curled into a tight ball. I gingerly close the distance between us by half. On closer examination, he has light brown skin framed by near-black hair. He wears the aforementioned yellow T-shirt, white shorts, white socks pulled up to his mid-calf, and red sneakers. I put his age at five, though I have nothing scientific to back this up.

Taking two more steps forward, I say, "Hey, kid."

He doesn't stir.

I take a couple more steps until I hover over him. I watch his chest move up and down three, four, five times, then I lean down on my haunches. I place my hand gingerly on his right shoulder and lightly rock him.

His eyes flutter open.

I wait for him to backpedal in fright, but he doesn't. He simply stares back at me with almond shaped eyes the color of milk chocolate. He looks at me, then down at where my hand still rests on his shoulder.

I pull it back.

He pushes himself up into a sitting position, ending up cross-legged.

He continues to stare.

"Hi," I say.

He says something back. It is not hi, hey, or hello. It is not a sound I've ever heard.

"Can you speak English?"

A series of weird sounds come from his mouth.

Oh, brother.

I mimic picking something off the ground and putting it in my mouth, then say, "Thank you for the berries."

He smiles.

His teeth are small, white, and even.

I stand up.

He stands up.

His head comes up to just above my hip.

I walk forward a couple steps, then turn. He hasn't moved. I say, "Come on, I want to show you something." Although my words mean nothing to him, my "follow me" gesture translates and he runs forward and falls in step behind me.

Ten seconds later, my feet find the sandbar and I step to the side.

"PUSSI!" he screams.

He runs up to Lassie, whose mouth opens in terror. With his injured leg, he is helpless to move. The boy falls to his knees and begins stroking him.

"Pussi [gibberish][gibberish] pussi [gibberish][gibberish][gibberish] pussi."

I laugh. I suppose I know one word in Eskimo now.

Lassie resigns himself to his fate, closing his eyes, and embracing the belly rub.

After a long minute, the boy releases Lassie from his clutches.

Lassie flicks his head at the boy.

I know, I know.

More berries.

The small meal of berries brings me back to the world of the living, but only to the point I am now profoundly aware of how hungry I am. "Where can we get more berries?" I ask, augmenting the words with the mimicry of picking fruit, putting it in my mouth, and rubbing my full and satisfied belly.

The small boy nods and points at the hills.

I look at my watch.

It is 3:31 a.m.

Twenty-nine minutes.

I lean down and pick up Lassie and the three of us head into the brush.

...

The berry bushes aren't far, a five-minute hike into the hills. Lassie insisted on being held by the little boy, and I follow behind the pair. Halfway through the journey, a black swarm of insects finds me and I am assailed by a blitzkrieg of bites. I cinch my hood tight, but the cotton sweatshirt and sweatpants do little to impede their inch long syringes and razor sharp teeth. The swarm doesn't seem to be remotely interested in the little boy, and I wonder if he is hiding a can of OFF somewhere or if his people have a long-standing treaty with the mosquitos.

The swarm evaporates leaving me counting my bites, and I trudge through the tall grass to catch up.

The little boy is standing near a bush. He picks a red berry from a bush and says something. All that matters is the shake of his head. I make a mental note the "small red berry with black dot" is bad. He shows me another couple berries that are head-shakers, then a couple that are head-nodders. I fold up the bottom of my sweatshirt into a basket and we spend the next ten minutes filling it with an assortment of head-nodders.

When we return to the sandbar, it is closing in on 3:45 a.m.

The three of us sit in a small circle and gorge ourselves on the berries in silence.

I watch the little boy hold out a berry to Lassie, then pull it away at the last moment. Lassie paws at his hand and the little Eskimo opens it and Lassie eats the berry from his palm.

I walk to the water and cup my hands in the water. My lips are about to touch the water when I hear a sharp sound.

The little boy runs up to me. He shakes his head.

He doesn't want me to drink the water.

"We've been drinking the water for the past four days," I say, making a four with my fingers.

He pats my stomach with his hand and shakes his head. He walks five feet up the sandbar, falls to his knees and starts digging.

After a couple minutes he has a three-foot hole dug.

I stand over him and look down.

Nothing happens for a long minute.

Then slowly the hole begins to fill with water.

It is coming up from the bottom, through the sand, which acts as a filter.

The little boy cups his hand in the growing pool and drinks.

He waves me forward.

I take a drink.

It tastes better than it had previously. The coarse sand, which was actually just tiny rocks, filters out the silt from the river bottom. I'm dubious this method makes the water safer to drink than from the river directly, but I'm not going to turn my back on three thousand years of Eskimo-ing.

At 3:58 a.m. my watch beeps.

The little boy is feeding Lassie water out of his hand.

I take a deep breath.

How do I tell the little boy, convey to him, that I would be asleep for the next twenty-three hours? How do I tell him that he has a better chance of survival, of making it back to Fairbanks, of finding help, if he continues on without me? How do I tell him that I am a one-hundred-and-fifty-pound rock tied to his ankle?

For some reason, this starts me thinking.

Where was Ingrid? Did she die at the hands of the earthquake? Was she alive, mourning my death? Did the news travel to my dad? What if I survived? What if I found my way back to her? What if she ended up giving birth to a little boy? How would I tell him that daddy was going to go lie down for a while, that I wouldn't see him again for twenty-three hours?

The little boy holds onto Lassie's hurt paw, inspecting it closely. Lassie winces and the little boy pets his head in apology.

I grab a stick and walk back to the two of them.

I sit down next to him Indian-style (or Eskimo-style.) I extend my wrist and point at my watch. I say, "I need to lie down now." I steeple my hands together and lean my head on them like a pillow. "I'm going to be asleep for twenty-three hours."

His thin eyebrows furrow.

I show him my watch. It is both digital and analog. I point to the hour hand. "I am going to be asleep until it goes around twice," I say, slowly tracing my finger around the clock face two times.

I can tell it doesn't register.

I put up two fingers, then three. "Sleep for this many hours." I flash my fingers again.

He shakes his head.

Of course he doesn't understand.

Because it is absurd.

Half the people I tell don't understand. How is a little kid who doesn't speak a lick of English supposed to understand?

I point at him, then point up the river. "You keep going. Don't wait for me."

He shakes his head.

"Go," I say, pushing him toward the brush. "You have to go."

He stares at me, then like the moose, he darts into the brush and disappears.

:09

June 26th
Sunrise 3:13 a.m.

Lassie and I feast on leftover berries for breakfast.

Halfway through our meal, Lassie glares at me. He has something on his mind.

"What?" I prod. "Why are you looking at me like that?"

Meow.

"You miss *what*?"

Meow.

"What is Opik? Is that some brand of catnip or something?"

Meow.

"The little boy? Why did you call him Opik?"

Meow.

"He told you? What, now you speak Eskimo?"

Meow.

"I was not mean to him. He has a much better chance of surviving if he goes at it by himself. We were holding him back."

Meow.

"Right, *I* was holding him back."

Meow.

I reach out a berry for him to eat, then pull it away.

Meow.

"How is it not the same?"

He shakes his head.

I take a deep breath. If I am completely honest, I miss

Opik too. Though I told him to leave, told him *you have to go,* I didn't want, or expect him to actually leave. How selfish am I? I wanted to keep him around, to help us find berries, to help us find our way out of here, knowing full well he stood a far better chance of making it on his own. He could be twenty miles upstream by now. He could already be saved. Hell, he could be back at the Olympics competing in some weird staring contest as we speak.

But it doesn't matter. He is gone.

I pick up Lassie, who squirms in my arms until his back faces me.

"Real mature."

Meow.

"He was not the best friend you ever had," I say. "And that hurts by the way."

We trudge through the brush, back to the berry bushes. I pick berries for five minutes, then we head back to our camp.

It is 3:17 a.m.

I dig a hole in the sand, about two feet from where Opik had dug his the previous evening, and take a long drink. I pick up Lassie and feed him water from my hand. He is pouting. I say, "Drink. We don't know if there will be a sandbar up ahead."

He drinks.

I find a stick and scribble an updated message in the sand: *Stranded. June 26th. Headed east with river. Henry Bins. And Lassie the Cat.*

Meow.

"No, I'm not adding Opik's name."

Meow.

"Because he's gone, he's probably twenty miles from here."

Meow.

I turn.

Opik is standing at the edge of the brush.

He is smiling.

And he is holding two fish.

...

Lassie and I watch as Opik slices open the fish with a small stick. I thought he was *gutting* the fish, but he isn't, he is simply making it easier to eat the fish's *guts*. He pulls out the slimy mass of fish hardware and offers it to me.

"No, you go ahead," I say, with a slight shake of my head. "You caught them,"

I'd only eaten sushi once in my life and it wasn't for me. It was a textural thing. The slime of the fish as it moved down your throat.

No thank you.

Opik offers the guts to Lassie, who can't eat them fast enough.

Sensing my hesitation with the fish's eyeballs, heart, kidneys, and a couple other things I didn't know were part of a fish's anatomy, Opik rips off a large filet of meat and hands it to me. It is translucent white.

I take a bite, ripping at the fish's thick silver skin.

After five days of near-starvation, I can't devour the fish fast enough. I even try one of the second fish's organs — I think one of his kidneys — which is less disgusting than I'd anticipated. I draw the line at the eyeball, saying, "Maybe tomorrow," and Lassie gulps it down.

I pat Opik on the shoulder and say, "Thank you."

He smiles.

"My name is Henry." I point at myself. "Henry."

"On-ray," he says.

"Close enough."

"Opik," he says, pointing to himself.

I nod and repeat his name.

I point to Lassie and say, "Lassie."

"Pussi!" he exclaims.

I laugh. "Close enough."

Lassie doesn't seem to mind. If Opik keeps bringing him food and rubbing his belly, he can call him whatever he wants.

Opik walks up to the brush and waves at me to follow.

I pick up Lassie. "Come on, *Pussi*, let's go."

I trudge behind him. He waits for me to catch up. I show him my watch. Point to the number four. "I need to be back before four."

He nods.

Is it possible he understood? Is it possible he left yesterday, then came back twenty-three hours later, knowing I would just be waking?

No way.

It is merely a coincidence.

Opik continues on. The brush falls away to wild green grass. I find myself gazing in every direction. With a half-full belly, I am able to appreciate the beauty of the landscape around me. For the first time since the earthquake, I once again marvel at the power of the sun. It has moved over the faraway hills and basks the valley in its gold.

I feel a tug on my hand.

Opik.

I follow behind him, his small hand clasped in mine.

Ten minutes later, we approach a thicket of bushes. Opik releases my hand. His eyes move over each bush, examining it, scrutinizing it.

"What are you looking for?" I ask.

Was he looking for more berries? Potatoes? Did potatoes grow on bushes? Nuts? Some animal that lived in the bush? Was he going to shake out some giant Alaskan boar that would run right at me?

My body goes on high alert.

Opik pulls off a yellow flower. Smells it. He reaches his hand out to me.

I shake my head.

He reaches it out toward me a second time.

I take a sniff.

The fragrance is sweet.

He shakes his head and throws it away.

He moves ahead fifty feet and comes to another round of bushes. They have small purple flowers. He sniffs one. Nods. He reaches it out for me to smell. It is sharp and herbal.

He breaks off a stem and pulls off a giant section of long, narrow, green leaves.

It is 3:47 a.m. when we get back to our camp on the sandbar.

Opik stands at the water, pulling the green leaves off the stem until he has a pile of fifteen or twenty on the sand next to him.

Lassie and I sit on the sand behind him, watching in rapt silence.

Meow.

"I have no idea. Maybe we are supposed to eat them? Maybe it's like kale."

The thought of kale conjures the image of Ingrid. I wonder where she is. If she's alive, had she given up hope that I am alive? Was she back at our apartment in Alexandria? Had she already properly grieved? Was she back at work? Back fighting crime? What would she eat tonight?

Opik tosses what is left of the bush, purple flowers and stems, into the river. He bends down and picks up one of the leaves and dunks it in the water. He crushes it up in his hand. He does this several more times. Then he walks back to us. In his hands he holds a sludge of the green leaves. He eases himself down to his knees, then gingerly holds out his hand to Lassie.

His paw.

Lassie extends his paw with a whimper.

Opik wraps the green leaves around his foot one by one until it has disappeared into a thick cocoon of green.

When he is finished, he holds onto Lassie's paw and says a couple words.

He stands up and disappears.

He is still gone when I lie down to fall asleep.

:10

A feast surrounds us when we wake. Fish, berries, and nuts in several different varieties.

Opik is twenty feet from us, sleeping on the sand.

I push Lassie off my chest and stand up.

I cock my head to the side.

Something is different.

I feel different than I had the previous five days.

My eyebrows furrow.

The itching.

I'm not itching.

I look down at my clothes. They are covered in a white powder. So are my hands. I wipe at my face. It too is covered in the white powder.

I smile.

Whatever it is, it has warded off the mosquitos for the past twenty-three hours.

I amble to where Opik is sleeping and gently rock him.

He opens his eyes.

"Hi."

He smiles.

"Thank you for the powder," I say, pointing to my clothes and smiling.

He wraps his hand around his throat.

"Right, makes them choke."

I help him to his feet and we eat from the pile he has foraged. He checks on Lassie's foot, which according to

Lassie, feels better. Opik makes another wrap with the left-over leaves. While he rewraps Lassie's paw, I point up the river and make walking feet with my fingers.

He nods.

At 3:07 a.m. we pack up camp and head out.

We make good time for the next fifty minutes, then find a place to lie down on the sandbar. Lassie and Opik disappear into the brush. I'm not sure, nor do I care, what the twosome do while I sleep, as long as they come back with food and magical-mosquito-choking powder.

And they do.

Three fish, a collection of different berries, and a squishy cactus-like plant that is delicious if you don't mind getting poked a couple times in the face.

We eat quickly in the morning, then cover as much ground on the never-ending sandbar as we can. Lassie recounts his twenty-three hours with Opik. How Opik climbed a tree and came down with these delicious nuts. How he massaged Lassie's foot and chanted, and how Lassie could almost put weight on it without flinching. How Opik used a stick to catch the fish. Not like I had. He would wade into the water and he would lightly tap the river, creating tiny little rivets, the kind a bug might make, which apparently attract the fish, and then he would cane the fish with the stick, paralyze it, and snatch it with his hands.

By my best estimate, we'd covered six miles each of the past three days, plus the eight to ten we made before we met Opik. As it stood, we were getting enough food to get by and I was confident if we continued at the same pace, we would arrive back at Fairbanks within ten days.

My confidence was boosted even higher ten minutes earlier, when Lassie had pointed out something floating between three logs on the opposite side of the river. It was bright yellow. A flag. One of the flags from the bridge.

We were on the right track.

We continue running up the sandbar for another mile, then watch it gradually disappear into the river.

Opik takes my hand. I think he senses my anxiety of walking through the tall grass, where anything could be hiding. Like, say, for instance, a moose. It was one thing to be on the sandbar where you had a clear vantage of everything around you and anything rushing toward you — not to mention the river was there as a last resort — but in the trees and thick brush, I feel like an antelope on the African savannah.

We move through the brush, weaving in and out of the trees, over thick roots, under rogue branches, between bushes, over rocks.

It's 3:43 a.m. when we see it.

The breath is pulled out of me.

It is overgrown to the point it appears to be part of the forest. It is covered in grass, and trees are growing on top of it. But there is no mistaking it.

A log cabin.

...

The cabin is in ruins.

The logs are dry and brittle, an acid wash of black and gray. The weight of the forest growing on top of it has caved in the roof in multiple spots and caused the bottom row of logs to sink into the earth. What should be a ten-foot high cabin is closer to six feet. What appears to be a log window cover, leans up against the cabin, underneath a rectangular hole nearly the same size. A ladder, built from the same aged logs, leans against the roof.

Opik ducks into the large dark opening — if there ever was a door it has long since disappeared or is on display in a museum somewhere — and Lassie and I follow.

There is enough sunlight shining through the windows and the natural *skylights* in the roof, to light the compact structure.

For as unkempt as the outside of the cabin is, the inside is relatively clean. It is riddled with dust and cobwebs, small plants, and some rodent squatters, yet it's evident that whoever had lived there, kept things tidy. There is a small mirror, about the size of a hardcover book, hanging on the wall. I run the side of my hand down the middle, etching out three inches in the dust. I lean down and examine my face. I shaved with an electric razor in the shower every couple days and I usually had some degree of stubble. After eight days, I now have a dingy brown beard. And though I attempted to stay out of the sun as much as possible the twenty-three hours I was asleep, my skin had darkened five shades.

I look worn, rugged, a man who lived. Not a man who slept his life away.

I smile at the man in the mirror, then continue on to a small area with a wood stove. Dishes are still stacked on the wooden counter. Salt and pepper shakers are still centered on the aging table. There are canned foods of different sorts, some dented, some not. Next to the nonperishables, which have long ago perished, is a dusty bottle. I run my finger over the plastic and smile.

I call over Opik and Lassie.

I don't remember where I read it, or heard it, some obscure fact that there was only one food on the planet that could never go bad.

Honey.

I unscrew the top and squish a dollop on my finger. I taste it. It is perfect.

I hand the bottle to Opik, and after squeezing some in his mouth, he lets Lassie lick honey off his hands. There is a large chest under the window and I pull it open with a loud creak. There are snow shoes, a fur hat, a fur jacket, a lantern. All great, but not what makes the hair on my arms stand on end.

I reach my hand in and pull it out.

A map.

...

It is 3:57 a.m.

I run to the table and spread out the map. I'd seen a road map a couple times before and this isn't much different. But it isn't roads. It's rivers.

Opik and Lassie huddle around me.

There is a black dot with a circle around it, which I assume is the location of the cabin.

I stare at the map for a long minute.

"Oh my God."

I pound the table with my fist, sending Lassie springing into Opik's arms.

"We followed the wrong river!" I yell.

I thought we'd been on the Chena River the whole time. We hadn't.

I stare down at the map.

The Chena River is a small tributary that runs southwest down through Fairbanks then empties into the much larger Tanana River. The Tanana flows northwest for ninety miles before emptying into the Yukon River, which flows west all the way from Canada, through Alaska, then empties into the Bering Sea.

When I'd come to on the canoe, I'd been floating on the Yukon River. Lassie and I had hiked ten miles upstream, where we'd encountered Opik. Then the three of us had continued upstream, staying on the northern riverbank and either due to the darkness or at a point when the sandbar was gone, we were forced inland; we missed the "Y" in the river where the Yukon and the Tanana converged. Our fatal mistake was continuing *northeast* along the Yukon instead of *southeast* along the Tanana toward the Chena, Fairbanks, and salvation.

I think back to the yellow flag I saw stuck in the logs. It wasn't from the Olympics. It couldn't have been. It couldn't have flowed *upstream.*

I find the scale in the bottom right corner of the map and measure it with my finger.

"A hundred and twenty miles," I say, lying down on the table. "A hundred and twenty miles."

:11

June 29th
Sunrise 3:20 a.m.
Yukon riverbank

I wake up on the kitchen table. Lassie and Opik are gone. The map is next to me.

I reach for the map and measure the distance a second time, hoping somehow I read the scaling wrong, that one inch equals two miles and not twenty. The scaling is right. By river, we are six inches from Fairbanks. A hundred and twenty miles.

As the crow flies, a direct shot from where we are positioned on the Yukon, southeast to Fairbanks, is four and a half inches, ninety miles. We would have to traverse through thick brush and up and over a series of small rolling mountains, between which the rivers were carved. Not to mention we could easily get lost on the way, adding days or even weeks to our journey.

We would have to follow the rivers.

Which meant:

1) Crossing from the north riverbank to the south riverbank of the Yukon.

2) Backtracking fifteen miles downstream to where the Tanana emptied into the Yukon.

3) Following the Tanana ninety miles upstream southeast to the Chena.

4) Following the Chena the last fifteen miles upstream northeast to Fairbanks.

If we headed out today, it would take a month.

We'd be lucky to get back by the end of July.

I let out a deep exhale.

I've never felt so defeated.

All I want is to hold Ingrid. To spend all sixty minutes of my day with her head tucked to my chest.

I look at my watch.

It is 3:04 a.m.

I climb back on the table and lie down. I close my eyes and pray for 4:00 a.m. to come early.

...

It doesn't.

I feel hands on my shoulder, rocking me.

I open my eyes.

Opik smiles at me. He has a fruit or a nut in his hand, one I'd yet to see. He offers it to me. I shake my head.

I don't want to eat.

He places the food next to me, then he climbs up on the table. He puts both hands on my side and pushes.

"Stop."

He pulls the map out from under me and climbs down.

A minute passes.

"On-ray! On-ray!"

I open my eyes.

He jabs his hand at the map.

I sit up.

"What?"

He waves at me to get off the table.

I slide off and he spreads out the map, then climbs onto one of the creaking log chairs and settles on his knees. He points to the small black dot that signifies the cabin, then he traces his finger down the Yukon eight inches to another small black dot on the river.

I shake my head.

He points at the spot on the river and begins rambling in Eskimo.

"What? Dude, I don't know what you're saying."

He shakes his head, blows out his cheeks. His eyebrows raise. He points to his shirt, to the word *Indian*.

"There are *Indians* there?"

He nods. He must know the word "Indian."

For a quick moment, I feel a glimmer of hope, until I realize eight inches is even farther away than Fairbanks.

"Too far," I say, then show him the route to Fairbanks with my finger. "Better to go this way."

He shakes his head, moves his finger over the route to Fairbanks. He moves his finger slowly. Then he moves his finger over the Yukon River to where I suppose he knows there is an Indian settlement on the river. He moves his finger fast.

I don't understand for another five minutes.

Not until he grabs my hand and leads me from the cabin, down through the heavy brush, and to the river.

Lassie is there.

Sitting in a small boat.

...

Meow.

"You were guarding the boat? From what?"

Meow.

I point at the wooden eyesore of a boat. The boat is ten feet long and five feet wide. "That thing has been sitting out here for thirty years. You think someone is going to steal it in the ten minutes it took Opik to come get me?"

Meow.

"A bear? You did not see a bear!"

Meow.

"You did not scare him off twice already."

I feel a tap on my wrist.

It's Opik, tapping on my watch.

It is 3:18 a.m.

He knows I only have a little bit of time left. He wants to get a move on.

I nod.

Having Opik with us changes everything. If Opik knows half about navigating the river as he knows about fishing or foraging, then we are in good hands. With him at the helm, we could float the Yukon River and make it to the Indian village within two days. I can see the headlines of the *Fairbanks Forager* or *Yukon River Daily* now: THIRTY-SEV-EN-YEAR-OLD MAN AND HIS CAT SAVED BY FIVE-YEAR-OLD ESKIMO BOY.

Opik and I run back to the cabin and grab everything we can — map, honey, the fur hat and jacket — then run back to the boat.

The horizon is pink as we lay the items in the front, and I give the boat a quick inspection. That it is made of wood worries me, although I suppose boats were made of wood for centuries and they managed fine. It appears to be in working order and, as an added bonus, there is a wooden paddle lying in the bottom.

Opik and I position ourselves at the back of the boat. It is flat, nearly concave, and we both place our hands against the soft wood and dig our feet into the brush.

"Ready . . . Go—"

There is a loud roar and Opik and I snap our heads around. It's just like the one in the pictures I'd seen. Back on its hind legs. Mouth open wide. Razor claws thrashing at the air.

Meow.

Yes, you did tell me.

"What should we do?" I plead to Opik.

Opik picks up a rock and throws it at the brown grizzly bear. This seems to upset the bear even more and he slashes at a small tree with his giant claws, cracking the trunk and sending the tree to the ground.

I judge the distance to the water. It will take us at least a five-count to push the boat to the edge of the river. Unlike the sandbar, where it gradually eases into the moving water, the river flows swiftly directly off the edge of the bank. When the boat hits the water, all three of us will need to be inside.

The bear is fifteen feet away. If it is the boat he's after, and he sees us pushing it away from him, he might charge.

I think back to a joke my father likes to tell.

Two friends are in the woods when a bear starts chasing them. The first friend begins to run as the second exclaims, "You can't outrun a bear!" The first friend replies, "I don't have to. I only have to outrun you."

"Get in!" I yell to Opik.

He does.

The bear slashes at another tree.

I run to the front of the boat. My plan was to scare him

off with the paddle, but while reaching for it, a better plan materializes. I dig my hand around, find what I'm looking for, then run to the back of the canoe.

Lassie whines.

At first I think he is concerned about me. It takes me a long second to realize his only concern is the bottle of honey in my hand.

I squeeze out as much honey as I can, then coat the outside of the bottle. I rear back and throw the bottle over the bear's head.

I don't look to see if he takes the bait.

I turn, dig my feet into the dirt, and push with all my might.

The boat doesn't move.

I turn around.

The bear hovers over the bottle of honey, now twenty feet away.

I take a deep breath and push.

The boat slides a couple inches forward. Opik wants to jump out and help.

I wave him off. "Stay in the boat!"

I turn around. The bear rears up on its back legs. Then he charges.

I scream.

I push the boat forward. It rocks. I push again. There is a grinding as the boat discharges from whatever is holding it back and it begins gliding over the soft brush. I can hear trees being trampled behind me as I shove the boat the last five feet, then dive in the canoe headfirst.

...

Lassie licks my hand, his way of telling me that I'm okay.

"Thanks, buddy."

He glances up at me and I realize for the second time my well-being is the least of his concerns. He is licking the honey that caked to my hands when I coated the outside of the bottle.

Sheesh.

Opik stands near the back of the boat. "On-ray," he

says, waving me toward him. I push myself up and join him. He points at a section of wood that is chipped.

"Aklark," he says.

It takes me a moment to understand. The chips in the wood. The four scrapes directly below.

Opik puts his hands up and curls all his fingers in. He opens his mouth wide and growls.

Aklark.

Bear.

The bear must have swiped at me right as I dove. He must have just missed me.

My heart races.

I'd come inches from being mauled by an Alaskan brown bear. My first thought is: I can't wait to tell Ingrid.

...

At 3:53 a.m., I divvy out all the food in the fur hat and we eat.

At 3:55 a.m., I tuck the fur coat under my head and lie down.

At 3:56 a.m., Lassie crawls onto my chest.

At 3:57 a.m., the boat begins to sink.

...

"Where is all this water coming from?"

It started as a trickle. Now it rushes in at a feverish pace. Opik and I search the boat floor for the breach.

Meow.

"We are not abandoning ship!" I yell. "We need to find the hole and plug it."

After thirty seconds, I find a small gurgling hole between two of the wooden boards. "Here it is!" I yell, stamping my foot down on the hole to impede the flow. There is a loud cracking, as my foot breaks through the bottom of the boat, leaving a giant gash.

The water pours in.

I pull my leg out, rip the paddle from Opik's hands and turn the boat toward the riverbank. We are only fifty feet into the river.

I have less than a minute before I conk out.

I dig the paddle into the water.

"Grab Lassie!" I scream at Opik.

He looks at me confused.

"Pussi!"

He picks up Lassie.

We are halfway to shore. The river helps us out and after three more paddles, the nose of the boat sinks into the soft brush of the riverbank.

"Go!"

The boat is half underwater. It will sink any second.

Opik jumps into the brush with Lassie. I hand him the paddle, then the fur hat and coat. I double-check to make sure the map is tucked deep into my pocket, then I leap into the brush, pulling myself up with the long grass.

I look behind me just in time to see the last inches of the boat slide under the water.

:12

June 30th
Sunrise 3:23 a.m.

I wake up to the sound of whimpering.

I roll over and open my eyes.

Twenty feet away, huddled next to a tree, are Opik and Lassie.

I'd heard the whimpering a couple times before. It was the sound Lassie made when he was having a nightmare. Sometimes I would wake up and he would be on my chest, a soft, guttural cry, echoing from his throat. The sound was usually accompanied by a twitch of his front paws.

I amble over to the duo and peer down.

Lassie is fast asleep.

Opik's head is buried between his knees, his body wracked in sobs.

How stupid am I? It didn't even cross my mind that the sound could be coming from Opik. He had been so stoic in the face of such adversity, as though this was all fun for him — a big adventure in the wild — it never occurred to me he might be scared. It never dawned on me he had a mom, dad, brothers, and sisters he missed dearly.

I lower myself down next to him and put my hand softly on his back.

"Hey, buddy," I say.

He sniffs.

"Can you look at me?" I ask, trying to lift his head.

He keeps his head locked between his legs.

"It's gonna be okay. We're going to find our way back."

I know he doesn't understand the words and even if he did, I doubt they would mean much coming from the white man who is only awake for sixty minutes a day and has been welching off his Eskimo hacks for going on a week, but I need to say them. Because for some reason, I believe them.

I lift his head with my hand.

He fights me, the muscles in his neck flexed.

He doesn't want me to see his tears. I know nothing about the Eskimo culture, though I can only imagine the importance manhood and toughness play in a society that survives each winter in Alaska. Not to mention the Ear Pull.

I sit rubbing his back for a long minute. He sniffs. A minute later, he raises his head. His eyes are puffy, their beautiful almond shape minimized to small slivers of brown.

"It's okay to cry," I tell him. "I cry all the time."

He stares at me.

I move my hand over a stick, act like it gives me a splinter, then ball my hands into my eyes.

He smiles and laughs.

Lassie wakes up and jumps on Opik's lap. He licks the tears from Opik's cheeks.

Opik shakes off the tears a couple minutes later, yet you can still see the anguish in his eyes. Lassie has it too. It is as though all our hopes sunk with the boat. I know mine did.

Until I remember something. I remember we have a canoe.

...

Ingrid and I played *Pictionary* once. We took turns drawing and guessing. If we got the answer right in the allotted time, we both took an article of clothing off. If we got it wrong, we had to draw another clue. And since we only had sixty minutes, to both unclothe and to entangle, we were under the gun. It was fun. At first. It turns out I am a terrible drawer. Had I gone to a normal school, I'm sure I would have learned to draw like all the other kids, but with only an hour a day, it hadn't been part of my father's curriculum. The only thing I'd ever drawn were the lines of the stocks I'd graphed on my bedroom wall.

So, when I got a clue, for instance, that was *Sneeze*, my hand didn't have the slightest idea, or the muscle memory, to move across the paper to make the shape of a nose or of a hand coming up. After thirty minutes of squiggles and arrows and Ingrid screaming at me to draw better, she ripped all her clothes off in protest and dragged me to the bedroom.

Now drawing *Canoe* is far easier than drawing *Sneeze*, or at least it should have been.

Opik stares at my drawing in the sand and shakes his head.

"It's a canoe," I tell him for the fifth time. "Ca-new."

Meow.

"It's not a banana."

I wipe my hand over the dirt and try again.

I could see the outline of the canoe in my head, yet each time I etched it in the sand, something went wrong.

Meow.

"Murdock?"

Meow.

I laugh. "Right, no balls."

Opik takes the stick from me. I watch as he expertly draws a canoe holding two people, each holding a paddle.

"Ca-new," he says.

I nod.

...

The sky is still more dark than light when we begin our journey back the twenty-five miles to the canoe. After twenty minutes, the sandbar returns. We run fast for the remaining time, then settle in and make camp. The magic anti-mosquito powder has lost its mojo and a swarm of black descends upon me.

After sucking me dry, the cloud evaporates and I plead with Opik to find me some more choking powder.

He shakes his head.

It must have been something he'd lucked upon just that once. I doubt I will ever would find out what it was.

As my last minute ticks away, I get to witness Opik's *fishing* in action. He wades into the river with a stick and begins tapping the water lightly, then smacking the stick down with all the force he can muster out of his forty-pound frame. He doesn't catch a fish in the time I watch, but I know he will have a couple waiting for me when I awake.

Which he does.

Opik's head is resting in the crook of my arm and he has his hand wrapped around Lassie's tail. I want to get up, to get a move on, but I find myself lying there listening to him breathe. I let them both sleep for another five minutes, then wake them.

By my estimate, it will be another ten miles to the Yukon River/Tanana River confluence, then another eight to ten miles to reach the canoe.

We eat as we run.

The next day is the same, the only difference the three less minutes of sunlight.

On the third day, the rains come.

According to Lassie, the storm rolled in twelve hours after I'd gone to sleep. An hour later, the heavens opened and a torrential downpour ensued.

Luckily, I'd fallen asleep high up on the sandbar, or I would have been at risk of being swept away by the rising water. It rode three feet higher on the banks than when I'd last seen it, and the river flowed at double the speed of the day before.

It is impossible to stay dry.

There is no haven, no tree, no bush, nowhere to hide from the torrential downpour. It makes fishing impossible. It makes foraging nearly as difficult and we go a full day without food.

July 3rd
Sunrise 3:32 a.m.

The rains wreaked havoc on the trees and bushes, and most of the fruit Opik finds is either in pieces or smashed beyond recognition. And with the rivers running so high and murky from the downpour, Opik is unable to catch a single fish.

The lack of protein is taking its toll. I can count every one of my ribs. When I run my fingers over them, across the rivulets, it makes a sound. I can wrap my fingers around my forearm and nearly touch them. My sweatpants are tied as snugly as possible, yet they repeatedly fall down as I run. After eleven days in the Alaskan wilderness, I've lost more than fifteen pounds.

We'd passed where the Tanana empties into the Yukon as we'd trudged through the rain the previous day. It was easy to see how we missed it as the brush was considerably thick for a long stretch, shielding the "Y" in the river.

As for the Yukon, it was still running high from the rain, but it had receded by half, and we were able to return to the sanctity and speed the sandbar offered.

Lassie is tucked in my arm and Opik sprints just behind me. I keep my eyes locked ahead as we run, waiting for the three rocks and the canoe to climb over the horizon.

At 3:40 a.m., the first rays of sun peek over the mountains.

A mile later, I stop.

"There they are!" I yell, pointing with the paddle at the three black rocks around the bend.

But I soon realize it is only the rocks.

The canoe is gone.

...

"The river swept it away," I utter. "The river *swept it away.*"

The river laps fifteen feet below the rocks. At the peak of the torrential downpour it could have easily risen to where the canoe was leaned up against the rock. I suppose I should have foreseen it as a possibility, but I hadn't. I was blind-sided by unbridled optimism.

Opik is perched on the rock where I rested the canoe nearly two weeks earlier. I wonder what he is thinking. Is he thinking what I'm thinking, that we are back where we started? That we are a hundred miles from Fairbanks? That if we'd gone in the right direction from the start we would be nearly halfway home. Or is he thinking about the Indian settlement that is a hundred and forty miles downriver?

I take out the map and unfold it.

Downstream or upstream?

A minute later, I grab a stick and I etch a message in the sand.

Stranded. July 3rd. Headed downstream. Henry Bins, Lassie the Cat, and Opik the Eskimo.

When I finish, I say, "Let's go."

:13

July 4th
Sunrise 3:35 a.m.

I wake up to loud meowing and Opik's face nearly an inch from mine. The day before, we'd jogged another ten minutes down the sandbar — downstream toward the Indian settlement — before finding a spot to sleep high up on the sand.

"What?" I yell, jumping to my feet. "A moose? A bear?"

Meow.

"You found it?"

Meow.

"You found the canoe?" I holler, then find myself picking up Opik and swinging him in a circle. It was the reason I decided to go downstream. To take our chances on the Yukon. I felt there was a chance the canoe might have gotten swept into one of the many log jams along the river.

Finally, something went our way.

We pick up camp and run two miles downstream. It is still dark, sunrise still thirty minutes away, but it is light enough to see the canoe on the opposite side of the river.

Without a moment's hesitation, I strip down to my underwear, grab the paddle, and wade into the water. It is colder than I remember, and my breath is sucked from my chest. I grit my teeth and using the paddle as a glorified kickboard, I start kicking for the opposite bank.

I pull myself out of the water a half mile downstream from the canoe, then run back up the riverbank to where it is tangled in a web of logs and brush. It takes me five minutes to pull it free, then another five to paddle the canoe across the river and dock it on a sandbar where Lassie and Opik wait for me.

It is 3:28 a.m.

My body shakes from the cold, and Opik wraps the fur coat around me and pulls the fur hat down over my head and ears.

He disappears for ten minutes. When he returns, he has a handful of nuts. It is all he can find he gestures with a soft shake of his head.

It is remarkable how the two of us communicate now. I'd only been around him ten days, yet I could understand him when he gesticulated, *you stay here and try and warm up while I go run and see if I can find some food for us, then we will jump in the canoe and head downriver when the sky begins to lighten.*

At 3:42 a.m. with the sky a fire orange, the three of us set off downriver in the canoe.

July 5th
Sunrise 3:39 a.m.

When I wake up the next morning, we are still on the Yukon. Opik is on the back bench of the canoe, the paddle draped over the side of the boat. I stand up and walk over to him. I gesture for him to hand me the paddle.

"Time for you to take a break," I say.

He nods.

I gaze downriver. It is wide, the widest I'd yet to see it, a third of a mile across. The canoe floats down the middle.

I sweep my gaze on both sides of the water, looking for signs of life. A light, a fire, a man on the edge of the river fishing.

We are all alone.

I'm curious if Opik and Lassie docked the boat at any point. My question is answered moments later when Opik hands me the fur hat overflowing with fruit and nuts. I eat a handful of what I've come to think of as *Alaskan granola* and tell him, "Go to sleep."

He nods.

Lassie climbs back to where I'm sitting and lies down on my lap.

"I take it you guys didn't see anything worth stopping for yesterday."

He shakes his head.

"You okay?"

Meow.

"The poops?"

Meow.

"Oh, diarrhea."

I let out a deep exhale. I'm surprised it took this long for dysentery to strike. After drinking the river water for the first couple days, I expected the worst, but neither Lassie nor I had been affected. Then we'd adopted Opik's dig-a-hole-in-the-sand system which, by virtue of my not waking up with my bowels next to me, appeared valid. So it might not be the water that was wreaking havoc on Lassie's insides. It could have been the diet of nuts and berries, or some rotten fish, or something he got into when I was asleep, or he might just be sick.

As if on cue, Lassie lurches forward and throws up.

When he finishes, he gazes up at me.

If we were home in Alexandria, we would be on the back of my scooter, headed to the emergency vet.

I can't help him. All I can do is make him comfortable and hope we find the Indian settlement in the next day. I pick him up and tuck him into the fur coat.

He whimpers.

"We're gonna find help tomorrow."

Meow.

"You never had a chance? To do what?"

Meow.

I shake my head. *The arctic fox.* Only Lassie on his deathbed would be concerned with getting some action.

I check on Opik. He is curled into a ball at the front of the canoe.

I lean down and whisper in his ear, "If I have a son, I hope he's just like you."

Then, as if hit in the stomach by a shotgun blast, I remember the odds Ingrid and the baby survived the earthquake are grave, if not graver, than of the three of us being rescued.

...

I spend the next half an hour squinting at the river-banks.

At 3:45 a.m., I start paddling toward the southern river-bank in hopes of a sandbar I can dock the canoe on, but the banks are all heavy brush.

At 3:55 a.m., I wake up Opik.

"You're up, buddy."

He smiles and takes the paddle from me.

I point toward the shore and he nods.

He will dock at the next sandbar and get some much needed rest. I move my hand back and forth.

"Fishy," he says with a smile.

I lean down and wrap my hands around him in a tight hug.

:14

July 6th
Sunrise 3:43 a.m.

I wake up wet.
Soaked and freezing.
I push myself up, then cover my face.
We hit a giant rapid, a wall of freezing water splashing over my body.
The boat jerks, nearly rolls.
I push myself up.
Opik is curled up in a ball, his eyes open wide in terror. Lassie is huddled next to him looking equally horrified.
"What is—"
I turn around just in time to see the next rapid. I sit down and cover my head. The water crashes over the three of us.
I grip the seat with white knuckles as the canoe makes its way down a narrow channel. The small boat is at the mercy of the rocks and white water. Even an expert guide would have few options other than to let the boat bang around and hope for the best.
But a guide *would* try and position themselves to take the path of least resistance. I glance back at Opik.
"Where's the paddle?" I yell.
He shakes his head.
Gone.
I take a deep breath and turn around. Another set of rapids. Another burst of freezing water.
Five seconds later and the river returns to calm.
The river appears flat for the coming quarter mile, but

it is dark and I don't want to risk running the gauntlet on another set of rapids.

"Lassie, are you okay?" I ask, turning to survey my two fellow passengers.

He is soaked. Shivering. He looks like he weighs no more than two pounds.

"Are you still sick?"

He doesn't answer.

Not a good sign.

Opik is crying. I have no idea how he lost the paddle, but I know he feels terrible.

"It's okay, we got through it. We're okay."

I dig my arm over the side and begin trying to paddle toward shore. It is still narrow and if we can get the canoe fifteen feet in either direction, we can try to grab a branch or the tall grass and get the boat out of the water, which would give the three of us a chance to recover and make a game plan, and possibly find a stick or something else that could double as a paddle.

"Oh, shit."

Up ahead, even in the darkness, the white froth of the churning rapids is visible.

There is no way we can make it to shore in time.

"Get up front," I yell, waving at Opik.

He plops down on the front bench.

I figure my weight will be better served in the back and I crawl to the bench near Lassie. I grab him by the collar and yell, "Hold on!"

The canoe zips down between two rocks, bangs around, and then we are hit by a giant wave. Before we can recover from the first blast, we get hit by a second.

The canoe rolls hard to the right. We smash into a rock.

Opik rolls forward and disappears over the side.

"Opik!"

The canoe lurches forward. I look back over my shoulder. Opik's head pops up in the whitewater, and then I watch as he is pin-balled down through the rocks.

OMG!

The canoe moves through the last of the rapids.

I squint at the whitewater, searching for Opik's body.

"Come on, come on."

I see him.

He is forty feet to our left, his hands splashing frantically against the water.

For all his wisdom and tricks, he doesn't know how to swim.

I gaze down at Lassie then back to Opik.

Meow.

"NO."

Meow.

"How—"

MEOW.

I jump over the side.

Two seconds later, Opik's small body rushes toward me and I tackle him in the water.

The last time I ever see Lassie, he is up on the back of the canoe, staring back at us.

...

When I was fourteen years old, I was wrestling with my dad. We were in the living room of the same house where he lives today. I'd finished eating breakfast and we were sitting down to do twenty minutes of algebra. I think he could tell how badly I didn't want to spend twenty of my precious minutes doing word problems, and he told me that if I could pin him to the ground, then I would get out of "school" for the day.

We'd wrestled plenty of times, but each time the small frumpy man in the sweater would eventually pin one of my shoulders to the ground and count, "One, one thousand . . . two, one thousand . . . three, one thousand," then celebrate with a victory dance.

I knew when we wrestled, he took it easy on me, but what he didn't know was that for the past six months I'd been taking it easy on him. I'd started doing three minutes of push-ups and sit-ups during my ten minutes of "me" time in my room. Though it didn't show much physically — I was still a scrawny little thing — I was much stronger than my father thought.

And today was the day I unleashed the fury.

Algebra be damned.

"What have you been eating?" my dad asked after two minutes.

I laughed and wiggled out of his hold.

Fast-forward a couple more lame attempts from my father to pin me and I could feel him getting tired.

I rolled on top of him. Twisted my body so my legs hovered near his head. Grabbed his elbow with my left hand. I snaked one leg around his head and locked my ankle under my opposite leg.

"Did you just put me in a Figure Four?" my dad wheezed, his head locked between the "4" shape of my thighs.

"Yes sir," I replied, tightening my legs and pressing all my weight down on his shoulder.

"One, one thousand . . . two, one thousand . . . three—"

With a burst of strength, my dad flipped me over.

Now on top of me, he smiled and said, "Did you really think I was gonna let you beat me?"

"My foot," I gasped.

He rolled off me.

When my dad flipped me over, all his weight had landed on my right foot locked behind my left knee. And it snapped.

We made it to the emergency room ten minutes later. The doctor set my foot, which quelled the pain from a ten down to about a six, then began wrapping it in a cast.

4:00 a.m. came halfway through the cast, and I woke up the next day in bed.

I remember looking down at my lime green cast and smiling. I'd been worried the previous day that I wouldn't have anyone to sign it, but my dad had wheeled me around the hospital having people sign my cast, and it was covered in well wishes.

Opik wouldn't have a cast for anyone to sign.

He must have smashed his foot against a rock and his left ankle is rotated outward twenty degrees farther than God intended. As bad as his ankle looks, it isn't the most pressing of his injuries. There is a gash in Opik's side that is gushing blood.

I rip off part of my T-shirt and push it against the rock's nasty signature.

Opik screams.

It is 3:11 a.m.

Forty-nine minutes.

I hold pressure on his side for five long minutes, then I pull away the T-shirt. It is colored red with Opik's blood. It is still relatively dark, yet I don't need the light of day to know the gash on his side is bad. The skin is splayed apart and if I stick my finger in the wound, I won't have to dig far, and possibly not at all, to touch bone.

Opik wails. From the pain in his side or from his broken foot, I'm not sure.

I shake my head.

I don't know what to do.

He needs to go to the emergency room. He needs fifteen stitches. He needs to have his leg set. Most importantly, he needs pain meds.

I take two deep breaths, then create a triage list in my head.

I put Opik's hand over the T-shirt and push down his hand. "You have to keep pressure on this!"

I crawl down the sand until I hover over his leg.

"This is going to hurt," I say.

I grab his shoe with both hands and twist it to a neutral position.

Opik's scream makes his previous one seem meek by comparison.

I pack sand under his ankle so it's elevated, then pack sand around it to keep it from moving.

"I know it hurts, buddy," I say, grabbing his hand and squeezing it. "I have to go grab some stuff. I'll be back as quick as I can."

His teeth gritted together, he gives me a soft nod.

It is 3:22 a.m.

Daylight is still twenty minutes away, but I can see well enough in the pre-twilight to navigate my way through the brush. It takes me ten minutes to find the bush that resembles the kind Opik used to make Lassie's bandage.

I rip out two entire fronds, then I set about finding two decent sized sticks.

I make it back to Opik and the sandbar at 3:43 a.m.

He is still crying.

Still screaming.

I take the two sticks I found — a foot long and an inch

thick — and set them on either side of Opik's ankle. I untie his shoe and slide out his ghastly swollen ankle. He thrashes and I tell him, "I'm sorry."

I slip out one of the strings from his shoe, then make a splint around his ankle with the two sticks. The finished product isn't pretty, but it will keep his ankle from moving from side to side.

Next, I dip the leaves in the river and crush them in my hand until I have a thick green paste.

I pull the T-shirt from Opik's side, then wash away the blood with a second strip of T-shirt.

The sun is up and I can't help but cringe at the two-inch, jagged cut halfway down his ribs. I gently cover the wound in green sludge. Opik's body flexes in pain. His screams elevate two octaves at each touch.

At 3:55 a.m., I curl up next to him, pulling his head into the crook of my shoulder and begin stroking his head.

"It's gonna be okay, buddy. I've got you."

A couple minutes later, he stops crying.

:15

July 7th
Sunrise 3:47 a.m.

The sun and the mosquitos have both attacked my flesh and I pant wildly as I push myself up on the sand. I crawl to where Opik lies. His foot looks like a snake trying to digest a grapefruit. If it looks anything like my ankle did the day after I broke it, it is a purplish black, not too different than the summer sky overhead.

There are crawl marks on the sand leading to the brush, and I deduce that at some point over the course of the past twenty-three hours, Opik needed to go to the bathroom. Instead of crawling a couple feet away and relieving himself on the sandbar, he crawled fifty feet to the edge of the brush. I can only imagine the amount of agony this pilgrimage caused him.

I spend the entire hour foraging for berries and find less than a handful. I keep three berries for myself and feed the remaining berries to Opik. He swallows with eyes closed. I dig a hole in the sand and drip water into his mouth. I carry him to the edge of the brush to go to the bathroom. He is only forty pounds, but I am so weak, he feels like forty kilos. I change the wrap on the wound on his side.

I find a large stick and wade into the river. I attempt Opik's fishing method for twenty minutes, but am unsuccessful.

July 8th
Sunrise 3:51 a.m.

It seems so long ago that I was out on the back deck of the cabin with Ingrid, seeing the sun for the first time. My appreciation then was strictly superficial. Yes, the sun was beautiful. Yes, it turned the black and white photograph that was my life into a living, breathing landscape. Now, after nearly three weeks in the wild, I see it as so much more. Its heat kept me from freezing to death after falling in the river. Its sunlight fed the plants and trees whose offerings kept me alive.

I want to enjoy my last minutes of sunlight — tomorrow the sun won't make it above the rolling hills before I fall asleep — but I can't. It is that superficial light which illuminates the angry, virulent infection that has taken hold of the gash in Opik's side.

I prod the raised red flesh with my fingers.

I fall asleep to the sound of Opik screaming.

July 9th
Sunrise 3:55 a.m.

I smash the rocks together. There is a small spark, but the grass doesn't catch. I smash them together again. And again. And again. My arms burn. My hands bleed.

I smash the rocks together. And again.

"Come on. Come on."

A piece of grass catches. I push a small clump of grass on top. This too, catches. A bigger clump. An even bigger one. I set the first twig on the smoldering pile. I blow on the grass. The stick catches.

Two minutes later, I have a small fire. I add as many sticks and as much brush as I can. I need the fire to burn into the daylight. I find two large tree stumps and roll them into the fire.

When I lie down next to Opik to fall asleep, the fire rages.

July 10th
Sunrise 4:00 a.m.

Opik's forehead is giving off as much heat as the fire that failed to bring us salvation. Neither of us has eaten in days. His normally robust, rounded cheeks have been swallowed by hunger, leaving shallow craters in their place. His breathing is shallow.

I drip water into his mouth with my hand.

"We're going to make it," I lie. "We're going to be just fine, you and me."

I fight to take a breath after I speak. I'm dizzy. The tunnel vision has returned.

I hobble to the riverbank. My body is giving up. It has been burned, bitten, and starved.

Tears are streaming down my cheeks.

"Help!" I scream. "Help! Anybody? Is there anybody out there? Please help us! We need food! And antibiotics! Anybody? Please!"

I look down at my watch.

The numbers swim in front of me.

It's 3:38 a.m.

I've been yelling for thirty minutes.

I take a deep breath, stagger for a quarter mile farther down the riverbank, and cup my hands around my dry, scaling lips.

"Help!"

July 11th
Sunrise 4:05 a.m.

"Opik. Opik." I crane my neck to the side. I want to get up. To check on him, though I'm certain he's dead. If I don't check on him, then I won't know for sure. And I can't know.

Know that I failed him.

I lick my sunburned lips and mutter, "So there is this red folder at my house."

I take a long breath.

"It's my mother's file. She did horrible things. To other

people and maybe to me. The reason I'm only awake for an hour a night, the reason I only get sixty minutes a day, is because she conditioned my brain. Brain conditioning. Sleep amplification. Who does that to their son? But that isn't what scares me. Opik? Opik, are you listening to this? I don't want to know the truth about her. If I never open the folder, then there's a chance my mom isn't this monster who they say she is. She is just this lady who walked out on me. Like the moose and the bear. The moose just wanted Silver. He just wanted to eat the fish. That's what my mom was to me growing up. She just left. Now the bear. The fucking bear wanted to eat *me*. I don't want my mom to be a bear. Opik? You hear me? I don't want my mom to be a bear!

"If I, if we, make it back. I'm gonna do three things. I'm gonna kiss Ingrid. I'm gonna kiss her for like an hour. Then I'm gonna rub her belly. I'm gonna tell her that I'm in. Boy, girl, one hour a day, a hundred hours a day, doesn't matter, I'm in. Then I'm gonna go buy a cat. A pussi! I didn't think I would like a cat, but I loved Lassie. He was the best. Kind of pervy sometimes, like this one time he licked Ingrid's nipple. But can you blame him? Man, he was great. Don't you think? Opik? Wasn't Lassie the best? Yeah, so kiss Ingrid, rub her belly, go buy a cat, then I'm gonna open that folder.

"I got to know, you know. I got to know if my mom is this monster. That's not all. My dad. If my mom is this monster, then where is he? He isn't picking berries for me in Alaska, that's where. And guess what he has in his basement. Well, you would never guess. You couldn't, Opik. You could never guess what is in my dad's basement. It's a hobby cemetery. It's where hobbies go to die. Kites. Drones. Magic. Those stupid boats with the glass in them. Boats with glass in them. Glass with boats in them, I mean.

"What was I telling you — oh, these boxes. My dad has these boxes. In his basement, hidden away. I think they're my mom's. But guess what? Me and Lassie and Ingrid are over there for Christmas and I sneak downstairs. Oh, and Murdock. Murdock is there. He still had his balls then. What? I can't hear you? Talk louder. Guess what? The boxes were gone.

"Opik? That's crazy, right? The boxes were gone. I almost opened the red folder the next day. I had it in my hand, but I couldn't do it. What if my dad is a monster too?"

I wait for him to respond.

But he's dead.

Ingrid.

Lassie.

Opik.

All dead.

"Right there. OVER THERE."

"You see them? On the bank, looks like two of them."

I open my eyes.

Push myself up.

A beam of light shines in my face.

"Henry?" the light asks.

Salvation.

:16

June 20th

"Henry?"

I snap open my eyes. The room is all white. An IV sticks out of my right arm.

"Where am I?" I ask. "Is this the hospital in Fairbanks? Where is Opik? Is he alive?"

A doctor hovers over me. He is wearing blue hospital scrubs. He has a white mask over his face.

"Did you have a good sleep?" he says.

I take a deep breath. My brain is groggy, but that is to be expected. "Yeah, I did. Thanks for rescuing me."

He cocks his head to the side and looks at someone. There is just enough room under his blue cap to see his eye-brows furrow together.

"Is Opik here? Is Ingrid?"

He ignores me.

A door opens and I hear footsteps.

A man in a black suit hovers over me.

"Hello, Mr. Bins."

"Are you the kayaker who found us?"

He has nearly the same reaction as the doctor in the scrubs. Head to the side. Eyebrows furrow.

"Do you know what day it is Mr. Bins?"

I think back. "July 12th."

Look away. Head to the side. Eyebrow furrow.

"Where is Ingrid? Is she okay? Did she survive?"

He turns and leaves.

A long couple minutes pass. I notice my hospital room has zero TVs and zero chairs.

A voice over an intercom says, "Ingrid is safe."

"She survived the earthquake?"

There is a long pause.

"There was no earthquake," the intercom shouts.

"Uh, yes there was. I can assure you there was a giant fucking earthquake. I watched the buildings fall myself."

A door opens. More footsteps.

This time it is a woman.

She is wearing a long jacket. Her salt and pepper hair is held back in a ponytail. There is a white surgical mask over her face.

"You never made it to Fairbanks," she says.

"Yes, I did."

"The pilots took you here, to our facility. You don't remember?"

"You're crazy. I went to Fairbanks. There was an earthquake, I fell in the river and was washed a hundred miles downstream, and I spent the last twenty-one days trying to survive in the Alaskan wilderness."

"You don't look like you've been in the wilderness for three weeks."

I look down at my arm. I wrap my fingers around my wrist. They don't even come close to touching. I pull my hospital gown open at the neck and peer down. I expect to see gaunt ribs. I don't. I feel my face with my right hand. My thick matted beard has been replaced by a single day of stubble.

"What the fuck is going on?"

"How long were you in Alaska?"

With all the thoughts racing through my head, it's hard to think. I was in the wild for twenty-one days, plus the two days before the earthquake. "Twenty-three days."

"How many hours awake is that? For you?"

"*Twenty-three.*" I gulp as I say the words.

The woman nods. "Twenty-three hours ago you boarded a plane for Fairbanks. The plane took you here instead."

Chills run down my arm.

"Wait. Why? And where is Ingrid? And where is here?"

"Ingrid is fine. So is the cat. They were given a mild sedative before takeoff and left in the car."

Mild sedative? Left in the car?

"Okay, but why I am here?" I ask. "What is this place?"

The woman stares down at me with blistering green eyes.

"This is the future of enhanced interrogation."

It hits me.

The last twenty-three hours I'd been asleep.

I was being *tortured.*

Tortured by my own brain.

I think back.

A white room.

A doctor in blue scrubs.

An IV in my arm.

Where is it?

I don't know.

Where is it?

Where is what?

The flash drive.

What flash drive?

A syringe of pink liquid.

I squirm.

He injects the syringe in my IV.

I scream.

That was real. Everything else, the cabin, the sunrise, the pregnancy, the earthquake, the river, the canoe, the moose, Opik, the cabin, the bear, the anger, the hunger, the pain, the death, it was all...

"What did you inject me with?"

"Just a cocktail we've spent the better part of forty years perfecting."

"A nightmare serum?"

"Something like that."

She watches me for a long moment. She knows exactly what I'm thinking. "We don't create the nightmare," she says. "We simply manipulate your sleep architecture, and you do the rest."

The earthquake statistics. The Eskimo-Indian Games. The moose. The bear. All things I'd looked up on the internet. Ingrid getting pregnant. Lassie getting sick. Opik dying. My father lying to me. Being lost, hungry, and alone. All my biggest fears.

I had created this world.

The woman lowers the white surgical mask.

The heart rate monitor to my right jumps eighty points.

I gulp.

"Welcome to the CIA's Sleep Control Program," my mom says. "It's been a long time since you were here."

...

The doctor with the blue scrubs returns.

"I'll ask again," my mother says. "Where is the flash drive?"

"What flash drive? I don't know what you're talking about."

"The flash drive," she says, then pauses.

The doctor in the blue scrubs raises a syringe.

"The one the President gave you."

3:34 A.M.

:00

I am in the White Room. My mother gazes down at me with green eyes. She pulls back her predominantly gray hair and puts it in a ponytail. She raises her right hand. In it, she holds a mallet. The handle is scarlet, or at least it appears scarlet, a consequence of all the dried blood. It might have been wood underneath, or metal. It's hard to tell. The chrome head of the mallet, which has been cleaned, polished to perfection, catches the glare of the bright light overhead and shimmers a white gold. I flex my arms against the velcro restraints, but they have no give.

The mallet slams into my left hand.

My knuckles break. I have no idea how many.

The mallet slams down a second time.

Then a third.

She continues until my left hand is a pulpy mess. Until every single bone is broken.

The pain is indescribable. Unimaginable. A pain you don't think, don't *want*, to exist in this world.

My mother walks around the table until she is standing on my opposite side. As hard as she's tried, she is covered in my blood. Bits of spray clinging to her lab coat, sprinkled on her neck and chin. Little freckles of pain and destruction.

"I will ask you this one last time," she says, nearly emotionless. "Where is the flash drive?"

I shake my head. I don't know. How many times can I tell her? The President didn't give me a flash drive. He didn't. I promise.

She raises the mallet.

Brings it crashing down.

I wake up gasping.

It takes me twenty seconds to realize I'm not in the White Room with my mother. That I haven't been for over two weeks now.

I push myself up and glance at the fancy weather clock on the nightstand.

3:01 a.m.

July 7th.

69 degrees.

I am in the bed I grew up in, in the house where I was raised.

My condo is still uninhabitable. It had been ransacked, torn apart in the search for the flash drive. I hadn't seen it, but Ingrid had shown me pictures on her phone. Every cabinet was dismantled, every food container emptied, every cushion shredded, every wall systematically cut away, every inch of insulation ripped out. Every nook, every cranny: opened, searched, and then destroyed.

My mother's henchmen had ample time to search the house. They had from 4 a.m. on June 18th — the time Lassie, Ingrid, and I boarded the plane headed for Fairbanks, Alaska — until 10 p.m. that same day, when Ingrid and Lassie finally shook off their sedation and Ingrid called the police. An eighteen-hour window to find it. To find the supposed flash drive.

While Ingrid and Lassie were sedated and stashed in the car, I was transported to an unknown location — the White Room — where my mother administered what I can only describe as a synthetic nightmare. For the next twenty-three hours, or what felt like twenty-three days to yours truly, I attempted to survive in the Alaskan wilderness.

Even half a month later, it is hard for me to believe the events were fictional: the earthquake, the river, the wilderness, Opik, Lassie, all of it, a neurological trick. My own brain, stimulated by whatever was injected into my bloodstream — a concoction perfected by an outfit my mother called the Sleep Control Program — had betrayed me.

If I closed my eyes I could still see Opik lying on the sand bank. His breathing ragged, the gaping wound on his side blistering red and oozing death. I could play the footage of

Lassie and the canoe in slow motion, floating away, never to be seen again.

I gaze to my left where the black and tan cat is curled into my hip.

I gently rub one of his ears between my thumb and forefinger. God, I would have missed him.

Anyhow, after Lassie and Ingrid woke up in the car, Ingrid called the police and they came to the private airfield. The plane was gone, and after hours of investigation, it turned out the plane had disappeared off the radar completely.

And with it, one Henry Bins.

It wasn't until Ingrid drove back to our condo that she discovered the carnage.

But the condo was of little concern.

I was missing.

She called in all her favors at the Alexandria Police Department, the DC Police Department, even the Feds. Twenty-four hours after I went missing, everyone within a two-hundred-mile perimeter was looking for me.

The search wouldn't last long.

I was found the next day — at 8:30 a.m. on the morning of June 20th — by a farmer. I was asleep in his tomato garden.

In Michigan.

When I woke up, I was at a hospital in Lansing. I'd awoken in hospitals plenty of times in my life — concussions, stitches, a dislocated shoulder, a ruptured ear drum — yet I couldn't help from screaming.

I thought I was still in the White Room.

The last thing I remembered before waking up was my mom asking me about the flash drive, then a man in blue scrubs holding a syringe filled with pink liquid. I expected that I was headed for another twenty-three day nightmare, that I was headed for another round of torture — sorry, *enhanced interrogation* until I cracked and told them what they wanted to know.

Apparently, my mother believed me, or maybe she felt a touch of mercy for her son, perhaps a twinge of regret at having used her own flesh and blood to experiment on when he was just an infant. Maybe having caused his condition, his one-hour-a-day existence, she might finally show some compassion.

More likely, she knew that if she let me go, then I would start searching for this flash drive and lead her directly to it.

So, she let me go.

Dumped me in some guy's tomato garden.

Luckily, Ingrid, my father, and Lassie were in the hospital room when I awoke, but even then, it had taken ten minutes to get my heart rate below 180.

The next days passed in a blur.

After it came out what happened to me, that I was abducted by one of the CIA's most illustrious torture specialists, who also was one of the most wanted fugitives in the world, everyone wanted to speak with me.

Ingrid interceded on my behalf, and I spent three hours — *three days* — in front of a video camera being questioned by her, the new Director of the CIA, and Red, the head of the President's Secret Service detail.

The new Director of the CIA was especially interested in what my mom had referred to as the CIA's Sleep Control Program.

If it existed, he'd never heard of it, nor had any of his colleagues.

I detailed the White Room, but there wasn't much to go on. Because I was found in Michigan, that's where the CIA was focusing its search, though the White Room could have existed anywhere within a four-hour flight time of Michigan, an area of roughly two thousand square miles.

Once the video cameras were off and the Director of the CIA had left, I confided to Ingrid and Red that my mother wasn't just searching for a flash drive; she was searching for a flash drive given to me by the *President of the United States*. Red, who had known Conner Sullivan since college, confirmed the President hadn't given me any flash drive. And in a short conversation with Sullivan himself, he said the same.

Everything else, the description of the room, the doctor in blue scrubs, my mother, the CIA's Sleep Control Program, my being used in the early stages of the outfit's experimentation and research, and everything else I could recount was on record and distributed to an alphabet soup of agencies.

The CIA wanted to find my mother.

The Department of Homeland Security wanted to find my mother.

The FBI wanted to find my mother.

But none of them wanted to find her as much as I did.

She caused my condition. And I hoped, if I could find her, she could reverse it.

There was only one way I could think to find her. I would have to locate this flash drive before she did.

And then she would come to me.

:01

"Hey, dork."

Lassie blinks his yellow eyes a couple times, then paws at me. I blow in his face, which he hates, and he shakes his head, his whiskers bobbing up and down.

"Time to wake up."

Meow.

"You had a nightmare? About what?"

Meow.

"Justin Timberlake died. That's your nightmare?"

Meow.

"Oh, sorry. He didn't die. He was just paralyzed so he couldn't dance. Yes, that is terrifying. Makes my nightmare of my mother smashing my hand to smithereens with a mallet seem meek by comparison."

Meow.

"Yes, I *suppose* I would still be able to dance."

I flip him over and tickle him. We wrestle for a long minute until he taps out.

I look at the clock. 3:04 a.m.

Four minutes gone.

I throw off the covers and stand up.

My childhood room hasn't changed much in the decade I've been gone. It isn't filled with pictures, trophies, or video game consoles. I didn't have time for that stuff, though there is a single poster of Prince, to whom I allocated my minimal amount of adulation. There is a giant whiteboard I used when I first started online trading, on which I would write down the stocks I intended to buy and would graph their progress. But aside from these two eccentricities, the walls are bare.

There is a small dresser, bed, and nightstand. Next to the closet sit two ten-pound weights and an abdominal wheel.

The room feels claustrophobic.

I can't wait to get back to my condo in Alexandria.

According to the contractor who is doing the remodel, it will still be another two weeks until Ingrid and I can move back home.

I am counting the seconds.

Then again, I am always counting seconds.

I pick up Lassie and walk from the bedroom. My dad's room is just to the left and I poke my head in. He is fast asleep on the right side of the bed. On the left side of the bed, looking all-too-human, is his one-hundred-and-sixty-pound pup, Murdock. The English mastiff has his head on the pillow and is stretched out the length of the bed.

A box fan swirls the sticky Virginia summer air through the room.

Another reason I can't wait to get back to my condo in Alexandria — air conditioning.

Lassie jumps out of my arms and leaps onto the bed and snuggles into Murdock's side. Murdock opens one large amber eye, then slowly lifts one of his giant paws, wraps it around Lassie, and pulls him in tightly.

I close the door three-quarters of the way, then descend the stairs.

For the first week of my stay here, when I woke up, my father would be sitting at the kitchen table drinking a cup of coffee.

"How you doing, Sonny Boy?" he would ask. "You tossed and turned all night," he might add.

That is the problem with having Henry Bins. If you are having a nightmare, you can't wake up.

It became too much, the daily interrogation of how I was coping. By the time I finished assuring my dad that each night was getting easier, that my mother hadn't pulled out a single fingernail throughout the night, that I hadn't been waterboarded even once, a third of my day would be gone.

Thankfully, for the past couple days he'd slept through my hour, giving me my space.

As for Ingrid, after a tearful reunion at the hospital and then after three grueling days of interviewing, we were finally able to spend the night together. Waking up next to her the following night, watching her sleep, I couldn't help thinking back to the nightmare; I couldn't help thinking back to when she told me she was pregnant.

The idea of being a rent-a-dad, of raising a child, of being a father when I only had an hour a day had made me furious at the time.

"I'm only awake one hour a day!" I yelled at her. "What don't you understand about that? Sixty minutes is all I get, and now you want me to take care of a *baby*?"

Sure, it wasn't reality. It was a world being simulated by chemicals and neurons, but it was exactly how I *would have* reacted.

Then there was the earthquake.

And Opik.

I hadn't told anyone about Opik. It was too painful. Plus, I didn't know where he fit into my nightmare. How had a small Eskimo boy crawled into my subconscious? How had I decided upon the name Opik? I had so many questions.

Regardless, the small boy, a figment of my imagination, had impacted me greatly.

If there was one certainty that came out of my nightmare, it was that I wanted to be a father.

I felt horrible, keeping this to myself, not sharing it with the woman I love, the woman I share a home with, but before I told her how I felt, I needed answers.

Answers about my mother.

And my own father.

...

Isabel had been stopping by my dad's every couple days, which at first irritated my father, and understandably so. To him, her presence was a suggestion that he couldn't take care of his baby boy, which he had done magnificently for twenty-seven years. After three bites of Isabel's famous enchiladas and my dad waking to find his house spotless, my father changed his tune and was now her staunchest supporter.

I open the fridge and grab one of Isabel's legendary Reuben sandwiches — thinly sliced pastrami, extra sauerkraut, extra mustard, on toasted rye — then head to the kitchen table and flip open my laptop.

I eat half the sandwich and check my stocks. Everything looks good and I keep all my algorithms in place. I spend the next five minutes watching the first episode of season three of *Game of Thrones* and devouring the second half of the sandwich.

At 3:17 a.m., I open up my email and find the thread from AST, Advanced Surveillance and Tracking.

The last email I received from AST was the past October. It was an invoice from the company owner, Mike Lang, who for the previous three years I had been paying to locate my mother.

Which he did.

Except, the woman he thought was my mother wasn't actually her.

I never told Mike what actually happened: that even though the Jane Doe who was pulled from the Potomac River had matched my mother's fingerprints, it was all an elaborate ruse by President Sullivan to smoke out the location of CIA black sites operating illegally here in the United States.

However, it isn't my mother I'm contacting Mike about.

It's my father.

I couldn't help but wonder where my dad was when my mother was professedly *experimenting* on me as an infant. What was he doing? Did he have his head buried so deep in the sand that he failed to realize my mother was using me as her own personal guinea pig? How could he not have known?

Plus, I was having trouble believing his long-standing narrative of how he and my mother brought me home from the hospital the day I was born, then realized something was wrong with me the next day when I was only awake for a single hour. This implied I was born with my condition which, according to both John LeHigh, the ex-Director of the CIA, and my mother, wasn't the case.

Something didn't add up.

I hit reply and type:

Hey Mike,

*I have a project for you if you have time. I'm putting to-
gether a scrapbook for my dad and I don't want him to
know. I was wondering if you could dig up his birth certificate for me. And mine while you're at it (I can't find it
anywhere.) And if you find anything on my grandparents,
could you send that along as well?*

*His name is Richard William Bins. Born 8/1/1950. Des
Moines, Iowa, I think. Name a price and get back to me.*

Henry

I hit send.

I make my way back upstairs. Back in my room, I fall to
my knees and lift the mattress off the box springs (this is
where I hid a *Playboy* in my youth — I only ever had one, December 1995, Samantha Torres) and retrieve the red folder.

I was surprised when Ingrid told me the folder was sitting in the safe when she returned to the condo. An oasis
in a desert of mayhem, the safe stood open, the red folder
sitting benignly on the middle shelf.

The only other things that were in the safe were two of
Lassie's prized jingle balls, and they were taken by one of
the goons who destroyed the condo.

To say Lassie was mortified to learn this would be an
understatement. I didn't even know cats *could* cry.

I walk back downstairs, grab a peanut butter smoothie
from the fridge, and find my dad's tan leather La-Z-Boy
and fall into it.

Lassie pitter-patters down the stairs and jumps into my
lap.

"Hey, buddy." I scratch behind his ears. "You looked
mighty comfortable last time I saw you."

Meow.

"Murdock kept farting, huh?"

Meow.

"My dad too?"

Meow.

"Yes, it must have been from the sauerkraut."

Meow.

"Murdock ate seven Reubens. Wow, yeah, that is a national security risk."

I give him a spoonful of peanut butter smoothie and he laps it up. We spend the next five minutes sharing the smoothie, then he settles onto my lap and falls asleep.

I set the empty glass on the small chair-side table and pick up the red folder. I'd spent ten minutes pouring over the pages every day for the past week.

The first page is an eight-by-ten picture of my mother. The landscape is green and lush. My mother stands in front of six men, all of South American descent. They are covered in filth and three are shirtless. My mother has a gun leveled at them. She is wearing blue jeans and a tan shirt. Her head faces the camera, chestnut brown hair cascading to her shoulders and emerald green eyes shimmering under a high afternoon sun. High cheekbones and a square jaw scream of her eastern European ancestry. I would guess her to be in her late thirties.

I know from the file that the picture was taken in Honduras between 1985 and 1988, the years my mother spent teaching the Honduran nationals how to best interrogate prisoners.

I flip to the next page in the file.

My mother was born Elena Janev on April 23, 1948, in the former Yugoslavia — what is now Macedonia.

At the age of eleven, she boarded a ship and made her way to the United States and to a small hamlet in Vermont. She had an uncle who lived there, who helped her perfect her broken English. She was the top of her class in high school and was awarded a full-ride scholarship to MIT where she studied chemistry with a minor in psychology. She graduated in 1970 — what would be the tail end of the Vietnam War — and with her eastern European background and her off-the-charts intellect, she had many suitors, one of which was the United States Central Intelligence Agency. In 1971, she began her CIA training in Langley, Virginia.

After she completed training, she was recruited into what the CIA refers to as its Extraordinary Rendition Program, a fancy name for capturing and interrogating enemy combatants and using enhanced interrogation, aka torture, to retrieve human intelligence.

The years 1973 to 1981 are redacted — huge blocks of blackened text — but I can put the pieces together from what I learned at the hands of the ex-Director of the CIA as well as my mother.

My mother became part of a clandestine operation to develop the best and most effective strategies of enhanced interrogation, an off-the-books black op she referred to as the Sleep Control Program.

At the same time, the CIA was setting up black sites — secret underground torture chambers — both domestically and abroad, which gave my mother and her team ample opportunity to test their new techniques.

Then, according to my father, he met my mother at a coffee shop in November of 1976.

He knew her as Sally Petracova.

A year later, she became Sally Bins.

I was born on December 12, 1978.

According to my father, I was born with my condition, but according to both LeHigh and my mother, I was one of her first experiments, so it's anybody's guess what actually occurred.

The next date that isn't redacted in the file is April 15th, 1981, when she traveled to Afghanistan. The Soviet-Afghan War was raging during this time period, and my mother stayed for six weeks. My mother was often away for long stretches, but six weeks was a long time to be away from your three-year-old, and I vaguely recall this period when she was away. (Of course, I thought my mother worked for a company called Global Geologist Unlimited identifying oil reserves in different parts of the world. I had no idea she was waterboarding secrets out of enemy combatants.)

The next four years are redacted, then in January of 1985, she traveled to Honduras where she stayed for three years.

This fit with my personal timeline, as the last time I saw her was on my sixth birthday, December of 1984.

From 1988 to 2001 is redacted.

Then in November of 2001, two months after the Twin Towers fell, my mother was sent to the Middle East, no doubt to put her skills to use in the attempt to destroy Al-Qaeda and Osama Bin Laden.

She returned to the States fifteen months later.

The next date in her file is August 19, 2007.

In line with what LeHigh told me, my mother had tortured a young man to death only to find out days later that
he was completely innocent.

She disappeared the next day.

No one had seen her since.

No one, except me.

...

At 3:58 a.m., I pick up Lassie and head back to my bedroom. I poke my head into my father's room as I pass and
my eyes begin to burn.

The air is toxic with Murdock's and my father's fumes. I
plug Lassie's nose with two fingers and he laughs.

We settle into bed, and I text Ingrid that I will see her
tomorrow.

My heart begins to race as the seconds tick toward four
in the morning. I don't want to fall asleep. I know that for
the next twenty-three hours, I will be running.

Running from my mother.

:02

I wake up early for the first time in over a year.

2:57 a.m.

Three extra minutes.

In the past, I would have been ecstatic and I would have spent the minutes like a gift card, going on a shopping spree. Thirty extra seconds in the shower. An extra minute working out. Twenty extra seconds to floss (which according to the dentist who made a house call twice a year to clean my teeth, I needed to MAKE time for). But not today. By the time I process the nightmare and calm my breathing, the extra minutes have evaporated.

In my nightmare, my mother had injected me with another twenty-three day nightmare.

I was lost at sea.

In a small boat.

With a tiger.

Yes, it was oddly similar to *Life of Pi* — which I read in my early twenties (four minutes a day over the course of 204 days) — but with one big difference: the tiger wasn't a tiger but a really big version of Lassie.

Speaking of whom, I gaze around the bed, but he isn't there.

With my nightmare fading and my breathing under control, I begin to notice a slight stinging sensation on both my arms and my face.

I flip on the light and survey my arms.

They are covered in bright red scratches.

I jump out of bed and race to the small attached bath and look in the mirror. My face, neck, ears, arms, every inch of exposed flesh, is covered in raised red welts. I look like a monster.

"LASSIE!"

It takes me a couple minutes to find him. He's hiding in the clothes hamper in the laundry room. He tries to swim to the bottom of the clothes, but I grab him by the scruff of the neck and lift him up.

Meow.

"I'm crazy? I'm *crazy?*" I scoff. "Dude, you scratched the living shit out of me."

Meow.

"I attacked you? What are you talking about?"

Meow.

"I did not yell, 'I'm gonna eat you,' then bite your ear."

He shows me. There is dried blood on his ear.

And then it all comes back to me.

The nightmare. How, after two weeks without food, I decided to eat the tiger, aka Big Lassie. I tackled him, took a huge bite out of him, but then he clawed me to death and ate me.

"Oh my God."

I explain to him what happened. My nightmare. That I must have acted it out in my sleep.

"Sorry I tried to eat you."

He forgives me.

I give him a Slim Jim beef jerky stick I was saving for a special occasion, then find some Neosporin and spread it on the thirty-feet-worth of scratches on my body.

At 3:07 a.m., I sit down to eat breakfast.

A minute later, the front door opens and Ingrid walks in. She is wearing jeans and a blue tank top. Her auburn hair is pulled back in what she likes to call her "work pony." She is holding a medium-size cardboard box. Her normally chestnut brown eyes are red and puffy.

I jump up.

"Hey, what's wrong?"

She sets the box on the counter and falls into me.

She sniffs and says, "My mom had a stroke."

"I'm so sorry."

"Yeah, I just got off the phone with my dad. She got up to get a glass of water and my dad heard a loud crash."

She pushes me away a couple inches, glares at me, then asks, "What the hell happened to your face?"

"Lassie and I had a disagreement."

"Over what?"

"Over him eating me in my nightmare. It's a long story." I change the subject back to her mom. "Where is she now?"

"The ER in downtown Atlanta."

"What's going on?" my dad asks, stumbling down the stairs and cinching a blue robe around his widening girth.

"Her mom had a stroke," I tell him.

"Oh, honey," he says.

Ingrid breaks free of me and falls into his arms.

"It's gonna be okay," my dad says softly. "They have some of the best doctors in the country down there in Atlanta. They're gonna take real good care of her."

He rubs Ingrid's back with one hand and asks me, "And what happened to you?"

"Lassie used my face as his new scratching post."

There is a loud bang, then Murdock gallops into the room, his face unable to contain the million watts of energy churning through him. At the sight of Ingrid crying in my dad's arms, his face falls. *What happened? Why is everyone so sad? What's going on? Wha, wha, wha...*

He runs up to Ingrid and snuggles his head into her side.

She falls to her knees and lets him lick the tears from her face.

"Thanks, big fella," she says, half laughing, half crying.

I pull out a seat at the kitchen table for Ingrid, and Lassie jumps on her lap.

"So, do the doctors know anything yet?" I ask her.

"Not much. They're doing tests right now. According to my dad they have her listed as critical."

"How is Hal handling it?" my dad asks.

A couple months earlier, my dad and Ingrid's dad started chatting on the phone every now and again. It seemed odd my dad was friends with my girlfriend's father, a man I'd never exchanged a single word with.

"He's doing alright. My aunt Rita, his sister, lives on the same street, so she's been trying to keep him calm."

"You should probably head down there," I say.

She nods. "I am." She looks at my dad and says, "I was actually gonna try to grab the five a.m. flight and was wondering if you could drop me at the airport."

"Of course, sweetheart."

"It's out of Dulles," she says, which is a forty-minute drive due west, nearly a half hour farther than Reagan International which is a short four miles directly north.

"No biggee," he says, nodding. "We should probably get a move on though."

I look at the clock.

3:23 a.m.

My dad heads back to his room to put on some clothes.

"What a shitty day," Ingrid says, then stands up and gives me a nice long kiss.

We separate and she tells me that on top of her mother's stroke, she was also pulled off all her cases by her captain and forced to look into a thirty-year-old cold case. "I spent five hours doing paperwork and filling in the detectives taking over my active cases."

"Couldn't Billy have done that?"

Billy is her partner, a second-year kid whom I have met a handful of times. He is a sarcastic little punk. I adore him.

"I didn't tell you. Billy was suspended for two weeks for punching a suspect in the face."

"Did the guy deserve it?"

"Girl."

"It was a woman?"

"Yes, and yes she did. She kicked him in the balls, then slapped him, then spit in his face. And Billy didn't punch the woman, he more or less shoved her away from him and accidentally hit her in the face. But the woman claims he punched her and her two friends backed her up, so they suspended him."

"Shit."

"And I guess I was the obvious candidate to look into this cold case because I would be working solo for the next couple weeks anyhow."

"Alright," my dad says, now clad in shorts, socks and sandals, and a mock turtleneck. "Let's boogie."

I give Ingrid a long kiss, tell her I love her, and then watch as she and my dad push through the front door.

I look at the clock.

3:29 a.m.

Murdock and Lassie are both staring at me.

"Looks like we have the house to ourselves, boys," I say, then start chasing them.

...

After three minutes of wrestling with the two buffoons, I make a quick trip to my dad's bedroom. I find what I'm looking for, then place it in an envelope, and set it outside under a bush in the front yard. I then text Isabel to give her instructions and ask her if it isn't too much trouble, if she could whip up some of her legendary lasagna as well.

At 3:40 a.m., I make my way downstairs.

The basement is in as much distress as I've ever seen it. My father's latest undertaking is to organize all his hobbies — what he refers to as Basement Organization Extravaganza — but if he has a system, I can't discern it, unless it is to systematically place common items as far away from each other as physically possible.

Heaps of refuse are piled four feet high in every direction. A foot-wide path has been cleared which weaves its way through the one-thousand-square-foot space, and I slink my way through.

The last time I was down here was seven months earlier when I was trying to evade a couple of goons who were following me. I needed a tarp to cover my dad's car while I slept, and I found one down here. Under the tarp were two cardboard boxes. The boxes were so neatly taped down, I had a hard time believing they were my father's.

I'd been meaning to check the basement for the boxes since living at my dad's, but I didn't want my dad to know. I thought about heading down the last couple days while he was sleeping, but I didn't trust myself to navigate the labyrinth in silence. On cue, my hip smacks into a table, and a box full of bolts and nails clatters to the ground.

A floor above, Murdock starts barking.

By the time he's finished his monologue, I've made my way to the far back of the basement. I lean down on my haunches and run my hands over the two pristine squares of concrete among the filth.

The boxes are gone.

...

I spend my remaining time searching the basement for the two boxes, but I don't find them.

At 3:59 a.m., the alarm on my phone sounds. I barely have enough time to weave my way back to the stairs, run to the kitchen and grab an energy bar, swallow it in two bites as I climb the stairs to my bedroom, and flop onto my bed.

As the seconds tick away I wonder what happened to the boxes.

Were they moved?

Or were they hidden?

:03

"What are you doing?" I ask my dad.

He is sitting at the kitchen table, a barrage of papers spread out in front of him.

"Good morning, Sonny Boy," he says, pushing his glasses up from where they rested at the tip of his nose. "How'd you sleep?"

"Pretty good." Which isn't a lie. If I had any nightmares, they hadn't stuck with me. And according to Lassie, I hadn't attacked him once throughout the night.

"I put another round of Neosporin on your scratches when I got back from dropping Ingrid at the airport."

No wonder the scratches had healed so quickly.

"Thanks."

"I don't want you to scar."

I smile, then ask, "What are you doing? You have a big final exam that you haven't told me about?"

"Oh, this," he says, spreading his hands over the table and laughing. "This is a cold case Ingrid is working. She told me about it during the drive, and I asked her if I could take a look at it while she was gone."

I nod.

My father's next hobby.

Cold Case Detective.

"Well, make sure you keep everything in order. You have a tendency to, well, not do that."

The previous day's search of the basement comes rushing back.

The boxes.

Gone.

I'm tempted to ask my dad about them, but he interjects

before I have a chance. "Isabel dropped off some amazing lasagna," he says, beckoning to the refrigerator. "Then come sit down for a few minutes. I want to tell you about this."

I haven't seen my dad this excited since he helped me elude the two guys chasing me.

I open the refrigerator and grab a huge slice of lasagna and throw it in the microwave.

While it's heating, I text Isabel "thank you" and ask her if she did the other thing I asked.

She texts back immediately that she did.

Next, I read five texts from Ingrid. She arrived in Atlanta. Her mom is still in critical condition. Her dad is a mess. It is way too humid down there. She loves me.

I text back that I love her and to keep me updated.

Lassie and Murdock, perhaps awakened by the smell of the lasagna, enter the fray, and I pull out another piece, grab two plates, and divide the lasagna as I see fit.

Lassie looks down at his portion and cuts his eyes at me.

Meow.

"Why is your piece smaller? Well, maybe because you are a little squirrel and Murdock is gigantic."

Meow.

"But you are a little squirrel. In fact, you're smaller than most squirrels."

Meow.

"Yes, my scratches *are* just starting to heal. What are you getting at?"

Meow.

"You wouldn't."

Meow.

"Pinky promise?"

I touch my pinky to his paw, then tear a chunk of lasagna off my plate and give it to him.

"If I wake up with even one little scratch on me, I'm going to feed you to Mayweather." Mayweather is a big raccoon that likes to pick on Lassie.

Meow.

"Try me."

I pour myself a large glass of milk and join my dad at the table.

It is 3:06 a.m.

"Okay, you got five minutes, old man."

My dad smiles, then begins.

...

Jennifer Nubers was reported missing by her father on January 11th, 1985. A day later, her body was found in a park. She was just sixteen years old.

A sophomore at Theodore Roosevelt High School in the Columbia Heights neighborhood of Washington, DC, Jennifer was last seen departing the school grounds Wednesday, January 10th, by Megan Nubers, her best friend and cousin.

Jennifer's parents had recently divorced, and she and her little brother split time between both the mother and father. Their respective homes were less than three miles apart and it was understood that both children would stay Sunday through Wednesday at their mother's, then Thursday through Saturday at their father's.

When Jennifer didn't come home to her mother's that evening, the mother simply assumed she went to stay at her father's, which she was prone to do. The mother never picked up the phone. Never checked to make sure her daughter was there safe and sound.

It wouldn't be for another full twenty-four hours until the father would call to report Jennifer missing.

It didn't take long for the DC detectives to uncover a motive for Jennifer's murder. According to her cousin, Megan, for the past year, Jennifer had been engaged in something extremely dangerous, something Megan had begged, pleaded with her to stop doing on multiple occasions.

It started off innocently enough. Jennifer, a lover of photography, was walking downtown DC — one of her favorite places to photograph — taking snapshots of a fountain outside an office building, when she noticed a man and a woman.

Having caught her own mother in an affair with another man, Jennifer knew the telltale signs of a clandestine encounter.

She followed the couple to a motel a half mile away and snapped a dozen pictures of the two walking to and from the motel room. Two days later, she staked out the office complex, patiently waiting for the gentleman to leave the building. When he did, Jennifer skipped up to him and said, "Nice wedding ring."

He nodded absently and said, "Thanks, I guess."

"I couldn't help notice the woman you were with two days ago didn't have a wedding ring on."

"Which woman?"

"This woman," she said, slipping him a manila envelope.

After glancing at the pictures, he took a deep breath, and asked, "What do you want?"

"Two hundred dollars."

It was such a reasonable sum that the man hardly hesitated before walking to a nearby ATM and pulling out the money.

"How do I know you won't come back asking for more money?" the man demanded before payment.

"I won't," she said simply, leaving the man to watch her as she skipped away.

Jennifer's blackmailing hobby quickly turned into a blossoming enterprise.

She was always on the lookout for impropriety, and her business model was sound: 1) she only charged small sums, 2) she never went back to the well, 3) if they refused payment, she shrugged it off and moved on to the next mark.

According to Megan, over the course of the year, Jennifer had made upward of $4,000.

"Don't you get scared that someone is going to hurt you?" Megan asked her repeatedly.

The petite brunette would always flash her the same coy smile and say, "Who would hurt little ol' me?"

Someone did hurt her. Badly. Cause of death was blunt force trauma to the base of the skull.

...

"Time's up," I say, putting up my hand.

My dad puts the file down. He is breathing heavy. Smiling ear to ear.

"I'm glad you're getting so much satisfaction out of this young woman's murder."

He shakes his head, fights down the smile.

"No, no, it's terrible what happened to her," he says. "But a little sixteen-year-old girl blackmailing a bunch of cheating businessmen — I mean, come on, that's something."

"True, but it also got her kind of killed."

I know the prospect of finding out who killed this girl all those years ago and bringing him to justice is only half of his excitement. It's the thought of the answers to a decades-old mystery sitting in a box on the table — at his mere fingertips.

The box and the mystery remind me of the case of the mysterious missing boxes.

"So, Pops," I say, still unsure how I want to phrase what's coming. "Do you remember when I was trying to evade those guys staking out your house way back when?"

"Of course I do. Fricking fireworks and Murdock sitting on the car's front bumper. It was amazing." He continues on about how he jumped on my Vespa, dressed as me, and sped away, leading the goons on a wild chase.

I interrupt him, "Right, well, when I was downstairs grabbing the blue tarp, I noticed two boxes underneath. They were the only two boxes down there."

He nods along.

"I was downstairs last night, checking on the progress of Basement Organizational Extravaganza or whatever, and I couldn't help but notice that the boxes are gone."

"Boxes, boxes," he mutters, his hairy caterpillar eyebrows kissing. "Boxes..."

I glare at him. I'd been playing poker with my dad for over twenty years and I knew his tells backward and forward. I watch for him to scratch his nose. To thrum his fingers on the table.

He does neither.

"Oh, right, the boxes," he exclaims. "I moved them."

"Moved them?"

"Yeah, they were getting in the way."

I want to ask him what they could possibly have been getting in the way of; they were the only thing in the entire basement that *wasn't* in the way.

I don't.

"Where?" I prod.

"Where?"

"*Where* did you move them?"

"Oh," he says with a laugh. "I put them in the shed."

Right, the shed.

"Yeah, with the rest of your mother's stuff."

:04

"What?" I shout, loud enough that Murdock lifts his head off the linoleum in the kitchen.

"I put the boxes in the shed with the rest of your mom's stuff," he repeats.

"Yes, I heard you. What I don't understand is why you are just telling me this now. You know I'm searching for her, you've known I've been searching since that whole black site thing. How could you keep this from me?"

"I didn't think—"

"What? You didn't think I would want to know about a shed full of my mom's stuff? What about when I came to you last year asking about her? How could an entire shed of her stuff slip your mind?"

He stands up from the table, his face growing flush.

"I didn't want to poison you again. You don't have enough time in your life to be mad at your mother."

"You don't get to decide what I have time for, okay? If I want to spend all sixty minutes of my day for the rest of my fucking life pissed off at my mom, then that is my right."

I take a deep breath.

Lassie has wandered over and glares up at me.

Meow.

I don't want to chill out.

"Do you know what that woman did to me? She caused my condition. She fucking *experimented* on me."

I am too furious to continue.

"Get me a flashlight."

My dad's eyes are moist. I don't care.

"Go get me a flashlight," I order.

He shakes his head, obviously frazzled, then opens a couple drawers until he finds a flashlight.

He hands it to me and says, "I just—"

I shake my head and he stops.

I pick up Lassie and flick on the flashlight, then open the sliding glass door that leads to the backyard.

Lassie climbs on my shoulder and gives my ear a lick. Somehow it calms me, and by the time I'm halfway to the clapboard shed in the back corner of the yard, it no longer feels like my temples are going to implode.

There is no lock and I pull the door open.

It creaks, and a musty wave of air flows over me.

My father must have moved the boxes weeks, if not months, ago.

I cough, then take two steps into the fifteen foot by ten foot space and splay the flashlight across the contents. Lawnmower, weed wacker, hedger, and various other grounds-keeping implements, which have long ago retired from active duty.

Something skitters across the ground and out the door of the shed.

Meow.

"No, I don't think that was a possum."

Meow.

"No, I don't think it was a raccoon either."

Satisfied the creature isn't either of his two biggest nemeses, Lassie jumps off my shoulder and darts from the shed in pursuit.

The two boxes are stacked next to three slightly larger boxes.

My mom's stuff.

I peel the tape off of Box #1.

Clothes.

Eight sweaters and two winter jackets.

Box #2 is even less exotic.

Jeans and a couple blouses.

I shake them out, then stuff them back in the box.

Why would my dad keep this stuff?

Did he silently hope the woman who walked out on him over thirty years ago might come back?

Box #3 is full of shoes. Heels, flats, boots. Twelve pairs

altogether. I pull out a pair of brown boots. They are the boots my mother was wearing the last time I saw her. She put them on, then helped me to ride the new Huffy I just got for my sixth birthday.

I replace the shoes, then move to the two smaller boxes, opening the first.

It is filled with two enormous bags of Tootsie Rolls. Thirty-year-old Tootsie Rolls. I shine the flashlight through a thick layer of dust expecting to see mounds of mold, but they look pristine, which speaks volumes to whatever ingredients and preservatives comprise the candy.

I'm guessing she bought the candy for Halloween the year before she left. I would have been five then. My mother was gone that year, though she was often gone for long stretches. I try to remember what I dressed up as for Halloween when I was five.

A skeleton.

My dad painted my face like a skeleton while I slept and dressed me in a black costume with glow-in-the-dark skeleton bones. The moment I woke up, we hit the streets. My dad paid the neighbors, sometimes hundreds of dollars — of course, a few did it for free — to wake up at three in the morning and turn their porch lights on so that I could go trick-or-treating.

I gaze over my shoulder, out the door of the shed and to the blanket of light cascading onto the grass from the back floodlights. Did I really just scream at the man who went through all this trouble so his little boy could have a taste of what Halloween was like?

I replace the candy, then open the second of the small boxes.

Probably my Easter basket.

Nope.

More sweaters.

"Shit."

I check the time on my cell phone.

3:46 a.m.

I let out a deep exhale.

What a waste of a day.

A shadow moves into the doorway.

Lassie.

Meow.

"Nope, just a bunch of clothes and some thirty-year-old candy."

"You *find* what you were looking for?" I ask.

Meow.

"But you love rabbits."

Meow.

"A boyfriend? Really? Well, you win some, you lose some."

He jumps up on one of the boxes.

I stare at him, then stare at the box he's standing on.

The box full of shoes.

I tell him to jump off.

He does.

When Ingrid moved in several months earlier, I'd helped her unpack — only for about ten minutes, but still — and I was in charge of unloading her many, many pairs of shoes.

She'd stuffed all her boots with newspaper, which she explained kept them from getting wrinkles in the leather.

I'd been too preoccupied with the prospect of what might be in the next box to notice that my mother did the same thing with her boots.

I rifle through the box and grab the boots my mom was wearing the last time I saw her. I stick my hand into each boot and extract a thick cylinder of crumpled newspaper. I do the same with the other three pairs of boots until I have a small pile of newspaper in front of me.

I unfold the pages.

The pages are from two different copies of the *Washington Post*: one from 1980 and one from 1984.

If my mom left in early 1985, why would she stuff her boots with a newspaper from almost five years earlier?

She must have been holding onto the paper.

Saving it.

I find all the pages from the 1980 edition, then begin scouring the articles. It isn't until I find the front page of the paper that I realize why she kept it. The top headline reads, "CIA's Top Secret Project MK-Ultra Uncovered."

I sit down on the dusty floor and skim the article:

...Project MK-Ultra was a top secret program

created by the Central Intelligence Agency to
examine methods of influencing and con-
trolling the mind, and of enhancing their
ability to extract information from resistant
subjects during interrogation . . . they used
numerous methods to manipulate people's
mental states and alter brain functions, including the surreptitious administration of
drugs (most notably LSD), hypnosis, senso-
ry deprivation, sleep amplification, isolation,
verbal and sexual abuse, as well as various
forms of torture.

"Sleep Amplification," I hear myself say.
Looks like I found my mother's missing years.

:05

I didn't see my dad the next day. Or the one after that. He remained asleep while I logged nearly every one of my sixty minutes on the computer finding out as much as I possibly could about Project MK-Ultra.

Basically, Project MK-Ultra was the code name given to an illegal program of experiments on human subjects, designed and undertaken by the CIA. Experiments on humans that were intended to identify and develop drugs and procedures to be used in interrogations and torture in order to weaken the individual to force confessions through mind control.

The program began in the early 1950s, was officially sanctioned in 1953, was reduced in scope in 1964, further curtailed in 1967, and officially halted in 1973.

It was difficult to piece together all of Project MK-Ultra's past and players because they destroyed nearly every file, but one surviving document from 1955 was beyond frightening. It listed a number of different subprojects, CIA speak for *experiments*, and what they were trying to accomplish:

- Subproject 19: Develop materials which will cause the victim to age faster/slower in maturity.

- Subproject 27: Develop materials which will cause temporary/permanent brain damage and loss of memory.

- Subproject 34: Develop substances which will enhance the ability of individuals to withstand torture and coercion during interrogation and so-called "brain-washing."

- Subproject 39: Develop materials and physical methods which will produce amnesia for events preceding and during their use.

- Subproject 44: Develop physical methods of producing shock and confusion over extended periods of time.

- Subproject 49: Develop a chemical that can cause blisters.

- Subproject 53: Develop materials which will cause mental confusion of such a type that the individual under its influence will find it difficult to maintain a fabrication under questioning.

Seeing as the program was officially halted in 1973, none of these experiments could be the one I was a part of — the one ex-Director LeHigh and my mother alluded to.

After two days of research and lining up the dates with my mother's file, I now had a theory.

In 1970, my mother is recruited into the CIA. While undergoing CIA training at "The Farm," she shows a certain proclivity for enhanced interrogation.

Meanwhile, Project MK-Ultra is on its way out.

My mother, with a background in chemistry and psychology, and with three years of torture school under her belt, is the perfect candidate to be the phoenix that rises from the ashes of Project MK-Ultra, and the Sleep Control Program is born.

That would account for the eight-year gap, 1973 to 1981, redacted from her file.

For these eight years, she is working double duty as both an interrogation specialist and as the head of the ultra top secret Sleep Control Program.

During this period, I am born, she uses me in one of her experiments, and as a result I develop my super awesome condition.

Something happens in 1985 and my mother leaves. A couple months later, she shows up in Honduras.

What happened in 1985?

Someone had to know.

But if I believed what the new Director of the CIA said — and I had no reason to doubt him as he was brand new and was selected by President Sullivan to clean house and bring about transparency in the 70-year-old agency — no one had heard even a whisper about the Sleep Control Program.

As for MK-Ultra, although the scope of the project was broad, and the program consisted of some 149 subprojects which the Agency contracted out to various universities, research foundations, and similar institutions — at least 80 institutions and 185 private researchers participated — there were only two names deeply connected to the program: Allen Dulles and Sidney Ewen.

Allen Dulles was the Director of the CIA from 1953 to 1961, serving under both President Eisenhower and President Kennedy. Covert operations were a top priority under Eisenhower's Cold War national security known as the "New Look," and under Dulles' direction, the CIA created Project MK-Ultra.

The code name MK-Ultra is made up of *MK*, an arbitrary two-letter code, meaning the project was sponsored by the Agency's Technical Services Staff, followed by the word *Ultra*, which designates the most secret classification.

Dulles chose Sidney Ewen, the son of Hungarian, Jewish, immigrant parents, to head up the project. Ewen was born in the Bronx in 1926. He received a Ph.D. in chemistry from the California Institute of Technology and joined the CIA in 1951. As a poison expert he headed the chemical division of the Technical Services Staff, earning the nickname "The Sorcerer."

In 1953, he was chosen by Director Dulles to head Project MK-Ultra. Over the next 20 years, Ewen would oversee more than 150 "experiments." Under his supervision the program engaged in many illegal activities; in particular, it used unwitting US and Canadian citizens as its test subjects, many of whom died or suffered permanent brain damage.

Although he testified at numerous Senate hearings over the years, he was never convicted of a single crime.

He retired from the CIA in 1972, stating at the time that he did not believe his work had been effective.

I didn't have a shred of doubt that these men had answers to many of my questions.

Allen Dulles died in 1989.

But according to everything I read, Sidney Ewen was still alive.

...

I search for any sort of contact information for Sidney Ewen, but come up empty. I have no doubt he would want to stay off the radar, having inflicted so much pain on so many people. Someone might want to come after him. Someone might want some retribution.

Someone like me.

Many of the articles I skimmed online compared Ewen to Josef Mengele, the doctor responsible for many of the horrible experiments conducted during the holocaust. This was particularly objectionable, as Ewen, himself, was a Jew.

Now, he was far from Mengele — who I didn't know much about until I read up on him — but he was still a monster.

And he created an even bigger monster.

My mother.

I look at the clock in the bottom right corner of the laptop screen.

3:56 a.m.

I open up my email to write Mike Lang at Advanced Surveillance and Tracking to inquire if he could track this Sidney Ewen down for me, when I stop.

Mike still hadn't gotten back to me about my dad.

My *dad.*

Sidney Ewen is 89 years old and if he was anything like my dad, he was bored out of his mind. Sure, my dad had his hobbies, but when he wasn't trying to invent "Rollerblades for the new millennium" or "get back into the best shape of his life" — said the Stairmaster that is holding five boxes of different sized hinges — or playing Cold Case Detective, he was trolling websites. Mostly he was on Facebook. He was either posting pictures of Murdock, or some stupid video, or his new favorite thing, something called Dubsmash.

I don't want to even get into that.

I log into my account and search for Sidney Ewen. There are seven Sidney Ewens.

The fourth one is a picture of an old man sitting in a rocking chair with a huge orange cat on his lap.

Bingo.

I type a quick message, then run upstairs.

:06

It's 3:04 a.m. when I make my way into the kitchen the following day.

My dad is at the kitchen table.

He hardly glances up.

We haven't seen each other since I screamed at him about my mom.

"Hey, Pops," I say.

He gazes up at me. "Heyya."

"Making any headway?" I ask, grabbing a container of Isabel's delicious green chili and tossing it in the microwave.

He takes his glasses off and swivels around.

"You wouldn't believe this case. This Jennifer girl had a journal where she kept notes on all the people she was blackmailing."

"No kidding."

"Yeah, but the pages were all torn from the journal and scattered about at the crime scene. The detectives tried to put them together chronologically, but I think they got a couple things wrong. I've spent the last couple days reading them and piecing them together."

I nod along, grab my bowl of chili and a protein shake, and join him at the table.

My dad's Adam's apple bounces up and down as he shuffles through papers. A nervous tick, the same thing he would do with his cards when he had a full house or better.

"Listen, Dad," I say.

He holds up his hand and says, "No, me first." He takes a deep breath. "I'm sorry I didn't tell you about the boxes. When you came to me last year asking about your mother, I told you everything I knew about her, which wasn't all that much."

And he had, though nearly everything he knew about "Sally Bins" was fabricated by my mother.

The only true revelation had been that my father knew my mother worked for the CIA. He found out when I was two years old, when he accidentally stumbled on one of my mother's fake passports. She didn't tell him much, only that she was an agent with the CIA. He thought her some sort of spy; little did he know, she was the preeminent torture specialist in the world.

I remember asking him how he was okay with this. How he was okay with being lied to. I'll never forget what he'd said:

"When you love someone, you look past that. When she was here, with us, she was Sally and she was great. When she walked out the door, she went to work. If she had to be somebody else, I was okay with that."

My dad is still speaking and I tune back in.

". . . I noticed the boxes a couple months back and I should have told you. I thought it was just clothes and I didn't think it would be any help to you and would only conjure up old memories that would cause you pain."

"I know why you did it and I shouldn't have flipped out on you. I'm sorry."

"Me too," he says and I can see a thousand pounds slide off his shoulders. "So, did you find anything — in the boxes, I mean?"

I tell him about the newspaper. About the article.

"MK-Ultra," he repeats. "I remember when that was big news in the early 80s."

I tell him my theory about how I thought his estranged wife fit into the fold, how I thought she was recruited by this Ewen fellow to head up an off-shoot black ops project, the Sleep Control Program.

I didn't want to get into it any further. Every time I mentioned to my father what she did to me, he would excuse himself from the room. It was too painful for him. And it hurt me to see him in pain.

I decide to change the subject. "So, tell me more about this case."

His eyebrows jump.
I look down at my cell phone.
3:08 a.m.
I'm feeling generous and tell him, "Ten minutes."
He picks up a stack of journal pages — their left edges
jagged from where they were ripped from the binding —
and begins reading.

...

*So, Mr. Langon, or should I say, Mr. Lan-GOON, made another
pass at me today.*

*What a creep. Aren't you married with like six kids? Don't
touch my shoulder when I turn in my paper. I don't want your
super hairy hand touching my favorite blue sweater.*

Ugh.

*Megan said he did the same thing to her last year. She almost
reported it, but decided not to. I'm wondering if I should report
GOON.*

*Yeah, uh, Principal Derry, I think you need to hire a new Hu-
manities teacher. Yeah, one that doesn't stare at your tits — not
that I have tits (come on, girls, get growing) — the entire class.
Poor Bethany, Big Titty Bethany in the front row. I swear thirty
minutes each hour, GOON is staring right at her huge tits.*

*Anyhow, Megan got her license last week, so we went
off-campus for lunch. Subway. So much better than eating in the
cafeteria. John McCannis and Luke Segurs were in the booth next
to us. Megan said that she made out with Luke in eighth grade. He
had braces and she had braces and she said it was gross. But he
got his off — she gets hers off in a couple months — and she said
she wants to give it another shot.*

Makes me wonder when I will get to kiss a guy.

*Fifteen and still haven't kissed a guy. Or do I count Bennie
from summer camp? No, he just licked my face. Plus, I don't want
him to be my first kiss. Yuckaroo.*

No, I want my first kiss to be Jason.

Yeah, like a senior is going to kiss me.

Plus he's going out with Martha, who is smoking hot.

A girl can dream.

...

Working late again. That's what she said. Just tell Bob to heat up the leftovers from yesterday for you guys. Yeah, cause the only thing better than Hamburger Helper is day-old Hamburger Helper.

I asked her what she was working on, you know, what the case was about, why she had to spend all these late nights at her office. "Oh, Honey, you know I can't talk to you about my cases."

Yeah, I know, you can't talk to me about anything.

Pft.

That's funny.

Pffft.

I just tried making the sound and spit on the pages a little.

Sorry.

Like anybody is going to read this.

Yeah, I'm talking to you, Markus. Put my journal down right now or I will smother you the next time you fall asleep.

Hahahahahha.

Yeah right, you will never ever find this thing again. I found the perfect hiding spot.

So, yeah, something is up with my mom.

Like six weeks in a row that she has been staying late one or two nights a week at the office.

I mean, that's not too weird, but she'd been acting weird too. (Too weird then weird too. That's WEIRD.)

The phone rang last Saturday and she ran from outside to grab it. Never seen my mom run a day in her life. The fat on the back of her legs jiggled and I was going to tell her, but that's mean. She's forty-five. I think most women have some of that chunky stuff on the back. I don't, thank God. Everybody says I got great legs. But I want tits. Come on, girls.

Same thing happened on Sunday.

Bob was watching the Redskins game and didn't even notice.

Uh, your wife is acting strange, Bob. Get it together, Bob.

Speaking of Bob, Hamburger Helper is ready.

Yay.

Barf.

...

My mom is having an AFFAIR.

Megan and I went to the mall after school. The mall in Bal-

timore. I guess some guy from her Trig class asked her out to the movies and she wanted to get a new sweater from some place called The Gap. I asked her if she wanted to be alive for her date and if so, then we shouldn't go to the mall in BALTIMORE.

I told her I would only go because they had a GREAT STEAK ESCAPE there. And she was going to buy me one.

(He was taking her to some like big romance movie called Romancing the Stone.)

BARFFFF!

FINE, I'm jealous.

I want to go on a date to a STUPID movie with a boy from my class.

Someday.

She showed me a picture of him from the yearbook. He's not that cute. And get this, he's in the Audio/Visual Club. What a DORKO.

But that's not the big news. Crazy news. AWFUL news.

When we were leaving The Gap, Megan pushes me and says, "Isn't that your mom?"

It was.

With some guy.

In the food court. At a mall. In BALTIMORE.

We snuck around to get a closer look.

They were eating at the Great Steak Escape.

Not only was she having an affair, now I would never be able to eat GSE again!

Here is the weird part. The guy looked just like Bob. I thought it was Bob for the first five seconds. But Bob doesn't wear suits. And Bob has a gut.

This guy was skinnier, but his face, his dark hair, were just like Bob's. And Bob look-alike had his hand on my mom's leg.

GET YOUR HAND OFF MY MOM, CREEP. GOON.

I wanted to punch him. To punch her.

How could she?

Sure Bob wasn't the smartest guy in the world. But he was the nicest. He had been so good to her, so good to me and Markus for the past eight years. How could she?

Then she leaned forward and kissed him.

I wanted to scream.

God, I hate her.

Oh, wait, I think she's here.

Fucking Bitch.

...

You will not believe what Crazy Bitch, aka my mom, did.

I told her that I needed her to drive me to the pharmacy, that I was having girl problems.

She let me drive.

She was really nice.

She probably felt guilty for not being home that much lately and for CHEATING on Bob.

When we got there, I drove to the very back of the lot and parked.

She asked what I was doing.

I started crying.

I tried not to, but I was so mad.

She asked me what was wrong. She asked me if I was pregnant.

Yeah right, mom. I've never kissed a guy but I'm fucking pregnant.

I told her that I saw her at the mall with Bob-look-alike. Eating Great Steak Escape and kissing him.

And guess what Crazy Bitch does? She didn't cry, she didn't apologize, she didn't say she was going to end it with Brad or Chuck or whatever the guy's name is from her office. No, she says that if I keep quiet, don't tell Bob, that she will buy me a car for my sixteenth birthday.

A brand new one.

Any car I want.

I tell her I want a Range Rover.

A green one.

She says okay.

Then I tell her to FUCK OFF.

I get out of the car and walk home. Bob is watching TV when I walk through the door.

"Your wife is having an affair, Bob."

I tell him everything.

The guy, the kiss, my mom offering to buy me a car to keep me quiet.

He starts crying.

Then he leaves.

...

Sorry it's been so long. Been a CRAZY couple weeks. The worst weeks of my life. I've been staying at Uncle Ray and Aunt Joan's for the past week, sharing a bed with Megan.
My mom and Bob are getting divorced.
Bob moved out and he is staying at a hotel.
Markus is staying with my mom.
He thinks this is all my fault.
He says that he hates me.
I don't blame him.
I should have taken the car.

...

My dad stops reading. I don't want him to stop. I want him to keep going.

"Poor girl," I find myself saying.

I don't know if it was my dad's plan to read this particular journal entry so I would relate with this young woman's contempt for her mother, that I would somehow become emotionally involved in finding her killer.

If it was, it worked.

I'm almost as pissed off at this girl's mom as I am at my own. She offered her daughter a car to keep her quiet, to conceal the affair from Bob (who I assume was Jennifer's stepfather, one whom she loved dearly.) Her affair not only destroyed the family, created an irreconcilable rift between she and her daughter, and caused the little brother to hate and blame Jennifer for the family falling apart. It also inadvertently sent her daughter down a road of blackmail, one that would eventually get her killed.

I want to dive into the case headfirst with my dad. I want to read the entirety of her journal entries. To spend hours poring over the case files from the DC detectives.

But I can't.

I have bigger fish to fry.

I tell my dad that he should keep pressing on the case and to keep me updated, then I grab my laptop and head to my room.

I have two new emails.

The first is from Ingrid, detailing everything that has happened in the last couple days. Her mother is still in a coma, but the neurological scans look promising and they just have to wait and see. Her dad is going crazy, and she was forced to introduce him to Candy Crush on her phone, which appears to at least temporarily take his mind off his wife for short stretches. They are taking turns keeping vigil at her mother's bedside and going home to shower and eat. She misses me and she even misses Lassie and Murdock, and she can't wait to move back into the condo when she returns. Kisses.

I email her back quickly, then open the second email. It's from Mike Lang at AST.

Henry,

This is all I could dig up. It was easy enough, no charge.

Mike

P.S. Bummer about your grandparents. And on V-Day, no less. My condolences.

I open up the zip drive he's attached to the email. There are four PDFs.

The first is my father's birth certificate: Des Moines, Iowa, Richard Jeffrey Bins, 8/1/1950, born to Jack and Margaret Bins.

The second is what Mike was referring to in his email. My grandparents were killed by a drunk driver on their way home from dinner on Valentine's Day. My father was twenty-one at the time, a junior at the University of Iowa. The PDF is a death certificate for my grandmother, dated 2/14/71. The third PDF is identical to the second, only it has my grandfather's name.

The fourth is my birth certificate.

It matches the birth certificate I have, or *had* — I'm not sure if it survived the flash drive massacre — in a file at my condo: Manassas, Virginia, Henry Grayson Bins, 3/20/1978, born to Richard and Sally Bins.

My dad's unmistakable signature — nearly illegible, each letter nearly half-an-inch-high and the "d" from Richard and the "b" from Bins overlapping — at the bottom.

My mother's signature is a quarter the size of my father's. Neat, each letter skillful, each spacing perfect.

I let out an audible sigh of relief.

My dad is my dad.

Thank God.

...

3:22 a.m.

I check my stocks. I lost nearly $60,000 over the last two days. I cut my losses and move what remains from a handful of fledgling investments into safe, low-yield bonds.

I haven't exercised in nearly a week, and I pull my Asics from beneath the bed and slip on the first one. Tying the double knot, it dawns on me I forgot to check something. I was so preoccupied — nay, relieved — to find out that my dad was exactly the man I thought he was, I forgot about the message I sent last night.

To Sidney Ewen.

I log into Facebook.

One new message.

It's from him.

My heart rate doubles.

Last night I'd messaged him: *Mr. Ewen, I'm guessing you know who I am. I have some questions for you. Please message me back when you get this.*

I click open his message.

Mr. Bins,

I am quite familiar with who you are and the condition you suffer from. Frankly, I'm surprised it has taken you this long to contact me. I will answer all your questions to the best of my ability, but I must warn you, you may not like the answers.

Sidney

I take a deep breath and begin typing questions. In the end, I delete them all, then type four words: *Can we meet tomorrow?*

I hit send, then pull on my second sneaker.

Murdock, who has a sixth sense for when I'm heading for a run, gallops into the room.

He cocks his head at me and pants.

"Yes, you can come."

His tail helicopters in a big circle, and he jumps up and licks my face.

I give a cursory glance for Lassie, but I don't find him.

By 3:43 a.m., Murdock and I have made our way halfway around the park near my father's house. It's not quite as sweltering as it was the previous week, but I'm still drenched in sweat. It's the first time I've run the loop in close to nine years, and it feels both eerie and satisfying at the same time, like being able to feel your way to the bathroom during a blackout.

I let Murdock off his leash. He is marginally well-behaved — at least, compared to Lassie, who is constantly running off to try to weasel his way into, well, in one case, an actual weasel — and when he scampers ahead, he waits for me to catch up, then takes off again.

When we are on the final straightaway that leads to my father's cul-de-sac, my cell phone chirps.

I pull it out.

I synced my Facebook account to my cell before I left, and my phone shows I have a new message.

The old coot must be up.

Probably playing Candy Crush like Ingrid's father.

His message is nearly as simple as mine.

"Tomorrow," it says, followed by an address.

...

The moment I walk through the door, I ask my dad if he'll do it.

"Of course," he says without hesitation.

I tell him the address and he plots it into his phone. He says it will take two hours.

In my dad's younger days, if we went on a trip, he would carry me to the car, but after seven slipped discs and soon-to-be osteoporosis, the days of transporting his one-hundred-and-sixty-pound son were over.

That means I would have to sleep in the car tonight.

I look at my cell.

3:56 a.m.

I run to my room and take a minute long shower, then throw on sweats and a tee, then grab jeans to change into when I wake up.

With a minute to spare, I open the door to the garage.

Lassie is sitting on the hood of my father's Lincoln, swatting at the metal hood ornament, which springs backward and forward.

I laugh and say, "Dude, what are you doing?"

Meow.

"This relaxes you?"

Meow.

"Are you sure it isn't just because its shiny and it springs around?"

Meow.

"A poor man's jingle ball? Don't you mean a poor cat's jingle ball?"

Meow.

"Maybe if you start doing some chores, I'll give you an allowance."

This could have gone forever, but I only have a few seconds left in my day. I open the door, recline the passenger seat, and climb in. Lassie hops off the hood of the car and settles into my lap.

Meow.

"You'll start emptying the dishwasher?"

Meow.

"How *exactly* are you going to mow the lawn?"

Luckily, my dad comes in and tucks a pillow under my head and covers Lassie and me with a blanket. He hands me a big glass of water to drink and makes me scarf down an energy bar.

Just like old times.

"Thanks, Dad," I say, then wade into the blackness.

:07

Culpeper, Virginia is seventy miles southwest of my father's house. It has a history steeped in both the Revolutionary and Civil Wars, which isn't uncommon among the many towns littering Virginia, but because the town was originally surveyed by a young George Washington, it is revered by many as one of America's premier historical towns.

This, of course, is all being relayed to me by my father, who has obviously taken a break from Cold Case Detectiving to brush up on his American history.

I'm tempted to tell my dad I'm only interested in one of the "18,247 people who reside in Culpepper, at least according to the last census," but he just spent two hours driving here and he would spend another two hours driving back.

He's earned his rant.

I nod along as I take off my sweats and swap them out for jeans, an easy task made impossible by the bulk of Murdock, who has pushed up from the back seat and is licking my face.

"Did you really need to bring Tweetledee and Tweetledum?" I ask, interrupting my dad's diatribe of how the town went from initially being named Fairfax to its now modern day Culpepper.

Lassie appears magically on top of Murdock's head.

Meow.

"You are Tweetledee," I tell him.

Meow.

"Yes, he gets to boss Tweetledum around."

I shove the pair backward and finish pulling on my jeans.

"Is that the house?" I ask my dad, gazing out the window at the two-story colonial sitting back on a couple acres.

"Sure is," he nods. "I even did a walk up to make sure the address on the house was the same as on the mailbox. It is. Couple a goats running around on the side of the house scared the bejesus outta me."

The house, with its green clapboard siding, picket fence surrounding green acreage, and tall oaks, seems so serene and innocent — the antithesis of the man who resides there.

"You want me to come with you?" my dad asks.

I don't want him to, but I also don't want to deny him a little adventure.

"You might not like what the guy has to say."

"I can handle it," he says, his lips gluing together. "It's about time I accept who your mom really was."

"Denial isn't just a river in Egypt," I say giving him a soft punch on the arm.

"Hey, that's my line," he says, erupting in a soft laugh.

I look down at my cell.

3:03 a.m.

"Okay, dingbats," I say, turning around. "Try to stay out of trouble while we're gone."

They both flash their best *Who? Us?* faces.

"Yes, you. Murdock, you're in charge. Don't let Twee-tledee get out."

Meow.

"I lied," I say, then open the door and quickly shut it.

...

The walk up the long dirt drive to the house takes two minutes. A full moon overhead illuminates the house in a soft glow, which appears to be in great shape for its age, though I surmise it had a face lift and a tummy tuck at some point.

My father points out two shadows patrolling the tall weeds under a giant birch to our immediate right — the two goats getting a late-night snack.

They raise their heads as we approach the porch, but don't appear overly concerned with our presence.

Guard goats, these are not.

After an unsuccessful couple seconds of searching for a doorbell, I reach up and grab the brass door knocker and bang it softy against the wood three times.

Nothing happens for thirty seconds, and my dad lifts the door knocker and bangs it five times loudly.

"Well, if that didn't wake him, at least now all the neighbors in a five-mile radius are up," I say.

He shrugs. "We didn't come all this way for nothing."

Fifteen seconds later, the creak of aging floorboards can be heard from behind the door, which is opened by a black woman in a purple robe.

"Good evenin'," she says with a bright smile. "Sorry it took me so long to get to the door; my hearing isn't so good anymore."

She is maybe in her early sixties, and I wonder if she is Mr. Ewen's wife, maid, or both.

She answers the question for me. "I'm Maggie, Mr. Ewen's help."

I thought *help* an outdated term, but this is Virginia and we are below the Mason Dixon line, where I know the rules are different.

"Mr. Ewen is expecting you. He's in his study. I'll show you the way."

My dad and I follow in behind her.

We enter a narrow hallway. The lights are low and everything is a different shade of brown. I pull out my cell phone and look at the time.

3:06 a.m.

I flick on the voice recorder app I installed and hit record, then put it back in my pocket.

"May I make you some tea or pour you a drink?" Maggie asks over her shoulder.

"I'm fine," I say.

"Do you have any scotch?" my dad asks.

I turn and glare at him.

He puts his hands up as if to say, "What?"

"Sure do. Good stuff too," Maggie replies, then stops at a closed door.

She waits for us to get closer, then leans forward and whispers, "Mr. Ewen, he sometimes will hear something that will trigger him to lose track," she points to her head. "If he starts prattling on about the war or whatnot, just give it a minute and he should snap out of it."

My dad and I both nod.

Maggie knocks on the door and says, "Mr. Ewen, your company is here."

There is a loud grumble and Maggie turns the knob on the door and pushes it in.

My father and I walk into a sprawling study. The lights, if possible, are set even lower than the hallway, and I find myself squinting at the man behind a giant desk.

He is bald, save for a few whispers of white hair. His nose and ears take up a third of his face and his Adam's apple sags down a good three inches. His back is stooped, and his shoulders are in the process of swallowing his head. He's eighty-nine going on a hundred and twenty. But even in the low light, his blue eyes sparkle. They appear as if they were plucked from a young kid on his skateboard and jammed into Mr. Ewen's aging carcass.

Books are stacked in giant columns of various heights, some a head taller than myself, and feel as though they will topple over as my father and I amble past.

"Mr. Bins," Ewen mutters, his voice breathy, heavy. "And who is this, your father, I presume? Mr. Bins Sr."

Six feet of desk separate us.

I nod, then decide against sticking my hand out.

My father extends his hand and says, "Richard Bins."

Ewen lifts a feeble arm and takes my father's hand. "And I am Sidney," he says.

A blur of orange bounds onto his lap, then once more onto the desk.

"And this is Peaches."

Peaches is an orange tabby.

A *big* orange tabby.

The Queen Latifah of tabbies.

She flops down onto the desk, then settles in, her head sinking into the many folds of her neck and back.

My dad reaches out his hand and strokes her long fur. She purrs in delight.

"I know our time is limited," Sidney says with a curt nod. "So, if it pleases you, we will do away with tireless pleasantries."

I look down at my cell.

3:11 a.m.

I'm set to ask my first question when Maggie enters with two glasses of brown liquid on a tray. She hands one to my father, then sets one down next to Mr. Ewen.

She leaves without uttering a word.

Both Ewen and my father take small sips, then exhale a satisfying breath. "The nectar of the gods," Ewen says with what amounts to a grin of his cragged lips. "Perhaps what I will miss most."

Something tells me Sidney Ewen doesn't have many days left on this earth. Perhaps that is why he agreed to see me. To rid himself of the mountainous guilt weighing so heavily on his stoop.

"Small batch?" my father inquires.

"Indeed," Ewen says, taking another sip. He spends the next minute telling my father about an old acquaintance's distillery in northeastern Scotland and the peat that grows there.

My dad offers me the glass and I take a sip.

It is marvelous, but all I can think about is how I have two less minutes, two less questions I can ask.

"But we did not come here to talk of scotch," Ewen says, moving his eyes from my father to me. "Let us begin."

"Where did you meet my mother?" I ask.

He takes a deep breath.

"I met Elena when she was twenty-three years old, when she was at Camp Perry, or what many people call 'The Farm.' This would be 1970 or '71. Each year, I would give a lecture to the new recruits on the latest breakthroughs in enhanced interrogation."

"Torture," I say.

"Yes, torture."

"And at this time you were heading up MK-Ultra?"

"I was. I'd been appointed by my dear friend Allen a decade earlier, but by 1971 the Senate was breathing fire down our necks. Two years later and Allen would officially pull the plug on the program."

"You talk about the *program* as if you were building houses for refugees in Haiti and not experimenting on unwilling American citizens in various forms of behavior modification."

"I understand you think me a monster, and I have neither the energy nor the time on this earth to argue otherwise. I did what I did."

He doesn't say this with indignation. He does, however, say it without the slightest air of remorse. To him, the people he experimented on were a casualty of war, no different than a man in the trenches.

Only the man in the trenches has a choice.

I want to scream at him that I was a casualty of this war.

I take two calming breaths, then say, "You were giving a lecture in Camp Perry in 1971 . . ."

"Yes, yes. I was speaking, as you might expect, about some of the findings from the program's many projects, and Elena, well, let's just say, she stood out among the crowd."

"In what way?"

"Well, as you might know, and your father can certainly attest to, your mother was a beautiful woman. A rose among thorns. Those eyes."

Yes, *those* eyes.

They haunted my dreams.

"But it was not her looks that intrigued me," he continues. "It was her insight. I'll never forget what she said near the end of my lecture. I was talking about how fear is your most powerful tool in interrogation when Elena raised her hand and said that she disagreed. She said your most powerful tool is hope."

"*Hope?*"

"She explained that fear might cause a prisoner to tell you something, but if you took away hope — any hope of rescue, any hope of ever seeing their family again, any hope of the pain abating, any hope of continuing on — they will tell you *everything*."

A chill runs down my arm, the hairs standing on end.

I glance at my father.

He is rigid.

I think back to my twenty-three hour nightmare: lying on the sand bank, having not eaten in days, Opik's corpse ten feet to my left, Lassie having been swept away to die, Ingrid and my unborn child never to be seen again.

Helpless.

*Hope*less.

I turn back to Sidney and say, "And this is when you recruited her to run a new program."

He nods. "The Sleep Control Program."

"Why sleep?"

"Over the course of a hundred and sixty projects on behavior modification, the results from the projects concerned with sleep modification were the most impactful. It was well known that sleep deprivation caused prisoners to physically wear down, to hallucinate, to go crazy, but the results from both sleep amplification and dream modification testing were incredible."

"By dream modification, you mean *nightmares.*"

He nods.

As if reading my thoughts, he says, "How do we do it? Well, it is far from an exact science. I will give you the short version." He takes a sip of his scotch and two deep breaths. "Creating a nightmare is like trying to create a tornado. You can't do it. However, if you have the right conditions, a blanket of warm moist air near the surface and a layer of cold air above that, and perhaps some southwesterly winds, then you create an *instability* where a tornado might form. That is precisely what we try to create in the brain, an instability."

Ewen glances at both of us to make sure we are still with him, that he isn't shooting scientific gibberish three feet over our heads.

My father and I both nod our understanding.

"We use three compounds," Ewen says. "The first, our warm air, suppresses certain neurotransmitters — serotonin, dopamine, several more — while enhancing others, mainly melatonin."

I was quite familiar with melatonin. In my teens, I had an operation to remove my pineal gland — a gland located in the center of the brain — which releases melatonin, the hormone that controls the sleep-wake cycle. My pineal gland was three times the normal size and was thought to be the cause of my Henry Bins.

It was not.

"The second compound, our layer of cold air, supercharges the limbic system, the area of the brain which controls primitive, *raw* emotions: fear, hate, anger, love, jealousy—"

"Hope," my father utters.

"Yes, and hope."

"And what is the third compound?" I ask, ready to move onto the next question in my arsenal but somewhat transfixed by the science of it all.

"Ah, the third, our southwesterly *wind*. Well, I'm sure you read up enough on the program to know."

I nod. "LSD."

"Correct."

Right, so my twenty-three day nightmare was just one big acid trip.

"The rest is up to the host," Ewen says. "Their experiences, their memories, their fears." He glares at me for a long moment, then asks, "Did your mother do this to you?"

I nod.

I can see, feel, his mind doing laps behind his blue eyes. Is he putting himself in my shoes? Living out a twenty-three hour — twenty-three *day* — nightmare?

"I can only imagine," he says under his breath.

This is when I realize just what a monster he is. He isn't sympathetic. He is curious. I can see him mentally placing electrodes on my body, hooking me to a series of machines, scribbling in a notebook as he hovers over my trembling body.

I want to climb across the table and smash my hand into his bulbous nose.

Instead, I look down at my cell.

3:26 a.m.

I want to know more about my nightmares, but I have a limited amount of time. "Keep going," I say. "My mother had just started the Sleep Control Program."

"Yes, yes," he says, then turns his gaze to my father. "Correct me if I'm wrong. You met Elena — well, I believe she was going by Sally at that point — in 1976."

My father nods. "That's correct. I met her at a coffee shop November of that year."

"Right, so she had been working on the Sleep Control Program for going on two — two and a half years. I was three years into what would prove a decade of Senate hearings, committee oversight hearings and whatnot, and I had little contact with Elena and the Sleep Control Program."

"Who was bankrolling the operation?" I ask.

"I was."

"You?"

"Yes. MK-Ultra had an annual budget of ten million dollars, today's equivalent of right around ninety million."

"And you were skimming?"

"I wouldn't say skimming. More like stockpiling. A rainy day fund."

"For when you were eventually shut down?"

"Correct."

"And just how much did you stockpile?"

"Around thirty million."

Thirty million dollars. What today would be over a quarter of a *billion* dollars.

"And you invested this all in the Sleep Control Program?"

"Heavens, no. The Sleep Control Program was only one of several black ops I funded after retirement."

I wait for him to elaborate.

He doesn't.

"So how much did you give her?"

"Ballpark—five million."

"And how much did you keep for yourself?"

I expect him to shake off the question, to say he was above stealing for his own gains.

"Enough," he says.

"Enough to buy a nice house on a big plot and a couple goats."

Another cragged grin forms as he says, "So I take it you met Marshall and Latimer?"

"We did."

"They wandered over from a neighboring farm several years ago and have yet to leave, though I must admit, they do bring a bit of joy into my static life."

I don't care about his stupid goats and say, "Okay, so my mom is running the show, you are bankrolling it from behind the scenes. Where do I come in?"

"Well, Elena and I never spoke face-to-face, but we did pass information back and forth through a series of different channels. In one letter, your mother told me she was going to take a step back from the program." He nods at my father and says, "She'd fallen in love and was getting married in the coming months."

My father let out a long exhale. "We were married on June 17th, 1977."

"Right. Well, I didn't hear from her for over a year, then I received a report from her that she and one of her partners — I never did know the ins and outs of the program, who exactly your mother was working with — had made a breakthrough in sleep amplification. In the animals they were testing on — I believe they were pigs, yes, pigs — they were able to keep them asleep for exact periods of time. After much trial and error, they had perfected a compound that kept the pigs asleep for exactly twenty-three hours a day."

My chest begins to tighten.

"This wasn't like giving someone anesthesia — that would negate what they were trying to achieve. This was twenty-three hours of regulated dream-sleep. However, that wasn't the breakthrough. The breakthrough was the hour the pigs were awake. They were disoriented, depressed, far less stable than the other pigs — the pigs being *deprived* of sleep. Elena theorized that if the compound were to be combined with our nightmare serum in interrogation — thus, giving prisoners twenty-three hour nightmares, followed by a single hour awake — they would crack in record time."

"And did they?" I ask.

Ewen puts up his hand. "You are getting ahead of yourself. At this point it was just a couple pigs, the next phase was—"

I finish for him. "—human trials."

...

"Right," he says. "Human trials."

"So that's where I come in, after the pigs? She tested this bullshit out on me?"

Ewen shakes his head. "You have it all wrong. Elena, your mother, she wasn't like me — at least back then. She wouldn't have dared test something out on an unwilling human, certainly not a baby. No, Elena tested it on herself."

My eyebrows jump. "She what?"

"Your mother was the first human trial of Compound-23," he pauses, then adds, "or should I say, you *and* your mother."

I lean forward in my chair.

"The next letter I received from Elena came three weeks later. She detailed that the testing of Compound-23 had been a success. For a week she slept for twenty-three hours a day, waking only at 3 a.m., then falling asleep precisely an hour later." He breathes heavily through his nose before adding, "The letter also said that she'd just found out she was eight weeks pregnant."

:08

An invisible fist clamps down on my chest.

My mother was pregnant with me when she tested out Compound-23 on herself.

My emotions are a whirlwind. In some ways, I am relieved. Relieved that my mother hadn't intentionally experimented on me. Also, in the back of my mind, I always wondered where my father was when, and if, my mother was experimenting on me. Why wasn't he there to protect me? Well, for one thing, he didn't know.

I gaze over at my father.

His eyes are moist.

I reach out and pat his leg softly.

"You couldn't have known," I tell him, though it doesn't appear to melt away any of his agony, or perhaps, anger.

"She must have known," I find myself saying. "That first night, when I was only awake for an hour, *she must have known* what she did to me."

"She did know," Ewen says. "The next letter I received from your mother came nearly ten months later. She detailed your condition. She feared she must have taken the compound during a vital part of your brain's formation and it hardwired a sleep-wake cycle of twenty-three hours."

"Can it be fixed?" I ask, the question jumping off my tongue nearly of its own accord.

"I fear there is only one person who can answer that question."

I nod.

But if my mom could have fixed me, she would have, right? Or did she view me as the greatest unintentional experiment of all time?

"I need to find her," I tell him.

I spend the next several minutes detailing my kidnapping by my mother, my twenty-three day nightmare, the White Room, and my mother's request.

"Tortured by your own mother," Ewen says, shaking his head. "The Elena I knew would never do such a thing. She was the ultimate patriot. The Elena I knew would lay down her life for the country that rescued her from a miserable existence on the other side of the globe. Everything she did, every experiment, every interrogation, she did to protect the country she loved."

My mother the ultimate patriot?

Sure, she came from a life of poverty in her youth. The divided nation of Yugoslavia was in the midst of a civil war at the time. Coming to the United States to live with her uncle must have been a godsend for her.

And I did have a memory of one July 4th in particular — the only one I remember when my mother was home — where she took me outside and we ran around the streets with sparklers. I remember her telling me it was the *most important day of the year.*

"If nothing else, your mother loved this country," my father mutters.

Something must have happened. What changed her from a patriot into a monster? Or could they be one and the same? Could one live without the other? Could the old man across from me also be deemed a patriot? Could he write off the killing of innocent Americans for the greater good?

I decide this is too heavy to process at this moment. I shelve it for later and ask, "You don't know of the White Room? Where it might be located?"

"I haven't spoken to Elena in over a decade. The last contact I had with her was just after 9/11. She was obsessed with something called Project Sandman."

Project Sandman?

Could this be what was contained on the flash drive she was searching for?

"What is Project Sandman?"

Ewen's face tightens. He squints one, twice, three times. Looks around the room.

"Who are you? Did Reagan send you?" he shouts.

I glance at my dad. He is as puzzled as I am.

"Someone over there is tipping off the Russians, and we need to find this mole before the entire war turns on its head."

"Mr. Ewen," I say softly, realizing I am witnessing what Maggie briefed my father and I on before we entered. "Take a deep breath. We are in your study. It's 2015."

"Who are you? You tell Reagan that I will do everything, will use every material we've created, to find the mole."

"Mr. Ewen," my father says. "Sidney!"

Ewen shakes his head back and forth. Then his eyes open. He looks exhausted, as if he's aged five years in thirty seconds.

"Uh, yes, I was saying, I haven't spoken to your mother in, uh, in over a decade."

A loud crash from behind the door sends Peaches scampering from the table.

"What in the dickens?" Ewen says, pushing himself up, which is a six-step process.

Another loud crash and the door opens.

Maggie sticks her head in and screams, "Oh, heavens, Mr. Ewen! I don't know how they got inside."

"Who?"

"The goats! It must be the goats!"

Marshall and Latimer.

"I closed the front door," she huffs. "I know I did."

My father and I glance at each other.

"Shit," we both say in unison.

Goats couldn't open doors.

But Murdock could.

My father and I run into the hallway. A blur zooms past us and into a room to the right.

A goat.

Another blur zooms past. This one three times bigger.

Murdock.

On his back, riding him like a cowboy in the Old West, is Lassie.

Oh my fuck.

There is a loud crash.

My father bolts after them, only to turn on his heel and race in the opposite direction.

I make for a room to the right. A large family room. One of the goats is standing on the couch, eating the only remaining cushion.

Me thinks we won't be invited back to Ewen Manor any time soon.

I hear a loud hiss and turn just to in time to see Peaches streaking down the hall. Two feet behind her is Lassie.

"Leave her alone!" I scream.

I look down at my cell.

It is 3:50 a.m.

The next five minutes prove futile as the five — Murdock, Marshall, Latimer, Lassie, and Peaches — thrash from room to room, destroying everything in their path.

Maggie is standing on the table in the kitchen with a broom, having what I can only describe as a very intense nervous breakdown.

"Ahhhh," she moans. "Make it stop."

A gunshot erupts.

Standing in the hallway, a smoking double barrel shotgun pointed at the ceiling, leaning at a seventy-five-degree angle against a thick cane, is Sidney Ewen.

You could hear a pin drop.

Latimer, still standing on the couch, lets the foam he's eating drop from his mouth and stares at the old man.

He points to the open doorway and says, "Everybody out."

...

"Where is Lassie?" I ask my dad, opening the passenger door and flopping into the seat.

It is 3:59 a.m.

I didn't have a chance to thank Sidney for his time. He looked in no mood to converse, though I couldn't blame him. Murdock and the goats destroyed well over $50,000 of his property.

At least he had his rainy day fund.

"There he is!" my father yells from just outside the driver's side window. He opens the door and I watch as Lassie scampers across the yard and jumps into the back seat.

He has scratches all over his face and body, yet he is smiling ear to ear.

"I didn't know you liked redheads," I say, then melt into the seat.

...

I wake up in the passenger seat. I push the lever on the side and bring the seat upright. My body aches from the two nights spent sleeping at such an odd angle, and I let out a groan. Something is attached to my right arm and I flip on the overhead light with my left hand. It has been awhile since I've woken up with an IV, and I gingerly peel off the tape and slide the needle and catheter from my forearm. The thin tubing runs to a drip bag hanging from the dry-cleaning hook in the back seat, which is two-thirds empty.

From the amount of pressure on my bladder, I can only assume there were others before this one.

For the first twenty years of my life I slept with an IV each night. For the first decade, my father would hook me up to the IV while I slept, but at least a couple times a week I would wake up with heavy bruising on my forearm, a clear indication my father had a difficult time finding the vein. For the second decade, I lived with a semi-permanent catheter in my arm, which I could hook up myself in the final minute before I would fall asleep.

The pros of having a saline/electrolyte drip over the course of twenty-three hours were that I would wake up feeling hydrated and refreshed, and I wouldn't need to spend a significant part of my hour awake consuming fluids.

The cons, or con, was that what goes in must come out.

I had a second catheter, one connected to a far more sensitive part of my body. Luckily my dad would attach, detach, and empty the contents while I slept, so I never had to deal with it. The notion of your father attaching a pee-bag to your penis when you are eight isn't a big deal. When you are about thirteen it gets a little creepy. That's when I started doing it myself, but it wasn't the easiest of processes and it always cost me two or three minutes of my precious sixty minutes a day.

Over the years, I decreased my IV drip from two bags to one bag to half a bag, until I finally phased it out completely. My body adapted to long periods without water, and after some trial and error I figured out the amount of water I needed to drink to avoid massive dehydration yet not piss myself throughout the night. (I went through a considerable amount of bed sheets.)

Yesterday, I was so preoccupied with Ewen, then the goat, dog, and cat tornado, that for the first time in seventeen years, I failed to drink a single drop of water. The only liquid I consumed was a sip of my father's scotch. If my dad hadn't hooked me up to the IV, it would have been forty-eight hours since my last dredges of water, and I would have spent my entire hour in misery, taking small sips of water and eating saltines.

And that is the best-case scenario.

I open the door and push myself out of the seat.

I've never had to pee so badly in my life. I ponder an attempt to make it to the bathroom, but there's no way. It's coming out. I pull down my pants and waddle over to a trashcan in the garage.

A minute later, I open the garage door and make my way into the living room.

My dad is at the kitchen table, once again Cold Case Detective-ing.

"Thanks for the IV," I say.

He smiles. "Yeah, after you went to sleep, I found the cooler I packed for you in the back seat. I totally spaced that you didn't touch it. How ya feeling?"

"Great, awesome actually. I think I just took the longest piss of my life, though it was in one of the garbage cans."

My dad laughs.

"How many drips did you hook up, like seven?"

"Just two."

I shrug and ask, "You still got that cooler you packed for me?"

"No, I fed it to the boys on the way back."

"After what they did, you gave them a treat?"

He shrugs.

"You pushover."

As if on cue, Lassie rounds the corner. He stops and stretches, his arms out front, his little butt high up in the air. Just another day in Lassie Land.

"Dude."

He gazes up at me.

Meow.

"What do you mean, *what*? Do you not remember what you morons did last night?"

Meow.

"Sorry doesn't cut it. Your little escapade cost me ten minutes of questions that I needed answers to. Answers I may never get because you guys had to chase around some stupid goats."

Meow.

"Oh, you're *super* sorry. That makes it all better." I get down on my haunches and reach down to pet him, then swat him on the top of the head.

I stand up and look at the clock.

3:06 a.m.

I ask my dad, "Hey, I'm a little behind schedule, could you whip me up something while I get to work?"

He jumps up and starts rummaging around the kitchen. My dad cooks three things well: spaghetti, grilled cheese, and pancakes.

"Actually, Isabel dropped some soup by this afternoon," he says. "It will go great with my *famous* grilled cheese."

I grab a seat at the kitchen table and flip open my laptop.

Lassie is facing the kitchen, his back to me, sitting on his back legs. A tiny little statue. He's pouting.

I'd never swatted him before.

I start to feel guilty.

I walk over and pick him up, turn him toward me. He is about three feet extended and dangling. He won't look at me, his head swiveling so his gaze won't meet mine.

"I'm sorry I swatted you."

Meow.

"I did not *thwack* you."

Meow.

"It did not feel like you were hit by a baseball bat."

Meow.

"It also didn't feel like I dropped a piano on your head." I pause, then tell him, "I'm sorry. Seriously."

I reach him up and blow on his stomach. An apology zerbert.

He laughs.

Licks my nose.

Best friends.

I set Lassie down and tell him to go cuddle up with Murdock and that my dad will bring them both some grilled cheese in a bit.

The first thing I do is check Facebook to see if I have a message from Sidney Ewen.

I don't.

Ewen's words come rushing back: *I haven't spoken to Elena in over a decade. The last contact I had with her was just after 9/11. She was obsessed with something called Project Sandman.*

I Google "Project Sandman."

There are no hits for "Project Sandman," though there are several for "Sandman."

The first result is a comic book called *The Sandman*. The second is a YouTube video from a band called Metallica, some song called "Enter Sandman." The third is from Wiki for "Sandman."

I click on the Wiki link and read the first line:

The Sandman is a mythical character in central and northern European folklore who brings good dreams by sprinkling magical sand onto the eyes of people while they sleep at night.

Sandman.

Sleep.

Sleep Control Program.

I let out an audible huff.

My dad asks over his shoulder from behind a skillet, "What?"

I tell him.

"I could have told you that."

Sometimes I forget my dad has 400,000 hours' worth of knowledge rattling around in his brain, a stark comparison to myself, who has less than 15,000.

"Project Sandman must be something she was working on for the Sleep Control Program." My eyebrows jump. "I bet that is what's on the flash drive."

He asks what I think might be on there.

"I don't know. A list of names? Of people they experimented on? Of people they interrogated? A list of locations?"

The White Room.

"It could be a whole history of the program."

It has to be.

But then why would President Sullivan have it? And why would my mother think he'd given it to me?

I need more information.

I continue reading the Wiki article.

The Sandman was a character from a folktale created in 1841 by Hans Christian Anderson. There were several instances of the Sandman in popular culture, from movies to music to books.

I click on the Metallica link and hit play on the music video.

I turn up the volume and my dad starts bobbing along. Soon he is singing the lyrics along with the song.

Say your prayers, little one
Don't forget, my son
To include everyone

Tuck you in, warm within
Keep you free from sin
Till the Sandman he comes

Sleep with one eye open
Gripping your pillow tight

Exit: light
Enter: night
Take my hand
We're off to Never Never Land

Something's wrong, shut the light
Heavy thoughts tonight
And they aren't of Snow White

Dreams of war, dreams of liars
Dreams of dragon's fire
And of things that will bite

Sleep with one eye open
Gripping your pillow tight

Chills run down my arm.

I stop the song.

"Hey!" my dad yells over his shoulder. "I love that song. It was your—" He stops and turns. His face is ashen.

"That song," he says. "It was your mother's favorite."

...

I spend the next ten minutes scanning a couple more of the "Sandman" search results. My dad brings me two grilled cheeses (cut diagonally and separated by a gooey bridge of cheddar and Monterey Jack) and a bowl of Isabel's sensational chicken tortilla soup, and I dip and eat while I read.

My father delivers a similar feast to Dee and Dum, and I hear Murdock gulp his down in two bites at which point I imagine he hovers over Lassie — who will savor each bite — and wait for possible leftovers.

At 3:35 a.m., I slip on my Asics.

I spend the next twenty minutes pounding the pavement, trying to imagine a scenario where President Sullivan somehow acquired a flash drive containing the known history of the Sleep Control Program. Every experiment, every compound, every person who ever passed through, every location, every last crumb.

I have so many questions. How did Sullivan stumble across the intel? And if he did, why would he ever give it to me? Why would my mom suspect he'd given it to me? And why did she want it so badly?

Obviously, she was still involved in the Sleep Control Program. Was she afraid if the contents of the flash drive became public knowledge the Sleep Control Program would go the way of the dinosaur, smallpox, and MK-Ultra?

I couldn't get the pieces to fall into place. Sullivan was all about transparency in the government. He'd gone on a crusade to find and close the illegal black sites the CIA was running on American soil. When he accomplished that feat — with the help of *moi* — he crucified the then Director of the CIA. Sullivan saw to it personally LeHigh spent the better part of the next decade in Leavenworth. If Sullivan somehow learned of the existence of another CIA clandestine black op, he would have put a stop to it immediately, and my mom would be in the cell right next to LeHigh's.

The biggest mystery of course: me.

Why me?

Where did I come into play?

Sure, the President and I had become, if not friends, then friendly. But why would he ever choose to give me something — not *just* something, a flash drive — and moreover, why would my mother suspect this?

And according to Sullivan himself, he didn't give me anything.

Nothing fit.

When I finish the three-mile loop, it is 3:55 a.m. I can barely feel the miles in my legs, but my brain feels like it just ran a marathon.

My dad is sitting at the table eating his own grilled cheese when I enter, fueling up for another long night of detective work.

"Thanks for the grilled cheese," I say, giving his shoulders a quick rub. "Don't stay up too late."

"I won't," he says, then adds, "Drink a couple glasses of water before bed."

:09

My dad is asleep at the table when I walk into the kitchen. His face is on a yellow notepad. I tap him on the shoulder and he stirs. I help him to his bed and tuck him in next to a snoring Murdock and Lassie.

Back in the kitchen, I grab a premade Cobb salad and a smoothie and sit down to my computer. Even with twenty-three hours of sleep, my brain still feels fatigued.

I flip open the laptop, then close it.

I reach across the table and grab my dad's yellow legal pad, wondering if he's made any progress. The pad is filled with my father's indecipherable gibberish. Nearly six pages of notes, Venn diagrams, bulleted lists. I don't know why he uses a legal pad when he doesn't use the lines; some notes are written vertically, some diagonally. It is chaos. I try to read a couple of sentences, but it is useless. The only thing I can make out are the small horses that fill the corners of each page. (Horses are my dad's doodle of choice. The same small inch-high horse. Wispy mane, long tail. Each one a carbon copy of the previous.)

I set the legal pad down and drag the closest pile of papers over. To my father's credit, he'd kept the papers organized and nearly free of coffee stains.

The pages are from Jennifer's journal.

I pick up the top page. It is eight inches high by five inches wide, the exact size I remember from the journal my father bought me in my teens. (I gave up writing after four entries. I enjoyed putting my thoughts down on paper, but it seemed I was just getting started when my hour would be over.)

I guzzle down half the protein shake, then begin reading.

...

Bob bought me this killer camera for my sixteenth birthday. Nikon. Zoom lens. And a red carry-case. He thinks I like red. I don't have the heart to tell him that I like green now.

He said we could paint my bedroom red if I wanted to.

Yeah, Bob, because I'm a serial killer.

No, I want to paint it SEA FOAM GREEN. Or maybe Apple Jolly Rancher. Ha, that would rock!

Anyhow, starting next week I have to split time between Bob's new house and THE BITCH'S.

Bob said that he was lucky that my mom agreed to split custody of me and Markus, because if she wanted to, she probably could have gotten full custody, him being our stepdad and all.

I told him that I would testify. HE should get full custody. She is the one who committed ADULTERY.

I wrote that on her bathroom mirror last time I was there with a bar of soap.

HAHAHAHAHA.

Bob asked me to do it (not write Adultery on her wall . . . but to split time with my mom.) If not for me, then for Markus. So I'm gonna bite the bullet for them. Sunday through Wednesday.

Why does she get four days????

DO IT FOR MARKUS.

DO IT FOR MARKUS.

DO IT FOR MARKUS.

Back to the camera. It is AMAZING. Bob bought like twenty rolls of film for me and I've already gone through seven. I dropped the first three rolls off to get developed two days ago and Bob said he would swing by and see if they are ready after he got off work.

I can't wait to see them. I took like thirty pictures of this spider web in the park. I was experimenting with the shutter speed and the lighting and I wrote down what I did with each shot, so when I look at them I should learn a lot about what I did right.

Man, I'm smart!!

Oh, and I took like fifteen pictures of Megan and Derrick. She wants to give him a framed picture of them for their two-month anniversary.

They are going to go see some stupid movie called Indiana Jones and the Temple of Doom.

She's SOOOOOO into movies now that she's dating Señor Dorko.

They are going on Friday and Megan said if I can find a date, I should go with them.

Right.

Though I did see Brian Truman like totally checking out my tits the other day.

THE GIRLS ARE COMING IN!!! (Hahahaha, like Paul Revere!)

But he's a freshman. I can't go out with a freshman. That's like illegal or something.

Anyhow, I'm gonna go take some more pics.

...

HOLY MOLY. You will not believe this. I totally caught some dude having an affair.

So Sunday, Bob drops me off at my mom's, sorry, THE BITCH'S.

She is like super nice. Has lunch all ready for us and wants to go the amusement park.

Um, what????

I'm sixteen, not twelve.

She said that since she didn't get to see me on my birthday, that this could be my birthday present.

Um, what about the Range Rover you wanted to buy me? To shut me up. To not tell Bob that you were FUCKING some dude from your office.

Was that offer off the table??

I wasn't getting a Range Rover. I wasn't even getting a little white Honda Civic like half the girls at my school. And because of the divorce, mom was pinching pennies. She said maybe in a year.

But I guess Six Flags is just as good.

I didn't want to go, but Markus was SUPER pumped and he was just starting to not hate me.

Six Flags was ACTUALLY kind of fun. I ACTUALLY forgot that I hate my mom for about three hours. And Markus had a blast. I've like never seen him so happy in his whole life. The only thing that would have made it better is Bob trying to squish his gut into the roller coaster.

Maybe me and Markus and Bob can come back.

Whatever, that's not why I had to like freaking run up here and grab this fricking journal.

So, everything is going great until me and Markus get off one of the roller coasters and are looking for my mom and we see her talking to like a group of three guys that are SERIOUSLY twenty years younger than her.

Like, closer to my age than hers.

I got SOOOOO pissed.

The whole drive home, my mom keeps asking me what's wrong. Uh, you like just got divorced, like aren't even legally divorced and you are throwing yourself at some freaking TEENAGERS.

I made her drop me off near the Capitol. Told her I'd be home in a couple hours. I needed to vent.

Luckily, I had Nicky, that's what I call my new camera, with me.

NIKON = NICKY.

There was this killer fountain in front of this office building and I was shooting it.

THAT'S WHEN I SAW THEM.

This guy walks out of the office. Looks over his shoulder a bunch of times, then meets up with this chick.

They were right behind the fountain and I zoomed in on them. The guy totally had a wedding ring on and the chick totally DIDN'T.

They started walking and I followed them. My heart was freaking pounding. It was like being on a rollercoaster times a million.

They walk up like three blocks to a MOTEL. I used up like half a roll taking shots of them walking up the stairs. They couldn't take their eyes off each other. They came out an hour later and I took another half a roll.

I thought maybe the guy saw me and I totally tried to play it cool. Just a girl taking a walk. I waited for him to run after me, but he didn't. He was too busy like still grabbing the chick's ass and stuff.

I ran to the pharmacy and dropped off the film. Paid like triple for them to do a rush job.

All I could think about for two days was the pictures. What was I gonna do with them?

They weren't ready until Thursday, RUSH JOB, MY ASS, and I took them back to Bob's. The pictures were fricking great. This

MARRIED dude and this chick totally going at it on the steps of a
scummy motel.
Megan came over and I showed her.
She FREAKED.
She asked me what I was gonna do with them.
What do you think?
I'm gonna BLACKMAIL him.

...

I set the pages down. I could perfectly see what happens next. She goes up to the guy the next day, shows him the pics, tells him to give her two hundred bucks, then follows him to an ATM where he pays her. It is too easy.

I pick up the pile and rifle through thirty pages or so. Some of them appear to be journal entries, more about Bob, Megan, Markus, THE BITCH; however, most are descriptions of the people she blackmailed. She never uses names. She nicknames them after streets intersections — 3rd and Mass, or K and Juniper, or 5th and Penn — purportedly where she spotted them, or perhaps even photographed them.

One of these people killed her.

It could have been 1st and Macon, or R and Mathis, or Lexington and Race.

Someone either didn't trust her to not show the pictures to their spouse or caught her in the act.

But who?

I suppose if they knew that, then it wouldn't be a cold case.

I set the journal pages down and reach across the table and grab a large blue binder. The investigation report.

The men investigating the death of Jennifer Nubers were Washington, DC, homicide detectives Albert Johnson and Devin Cornish.

The report was done on a typewriter. More than twenty pages long. There are several pictures of the crime scene, which I decide are images I have no intention of looking at. I open the three-ring binder and find the investigative report.

It is 3:27 a.m.

...

Homicide detectives Johnson and Cornish met with Bob Gillis, Jennifer Nubers' stepdad, on January 13, 1985. He was the one to call her in missing forty-eight hours earlier.

When the two detectives told him Jennifer's body was found in a park on the west side of town, that she had been murdered, the man fell to the floor. Cornish attempted to help the man up, but he was of considerable height and girth — 6'1", easily two hundred and ten pounds — and it took both detectives to raise him.

Johnson, the senior detective by more than seven years, had alerted more than fifty families to the murder of a loved one, and he immediately eliminated Gillis as a suspect in his stepdaughter's death.

The man continued to sob as they asked him questions about Jennifer. Who was she friends with? Was she dating anybody? Did she have any known enemies?

The only intelligible and perhaps audible answer he gave was the name Megan.

Megan Nubers was Jennifer's best friend and cousin. She was a year ahead, a junior, at Theodore Roosevelt High School.

The detective's next stop was Jennifer's mother's house, which was in the same Columbia Heights neighborhood. Marie Nubers was far less emotional than Gillis, whom she was in the process of divorcing, but Johnson had a hard time believing the woman was capable of killing her sixteen-year-old daughter. Though, of course, he'd seen far more sinister things in his days.

She did admit freely her relationship with her daughter was strained, that she had an affair, and her daughter probably hated her.

Possible motive for the daughter to hit the mother in the back of the head with a blunt object, but hardly the other side of the coin.

Markus, Jennifer's ten-year-old brother, was staying at friend's house during the interview. Both Johnson and Cornish, both of whom had two younger sisters and who agreed it was the sibling's reactions that were often the hardest to watch, were thankful for this.

When the two detectives entered the home of Megan Nubers, she was joined by her parents Ray and Joan. She was sandwiched between them on a blue couch.

The two detectives asked a few questions of Jennifer's aunt and uncle.

Johnson asked, "So Ray, you are brothers with Marie's first husband, John?"

"Correct."

"And what happened to him?"

"He died in a fishing accident when Jennifer was four. She doesn't remember much of him."

"And he was good dad?"

"As far as I know. I was working in Ohio at the time and I didn't see him all that much during that period. Part of the reason we moved back was to help Marie out with the kids after he died."

"And John's death, nothing suspicious?"

"No, freak accident with a marlin. Pulled it on board, thing harpooned him in the neck, bled out before they could get the boat back to shore."

Cornish, an avid fisherman himself, couldn't help but fight down a smile.

Johnson, attempting to cover for the snicker emanating from his partner's throat, turned his gaze to Megan.

"When is the last time you saw Jennifer?"

Megan's voice cracked as she told the detectives the last time she saw her cousin was 3:30 p.m. on Wednesday, January 10, 1985.

"Does she have any other good friends? Or a boyfriend?"

"Not really. She pretty much just hangs out with me and my boyfriend, Derrick. Just last weekend all three of us went to the movies on both Friday and Saturday night."

"Really, what did you guys see?"

"On Friday we saw *Dune* and on Saturday we saw *Beverly Hills Cop*."

"How was that one? Eddie Murphy, right?"

"It was good. Funny," she said with a forced smile.

"And Jennifer, you guys didn't mind her being a third wheel?" Cornish asked, finally composed.

"No, not at all."

"And this Derrick, he's a good guy? He would never want to hurt her?"

"No, never. It wasn't him. It was one of the guys she was blackmailing."

Both detectives and both her parents' eyebrows scrunched together in near unison.

"Blackmailing?" her father asked, beating both detectives to the punch. "What do you mean, blackmailing?"

Megan took a deep breath and told them.

Told them everything.

...

"Why didn't you idiots just read the journal?" I ask out loud, though I'm sure at some point they would have. Possibly they had to turn the pages over to evidence to look for fingerprints before they read them over. Or maybe the pages were found far from where Jennifer's body was found and only later were they connected to her.

I flip forward a half dozen pages.

It is 3:46 a.m.

...

Of the more than twenty-five people Jennifer Nubers blackmailed over a ten-month span, detectives Johnson and Cornish were only able to track down three.

3rd and F

22nd and New Hampshire

And *2nd and Mas.*

And this was only because there were banks located on these exact street corners. Using Jennifer's descriptions of the men from her journal and the intersections, they were able to use the banks security tapes to locate the gentlemen. It would have been nearly impossible to look through a year's worth of tapes, but luckily, in all three circumstances, Jennifer mentioned which movie Megan and her boyfriend (or all three of them) saw and the detectives could narrow the timeline to a couple weeks.

In all three cases, the men — Jack Newborn, Chase Wingleberry, and Montel Hermann — admitted to being blackmailed by Jennifer Nubers.

Both Jack Newborn and Montel Hermann said that they

paid her $250 after she showed them pictures of them having affairs (in Newborn's case, with another man), then never heard from her again. Wingleberry, perhaps the scummiest of the three, took money out of the ATM, then decided not to pay her. He said, quote, *I didn't give that little bitch a dime. My wife knows I fuck around. I told her to go right on and tell her. Shit, she'd probably love the pictures of me and the redhead.*

Newborn, an account executive at JP Morgan and Sons, a father of four, with perhaps the most to lose and therefore the biggest motive, was in London on business when Jennifer was murdered.

Hermann too, was on business, in Seattle.

Both men's trips were corroborated.

Wingleberry's alibi was his wife. Though when they interviewed her, she said she was NOT okay with her husband, quote, *fucking around*, but that he was with her the night of Jennifer's disappearance.

Johnson and Cornish knew the wife was lying.

It took her coming down to the precinct three times before she cracked. Before she admitted Chase wasn't with her that night. That he never came home. That he was gone for two days. The exact two days that Jennifer Nubers' was missing.

She said her husband was acting odd. That when she asked where he'd been those nights, he said he was at his parents. But she knew for certain he wasn't there; she'd talked to his mother just the night before, called her to ask for her oatmeal raisin cookie recipe.

They put out an arrest warrant for Chase Wingleberry, picking him up at the lumberyard where he worked.

After nearly twelve hours of straight questioning, Chase Wingleberry admitted, "Yeah, I killed that bitch. A week after she tried to blackmail me, I saw her with her camera walking down the street and I grabbed her and threw her in my truck. Fucked her silly for two days at a motel, then blasted her with a lamp and tossed her out in that park."

On January 27, 1985, Chase Wingleberry was arrested for the murder of Jennifer Nubers.

His wife posted bail a couple days later, using the lien on their house for collateral for the $200,000 bond.

That night, she shot him. Then she shot herself.

...

"What the hell?" I say, setting the report down on the table.

So this woman posts her husband's bail, then kills him, then kills herself.

That was curious, but not why I am so confused.

Ingrid said this was a cold case.

It isn't.

It is a *closed* case.

Then why is she working it?

:10

"When you were driving Ingrid to the airport, did she tell you they arrested the guy who killed Jennifer?"

My dad is perched up against the back of the bed with his cell phone in his hand — no doubt playing Candy Crush.

It is 3:03 a.m.

He nods. "Yeah, but she said the powers that be think the guy gave a false confession. I guess they were going at him for like twelve hours. You can't get away with stuff like that nowadays."

"But the guy admits to seeing her, throwing her in his car, taking her to a motel, having his way with her for two days, then hitting her with a lamp."

"You didn't pick up the other binder, did you?"

I shake my head.

"That one has all the forensic stuff in it. Nothing matches. For one, they found no evidence of sexual intercourse, said she was still a virgin, still had her cherry. They didn't find any trace of her in the guy's car. Not that back then they did much DNA testing or whatever, but they didn't find any hairs or clothes or anything. Checked all the motels, hotels in the area; no one recognized seeing the guy."

I nod along.

Then why confess?

I try to imagine twelve hours sitting in an interrogation room, two detectives asking me the same question over and over and over again.

I suppose in some way, it wasn't that much different than what my mother did to me, to all her prisoners. Of course, the detectives couldn't use "enhanced interrogation" techniques, though I'm sure they got away with plenty more back then than they do now. Who knows? Maybe they beat him with phone books, slapped him around, made him pee himself.

If my mother had put me through another nightmare, another twenty-three days of hopelessness, there is no doubt I would have admitted to having the flash drive, that yes, the President did give it to me. I would have said anything to make it stop.

Maybe that's how Chase Wingleberry felt.

He just wanted it to stop.

"Why aren't you out there working the case?" I ask him.

He tilts his head to the side. I'd seen the tilt before. After I asked him how the workout regimen was going, or how the two-thousand-piece puzzle of white doves was coming, or how the new fence in the backyard was coming.

"I, uh, well."

"You gave up."

"Well, you said it yourself, it's a closed case."

"And you just said it yourself, the guy didn't do it."

He lets out a long exhale. I know he's done. His new hobby had lost its magic. He'd find something new in a couple days.

I shut the door and go into the kitchen.

Lassie and Murdock are asleep on the linoleum floor, where they come when it's sweltering, like it is this evening.

"You boys trying to cool off?" I say, then open up the freezer and put a lime popsicle next to each of them.

"Do not eat the stick this time" I say to Murdock, rubbing his huge head.

He promises not to eat the stick, then eats the stick.

I spend the first part of my day sending Ingrid an email, telling her how much I miss her and that I can't wait for her to get back. It's only a couple paragraphs, but it takes me ten minutes to perfect.

I send it at 3:13 a.m.

I gaze over the top of my laptop at the stack of Jennifer's journal entries. The pages are riveting reading, and I want to spend the next hour drinking scotch and soaking up her sixteen-year-old wit.

I can't.

Thinking about Chase Wingleberry falsely confessing to killing young Jennifer keeps bringing me back to that table in the White Room.

I need to find it.

To find her.

To find that stupid flash drive.

But how?

I am at a crossroads. I tried to get back in touch with Sidney Ewen, hoping he might send me some of the letters my mother sent him, but he'd yet to reply to my messages.

He was probably too busy shopping for a new couch, and chairs, and carpet, and a china cabinet, and whatever else Team Rampage destroyed.

What I need is to find out who my mom was working with. Ewen mentioned she had partners. Maybe if I could track them down, they could give me some direction.

There is a loud thud against the front door.

Murdock and Lassie jump up and run to the door and start barking their heads off, or in Lassie's case, making some weird almost burping noise.

"STOP BARKING!" I scream.

They don't.

"It's the fricking newspaper, you hear it every morning."

I open the door and the two idiots retreat.

Good to know.

I lean down and grab the paper.

I slip the *Washington Post* from its clear sleeve, remarking at how much smaller the paper is than it was when I lived with my father over a decade earlier.

I am walking the paper to my father's room to toss it on his bed when I stop.

The newspaper.

The ones my mom used to stuff her boots.

They were two different copies of the *Washington Post*. The article from the 1980 edition about the CIA and MK-Ultra was so captivating, I didn't even look at the paper from 1984. If I remember correctly, it was from January of that year, which was still a year before my mother would pack up her stuff. She must have been holding onto the second paper for a reason as well.

I run into the kitchen and grab a flashlight.

Lassie paws at my leg.

Meow.

"I'm going back into the shed."

Meow.

I laugh. "Yeah, maybe she did break up with her boyfriend."

I ask Murdock if he wants to come, but he is at peace sprawled out on the cool linoleum.

I pick Lassie up, slide the glass door open, and make my way to the shed.

...

I'm not sure why I stuffed the *Washington Post* pages from 1984 back in the boots.

I pull out the crumpled balls of paper and sit on the dusty floor of the shed, leaning against the soft wood.

Lassie and the bunny who lives in the shed are busy discussing something in the far back corner, perhaps her relationship status on Facebook.

I set the flashlight between my legs and begin scanning the pages of the newspaper, this copy dated January 9, 1984.

It was a Monday, and the headline on the front page is: *Redskins Super Bowl Bound!*

Apparently the Redskins beat the 49ers, 24-21, staving off a huge comeback by the 49ers in the fourth quarter.

My dad was a huge Redskins fan; maybe he was the one who kept the paper. Or was my mother a Redskins fan as well? I thought I recalled my father telling me she hated American football. That like many European-born, she thought soccer was far better.

I unfold a second page. There is an article titled "Move to Stamp Out Corruption," which peaks my interest. It details how Nigeria's new military government arrested more than 200 individuals in an attempt to stamp out official corruption.

I move on.

I unfold several more pages, but nothing jumps out.

I'm about to give up when I find one last piece of newspaper tucked in the toe of one of the boots.

I pull it out.

Uncrumple it.

It is from page three.

The article is titled "POW Escapes from Russian War Camp."

Immediately, I know the article is the reason my mom kept the paper.

A CIA operative teaching Mujahedeen interrogation tactics during the Soviet-Afghan War disappeared without a trace on April 13, 1981. He was thought dead. On January 5, 1984, he showed up at the American embassy in Iran. He'd been held captive in a Soviet prison camp for the past two and a half years and had escaped.

The CIA did not disclose the captive's name, but I knew who the man was.

He was my mother's research partner.

...

Back inside, I flip open my mother's file.

I want to make sure I have the dates right.

I do.

My mom went to Afghanistan on April 15, 1981, two days after the CIA operative disappeared. She stayed there for several weeks before returning in early May.

This couldn't have been a coincidence.

Just as my mom went to Honduras a few years later to teach their militia interrogation techniques, this guy did the same with the Mujahedeen, who were the Afghani militants battling the Soviets.

My mother didn't go — as she had a small boy (I was three at the time) — but more likely she stayed behind to continue her work on the Sleep Control Program. When her partner disappeared, she jumped on the first plane to Afghanistan to assist in the search and perhaps put her interrogation skills to good use with the Mujahedeen's captured Soviets.

I flip open my laptop.

My gut instinct, the same gut instinct which tells me which stocks to buy and sell, the same one that made me millions of dollars over the course of the past decade, is telling me this guy was her research partner at the Sleep Control Program.

I need to find him.

They might not have disclosed his name in the *Washington Post* then, but certainly over thirty years later, his name had surfaced.

I Google search, "Escaped American POW from Soviet Prison Camp 1984."

The name was disclosed.

The CIA operative was named David Sullivan.

The President's father.

...

I was looking for a connection from my mom to President Sullivan and here it was. My mother's research partner at the Sleep Control Program was Conner Sullivan's father.

I let out a long exhale.

The pieces of the puzzle were starting to fall into place.

I do an internet search on David Sullivan and click on one of the images. I expected him to be extremely tall like his son, but evidently Conner Sullivan got that from his mother's side. David Sullivan is closer to my size. He has gray-blue eyes not unlike my own. The President has similar eyes, and that isn't where the similarities with his father end. Both have the same wavy brown hair and square jaw.

I click on his bio and read it.

He was born in San Francisco in 1938. He attended Cal Tech — the same University as Sidney Ewen — graduating with a degree in chemistry. He was recruited into the CIA in 1950, working in the Technical Services Staff, the same area where Sidney Ewen got his start.

I remember back to what Sidney said, "I didn't know the ins and outs of the program. I had no idea who your mom was working with."

My ass.

David Sullivan married wife Angela in 1959. Three years later, they would have their only child.

Conner Sullivan.

The future President of the United States of America.

In 1980, David Sullivan went to Afghanistan to teach interrogation techniques to the Mujahedeen.

He disappeared on April 13, 1981.

He escaped three years later.

Back in the US, he was considered a national war hero and decided he wanted to run for public office. He entered the Virginia Senate race and won a seat that November in a landslide, a seat he would hold for almost two decades.

In September of 2001, David Sullivan and his wife were visiting New York on business before heading to the Hamptons for their annual fall getaway. The couple was eating breakfast at Windows on the World, a restaurant located on the 107th floor of the North Tower of the World Trade Center when a plane flew into the building, killing the couple and sixty-nine other patrons.

"Shit," I say out loud.

I didn't know there was a restaurant in the World Trade Center. All those people sitting down for breakfast. All those morning meetings over coffee and a scone.

All of them dead.

And Conner Sullivan's parents were two of them.

My dad walks around the corner.

I suppose I look somewhat perplexed and he asks, "You okay?"

"Did you know President Sullivan's parents were killed in 9/11?"

He nods. "Of course. The President was a city councilman at the time and he used — well, didn't *use*, that's probably the wrong word — let's just say his parents' deaths definitely put him in the spotlight, even more so than as a senator's son, and that was probably part of the reason he was elected governor the following year."

"I don't know how I could have missed that when I read his bio."

To my credit, when I saw Sullivan leave the house across the street a year earlier, having thought him responsible for Jessie Kallomatix's murder, I looked him up on Wikipedia. I only spent a couple minutes scanning the article, more concerned with his picture matching the face I saw under the streetlight.

My dad reaches into the refrigerator and pulls out a half gallon of milk. "So I was thinking about what you said," he says, "about my giving up all the time. And you know what? I'm gonna see this Jennifer Nubers thing through."

"Good for you," I say mechanically, though my thoughts are centered on David Sullivan and the fact he's dead. That I'll never be able to question him about my mom.

I look at the clock in the lower right corner of the computer.

3:56 a.m.

Where did my hour go?

There is a scraping noise and I turn.

In my haste to get back inside, I forgot about Lassie.

I slide open the glass door and Lassie saunters through.

"So," I ask, "what is your furry friend's relationship status?"

Meow.

I find myself letting out a long needed laugh.

It's complicated.

:11

A Beautiful Mind.

That's the only way I can describe it.

The scene when Jennifer Connelly walks into Russell Crowe's office and sees all the papers stuck to the wall connected by a thousand pieces of string. That's what the long wall opposite the kitchen table looks like when I walk in.

"Uh, excuse me," I say to my dad who is tacking another piece of paper to the wall.

He turns.

His face is flush, in excitement or shame, I'm not sure.

"What in the world?" I ask.

"I know," he says with a big smile. "Isn't it great?"

Not exactly the word I had in mind.

More like *crazy.*

"How long have you been at this?"

"Since I last saw you."

"You haven't slept?"

"No," he says, picking up a big mug and taking a drink.

"How many cups of coffee have you had?"

"Way, *way* too many," he says wiping a hairy forearm across his mouth. "But I have to keep going. I made a couple big discoveries."

He ushers me to sit.

I tell him to give me a couple minutes and I grab one of Isabel's premade burritos and toss it in the microwave. I do push-ups and sit-ups for the minute and a half it heats — the only exercise I expect to get — then join my dad at the table.

"You ready for this?" he asks, his entire body shaking like a hummingbird.

"Yep."

"How long do I get?"

I think this over. I was at a dead end with the search for my mother and the flash drive. Sidney Ewen wasn't returning my messages, and David Sullivan was dead. I didn't have any other avenues at the moment that I could pursue.

"I'll let you know when to stop."

"Okay," he says, with a wide smile. "So, like I told you before, the detectives had the timeline all wrong. I don't know who put the journal back together, but he sure as shit didn't see any movies in 1984."

I nod.

"So, I figure there are three theories for who killed her. It was either someone she *already* blackmailed or it was someone she was *currently* blackmailing or it was someone she was *planning* to blackmail. You follow?"

I have a huge bite of burrito in my mouth and nod.

"I have a hard time believing that someone who she already blackmailed would kill her. I mean, she was this young girl, she was charging such small sums, she never went back to the well, and she said — and even that idiot Chase verified — that if they didn't pay her, she gave them the photos anyway."

"I don't know, I can see someone getting extremely pissed off they were being blackmailed."

"Yeah, maybe, but according to her journal, it sounds like most of them were pretty okay with it. Two hundred bucks and they are scared straight for the rest of their lives. Hell, Jennifer Nubers was probably responsible for repairing more marriages than Viagra."

I chuckle.

"And I figure if one of these guys killed her, he would just do it. He wouldn't keep her for two days."

I see where my dad is going with his logic. I say, "And there were no signs of sexual abuse, so they weren't keeping her all that time for that."

"I think they were interrogating her."

"Looking for whatever pictures she took."

"Right."

"Why wouldn't she just give them up? I mean, why would she care? They were just people having affairs."

"Yes, but what if this time it wasn't an affair? What if she stumbled on some people who were into something worse?"

"Did you read the whole journal?" I ask. "Does she mention something like that? Like drugs, or guns, or the mafia or something?"

"No, but lots of the journal pages are unaccounted for. The ending of some entries. The beginnings. Sometimes it's just the middle pages. They either blew away or someone took them."

"So, the journal entry we're looking for might not even be in that pile?"

"Right."

"That's disheartening."

"Well, we have to work with what we have and hope we get lucky."

"Which is why you've recreated the wall from *A Beautiful Mind*."

"Yeah," he laughs. "Please don't commit me."

"No promises."

He laughs again, then says, "It is fitting you would mention movies, seeing as how that is how I was able to piece the journal together chronologically. The way I figure it, the last few entries are the ones Jennifer hadn't dealt with yet. The ones she hadn't closed the books on."

I look at the journal pages thumbtacked to the walls of the kitchen. They are in stacks — three pages, two pages, four pages — arranged by entry. There looks to be around forty.

"How many entries?"

"Around eighty, but these are the only ones that detail the people she was blackmailing."

"And the strings?"

"I connected the entries to any other entry she mentions. So for instance, in the third entry, she calls a guy '4th and Lex,' and she mentions him again in the seventh entry, that he paid."

"And let me guess, that's what the red and blue sticky notes are for."

"Red is paid, blue is unpaid, yellow is unknown."

"And green?"

"Green has a list of each entry's highlights and any points of reference as to the timeline."

"Wow, I'm impressed. I've never seen you do anything so—"

"*Organized.* I know. I'm quite proud of myself."

"Slow down, hotshot, you have a long way to go." I add, "Okay, so how many of the guys paid?"

"Twenty-seven paid, four called her bluff, and nine are unknown."

"Did she ever blackmail any women?"

"Not at first, but eventually she blackmailed a few. Jennifer wrote that she couldn't deal with all the crying. The guys, they just paid. The women, they felt guilty and they wanted to explain to her why they did it. And Jennifer — she didn't much care."

"And, of course, there could be several more entries that are missing, that aren't even up there."

"Correct."

"Okay, I feel pretty up to speed. So, the order you have them in is different than the order they were put in by the detectives?"

"Not a whole lot different, but yes. I marked each page with how the detectives ordered them, but I don't think they were putting too much emphasis on the journal — there were quite a few little details they missed."

"And using the movies Megan and her boyfriend went to, you were able to put them in the correct order."

"It wasn't just the movies, though they were a big help. It was Megan and Derrick's anniversaries, Jennifer and James' relationship, and of course—" his face flushes in embarrassment, "— the size of her boobs."

I laugh at my dad's prudishness.

"Wait," I say. "Who is James?"

"Jennifer's boyfriend."

I smile. This makes me happy.

"I didn't read about him. And Megan doesn't mention him when the detectives interview her."

"He was Derrick's cousin. They only dated for a couple months, then James and his family moved to South Africa."

"So, Jennifer and Megan are cousins and they were dating Derrick and James who are also cousins."

"Right."

"And this James was never a suspect?"

"He was in South Africa."

"Right."

I get up from the table and grab a smoothie from the fridge, then I spend the next four minutes surveying my dad's wall of chaos. Mostly I am interested in the green sticky notes, the highlights.

I move down the line, reading them:

K and 1st
Guy in suit and red tie
Follows to car, takes pictures of him kissing woman.
Megan and Derrick go see Karate Kid
—

H and New York
Woman in black skirt
Meets up with woman in blue skirt
Go to motel
Derrick introduces Jennifer to James
All four go to Revenge of the Nerds
—

Ridge and 4th
Black guy in jeans and white T-shirt
Meets up with two women.
Sees her taking photos and shouts at her
She runs
Doesn't blackmail
Jennifer and James go on first real date
Chili's and a movie, Purple Rain
She gets first kiss!

I laugh. "Did you have to put an exclamation point after *she gets her first kiss?*"

"That's a big deal for a girl," my dad says with a big smile.

"Yeah, who was your first kiss?"

"Fifth grade. Jeannie McAndrews."

His gaze is far away; he's back in that kiss. When he returns he asks, "And yours?"

"I think it was the prom you set up for me. The lady from your work's daughter."

"Right, what was her name? Margaret Rooten's daughter. Jill or something?"

"That was it, Jill Rooten."

"She wasn't very cute," my dad says with a laugh. "Sorry about that."

"You tried," I tell him.

It couldn't have been easy to convince your coworker to have her daughter wake up at two in the morning and get ready for prom in a guy's living room for an hour.

"Margaret actually posted some of Jill's wedding pictures a couple years ago, and she really turned out beautiful. I think maybe she had the bump in her nose fixed."

Good for her.

My dad says he will be right back and disappears from the room.

I look up at the wall clock.

3:16 a.m.

He returns a moment later with a large atlas. He opens it up, rifles through pages, then rips out four of the two-foot tall pages.

I watch as he removes a framed picture from the wall in the living room and tacks the pages to the wall, creating nearly a four-foot map of DC.

He grabs a green thumbtack from his pocket, hovers over the map for a long couple seconds, then pushes it in. He says, "This is the park where Jennifer Nubers' body was found." He pushes in three more green thumbtacks. "This is the school where she was last seen . . . this is Bob, her stepdad's, place . . . and this is her mom's house."

He hands me the box of thumbtacks and walks into the kitchen.

"I think it will help to visualize where she photographed all her marks. Maybe it will spark something."

"Couldn't hurt," I say.

He starts calling out the intersections Jennifer nicknamed the people she was blackmailing. Washington, DC, is a grid of numbered streets and lettered streets and most have one or the other, some both. She shortened most of the longer street names: Lexington became Lex, Manchester became Man, Massachusetts became Mass.

2nd and R. Paid. Red.

3rd and H. Paid. Red.
D and Mass. Red.
H and North Capitol. Yellow.
7th and Kentucky. Red.
G and Man. Yellow.
Plymouth and Spruce. Didn't pay. Blue.
2nd and Lex. Red.
"What's at 2nd and Lex?" I ask.
"The Wilmore Motel. Seems to be a favorite spot for an illicit affair."
He keeps going.
Ten more.
Five more.
Until the entire four feet of map is littered with red, blue, and yellow thumbtacks.
He yells out the final five:
L and 13th. Red.
S and Man. Yellow.
3rd and Kentucky. Red.
4th and A. Blue.
4th and Constitution. Yellow.
"Is that all of them?" I ask.
"Yep," he says, walking over.
The two of us stand in the living room, gazing at the map.
"There are five at the Wilmore."
He nods. "Yeah, but they all paid."
"True."
"Let's concentrate on the yellows."
"Right, but wouldn't it make sense it would be the last one, the one on 4th and Constitution, that got her killed?"
"It would, though the last one she was working was a woman."
"The woman could have paid a guy to kill her. Or I mean, she could have done it herself. Jennifer was tiny."
He shrugs, but I can tell his gut is telling him it had nothing to do with the woman.
"Okay, so there are nine yellows," my dad says, pointing out each one with his finger.
He gets to the eighth one. The second to last.
"S and Man."

"Do we know what is there? Where they went?"

He walks to the kitchen and grabs the green sticky note off the entry and returns.

He hands me the green sticky note:

S and Man.
Guy in suit leaves Capitol Building.
Jennifer thinks he is a congressman.
Meets woman.
Went to A Nightmare on Elm Street with Megan and Derrick.

I stare at the green sticky note. Something on it is pinging, but I can't make out what.

A congressman?

That might be a big deal, but that isn't it.

It's the intersection.

S and Man.

S Street and Manchester Avenue.

For some reason, I feel like I know something there. I'd driven downtown DC with my father a handful of times, but mostly to see the touristy stuff: the Jefferson Memorial, the White House, the Smithsonian.

What was it about S and Man that intrigues me?

"Holy shit," I blurt a moment later.

"What?" my dad asks.

"S and Man," I say.

"What about it?"

"Put it together."

He shakes his head. "What do you mean?"

"S-and-Man. Put it all together."

"Oh my God!" he shouts. "S-and-Man. *Sandman.*"

"This is it," I say. "This is Project Sandman."

:12

"You think it could be?" my dad asks, unconvinced. "You think this could be the Project Sandman that Ewen was talking about?"

"Think about it," I say. "Think about what Maggie said before we walked in, that sometimes Ewen will hear something that triggers him and that's when he gets all loopy."

"Yeah, so?"

I pull out my cell phone and find the recording from our sit-down. It takes me a moment to scroll to the right spot. I hit play.

Me: You don't know of the White Room? Where it might be located?

Ewen: I haven't spoken to Elena in over a decade. The last contact I had with her was just after 9/11. She was obsessed with something called Project Sandman.

Me: What is Project Sandman?

Ewen: [shouts] Who are you? Did Reagan send you? . . . Someone over there is tipping off the Russians and we need to find this mole before the entire war turns on its head.

Me: Mr. Ewen . . . Take a deep breath. We are in your study. It's 2015.

Ewen: Who are you? You tell Reagan that I will do everything, will use every material we've created, to find the mole.

My dad: Mr. Ewen [shouts] Sidney!

I hit stop.

"You're right," my dad says, "Project Sandman is what set him off."

I nod. "Sent him back to when Reagan was president."

"Which was most of the eighties."

"And Jennifer Nubers was killed in 1985."

My dad inhales. "That's the same year your mom left."

I never made that connection.

"You're right."

"Jennifer Nubers was killed on January 12, 1985. The last time I saw your mother was four days after that."

The last time I saw my mom was on my sixth birthday, which would have been nearly a month before, then she went away on a work trip.

I never saw her again.

"January 16, 1985," my dad says. "Your mother came home, told me she was leaving and packed up those boxes. She said she would send me an address to mail them to her later, but she never did."

"It all fits."

His eyebrows jump.

He runs to the wall and rips off the "S and Man" entry. He skims, then reads out loud:

> *"I followed him from the Capitol Building. He was with a bunch of other guys in suits and there were a couple of television crews. I asked one of the guys videotaping what was going on and he said that they'd just finished inaugurating all the first-term congressmen in some ceremony. A CONGRESSMAN! He's all right looking I guess. He kept looking over his shoulder. That's why I followed him."*

"And then a page is missing," he interjects. "Or maybe two. Who knows? But then it continues."

> *". . . gets on the subway. I know I shouldn't keep following him, but I can't stop. He gets off on 3rd and H and goes into three or four shops. I can tell he's trying to lose anyone that might be tailing him. But he isn't looking for a sixteen-year-old girl, that's for sure. The last store he goes into, he comes out with a beautiful brunette. I zoom in real close and take a picture of her face. I wish I had her eyes. They are emerald green.*

"It's gotta be her," my dad says.

I agree.

"Keep reading," I tell him.

"I expect the guy to kiss her but he doesn't. I don't think they are having an affair, but they are up to something, that's for sure. They both look over their shoulders, then they walk for three blocks to an office building near S and Man. I snap a dozen photographs. These are going to be worth more than just two hundred bucks. A whole lot more.

"The Sleep Control Program," I say.
"Maybe," my dad says.
"What do you mean, *maybe?* This congressman must have been involved. Maybe he was funneling her money. Or maybe she was funneling them money to keep it quiet. Or passing along intel."
"Your mom was a CIA agent. It could have been any number of things."
"I wish there were more pages. I wish we knew what happened after that."
"I'm guessing she followed them a second time. We may never know what she found."
"Well, whatever it was, it was worth killing over."

...

I check something in one of the binders, then I tell my dad my theory.
"These two, for whatever reason, are not supposed to be seen together. Jennifer takes photos. She attempts to blackmail the congressman, but she gets greedy. Asks for a couple thousand dollars, maybe more. Who knows? He tells her it will take him a couple days to get the money. Maybe a week. Maybe two. She's patient. She has time, so she keeps blackmailing a few more people. When he doesn't pay, she threatens to send the pics to the paper or some other government official. They decide it's too big a risk. Even if they pay her, what's stopping her from leaking copies? So that's when mom steps in. This is what she does for a living. She interrogates people. She gets answers."
In the binder, I'd flipped to Jennifer Nubers' autopsy report, then skimmed to the line about toxicology.

"They found traces of LSD in her bloodstream," I tell him.

My dad's mouth opens wide. He says, "She tortured her. That's why she was gone for two days. She did to her what they did to you."

Yeah, but with one big difference.

She didn't *kill* me.

...

There is one more piece that needs to fit. One more link in the chain.

I pick up my cell phone and dial Ingrid.

She doesn't answer and I hang up and dial again. On the fourth ring, she answers groggily, "Hey."

"Hi, honey."

"I didn't expect to hear from you today."

"How is your mom doing?"

"About the same as yesterday. She'll have to go to a speech therapist, but they think she'll make a full recovery."

"That's great to hear." I pause, then add. "But, actually, that's not why I called."

I can hear her readjust herself in bed. "Is something wrong? Did something happen to Lassie?"

"No, nothing like that. Everyone is okay." I take a deep breath. "I need to know who wanted you to look into Jennifer Nubers' murder."

She lets out a laugh. "Don't tell me your dad sucked you into that old case?"

"He did."

"I told him it was a closed case, that they arrested the guy who did it, that his wife blew his brains out."

"Yeah, I know. I can't get into it now. I just need to know who asked you to look into the case."

She could feel the angst in my voice. "Um, my captain."

"Yeah, but it's not his jurisdiction. This happened in DC."

"He didn't tell me much. He just told me I was off all my active cases and I was supposed to look into this. He said it was a closed case and it seemed pretty open and shut, but if

I would spend a week looking into it, he would think of it as a personal favor to him."

"I need you to find out who wanted him to look into it."

"Okay, I'll call him tomorrow."

"No, I need you to call him *now*."

I'd never said anything like this to her before.

"What's going on?"

"I'll have my dad tell you after I fall asleep. I only have four minutes left and I need you to do this. Please."

"Okay, but promise me your dad is going to tell me what's going on."

"I promise."

She hangs up.

My dad and I look at each other, then look at the clock.

3:56.

3:57.

3:58.

My dad says, "'You better go lie down—"

My phone rings.

I put it on speaker.

"Did you get a hold of him?" I ask.

"Yeah, he wasn't thrilled, but I asked him who wanted him to look into the case."

"And?"

"He didn't know. He got the order from his boss, the Virginia Police Commissioner."

"Damn it."

"Don't worry. I made my captain call him."

"And he did?"

"Yeah, I had to promise some favors, but he came through."

"Who did the commissioner say asked him to look into the case?"

"He said it was President Sullivan."

...

When I wake up the next day and walk into the kitchen, Ingrid is sitting at the kitchen table with my dad. Lassie is sitting in her lap, and Murdock is under her chair.

Ingrid jumps up when I round the corner, sending Lass-ie flailing to the ground.

"Honey!" she yells, rushing me.

I pull her into a long kiss. I nearly forgot how much I loved her lips. Loved every inch of her.

"What are you doing here?" I ask.

"Well, after you went to sleep last night, your dad filled me in, and I booked the first flight out."

"Is your dad gonna be okay without you?"

"Oh, yeah, they're sending mom home today, and my aunt will be there. I was going to fly back the next day anyhow. Plus, I just missed you so much."

She gives me another long kiss, then breaks away.

"This is crazy. Project Sandman or whatever and your mom. It's hard to believe."

"But, do you?"

"After all your dad told me, yeah, I do."

"What about President Sullivan?"

"I don't know where he fits, but he is definitely the one who put the wheels in motion."

"I'm gonna call him."

My dad says, "Good luck. He's in Russia at some big conference."

I whip out my cell and dial the number the President gave me.

He doesn't answer.

I ponder leaving a message, something along the lines of, "Hey, Conner, it's Henry. Just wondering why you wanted my girlfriend to look into a thirty-year-old murder case that involves my mother. Holla back."

I put the phone down and head for the kitchen. I grab some yogurt and some Grape Nuts, then join Ingrid and my father at the kitchen table.

"So, we've made some headway," my dad says. "We made a list of all the congressmen in 1985. Because of what Jennifer wrote, we narrowed it down to just the first-termers."

"So how many were there?"

"Twenty-seven."

"You track any of them down yet?"

"About half. Others are unlisted, some moved out of country, some died."

"We've ruled out a few already," Ingrid says. "Guys

who didn't fit the bill. Who couldn't possibly be confused for handsome."

"How many are left?"

"Twelve."

"That's not too bad. Narrowed down from three billion, twelve guys who were possibly involved in Jennifer's murder?"

"Yeah, but they're scattered all over the globe. Arkansas, Colorado, Germany, Iowa. And it's gonna be nearly impossible to verify alibis for those days. I mean, we're talking over thirty years ago."

"What I don't understand is why the DC detectives didn't look into this back then. They said they could only track down three of the guys Jennifer blackmailed, but they obviously could have tracked down this congressman if they really wanted to."

"I'm sure they would have if Wingleberry didn't cop to the murder so early on. He'd confessed and taken a bullet through the head within two weeks of Jennifer's murder."

She's right. They would have no reason to stir up a political conspiracy after Wingleberry confessed.

After a long moment, I say, "We need to find the pictures."

Both my dad and Ingrid turn and glare at me.

"The pictures?" my dad asks.

"They interrogated her for two days and then they ended up killing her, which means that most likely, she didn't give them the pictures."

My dad nods.

"But why?" Ingrid asks. "I mean, she openly gave the pictures to the men she was blackmailing, even the ones who didn't pay."

"She got greedy. Maybe she wanted to buy a car. Maybe, this time she was trying to get a lot more money"

"Yes, but the second they grabbed her, began interrogating her, she would have quickly forgotten about the money and told them where to find the pictures."

True.

If they'd done to her what they'd done to me — given her a twenty-three-hour nightmare — there is no way she wouldn't have cracked, no way she wouldn't have given up the location of the pictures.

Unless.

"Unless, she didn't have them," I say. "Unless, she gave them to someone who she feared these people might hurt."

The three of us look at each other in unison. There were only two people Jennifer might have given the photographs to.

Megan.

Or her brother.

:13

"No, I haven't been ignoring you," I tell Lassie.

Meow.

"Well, I'm sorry if you feel that way. Maybe we can play with some string later."

Meow.

"I wasn't patronizing you."

I dangle fake string in front of him. His little head sways back and forth. He swats at the invisible string with his paw.

Meow.

"I know, you can't help it."

Meow.

"It *is* a sickness."

I stand up and move to my dresser.

It is 3:02 a.m.

"I was gonna wait to give this to you for your birthday next month, but I suppose I can give it to you now."

He perks up on the bed.

"Close your eyes."

He does.

I remove the contents from the Amazon box — the package came three days earlier, but I was waiting to give it to him — and put it behind my back.

"Okay, you can open your eyes now."

He does.

I move my hand from my back, revealing a pack of four jingle balls (four different colors), packaged in mesh netting.

Meow.

"No, this isn't some kind of sick joke." I toss the pack on the bed right in front of him. "Have at it."

He looks at the four balls, his yellow eyes starting to mist over.

"Are you crying?"

Meow.

"What are you allergic to? Cats?"

He ignores me.

"Go ahead, open it."

He slashes at the netting and the balls spill out, falling to the floor in a mass of jingling bells.

Lassie jumps down, darts toward the blue one. Then stops, darts toward the red one. Stops, yellow. Stops, green. He wants to play with all of them at the same time.

There is a loud crash, the sound of Murdock hitting the side of the doorframe as he tries to enter.

Now I remember why I was waiting to give Lassie the balls until we moved back home.

Murdock.

If they made Lassie crazy. They made Murdock down right psycho.

"Don't do it," I tell Murdock.

He ignores me.

Murdock grabs the blue jingle ball in his giant mouth and swallows it.

Then the green.

Then the yellow.

Then the red.

It is what Lassie will forever refer to as the Jingle Ball Massacre.

Murdock leaves as quickly as he came.

Lassie's jaw is slack.

He looks at me.

Meow.

"I am not going to go 'Old Yeller' him."

He takes a deep breath, then crawls under the bed.

...

"That's him," my dad says. "That's Jennifer's brother."

I look at the images on the computer. Markus Nubers is in the neighborhood of forty, slightly overweight, and balding. According to his LinkedIn profile — side note: I

learned my dad has a LinkedIn account, which is odd because he doesn't have a job — Markus is a father of three
and a regional sales representative for an automotive parts
conglomerate. He lives in Delaware City, Delaware.
"Have you heard from Ingrid?" I ask. "Did she talk to
him yet?"
He shakes his head. "I haven't heard from her all day."
"What about Megan? Did you find her?"
"Yeah, but she was much harder to find. She changed
her name a couple times, but there was an old photo of her
in the newspaper from after Jennifer's death, and I was able
to match it to one of the pictures that came up in a Google
images search."
He clicks on a separate tab on his laptop. It is Megan
Nubers', now Megan Klein's, Facebook page.
"We aren't friends so there are only a couple pictures."
He clicks on her photo.
She is a moderately attractive forty-something woman.
Dark brown hair, light brown eyes.
My dad clicks through three more pictures.
No husband.
No kids.
She does have a big fluffy dog.
"I think that is one of those goldendoodles," my dad
said.
"What are you, a breeder now?"
"No," he laughs. "The neighbors down three houses
have one. Doodles. Murdock loves him."
"Wait, they named their goldendoodle Doodles?"
He nods.
We both give a quick laugh. Once composed, I ask,
"Where does Megan live?"
"Somewhere up north. I'm sure Ingrid will have no
problem finding her."
Speaking of Ingrid, I check my phone for any updates.
Nothing.
Not to mention that the President still hadn't called.
Fricking Putin.
My dad lets out a long yawn, arms extending high to-
ward the ceiling, then tells me he's exhausted and is going
to bed. He does add that if Ingrid calls or texts to wake him.

I tell him I will.

I walk into the kitchen. It is spotless, evidence Isabel had been by the previous day.

I cross my fingers and open the fridge.

Lasagna.

"Yes."

I cut two huge slices, then get them heating. I walk to my bedroom and lift the bed skirt and peek underneath.

Lassie is on his side.

I reach out my hand and grab him by the tail and slide him out. He doesn't move.

I check his pulse.

Alive.

"Hey, buddy. I have just the thing to cheer you up?"

Meow.

"No, I didn't chop Murdock up into a million pieces and feed him to a bunch of ducks."

He sighs.

"I have a big piece of lasagna heating up for you."

He snorts.

"Come on, I know how much you love lasagna."

Meow.

"Who is Garfield?"

Meow.

"Seriously, I have no idea." I stand up. "Well, come out and eat with me if you want."

I leave the room.

A minute later, I'm situated at the table with half a foot of lasagna and thirty-two ounces of milk. There is a plate under the table with a small slice and a saucer of milk.

I snag my laptop and log onto Google Earth. I spent ten minutes playing around with the program when I was searching for accommodations for Ingrid's and my trip to Alaska.

I pull up the image of downtown DC, then scroll until I find the intersection of S Street and Manchester Ave.

I zoom in to street level and begin making my way down the street. The intersection is a hub of activity and businesses line both sides of both streets.

The corner intersection has a gas station, a Wendy's, an office building, and another office building.

I move the cursor down S Street, then down Manchester Ave, noting all the buildings the congressman and my mother might have entered, though over the course of the past thirty years, many of the businesses had presumably changed hands.

Was it possible that inside one of those buildings could be the headquarters of the Sleep Control Program?

Maybe back in 1985 that was the case, but certainly it was moved since then. They wouldn't put a black op within two miles of the White House? Would they?

No, the Sleep Control Program is located in Michigan, where they found me.

Or somewhere close by.

Maybe even Canada.

I hear a huff and I peek under the table.

Lassie is sitting there like a stone statue, staring at the lasagna. He looks like he just went fifteen rounds in the boxing ring.

I give his head a rub and tell him I ordered him another pack of jingle balls and that we can move back to our house at the end of the week.

This appears to cheer him up, and he begins nibbling away at the lasagna.

I order his balls off Amazon, then Google "Garfield." I skim the Wikipedia and read a couple of the sample comic strips they have.

I tell Lassie, "Garfield, lasagna. I get it now."

He laughs.

At 3:58 a.m., I carry Lassie to bed. I lay back on the pillow. There is a rustling sound.

I must have been too preoccupied to notice it when I woke up.

I reach my hand into the pillow and slip out a white envelope. "Henry" is scribbled on the front in Isabel's handwriting. She must have slipped it in my pillow while I was sleeping.

I open it and remove the contents.

It is one page.

The letterhead at top reads "DNA Testing of America."

When my father left to take Ingrid to the airport, I went into his room and pulled a couple of his hairs from a comb.

Then I plucked out a couple of my own. That's what was in the envelope I stashed in the bushes for Isabel.

I swallow hard as I read the words: *Not a paternal match.*

:14

My dad isn't my dad. My dad isn't my dad. My dad isn't my dad.

Those are the only five words I can think. The only five words in my vocabulary.

My.

Dad.

Isn't.

My.

Dad.

I gaze over at the clock on the dash.

3:05 a.m.

For five minutes, I'd stayed in bed, those five words running over my eyes.

I look down at Lassie asleep on my chest. I want to tell him. To tell him the guy in the other room isn't my dad. That he is an imposter. A fraud.

"You gonna ever get out of bed, Sonny Boy?"

I gaze up.

There is a man standing in the doorway of my room.

Gray hair, glasses pushed down on his nose, flannel shirt, tan khakis.

"Yep, just thinking."

"I've got some food ready for you."

I nod and smile. "Sounds good. Be out in a minute."

I push Lassie off me and spend the next five minutes in the shower. It is the longest shower I have ever taken.

When I finally get dressed it is 3:15 a.m.

A quarter of my day is gone.

My dad — sorry, Richard — has food waiting for me at the table. Spaghetti. Garlic bread. A tall glass of milk.

I stare at him.

Glare at him.

I'm furious.

Then I get furious for getting furious. How could I possibly be mad at this man? Whether or not he was my biological father, he was still my dad.

Right?

I contemplate telling him.

He asks, "Are you gonna sit—"

The front door opens. It's Ingrid.

"You are not gonna believe this," she says.

...

Ingrid woke up next to Henry for the first time in over ten days. It felt so good to sleep next to him. To feel the heat radiate off his body. Lassie was sleeping on her chest, nestled between her boobs — his new favorite spot — and she lifted him up and moved him to Henry's chest.

She then gave both her 'guys' a quick kiss on the forehead, then jumped out of bed and threw on her clothes.

Jeans and a gray top.

Homicide Detective chic.

On her way to the Alexandria Police Department headquarters twenty minutes away, she chatted with her dad over the phone.

Her mother had just been released from the hospital and her parents were driving back to their house. She was in good spirits though she would get frustrated whenever she tried to speak. Her first speech therapy session would be the following afternoon. Ingrid spoke to her mom briefly, telling her she would be screaming answers to Jeopardy in no time at all.

Her mother mumbled back something that sounded like, 'A boov yoog.'

"I love you too," Ingrid replied, hoping that's what her mother was trying to say.

Ten minutes later, she pulled into the parking lot of the police department.

By the time she reached her captain's office, more than fifteen people had asked her how her mother was doing. She gave the same reply to each: her mom was doing great, she was out of the hospital, and she was expected to make a full recovery. Ingrid had never been hugged so many times in her life.

She opened the door to her captain's office, stepped through, and let out an audible exhale.

Captain James Marshall was behind his desk. He was an impressive looking man in his fifties with the buzzed hair of a lifetime military man, of which he never spent a day in his life.

"I swear," Ingrid said. "If one more person asks me—"

"How is your mom doing?" the captain asked with a big smile.

Ingrid flipped him off.

"Oh, and thanks again for the four a.m. wake-up call two nights ago. That sure went over well with my wife."

"You're a police captain. You should be used to getting calls in the middle of the night."

"Not on the landline in my house."

Ingrid laughed. "Did I really call your landline?"

"Sure did."

"Sorry about that."

"Water under the bridge, though remember you promised to go to Linda's next Tupperware party."

"I will, I promise."

"Oh and you owe me a hundred bucks for the Nationals tickets I had to buy."

"What?"

"For the commissioner, for waking *him* up at four in the morning."

Ingrid opened her wallet and tossed a hundred dollar bill on the desk. "My dad gave me that two days ago to buy some duty-free stuff at the airport."

Marshall laughed.

Ingrid half expected him to hand the money back to her, but he folded it up and stuck it in his wallet.

"Okay," he said. "So are you back officially? Or is this a pop-in?"

"No, I'm back. I just wanted to fill you in on some stuff before I get to digging?"

"This have something to do with that phone call?"

"Yeah."

She spent the next thirty minutes filling Marshall in on the particulars. Ingrid had known James for nearly ten years. He was her first partner when she joined the force. After two years, he became her sergeant, then two years ago, he became her captain. Ingrid knew whatever she told him would stay with him.

"Holy shit," he said.

"I know."

"It will be difficult to prove one of these congressmen from thirty years ago had anything to do with the girl's murder."

"I agree."

"Is that why you figure Sullivan wanted you to look into it? To try to put a stop to this Sleep Control Program."

"I think so. I think maybe he got wind Henry's mother might be connected to the murder, and if I investigated it, I would stumble on the answers."

"Why not just call you and tell you directly? Or tell Henry? They're buddy-buddy, aren't they?"

"He probably didn't want to get Henry's hopes up. He knew that if I investigated it and came up with the same connection, then there was some truth to the rumors."

"Okay, so where do you go from here?"

Ingrid told him their theory that the photographs Jennifer took were still out there somewhere. That maybe Jennifer gave the pictures to her cousin or her brother.

"That's pretty far-fetched. I mean, it's been thirty years."

"It's our only hope."

"Okay, so what do you need from me?"

"I need help," Ingrid said. "I need Billy."

Marshall took a deep breath, pushed back six inches in his seat. Finally he said, "Fine, but if anybody asks, we never had this conversation."

"What conversation?"

...

I put up my hand to stop her.

"So, do you think that's true about the President?" I

ask. "Could Sullivan have wanted you to look into the case because he heard a rumor my mother might be involved?"

"That would make sense," Ingrid says. "Think about it. You called and told President Sullivan what your mom did to you. That she tortured you and that she is looking for some flash drive. A flash drive he gave you. He didn't give you one, but maybe this sparks something from his memory, that maybe your mother was involved with this conspiracy, a murder from thirty years earlier. He figures this is the only connection he can think of, so he calls the Virginia Police Commissioner and asks him to call my captain and have me look into the case."

I nod.

"Has Sullivan called you back yet?"

"No."

"He's in Russia," my dad says. "Trying to stop a second Cold War from happening. I think that takes priority."

For a quick moment, I remember he's not my biological father. I push the thought from my mind.

I tell Ingrid, "Ok, keep going."

...

"The Captain okayed this?" Billy asked from the passenger seat.

"Unofficially, yes. But if anyone finds out you're working a case while suspended, he'll deny it."

"Ok, you can drop me off here."

Ingrid turned to look at him. To make sure he was kidding.

He was.

Billy was so excited when she showed up on his doorstep that he nearly shed a tear. Ingrid spent the last half an hour filling him in on the case.

"So, which house are we headed to first?"

"Megan's. She lives about an hour north of here. Then we'll head up to Delaware and see if we can track down her brother."

"And you couldn't do this by yourself because?"

"Because you're an idiot and people tell you things they won't tell me." Which was true, but it also had to do with

Ingrid being an attractive woman. No matter how hard she tried to downplay it, sometimes when she interviewed women, Ingrid could feel they were threatened by her and would clam up. It was even worse with the men; they would boast and flirt and it was nearly impossible to get a straight answer out of them. Billy was harmless. Men and women opened up to him like no one she'd seen before.

"Touché," he said with a big smile, his too-big teeth white and even.

"And I missed you."

"Aww."

Ingrid did miss him.

Billy was full Italian and his forearms were covered in thick black hair. Some of the women on the force thought he was sexy, and he'd made his way through most of them in his short two years in homicide. Ingrid wasn't attracted to him at all and continually reminded him deodorant only cost $4. Regardless, she adored him, he was like the little brother she never had. Plus, the couple times Henry met him, the two got along amazingly.

Twenty minutes later, Ingrid parked in front of a condominium complex.

She called the number she had for Megan Klein.

Megan answered on the third ring.

Ingrid told her who she was and asked if she had time for a couple questions.

She did.

"Are you home?" Ingrid asked. Ingrid knew she was; a blue Nissan Altima that matched her plates was parked in the lot.

"I am."

"Well, we're right outside. We'll be at your door in thirty seconds."

Megan was standing in the doorway when Ingrid and Billy walked up the steps to her second story condo.

The three shook hands and introduced themselves.

"This is about Jennifer?" Megan asked.

"Yes."

"But they found the guy who did it thirty years ago."

"You're right, they did. We're just trying to tie up some loose ends."

"Okay, well, anything I can do to help," she said, her eyes lingering on Billy.

"We really do appreciate it," Billy said with a smile.

Megan invited them in.

"Sorry about the mess," she said. "I'm going through a divorce right now and I'm trying to sort through some things."

Ingrid couldn't help notice how she emphasized the word divorce. She wanted Billy to know that although she was Megan Klein now, she was single and ready to mingle.

She offered them drinks, which both declined, then met them in the living room. After some light pleasantries, Ingrid asked, "So, Jennifer — we understand that she was blackmailing people for money."

"Yeah, she was. I told her it was going to get her killed." She takes a huge breath. "And it did."

"All the pictures she took of these people, what happened to them?"

"Well, she gave them to the person. Whether or not she got paid for them. And she said that she never made copies. She said she didn't want them around."

Billy asked, "So she never gave you any, never asked you to hold onto some pictures for her?"

"No."

"Never?"

"Never."

Ingrid asked, "Could she have hidden them with you and not told you?"

"I mean, maybe, but I'm sure I would have found them by now." She gazed into the opposite room, at the five boxes of stuff scattered about on the carpet. "I've been divorced twice, moved four times, I think I would have come across them by now."

"What about your house?"

"Oh, I don't know. It's possible. She was living with us for some time, and she was welcome to come and go whenever. My parents gave her a key when she was about ten."

"Do your parents still live in the same house?"

"No, they moved to Florida about six years back."

"Do you know the owners?" Billy asked.

"No," she said, shaking her head. "But I'm sure I could find out if it would help."

Ingrid hid back a smile. Had she come alone, Megan wouldn't have been going the extra mile to help. But for Billy.

"That would be great," Billy said.

Megan promised to make some calls and to get back to them. Billy gave her his card. She took it with a smile.

After a quick bite, they headed toward Delaware.

The drive took an hour.

Billy slept most of the way and Ingrid listened to a classic rock station Billy hated. He was into hip-hop.

At 4:35 p.m., she pulled into an industrial complex.

America Auto Parts Inc.

They asked the secretary if Markus Nubers was in and were directed down a short hallway to an open office door.

Markus Nubers was on the phone. He looked much the same in person as he did in the photographs Ingrid had seen online. Balding, twenty pounds overweight. He was wearing a white polo with AAI embroidered on the front.

They waited patiently in the doorway for Markus to finish his call before walking in.

His eyes moved down Ingrid's body, then he smiled and said, "You guys the IRS folks?"

Ingrid and Billy looked at each other and fought down smiles.

"No," Ingrid said. "We're with the Alexandria Police Department."

"Oh, is this about that speeding ticket?"

"No, we're here about your sister."

His face fell.

"She was killed in DC. What's that have to do with Alexandria? Plus, they got the guy. His wife blew his brains out. Justice was served."

She gave the same story, "Just trying to tie up some loose ends."

He shrugged and offered them a chair.

Ingrid asked, "Were you aware your sister was blackmailing these guys?"

"No, not until the police told us."

"Who is us?"

"Me and my mom."

"Where is she now?"

"Same house."

"Remarried?"

"No, but she's got a guy."

Billy asked, "So your sister never showed you any of the pictures?"

"Nope."

"Could she have hidden them in your stuff somewhere? Or her stuff?"

"The cops went through a lot of her stuff during the investigation. As for my stuff, I don't know why she would."

"In her journal, she writes that you were always snooping around, trying to read her journal."

"You have her journal?"

"Just the pages that were found at the crime scene."

"Right."

He took a deep breath and said, "You don't think that I might be able to get those pages, do you? It would be great to hear her voice."

"I'll do my best," Ingrid said. "But back to the question, did you read her journal?"

He scoffed, "No."

Billy asked, "But you would look for it, right?"

He shrugged. "Yeah, I guess. The first time I found it by accident. I was looking for something in her room — these pink scissors, I think — and I found it." He let out a small chuckle. "I only read a little."

"So, you did read her journal," Ingrid said, a bit more brusquely than she intended.

"Just enough to get under my sister's skin."

Ingrid gave a slight apologetic nod.

He continued, "When she got home after school, I asked her who some boy was and why she wanted to kiss him so badly. She freaked out."

"Let me guess," Billy said. "Then she started hiding it a lot better."

"Yep, though I probably found it in like five different places."

"And then what?"

"And then I never found it again."

"When was this?" Ingrid asked.

"The last time I ever saw her journal was around April

the year before she died."

"That's right about the time she started blackmailing people."

"Right," he said. "Because I never read anything about that."

"So, she either kept it with her at all times," said Billy.

Ingrid thought back to what Jennifer wrote in her journal. "Or she found a much better hiding spot."

...

"She wrote that in her journal," my dad barks. "Right before she started blackmailing guys, she wrote that she found the perfect hiding spot and Markus would never find it."

"I know," Ingrid says. "And it was the perfect hiding spot."

...

"You don't have any clue where she might have hidden it?" Ingrid asked.

"I don't know," Markus said, shaking his head. "I must have looked everywhere. Must have searched the whole house twenty times."

Billy smiled and said, "Your room."

"What?" asked Markus.

"Did you ever check *your* room?"

His eyebrows scrunch together. "My room?"

"I bet she hid it in your room. Why would you ever look for it there?"

"I guess I wouldn't."

Ingrid jumped up. "Let's go."

"Where?"

"Your mom's house."

...

Ingrid followed behind Markus' white F150 for sixty miles, until they reached his mother's house in DC.

The house was in a middle class neighborhood, painted tan with mint-green trim, its only distinguishing factor from the house on either side.

Jennifer's mother met them at the front door. The years hadn't been kind to her. The pain of losing a daughter, perhaps the guilt of driving her daughter into her dangerous hobby, was evident in her white hair, wrinkled skin, and in each labored breath.

"What's this all about?" she huffed, holding her chest.

Markus took her aside and after a whispered conversation, she disappeared into the house.

They wouldn't see her again.

"Follow me," Markus said, leading them into the house, through the foyer, into a hallway, and finally into a bedroom. "This was my room."

There was a bed at the center, a small dresser, a mirror, a small bookcase.

"Not much has changed," he said. "Same bed, same dresser, same bookshelf. They took all my crap off the walls of course, but same layout."

Billy said, "Okay, if you were Jennifer, and you were gonna hide a journal in this room, where would you put it?"

The three of them glanced at one another and then started searching. Closets, beds, under furniture, lifting up carpet, looking for holes in the ceiling, the wood trim, behind the doors. Every nook, every cranny.

After twenty minutes, all three stood in the center of the room.

"Nothing here," Markus said.

Ingrid let out a long exhale. "Well, thanks anyway."

"Hold on," Billy said. "Did you say the bookshelf is the same?"

Markus nodded.

"What about the books?"

He nodded again. "Yeah, I mean, it's just an encyclopedia set. I didn't want to lug them off to college and it's not like my kids would use them; everything is on the internet now."

Ingrid knelt next to the bookshelf. The set was twenty-six books. One for each letter. Some of the books were thin, others thicker. Ingrid began pulling out the books one by one. Billy joined her and helped. Billy slid the V book off the shelf and opened it.

He showed it to Ingrid.

A hollow rectangle was carved out of the pages, the exact size of a journal.

Billy showed the book to Markus.

"Well, I'll be," he said. "I never would have looked there in a thousand years."

The excitement over finding Jennifer's hiding spot quickly faded. There was nothing in there.

They were all silent for a good twenty seconds, then Markus said, "Bob's."

Billy and Ingrid looked at him questioningly.

"When Bob and my mom got divorced, he went out and bought the exact same encyclopedia set. In fact, he set up our rooms exactly the same as they were here, so the transition would be easier."

Ingrid said, "So, you're telling me that at your stepdad's house, there is the exact same encyclopedia set?"

All three understood what was as stake. If Jennifer whittled out a hiding spot in a book here, what was to stop her from doing it at Bob's as well?

Markus nodded and said, "Yes."

...

Bob was out of town with his new wife, but Markus had a spare key.

Markus was telling the truth, his bedroom was a near replica of the one at his mother's house. However, Bob moved the set of encyclopedias from Markus' bedroom to a small study.

Ingrid moved her hand over the V book.

She slid if off the shelf and opened it.

She showed it to both Markus and Billy and shook her head.

...

"She didn't carve out a place for her diary?" my dad asks.

"No," Ingrid says, then adds, "At least not in the V."

She reaches into her bag and pulls out a book.

"J for journal," she says.

I fight back a smile, and ask, "Were the photographs inside?"

Ingrid nods and hands me the book. It is an inch thick, the heaviest book I've ever held.

Ingrid says, "I have to warn you, the photographs are upsetting."

"I don't think I can get any more upset."

"Not for you," she says, trying not to look at my father.

I flip the book open. There is a rectangle carved out of the pages, deep enough to hold a journal three-quarters of an inch thick. Resting in the space is a stack of four-by-six photographs.

I pick up the first and glance at it. It is thirty years old, the colors drab. It is a picture of a man and my mother walking down the sidewalk. The next four are of the two in an alley. Kissing.

She *was* having an affair.

I take a deep breath and pass the photos to my dad. I suppose part of him knew when Ingrid wouldn't meet his gaze the story the pictures would tell.

He looks at each one, taking a heavier breath with each shuffle.

"I'm sorry," Ingrid says. "I almost wish we hadn't found them."

I am looking at my dad when it hits me. If my mom had an affair with this man, then he could be the same man she had an affair with before I was born.

The guy in the photos.

He could be my dad.

I snag one of the photos back. I was too preoccupied with the idea of the two kissing that I failed to look closely at the gentlemen.

It is a profile picture of the man, his lips pressed to my mother's, but there is no mistaking it.

The man wasn't a congressman.

He was a senator.

Senator David Sullivan.

"Oh my God," I say.

"What?" Ingrid asks.

I think back to David Sullivan's picture. His gray-blue

eyes, the same gray-blue eyes his son had. The same gray-blue eyes *I* had.

President Sullivan and I might be brothers.

:15

Ingrid and my father are both looking at me. Waiting for me to explain my outburst.

I look at my father. What am I supposed to tell him? Am I supposed to say, "Listen, I know you just found out your wife was having an affair, and I think now would be a great time to also divulge that you are not my biological father"?

I couldn't do it.

Instead, I say, "The man in the pictures, do you know who he is?"

Ingrid shakes her head. "Billy and I tried to match him up with our list of congressmen, but we couldn't."

"That's because he wasn't a congressman. He was a senator. It's David Sullivan. The President's father."

"The President's father?" Ingrid blurts, then picks up one of the pictures. "Are you sure?"

"Positive," I say. "He and my mother were working together on the Sleep Control Program."

I give a small summary of his career, abduction, election to senator, then his untimely death in the World Trade Center.

"If they worked together," my dad says, "then they might have had an affair the entire time we were married."

"I suppose," I say, though I was nearly certain this was true. Perhaps even *before* they were married.

"Do you think the President knows?" Ingrid asks.

"I don't know, but it would explain why he had you looking into the murder. Maybe his dad told him. Confided in him."

"What? That they were being blackmailed by some little

girl and they kidnapped her, tortured her, and then killed her?"

My dad takes a deep breath and says, "After Jennifer's murder, David Sullivan stayed with his family, but your mother left."

"And you think that proves she was guilty?" I ask. "You think that proves she was the one who killed Jennifer?"

As much as I hated my mother, even after all she did to me, I still had a sliver of hope she wasn't the monster I thought she was, that she didn't kill a sixteen-year-old girl. I don't want to know half my DNA was from a woman capable of this. I shudder to even think about it.

"Well, both your mother and the Senator had a lot to lose," Ingrid says. "Both had families, children, and both would have been under heavy scrutiny if the affair leaked."

I say, "And perhaps under heavy scrutiny, they would have discovered the pair's connection to a black op."

Ingrid says, "The Sleep Control Program."

"Right. So when Jennifer goes to blackmail them for having an affair, she has no idea how much they stand to lose. That even if they pay her off, they can't trust that she didn't make copies and that the pictures won't get out."

Ingrid says, "And so they kidnap her and ask her where the photos are?"

"But she hid them in her brother's room," my dad says. "She was scared of what they would do to him if they thought he knew."

"So Jennifer doesn't tell them," I say. "Then they shoot her up with Compound-23, hoping that after a twenty-three hour nightmare she will give up the location of the pictures."

Ingrid says, "But she doesn't. She stays strong. Then they hit her in the back of the head with something and dump her body."

I say, "After the murder, they break off the affair and my mom leaves, goes down to Honduras for three years. When she returns, the case is long closed, a distant memory."

"And your mother moves the Sleep Control Program somewhere else. Maybe Michigan. Maybe somewhere in the Midwest."

I nod.

"So then where do you come in?" my dad asks. "Why kidnap you? What about the flash drive?"

It takes me thirty seconds to put it all together. "When we talked with Sidney Ewen, he said the last time he talked to my mother was right after 9/11."

Ingrid says, "Right after the Senator died."

"And his wife, which means everything the Senator owned was passed on to their only child."

"Conner Sullivan," my dad says.

"And I'm guessing somewhere in all of his valuables, maybe locked in a safety deposit box somewhere, is a—"

"Flash drive," Ingrid says.

I smile.

My dad says, "Maybe the President has a flash drive and he doesn't even know it."

"But what's on it?" Ingrid asks.

I know what's on the flash drive.

My dad was right.

"It's my mother's confession," I say. "She was the one who killed Jennifer Nubers."

...

I run everything we learned through my head. My mother's file. The interview with Ewen. My abduction. Jennifer's murder. David Sullivan's death. The President.

After a long minute, I say, "Here's how I see it. I think David Sullivan and my mother — in addition to working together on the Sleep Control Program — had a long-standing affair." I try to avoid my father's gaze as I add, "Who knows how far it went back."

"When he escapes from the Russian prison camp," I continue, "the two pick up where they left off. David Sullivan has moved up the ranks, he is now a state senator with far more to lose if the affair leaks. But what both fear most when they are approached by sixteen-year-old Jennifer Nubers is that if the press looks into their affair, the Sleep Control Program — what the two have been working on for over a decade — will be compromised.

"They tell Jennifer they will get her the money — whatever she asks for, probably ten or twenty grand being that David is a senator. A week later, they snatch her off the streets, keep her somewhere while they interrogate her about the photographs. She is worried for her brother's safety and doesn't divulge the photographs' whereabouts.

"My mother snaps and hits her with something on the back of the head. Maybe she wasn't trying to kill her, but regardless, she does. Possibly, David Sullivan isn't even present when this happens. My mother needs help moving the body and he offers to help, but only if she promises to write a full confession — or videotape a confession — one which absolves him of Jennifer's murder entirely.

"They dump the body and decide to break off the affair. A couple days later my mother comes home, packs up some of her stuff, then goes to Honduras for the next three years. Meanwhile, David Sullivan keeps the file on his computer or video camera or whatever. Jennifer's alleged murderer, Chase Wingleberry, is arrested two weeks later, falsely confesses to the crime after twelve hours of interrogation and is promptly bailed out by his wife and killed. Sullivan holds on to the confession, just in case new evidence ever arises in Jennifer's death. Flash drives are invented at some point in the late 1990s, though they were probably already in use by the CIA and other government types by then, and he transfers whatever proof he has to a flash drive. Then, when he and his wife die, all his possessions are transferred to his son.

"My mother has returned to the states by now and she calls Ewen to see if he knows anything about 'Project Sandman,' but he hasn't heard anything. She waits for the chips to fall, waits for President Sullivan to stumble on this flash drive and to have her arrested, but nothing happens. She continues her work, then according to the then Director of the CIA, she is interrogating — torturing — a suspect in 2007 when she freaks out. She is never heard from again.

"Conner Sullivan is elected President of the United States in 2012. By now, my mom is sick of being on the run. She wants to come clean, but she has Jennifer's murder hanging over her head. She gets wind somehow that Sullivan and I are buddy-buddy, that he's been to my house a couple times. The only reason my mother can imagine the President befriending her son is to share with him what is on the flash drive. She hears from someone — I don't know who fits here — that President Sullivan found the flash drive and gave it to me. Maybe because it was my mom, Sullivan thinks I should be the one to decide her fate.

"My mother somehow learns that Ingrid and I are scheduled to take a trip to Alaska. It would be easy to find out for someone with her skills, and all she had to do was put a flag on my credit card. She realizes it is the perfect chance to interrogate me. We get on the plane, they knock out Ingrid and Lassie, and toss them in the car. They fly me to Michigan or wherever the Sleep Control Program has been moved to and proceed to give me the worst fucking twenty-three day nightmare in the history of the known universe." I take a deep breath. "I can't tell her where the flash drive is because I don't have the flash drive, and she sends a team of goons to our condo to rip it apart."

Meow.

I look down at Lassie.

"Yes, and to steal Lassie's jingle balls."

I continue, "I'm found the next morning in some dude's tomato garden and I'm debriefed. The President finds out I'm looking for a flash drive he gave me. He didn't give me anything, he never found any flash drive in his father's possessions, but he does remember something, maybe something his father told him about a murder of a young woman in 1985. Maybe his father told him that my mother was the one who killed this girl. It's the only thing he can possibly imagine that connects the three of us. So Sullivan calls the Virginia Police Commissioner to get Ingrid's captain to have her look into Jennifer Nubers's murder. He knows if she reinvestigates it and finds a link to my mother, I will be the first to know."

Everyone stares at me.

My dad. Ingrid. Lassie. Murdock.

My dad says, "I think you're right."

"Me too," Ingrid says.

Meow.

Bark.

Everyone is in agreement.

"So what now?" Ingrid says.

"We need to talk to President Sullivan," I say. "I think

he has the flash drive somewhere and doesn't even know it."

"He's in Russia," my dad says.

"We know," Ingrid and I say at the same time.

...

The next three days, I wake up, I run into the kitchen, and each day, both my father and Ingrid shake their heads.

He didn't call.

The hour I'm awake, we try to make small talk, but we spend most our time staring at the phone.

On the fourth day, we've all but given up.

"Maybe we should just let it go," Ingrid says. "I don't know how much good will come out of this even if we do find the flash drive."

She has a point. My mom is already one of the most wanted women in the known world. Once a patriot, she is now considered a traitor, a threat to national security, and her name is at the top of every watch list in a dozen countries around the globe. They are looking for her domestically and abroad. It's not like the world would suddenly find out she was responsible for a young woman's death thirty years earlier and ratchet up the search for her.

Or would they?

It is one thing to be wanted for torturing enemy combatants on US soil and stealing government secrets. It is another thing altogether to have murdered a young girl in cold blood.

Then there was the family to think about: Markus, Megan, and her mother. Did I really want to make them wade through the muck of Jennifer's death for a second time?

No.

Certainly not.

And if President Sullivan had yet to return my calls, this obviously wasn't high on his list of priorities. He was, of course, trying to ward off a second Cold War, which did put the whole thing in perspective.

However, I did hold out hope that if we located the flash drive, my mother would surface. That she would come to me.

I stare at Ingrid.

I see into our future.

At the very most, I could hope to spend 20,000 hours with her, and that's if I lived to ninety and if we spent every minute together I was awake. If I were normal, if I didn't have Henry Bins, that number would be closer to 300,000 hours.

I still haven't told her I want a family. That I want to be a father.

"What do you think, Henry?" Ingrid asks. "Should we just let it be? Move on with our lives?"

"Yes," I lie.

...

Lassie is sitting on my lap when it happens. It is the day before we are set to move back into our condo.

It is 3:32 a.m.

My dad is asleep. Ingrid is brushing her teeth, getting ready for bed. The two are set to meet the contractor at our condo at 7:30 a.m. to sign off on all the work that was done.

"Are you excited to move home tomorrow?" I ask Lassie.

Meow.

"Yes, you can have the jingle balls the second we get back."

Meow.

"You want to leave one for Murdock? Well, aren't you a softy?"

Meow.

"Oh, you want to fill it with acid?" I can't help laughing. "I thought he was your best friend."

Meow.

"Who is Roger?"

Ingrid comes around the corner in her pajamas. She gives me a long kiss and says, "I'm gonna hit the sack. Your dad and I should be able to get everything situated and we can drive over tomorrow night when you wake up." She gives me another kiss. "Who knows, if I drive fast enough we might even have time to re-christen the place."

"I like the sound of that. Maybe you can put the siren on."

She laughs, gives me one last kiss, and then heads to the bedroom. A half second later, Lassie jumps off my lap and heads the same way, no doubt to snuggle up in her cleavage.

I grab a smoothie from the refrigerator and sit down to the computer. I pull up the Google Earth image for S and Manchester.

"Where were you two going?" I ask out loud.

I take down half the smoothie as I move along the street view, pausing at the intersection, then heading down S Street.

I double back, then head down Manchester Ave. Two-thirds of the way down the street, I pass a small two-story building. The sign on the outside reads, "Overseas Private Investment Corporation."

I continue moving down the street, but nothing else holds my interest.

I close the tab, then open up *Game of Thrones*. It had been nearly two weeks since I last watched and I move the cursor back five minutes — I am still on episode one of season three — and hit play.

After a minute, I realize I'm not even watching.

I'm still thinking about the building on Manchester.

Overseas Private Investment Corporation.

What is it about the name that is pinging in my brain?

I close the tab on *Game of Thrones* and do a Google search for the company.

There is no web page.

Odd.

I click on a tab for DC businesses and search Overseas Private Investment Corp. The company has been around for more than forty years, founded in 1973.

That's all there is.

I take a deep breath.

1973.

1973.

That was the year MK-Ultra was shut down and the year the Sleep Control Program supposedly began.

Could this have been where David Sullivan and my mother were going? And if it was the headquarters of the Sleep Control Program then is it still today?

Did we get it all wrong?

Did they never move it?

Is this where the White Room is?

Is this where I was kept?

No.

It can't be.

Then why was the name "Overseas Private Investment Corporation" running through my head on a loop?

Had I heard the name before? Maybe even subconsciously?

It had happened before. I would hear something Ingrid said to me during the night, and I would remember it the next day. Or in the case of my fight with Lassie, I attacked him in my dream, and he slashed me with his claws, and it became part of my dream.

My dream.

My nightmare.

It hits me.

"Holyyyyyyyyyyyyyy shittttt."

I wondered how I came up with his name. How had my subconscious decided to call him a name I never heard before?

Only in my dream I spelled it differently.

Overseas Private Investment Corporation.

OPIC.

The Eskimo boy from my dream.

Opik.

:16

I must have heard my mother or one of the others who kidnapped me mention the building. Of course they wouldn't call it the Overseas Private Investment Corporation; no one would ever call it that. They would call it OPIC.

"Where are we taking him?"

"OPIC."

It could have been as simple as that; the word entering my subconscious. Then when the little Eskimo boy popped up in my synthetic nightmare, that's what I named him.

It didn't matter how it happened. All that mattered is that it did.

The White Room is still in downtown Washington, DC.

I can only imagine my mom when she realized how fitting it was. How in Jennifer Nubers' journal, she named their affair "S and Man." Sure, the OPIC building was halfway down Manchester, closer to T Street than S Street, but it was too fitting.

Add in the fact my mother's favorite song was "Enter Sandman," plus the folklore tale, and with the CIA's affinity for the word "project," of course she would name it *Project Sandman.*

I look at the clock.

3:41 a.m.

I jump out of the chair and snag two premade sandwiches out of the fridge and throw them in a cooler with an ice pack. They won't stay cold for twenty-four hours, but they should still be edible when I wake up. I add a couple bottled waters, then grab my dad's car keys off the wall.

I'm a half-step from the garage when I turn around. I

rip a piece of paper from my father's legal pad and scribble a quick note.

A minute later, I have manually pushed up the garage door. I back the car out, pull down the garage door, and drive out of the cul-de-sac.

I drive as far as I can for the next fifteen minutes, then pull into a neighborhood three miles from where the OPIC building is located. All the windows in my dad's car are tinted except the windshield. I unfold my father's silver reflector and spread it out above the dash. If someone looks closely in one of the windows, they will see me asleep in the back seat, but hopefully that won't happen.

I turn my cell phone off at 3:59 a.m.

Tomorrow I am going to break into the OPIC building.

And if my theory is correct, I will find the White Room.

And I will find my mother.

...

No one saw my dad's car parked on the side of the street and thought it suspicious enough to peer through the windows. Or if they had, they figured I was an overworked politician trying to catch a couple winks before heading back to the Hill.

I grab a sandwich from the cooler, which is surprisingly still cold, and scarf it down, then I guzzle both bottles of water.

I'm afraid to turn on my cell phone.

I'm sure I have fifty missed calls from Ingrid and my father. Even after reading my note — my telling them not to worry, that I had something personal to take care of, and I would be back in two days — I'm certain they skipped the meeting with the contractor and have been searching for me since.

My feelings of guilt are outweighed by the bubbling, near bursting, need to confront my mother on my own. To show her that even with my one hour, even with the curse she bestowed on me while in her womb, I didn't need anyone's help.

I could fight my own fights.

Six minutes later, I take a left at the intersection of S

and Manchester, then park the car on the side of the street.

I'm wearing jeans and a dark blue T-shirt, so I'm not exactly easy to spot, but I don't resemble a cat burglar either.

After a brisk minute walk, I am standing in front of the two-story OPIC building.

There are three small stone steps leading to a wooden door. I try the handle.

Locked.

I walk around to the side of the building and find a glass window. I peek inside. I'd never been inside an investment firm, but the handful of desks and small offices resemble what one might look like. Of course, they *would* need to keep up appearances. This doesn't mean there isn't something sinister hidden a floor below.

I try the window, but it's locked. I move down twenty feet and try a second window. Again, locked tight.

I look down at my watch.

3:11 a.m.

I run around to the back where there is a second entrance. There is a numerical panel beneath the handle.

I try 1234.

It doesn't work.

I'm gonna have to break in. Though if the place is what I think it is — a CIA black op marauding as an investment firm — I doubt there is a security system. At least one that reports to the police. The last thing these spooks want is for the police to come inside, start poking around, and discover there is no ink in the printers. That being said, I assume some sort of security protocols are in place. If there is a break-in, a few people will be alerted; one of which, I hope, is my mother.

It takes me thirty seconds to find a worthy projectile.

I'm about to smash it against the glass when I stop. There might not be a security system that alerts the police to a break-in, but there is still the chance someone will overhear the breaking glass and call the cops. There is a law firm two businesses down which still has its lights on.

I run to the street, spot a relatively nice car, and I rock it back and forth.

The car alarm blares.

I sprint back to the side of the OPIC building and smash the brick against the closest window.

Even I have a hard time hearing the explosion of glass over the wail of the shrieking alarm — an alarm I know is unlikely to attract much attention. Even being awake one hour a night, I know the sound of a car alarm has become somewhat relegated to the white noise of the city.

I chip away at what is left of the window, then gingerly pull myself up and into the building.

I slip the small flashlight from my back pocket and flick it on. I look in desk drawers and a couple filing cabinets. Both are full of stuff and look as if they are used daily. There are four small offices, and I poke my head into each one and give a rudimentary search. Everything appears to be above board. There is actually ink in the printers.

There is a set of stairs, leading only upward, and I climb them, only to find a near replica of the ground floor.

"Damn."

Maybe I got this all wrong.

Maybe this was actually an investment firm.

Which means I probably tripped a security system and the police were on their way.

I ponder making a run for it before they show. I could still make it back to my dad's. I could make up a story about why I left. Anything is better than the truth: *I thought I discovered the location of the White Room, a conjecture based solely on the name I gave a small Eskimo boy while in an LSD-induced nightmare. Oh, and I also figured my mother would be there waiting for me, sitting on a table in the White Room — the same table she strapped me to before injecting me with Compound-23 — and I would force her to divulge all her secrets before giving me a pill which would erase my Henry Bins forever.*

I laugh at the absurdity of it all.

I head back downstairs.

I'm halfway down when the car alarm stops. From my experience, most car alarms last five minutes. I look at my watch and see exactly five minutes have elapsed since I broke the window.

I edge to the window I busted and crane my head, listening for police sirens. I don't hear any, though I'm not sure they would turn their sirens on at night, not wanting to alert the intruders.

"Dammit, Henry," I say.

Then I take a deep breath.

"Okay, you still have forty-three minutes. If the cops were coming, they would be here by now."

"You're right," a voice says. "They would be."

I turn.

Standing in the middle of the room is a man.

I shine the flashlight on him.

Sidney Ewen.

...

I walk toward him.

His stoop is gone. He is without a cane. He looks twenty years younger than the last time I saw him.

"You," I say.

He shrugs, then says, "Who were you expecting?"

"I don't know. Certainly not you."

"Your mother?"

"Maybe," I say coldly.

"Elena was here recently. Well, you know that all too well. Sadly, she was forced to flee the country in the wake of your release."

"Where is she?"

"Bermuda, last I heard, but she likes to move around."

I nod, then say, "Show me."

He stares at me. Doesn't answer.

"Show me the White Room."

He laughs. "Ah, the White Room. Alas, we don't call it that."

"What do you call it?"

"It doesn't have a name. Just a room."

"But it's here?"

He nods.

"Show me."

"Very well."

I follow him to one of the offices. He lowers the drapes. He flicks a switch and an overhead fan turns on. Finally, he picks up a paperweight and moves it to the opposite side of the desk. There is a soft click and the desk moves forward three feet, leaving a circular metal grate.

A sewer grate.

He leans down and lifts it, then slides it away. A remarkable feat for a man who acted as though he had mere days left to live the last time I saw him.

There is a ladder heading down into a gray abyss.

"The sewer?" I ask.

"What did you expect? Something fancier?"

"Kind of."

He laughs, then steps down into the hole. I climb down after him.

He tells me to make sure I close the grate.

I do, but only partially.

Just in case.

I climb down ten feet, then jump to the concrete below. The sewer is softly lit and surprisingly clean.

"This is an old sewer duct," he explains. "They did a big reconstruction project in the late sixties, and this quarter-mile section was decommissioned."

"So that's why you bought the OPIC building in 1973. Its location over an abandoned sewer duct."

"Precisely."

"So the maintenance crews can't get here?"

"No, it's sealed off on both ends. Above is the only entrance."

"And you had it cleaned?"

"Yes, of course. We aren't animals. Though, as you may notice, there is a still a lingering aroma."

It's there. More musky than rotten.

He ambles forward for a hundred yards, then stops at a door. He punches in a code and pushes through.

I follow him, then trip through the entrance.

"Be careful," he says.

I slide the flashlight in the door entrance, then push myself up, hoping Ewen doesn't notice the door failing to close completely.

He doesn't.

The corridor ends, and we push through a metal door and into what appears to be a wide laboratory. It is filled with computers, gadgets, terminals, and medical equipment. I know most of the machines by sight — MRI, CT,

EKG — since I'd been hooked to, or inside, every one of them at some point in my youth.

In another corner there is a small fridge and a cot, no doubt where Ewen was staying since I last saw him — patiently waiting for me to trip the alarm.

There is a long clear window against the far wall. Through the window, it is all white.

The White Room.

I let out a long exhale.

I found it.

I turn around.

Ewen is sitting in a chair behind a desk.

I stare at him, then say, "You said the last time you talked to my mom was shortly after 9/11?" I pause. "That's not true."

He shakes his head. "No, it's not."

I take another deep breath. "Did you know about her and David Sullivan?"

"I did."

"And did you know my mother killed Jennifer Nubers?"

He smirks.

He did.

"Tell me," I say.

"Shortly after 9/11 — shortly after David Sullivan's death — Elena did contact me. She wanted to know if David sent me anything. Something she called Project Sandman."

I smile.

I knew it.

"It had been years since I spoke to David, not since he escaped from the Russian prisoner camp, and I told her that he hadn't sent me anything. A week after that, I received something in the mail."

"A flash drive," I said.

He nods.

"Yes, a flash drive. It had one file on it: Project Sandman."

"My mother's confession for killing Jennifer Nubers."

He looks impressed. "Correct."

"Was it typewritten or a video?"

"A video."

"And she confesses to killing Jennifer Nubers?"

He nods, then asks, "Would you like to see it?"

...

"My name is Elena Janev," my mother says. "The date is January 15, 1985." She holds up a newspaper to confirm this.

She looks exactly how I remember her, which makes sense, because the last time I saw her was three weeks before she recorded the video. Her brown hair is held back in a ponytail. Her green eyes are the green of the deep Amazon jungle. Her high cheekbones taper gently to full lips.

She has bruising around her throat and a cut on her forehead, evidence that Jennifer Nubers put up a fight.

"Three days ago, I murdered a sixteen-year-old girl named Jennifer Nubers. My motive was that she was blackmailing me for having an affair with a man. As you may know from her journal, which we scattered around the crime scene, this was a hobby of Jennifer's. She approached me two weeks ago and requested a sum of ten thousand dollars or she would send the photographs to my husband."

I glance over my shoulder at Ewen.

He nods, as if to say, "Yes, she is a monster."

And she was.

She was even worse than Ewen. In Ewen's warped mind, he killed to protect America. My mother killed to protect herself.

My mother continues, "Five days ago, January 10th, I met Jennifer to pay her. I injected her with a sedative, put her in my car, and brought her to a motel room."

Liar.

You brought her here.

To the White Room.

"After two days of interrogating her to discover the whereabouts of the pictures, and failing, I lost my temper. I grabbed a lamp off the table and hit her in the head, thereby inflicting a deadly head trauma. I then transported her to McKinney Park, scattered her journal around her, and left."

The video cuts out.

I sit in silence for a long minute.

Half of this monster's DNA is inside me.

I want to wretch. To get a scalpel and attempt to cut away half of each cell.

But then whose DNA would I be left with?

I stand up and turn to face Ewen. "Is David Sullivan my father?"

He laughs. "How did you find out?"

I tell him about how I had doubts my dad was truly my biological father and how I sent out his and my hair samples to a DNA testing company and the results were negative.

Ewen says, "If you like, I can tell you for certain who your father is right now."

"You can?" But of course he could. Of course he had David Sullivan's DNA on file.

"Certainly, I would simply need to take a quick blood sample and run it through the computer."

I nod my approval and he moves to a metal drawer filled with medical equipment. He returns with rubber gloves, a tourniquet, and a small vial.

Thirty seconds later, the vial is full of my blood.

"This will take about ten minutes," he says.

I look down at my watch.

It is 3:32 a.m.

I need to be back in the car by 3:55 a.m. so I can drive a mile or two away before I fall asleep.

Ewen takes my vial to some fancy machine and turns it on. It begins spinning.

He returns and I say, "What I don't understand is, if you had the flash drive, why did my mother think I had it?"

He smirks.

"You were the one who told her I had it."

"When I received the flash drive from David, I was a bit confused, but then I pieced it together. He had Elena record the video just in case he was ever connected to Jennifer Nubers' murder, which he was an accomplice in through the affair and possibly the disposal of the body. When David died, he'd set up a system whereby the flash drive was sent to me automatically, meaning he feared something might happen to him. He must have feared your mom would attempt to get the flash drive from him. Maybe even kill him.

"Your mother knew about all my skeletons. If she came forward at any point, decided to trade her secrets for my secrets, I would spend the rest of my days behind bars. So I kept the video, knowing I could use it against your mother if need be.

"A few months after I received the flash drive, I contacted Elena and told her I watched it, but that I didn't feel it rightfully belonged to me. I told her that I gave it to David's son."

"Conner Sullivan?"

"Correct."

I am starting to see how this played out. "You never gave it to him, did you?"

"I did not."

"How does that benefit you? For her to think President Sullivan had it?"

"He wasn't president at the time; he was the Governor of Virginia. But that's beside the point. I merely wanted your mother to think there were two copies of her confession out there so she'd be less likely to cut any deals."

"Cut any deals? My mom was wanted by every agency in North America. What could she possibly possess that would make you think she could cut a deal?"

"The files."

Right, the MK-Ultra files that were all *supposedly* destroyed.

"She had a copy of the files?"

He nods.

"And let me guess, they proved that MK-Ultra did far worse things than anyone ever could have imagined."

"I would have spent the rest of my life behind bars. That is, if I didn't receive the death penalty."

"Okay, but that doesn't explain the connection to me."

Ewen helps me along. "Six months ago, I reached out to Elena to let her know I was diagnosed with stage four cancer."

"Which of course, you weren't."

"Nope, fit as a fiddle," he says with a smile.

"I also told her that I had a conversation with the President recently and I asked him about the flash drive. How he said it was impossible to keep anything private as the most powerful man in the known world and that he'd given the flash drive to someone — someone he felt deserved it more than he did."

"Me," I scoff.

"Right."

"Why go through all this trouble?"

He takes a deep breath. "Your mom figured I'd be dead in six months and my copy of her confession would die with me. That left you with the only remaining copy. If she could get that, there would be no stopping her from making a deal with the CIA, the Feds, and all the other agencies, in trade for all the destroyed MK-Ultra files. Trust me, the CIA would jump at the chance to get their hands on these files, and your mother would be granted absolute impunity."

"So she kidnaps me. Tortures me. Uses Compound-23 on me in hopes I will break."

"But you don't know anything about a flash drive because President Sullivan never gave you one."

"No shit," I say, my face flushing, realizing I am a pawn in this guy's sick game.

"I knew when she let you go, that you would come to me for answers. Then you came to see me, and I told you just enough that hopefully you would make the connection."

"But I never would have made the connection unless I started digging into Jennifer Nubers' mur—"

He smiles. "One last favor for a dying man."

"What did you tell the President? How did you get him to call the Virginia Police Commissioner? How did you get the case assigned to Ingrid?"

"Easy. I've known Conner for thirty years. He calls me Uncle Sidney. I told him there was an old case in DC, how the mother was an old friend of mine, and how she reached out to me and asked if I could pull some strings and have someone reinvestigate her daughter's murder. I told him that it couldn't be a detective from DC. Then I name-dropped Ingrid who, I knew from various sources, you were living with."

"So you put this whole thing in motion. Why?"

"I have dedicated my entire life to one thing."

It takes me a moment, then I say, "Behavior modification."

"Precisely."

I glare at him.

"I needed you to come here," he says. "I needed you to

think you would be coming to meet your mother."

"Why?"

"Because I knew then you would come alone."

His words are a cold breeze down my spine.

I glance at the door. It is thirty feet away.

I look at my watch.

3:42 a.m.

I ponder making a run for it, but even after Ewen's veiled threat, I don't find myself overly alarmed. After all, he is a ninety-year-old man.

What's the worst he could do?

There is a soft chime and Ewen gets up and walks to a machine. He returns holding a sheet of paper. He hands it to me and says, "A perfect match."

I take the paper and look at the results. "So David Sullivan was my father."

Ewen shakes his head. "That isn't David Sullivan's DNA profile."

I inhale.

"It's mine," he says.

:17

It is too much to handle.

This man is my father.

I lean forward and retch, sending the sandwich I ate earlier onto the concrete floor.

"You're my dad?" I ask, looking up, wiping the excess from my lips.

He nods. "It started the night I gave my speech when your mother was at The Farm. We ended up back in her barracks."

"And when did it end?"

"When she realized she was pregnant with you, she broke it off. She didn't want me to be a part of your life even if I was the father."

"Did you know you were my biological father?"

"Yes."

"And so did she?"

He nods. "She did a paternity test when you were an infant."

"And you didn't want to be a part of my life?"

"Not particularly," he says, nearly as coldly as my mother confessed to killing Jennifer Nubers. "But I think things turned out for the best. Richard was a far better father than I ever would have been."

"You bet your fucking ass he was," I nearly scream.

His veiled threat comes rushing back.

"So why did you want me to come here? You have a change of heart? You want to be my dad now?"

"No," he says. "I simply want to know more about you."

"What? What the fuck do you want to know? You want to know how I feel about my mother and father both being killers? You want to know if I have an Oedipus complex? If I want to kill my dad and fuck my mom? Well, I can tell you for certain that I want to kill my fucking dad."

I fight myself from rushing him. From smashing his bald head into the concrete.

"I'm not a psychologist," he says, laughing. "I don't give a shit what you think about me. I'm a scientist. I want to know how your brain works."

He points to the all the machines.

"You can go fuck yourself," I say, closing the distance between us. The next word he says, I'm going to smash my fist into his jaw, sending his ninety-year-old teeth scattering to the floor.

He doesn't say another word.

He simply pulls a gun from his waist and points it at me.

Then he looks at his watch.

I look at mine.

3:49.

Eleven minutes and then he can do whatever he wants with me.

...

I wake up.

I am strapped to a table.

I'm in the White Room.

I scream.

The door opens.

I crane my head upward.

"Good morning," Ewen says.

"Fuck you."

"Somebody is cranky. Didn't get enough sleep, did you?"

"What did you do to me last night?"

Ewen smiles, then leaves as quickly as he came.

I take three deep breaths. Luckily, last night he hadn't administered Compound-23, and I didn't have another nightmare, a fate I'm certain won't last another night.

I glance at the wall to my left, a wall I know is actually a long mirror.

I yell at the wall, "You fucking cowardly piece of shit! Get in here!"

I lay my head down.

I wrangle my hands against the velcro restraints.

There is little give.

I half expect my mother to come through the door with a mallet. To smash my hands to smithereens like in my nightmare. To ask me where the flash drive is.

I would be able to answer this time. I would be able to tell her that her mentor, lover, the biological father of her only child, had it. How I watched it. That I knew what she'd done. How she killed Jennifer Nubers. But I *wouldn't* tell her where it was. No matter how many knuckles she broke, no matter how many nightmares she gave me, I would tell her to go to hell.

The door opens and Ewen returns. He is holding an iPad.

He approaches, sits on the table near my ribs and says, "I must say, your brain is remarkable."

He turns the iPad toward me.

"Your brain has nearly twelve percent more synapses firing each millisecond than average. Do you know how many that is? Billions more synapses firing than perhaps even me."

He pats my leg. "Haven't you ever wondered why? Why you are so smart? How when you've only been awake, alive really, one-fifteenth that of an average person your age, how you could be more intelligent than most of these people?"

Actually, I had wondered this. *Exactly* this. Wondered why I wasn't intellectually a four-year-old.

"Fascinating," I say, then spit on the computer screen.

He wipes the screen clean, then says, "Well, the real fun will begin tonight. When we see how your brain responds to Compound-23."

The thought of another twenty-three day nightmare claws at my stomach.

I find myself begging, pleading. "Please . . . please . . . no . . ."

He smiles and pats my leg. "Don't worry, *son*. It will be okay."

He walks out, leaving me with my own thoughts for the next ten minutes.

What had Ewen said, that creating a nightmare is like

trying to create a tornado? You need to create an instability in the mind. With my synapses firing twelve percent higher than average, I should be able to control my brain. Keep it stable. Keep it free from tornadoes.

I start thinking of everything good in my life. My dad, my real dad — the greatest dad in the world; Lassie, my perverted BFF; Murdock, that amazingly stupid, loveable horse; and Ingrid. If I made it out of here, the second I saw her, I was going to propose. Tell her how sick I was of not being married to her. That I wanted to marry her and to knock her up.

I visualize our life together.

Me, her, Lassie, and a small boy, all wrestling on the bed. No one, not even me, worried about what time it is.

The door opens and my fantasy evaporates.

"I hate to get this party started early," Ewen says, a syringe filled with pink liquid in his hand. "But I simply can't wait any longer."

He walks forward until his stomach is touching the table.

"Oh, I forgot to tell you," he says. "My Peaches went in for her annual check-up last week and guess what?"

He doesn't wait for my guess.

"She's pregnant," he says. "Can you believe that? My Peaches, pregnant. Now, you wouldn't happen to think your stupid little cat had anything to do with it, now would you?"

I can't help laughing. "Yeah, I think he did. He probably fucked the shit out of her." I keep laughing. "I hope that fat bitch wasn't on top. She could have killed him."

Ewen's mouth tightens. It's the first time I've ever seen him truly upset.

"Now, she's gonna get even fatter," I say, in near hysterics.

He brings the syringe down.

I let out a scream and yank my left arm up.

Unlike my nightmare, where there was no give at all in the restraints, Ewen tightened the velcro on my left wrist fractionally looser than my right wrist.

It took me the last ten minutes, slowly, millimeter by millimeter, sliding my hand through. Half way, I felt my pinky snap. I nearly gave up, then I saw the syringe and gave one last yank, ripping the tendon off my thumb, and allowing my hand to slide free.

I slap away the syringe, sending it clattering to the ground. I reach out and grab the bottom of Ewen's shirt. I have limited motion with both legs, one arm, and my neck restrained, but it's as if the power of all of my extremities has been funneled into the three working fingers of my left hand.

I yank Ewen's shirt toward the table. He fights me, slapping at my arm, but he is a fruit fly.

I pull him on top of me. I release the bottom of his shirt and grab him by the collar. He tries to push off me.

He can't.

I push him up by the neck of his shirt, then yank him down violently. I angle my head upward. Ewen's face smashes into the crown of my head with a sickening crunch.

The blow dazes me.

When I shake it off, Ewen is lying on top of me. He is out cold.

I roll him off me with my left hand, sending him to the ground four feet below.

I release the velcro strap on my neck, then my right arm, then both feet.

I jump off the table.

Ewen is on his back. His face is destroyed, his nose turned upward and leaking blood by the gallon.

He begins to squirm and I kneel down and check him for the gun. He doesn't have it.

"Whaaa," he moans.

I lift him up and put him on the table. Then I strap him down with the velcro restraints.

Then I leave the White Room.

I find some gauze and tape in the medical supplies and I wrap my hand. The gun is on a table next to a computer and I stick it in the waist of my pants.

It is 3:19 a.m. when I return to the White Room.

Ewen is wide awake now.

He cranes his neck upward.

"What are you doing? You can't do this!" he screams.

"Little different being on the other side of things," I say.

I pick the syringe off the floor and hover over him.

"My mom was brave enough to test this stuff out on herself, but something tells me you were too big of a pussy. Well, it's time to rectify that. I can only imagine, with all the shit you've seen, what will haunt your nightmares."

He begs me not to. "Please! Please!"

I lower the syringe.

He screams four words.

They stop me cold.

"What?" I ask.

"I can fix you," he says.

:18

"Fix me?" I ask. "What do you mean you can fix me?"

His chest is convulsing in panic. He strains his neck against the restraint and says, "I can reset your sleep cycle."

"I thought you said only my mother would know if that was possible?"

He shakes his head. "Your brain is like a hard drive; all you have to do is wipe it clean."

I stare at him.

I look at the syringe.

I think of Ingrid.

I think of our limited time together.

"I swear," he says. "It will work."

I take a deep breath, recap the syringe and put it in my pocket. I decide to at least hear him out.

"Have you done this before?" I ask.

He lifts his head against the neck restraint, what amounts to a nod. "In several of our subprojects with MK-Ultra, we wiped the subjects' brains clean. Many had obsessive-compulsive disorders or disassociate personality disorders, and when we wiped their brains, these reset and went away."

"A personality disorder is far different than my condition."

"No, it really isn't. Like obsessive-compulsive disorder, your sleep cycle is learned behavior. Your brain learned to only be awake for one hour a night, just like someone might learn to be afraid of going outside. Your sleep-wake cycle isn't encoded in your DNA, say like having blue eyes."

"So, nature versus nurture."

"Right."

"But this happened when my mother was pregnant with me."

"Doesn't matter. It was still something learned by your brain. Something Compound-23 taught it."

"Okay, so how do you reset it? You gonna give me electroshock therapy? Because they tried that on me when I was little."

"No. God, no," he says, scoffing. "It has to do with electromagnetic radiation."

I cut my eyes at him.

He takes a long breath. "It is quite complicated, but the short of it is radio waves and brain waves are both types of electromagnetic radiation, waves of energy that move at the speed of light. The only difference is the wave's frequencies."

"I'm with you."

"When you remember something, your brain fires thousands of neurons — perhaps even millions in your case — creating a wave of energy. We simply created a machine that mimics these brain waves, and by concentrating the waves on specific areas of the brain we interrupt normal activity. It is a process called Transcranial Magnetic Stimulation."

"Transcranial Magnetic Stimulation," I repeat. I'd heard a thousand medical terms in my days, but this isn't one of them.

"We overstimulate the brain with trillions of electromagnetic waves the same frequency as brain waves, and the brain can't handle it, and to protect itself from imploding, the brain will basically dump everything it can, then shut down."

"What do you mean, everything?"

"*Everything* that has ever been encoded."

"So, what, like going back to being a baby?"

"Yes and no."

"What do you mean?"

"Yes, your brain will be completely blank, possibly even blanker than an infant's, but your brain will already have the wiring in place, the synapses, *connections,* that are formed as you mature. And as I mentioned earlier, you have billions more than your average person."

"So what you're saying is, my brain would be blank, but I would be able to learn faster?"

424   3 A.M. PREMIUM

"Correct. The subjects who we experimented on learned how to speak in less than two months, to write in four months. Most regained full brain aptitude within three years."

I let out a deep exhale. The idea of relearning how to speak, relearning how to write, relearning how to brush my teeth. Then again, I wouldn't have a one hour limitation. I would have as many hours as there are in a day. If your average person did it in three years, I might do it in two. Sure, the first couple years would be tough, but after that, I would have the next forty to sixty years to be normal.

We are talking 20,000 hours awake versus 300,000.

But there was more at stake than just walking and talking.

"What about all my memories?"

He shakes his head.

Ingrid.

My dad.

Lassie.

Murdock.

I would forget them all. Forget I even know them.

The thought makes me want to cry.

Was I being selfish? Thinking of doing this?

No, of course not.

These people love me. They want me to be normal. They want me to be awake sixteen hours a day.

Also, I wanted to be a father. If I didn't do it for myself, I had to do it for my future child.

I look down at my watch.

It's 3:26 a.m.

"Okay," I say. "Let's do it."

...

With my left hand destroyed, it takes me twenty minutes to write three emails.

The first two are to my father and Ingrid. I tell them what I am about to do and why I'm doing it. That it will be tough at first, but it will be worth it in the end. That they will have to be patient with me, to tell me stories of our memories. That I promise I will learn to love them each more than I loved them before. I thank them both for the amazing memories. That I cherish them, but that I am ready to be born anew.

The third email is to myself.

I push send, then walk back to the White Room.

It is 3:46 a.m.

I release Ewen from the restraints.

I point the gun at him and say simply, "I will shoot you in the balls if you try anything."

He nods.

Back in the lab, Ewen ushers me to a machine. It looks much the same as an MRI machine.

"You will have to get rid of the gun, you can't have anything metal in there."

I have no reason to trust Ewen, but I do. Not the person. The scientist. I can see the curiosity in his eyes. He could do anything to me, but at this point his biggest worry is if he can fix me.

I lay the gun on the counter.

"Your watch too," he says.

I take it off and set it next to the gun.

It reads 3:50 a.m.

I laugh at the thought this might be the last time I ever check the time. When I wake up, time will no longer matter.

"Lie down," he says.

I lie down in the machine.

It whirs to life.

"Okay," Ewen says. "Here we go."

I whisper to myself. "Goodbye, Henry Bins."

...

I open my eyes.

Shapes and sounds swirl around me.

Something hovers over me. Something touches me.

"Henry."

This sound means nothing to me.

"Henry."

What is going on?

Where am I?

"Henry?"

The creator of the sound shakes me.
"He doesn't recognize you," a voice says.
"We have to get him back to the house," says another.
I'm moving.
Upward.
I blink my eyes.
Look down.
Look at the two figures holding me up.
Touching me.
"Do you know who we are?" one of them asks.
I move my head up and down.
I do know.
"Yes," I say.
Ingrid and my father gasp.

My brain feels foggy. The thirty seconds I spent in the machine the previous night must have jumbled up my short-term memory.

Slowly, the events of twenty-four hours begin coming back.

Lying in the machine.

The loud whirring.

Running through all my memories, knowing they would be gone in the next few minutes. My dad teaching me how to leg wrestle. My dad teaching me to drive, then taking me to the McDonald's all-night drive-through. Playing poker with my dad every Wednesday for nine years. The first time I woke up with Lassie on my chest. Tickling him. Rushing him to the vet. Him licking my nose and telling me I was his bestie. Playing with Murdock when he was just a puppy. Murdock stealing and eating an entire Thanksgiving turkey out of my dad's fridge. Ingrid. The first time I laid eyes on her. Our first kiss. The first time my eyes soaked up her deliciously naked body.

I couldn't let these memories go.

No matter what price.

I jumped out of the machine.

"What are you doing?" Ewen roared.

"I am exactly who I'm supposed to be," I said.

"No, get back in there. We need to see if this works."

"I'm not an experiment," I said, then smashed my fist into his face.

I grabbed the gun and pointed it at him.

"Go lie down in the machine," I ordered.

"No way."

I pulled the trigger sending a bullet zipping past his head.

"I'm not gonna ask again."

He backpedaled, then laid down in the machine.

I pointed the gun at him for the next seven minutes, waiting for him to move.

At 3:59 a.m. I made my way into the hallway and laid down, exactly where Ingrid and my father had found me just minutes earlier.

"I didn't go through with it," I tell them.

"Thank God," my dad says, then pulls me into a long hug.

"No matter how many hours it would have added to my life, it wasn't worth losing the memories of the people I love."

The three of us hold each other tight for a long minute.

Wiping my eyes, I ask Ingrid, "Was it hard to find this place?"

She sniffs a couple times, then says, "Your directions in the email were pretty good."

Climb through the broken window, go into the back right office, pull off the sewer grate, climb down, there should be a door with a flashlight holding it open.

I spend the next fifteen minutes telling them all that happened: my OPIC/Opik realization, breaking in, seeing Ewen, how he had masterminded everything — even having Ingrid look into Jennifer Nubers' murder — that it was all just another experiment in behavior modification to see if he could control my actions.

I tell them how he strapped me to the table, how I'd escaped.

"Your hand," Ingrid said.

"Yeah, I don't even want to think what it looks like under all that gauze. I know for certain I broke my pinky, and I'm pretty sure the muscle and tendon on top of my thumb were torn off."

"We'll have to get you to a hospital," my dad says.

I nod, then continue my narrative.

I tell them how Ewen said he could fix me, how I sent them emails so they would know where to find me and how to act when I didn't know who they were. But that when I got into the machine, I started to have second thoughts. Then how I put Ewen in the machine.

"What happened to Ewen?" Ingrid asks.

"Good question."

I push through the door and into the lab.

Ewen is lying on the floor of the lab, he is curled up in the fetal position. With his bald head, he looks just like a newborn.

"He's Benjamin Button," my dad says.

I hadn't seen the movie, but he quickly explains it is about a baby who is born looking like an old man, then ages backward over time.

"Pretty much," Ingrid agrees.

I stand over him.

"Sidney?"

He looks at me with his wide blue eyes. Confused. Scared. He mumbles gibberish.

"What should we do with him?" Ingrid asks. "We can't just leave him here."

"You want to take him home with you, Dad?" I ask. "With Ingrid, Lassie, and me gone, you and Murdock might like the company."

"I changed enough diapers in my day," my dad says with a laugh.

I'm reminded that the drooling, ninety-year-old infant on the floor is my biological father.

I decide he isn't.

The man standing next to me, the man that changed all my diapers . . . he is my dad.

:19

"Here you go, punk," I say, tossing four jingle balls to Lassie on the bed.

His eyes bulge and he darts around, deciding which one to play with first.

I let out a laugh.

A lot had happened over the past three days.

After leaving the OPIC building, I asked my dad if I could have a minute alone with Ingrid.

I told her I didn't care how many hours I got in a day, just as long as I got to spend them with her.

I asked her to marry me.

She cried, said yes, and cried some more.

When we reached the car, my dad was in the front seat, and Lassie and Murdock were in the back. Murdock attacked me with slobbery kisses, and Lassie kept repeatedly asking me how many fingers he was holding up.

Ingrid and I broke the news of our engagement and everyone went crazy. We celebrated by going through a McDonald's drive-through. I ordered a quarter-pounder with cheese, a large fry, a large Coke, and a chocolate milkshake. Lassie, my father, and Ingrid all ordered the same.

Murdock ordered eight Big Macs.

4:00 a.m. came not long after the feast, and while I was sleeping, my dad drove to the hospital. Over the next twenty-hours, I had surgery on my left hand to reattach several of the muscles and tendons in my thumb, then another surgery to put two pins in my pinky, where I broke it in two places.

The doctor said my hand wouldn't be good as new, but in a couple months it would be good enough.

My second night in the hospital, my cell phone had rung at 3:10 a.m.

It was President Sullivan.

He said he was sorry it had taken him so long to get back to me, but that this whole thing with Russia was getting out of hand, and he couldn't even think straight.

I decided against telling him the whole story: that his father had an affair with my mother, that Uncle Sidney, a man he'd known for thirty years, was more of a monster than anyone could have ever known. He had enough to worry about with that Putin guy.

Sullivan explained that Sidney Ewen was the one who had asked him to look into the murder of Jennifer Nubers, and that he had obliged him as it was a dying wish of the old man. He wasn't exactly sure why Ewen wanted Ingrid to be the one who investigated the murder, but he figured she was as good as anyone and put in the call.

Sullivan said he didn't hold Ewen in the highest esteem, as he had been the head of MK-Ultra for its despicable tenure, but that his father had held a certain respect for the man, so the President had always tried to be cordial to him.

I told him about Ingrid and my engagement and he promised he would attend the wedding.

As for Sidney Ewen, aka Benjamin Button, we dropped him off in front of a fire station on the way to the hospital.

My idea.

As far as the OPIC building and the Sleep Control Program, Ingrid had relayed everything we learned to the Director of the CIA. It would be up to him to disclose any information to President Sullivan, though she urged him to try to keep the investigation in-house.

Last night, Ingrid and I had spent a magical night re-christening the new home, but she was now officially back on duty — they even let Billy come back a couple days early — and the two had pulled their first homicide investigation eight hours earlier.

As for Jennifer Nubers, Ingrid, my father, and I were all in agreement it was best to keep the case as it was. The files went back to whence they came, except for the journal pages, which may have gone missing and may have found their way to Delaware.

I watch Lassie play in jingle heaven for another couple minutes, then ask him, "How about you pick one and I put the other three in the safe?"

Meow.

"Yellow. Are you sure?"

Meow.

"Green. Is that your final answer?"

Meow.

"Okay, I am picking for you."

I pick up the red, green, and yellow jingle balls in my right hand — my left hand is heavily bandaged — leaving him the blue one. I walk into the closet and open the safe. I set the jingle balls inside.

There are two other things in the safe. My mother's file. And a flash drive.

On the way out of the laboratory, I snagged the flash drive containing my mother's confession from the computer.

I found it ironic that I now possessed the object the goons were looking for when they destroyed the condo.

"Where is the flash drive?" my mom had asked me.

"It's in my safe, bitch!"

That's what I would say to her if I ever got the chance. Of course, I uploaded a copy of the video to the cloud where it would sit in perpetuity, and Ingrid had a copy in a safety deposit box at her bank.

"Come and get it," I would add.

The condo was now equipped with a state-of-the-art security system. Stuff you couldn't even get commercially. Expensive stuff. If my mother's goons made another attempt to break in, they wouldn't get far.

I close the safe and spin the combination, then walk back into the bedroom. I stare at Lassie, thinking there is something I was meaning to tell him. It takes a moment for it to come to me.

When it does, I pick up the blue jingle ball, the only way to get his attention.

Meow.

"Just a sec," I say. "I have some big news to tell you."

Meow.

"You remember the redhead from Ewen's place. The big tabby."

Meow.

"Her name isn't Bertha. It's Peaches."

Meow.

"Yes, she should have eaten more peaches and less pizza." I pause, then add, "Guess what? She's pregnant."

His eyes bulge.

"You're gonna be a dad."

He coughs. Coughs some more. His impending fatherhood is a grapefruit-sized fur ball in his throat. He stops hacking, then glances up at the ceiling for a long moment. His whiskers twitch from side to side. He is in deep thought. Finally, he moves his glance to me.

Meow.

"Marry her? No, you don't have to marry her."

Meow.

"Ingrid and I are getting married because we love each other and we want to start a family."

Meow.

"Dude, you are a cat. Cats don't get married."

Meow.

"I don't know what will happen to them. They'll probably give most of them away."

Meow.

"You want one? Dude, you can't even take care of yourself. If it wasn't for me, you would die in thirty minutes."

Meow.

"So what you're really asking is do I want another cat? No, I don't even want *one* cat."

Meow.

"A boy. Why a boy?"

Meow.

"So you can name him Justin Timberlake Jr.?"

Meow.

"You and Justin are basically the same? Trust me, you could not be any more different."

Meow.

"Was that supposed to be a dance? It looks like you just had a seizure."

Meow.

"Archibald? I am not letting you name your kid Archibald. He'll get his ass kicked by every cat in town."

Meow.

"Tell you what. I'll call Ewen's maid in the next couple weeks and see if we can go over and visit when she has the litter."

Meow.

"You are not proposing to her."

Meow.

"You can get McDonald's without getting engaged. I will take you to McDonald's right now if you want."

Meow.

"I was kidding. Maybe next week."

Meow.

"Yes, we will go visit. And I guess if you really want one, we can ask them for one."

Meow.

"I told you, we are not ruining this little cat's life by naming him Archibald."

Meow.

"Archie? Yeah, I kind of like that."

Meow.

"Yes, you can have your stupid jingle ball back."

I toss it on the floor and he scampers after it.

I exit the bedroom and notice that on the kitchen table is a huge basket. It is three feet tall and covered in cellophane.

I peek through the clear plastic and eye the contents. A bottle of Cristal, some cheeses I can't pronounce, some meats, pears, strawberries, Swiss chocolates, a tin of caviar, and some crackers.

Easily a thousand dollars' worth of delicacies.

I pull the card off the basket and read it:

Henry and Ingrid,

Congrats on the engagement. Couldn't be happier for you. Looking forward to the wedding.

Conner

P.S. What time will the wedding be?

I smile and laugh.

I'm tempted to open the basket and dive in to some cheese and crackers, but since Ingrid had the self-control not to attack it, I suppose I can muster some as well. Instead, I grab some leftover Thai food from the fridge — Isabel had yet to stock the fridge — and throw it in the microwave.

I do push-ups and sit-ups while it heats, and it feels good to get back into a bit of routine.

I take the food to the table and I get on my laptop for the first time since I was on Google Earth and stumbling on the OPIC building.

I check my stocks, make a couple tweaks, and then log into my email.

I have two emails.

The first is from IhaveHenryBins@gmail.com, and it takes me a moment to remember I sent an email to myself right before I was set to have my memory erased.

I click it open and read it.

Dear Henry,

You wrote this email to yourself. Hopefully it hasn't taken you too long to relearn how to read. I wish I could write you fifty pages, taking you through the last thirty-seven years, explaining how we got here, and why we made the decision we made, but the clock is ticking, and I'll be honest, I'm writing this with one hand and it's taking forever.

Do me a favor and Google "Henry Bins." This is you. This condition is named after you. Crazy, huh? One hour a day. Seems like it would be impossible to live being awake just one hour a day. Now that you are normal, now that you are awake for as long as you like, it might be hard to imagine packing sixteen hours of life into sixty short minutes. Yet somehow, you not only lived, you thrived. But it wouldn't have been possible without one man, your dad.

I wish I could tell you all the great things this man did for you, all the sacrifices he made so your one hour a day could be amazing. How he spent nearly his entire day awake trying to think of ways to make your one hour as educational, as fun, and as normal as possible. Love this man for all he's worth. As for Ingrid, how hot is she? We really knocked it out of the park on this one. If she followed my instructions, then she has spent many hours telling you stories about how we met and fell in love. Marry this woman. Have children with this woman. And never, ever, take her for granted. Not for one minute. Not for one second. If there is anyone who should know how valuable one second is, it's you.

About Lassie. Yeah, he talks. It's weird. He's a pervert, but he's awesome. He likes lasagna — like Garfield, Google it — and belly rubs and jingle balls. Oh, and he knocked up some cat named Peaches. Remember to tell him that.

Lastly, there is a red folder in your father's house. It contains the file of your mother. Find her. Find her if it's the last thing you do.

...

There is a second email.

The sender is Izzy43457ii@gmail.com.

I call Isabel "Izzy" sometimes, so I assume it is from her, but the email account is one I'd never seen before.

It isn't until I read the email that I understand why she created the account. She didn't want the email to be traced.

I can barely breathe as I reread her words:

Henry...It's Isabel. Two men came to my house yesterday and they were asking questions. They wanted to know about the hair sample I sent. They said that one of the hair samples belongs to a man who they have been trying to find for almost forty years. They left me their card. They are from some agency called the CID. I Googled it. It means they are from the US Army Criminal Investigation Command. Henry, I think they are looking for your father.

3:46 A.M.

:01

I push myself up in bed and glance at the clock on the dresser.

3:01 a.m.

Friday, February 26th.

Twenty-six degrees.

Mostly Cloudy.

There is something off about the clock. It's at an odd angle. And it's much closer to the edge than usual.

It takes me another second to realize why.

Just behind the clock, with a tiny paw half-extended, is the newest addition to the Bins family.

Archie.

The orange and tan striped kitten peers at me with wide eyes, then extends his paw to the clock.

"Don't do it!" I shout.

In the three short weeks since Archie came into our lives, he has broken three wine glasses, two picture frames, Ingrid's favorite coffee mug, and one Samsung Galaxy S6.

He glares at me for a couple seconds, then extends his paw.

The clock teeters on the edge of the dresser.

"*Archie*, don't."

Another glare.

Another push.

"Seriously, Archie, don't push it again."

He pushes it again.

It crashes to the floor.

"Dammit, Archie!"

I push myself out of bed and pick up the clock.

The LCD screen is shattered.

I replace the clock and pick the three-month-old kitten off the dresser. I can still hold him in one hand. He might have the same green eyes as his tabby mother, but the *I-solemnly-swear-I'm-up-to-no-good* twinkle certainly came from his father.

I say, "Dude, you have to stop breaking stuff."

He gazes up at me. Eyes huge. Little pink nose wrinkling.

"That's not gonna work on me."

His little mouth opens and he licks my thumb.

It's so cute, my heart hurts a little.

"It's all fun and games until you break another one of Ingrid's mugs," I tell him. "Then you'll be living on the street, buddy."

It's a bluff. If Archie has me wrapped around his pinkie, then he has Ingrid wrapped around his whole paw. The first week we had him, nearly every one of my sixty minutes awake was spent looking at pictures and videos Ingrid took of him the previous day.

Look at this one of him asleep on the couch.

Look at this one of him playing with my keys.

Look at this one of him peeing on the carpet.

I spend the next minute wrestling on the floor with him, chasing him on all fours. He hides under the bed, and I drag him out and plop him on my chest. I tickle his little head, then stand up with him in the crook of my arm.

"All right, you little troublemaker, let's go find your dad and point out his lack of parental control."

We walk out of my childhood bedroom — and by childhood, I mean I lived there until I was twenty-seven — and make our way down the hall to my father's room.

My father isn't there, and with him gone, Murdock — my father's gigantic English mastiff — is sprawled across the bed diagonally, his one-hundred-and-sixty-pound frame taking up nearly half the mattress's real estate. Lassie is curled up into Murdock's belly. No doubt young Archibald had been snuggled into the mix before waking up and heading out on his seek-and-destroy mission.

"Hey, dingbats," I say.

They both stir.

Lassie stretches out his front legs, then slinks to the edge of the bed.

Murdock sees Archie in my arms and whimpers.

"Okay, settle down." I set Archie on the bed, where he quickly scampers to Uncle Murdock.

Murdock licks him a couple times with his enormous tongue, then curls Archie into his body protectively.

"Archie pushed my clock off the dresser," I tell Lassie.

Meow.

"How many pushes? I don't know, three."

Meow.

"He just needs more *practice?*"

Meow.

"I'm not mad because it took him *three tries* to push the clock off the dresser. I'm mad because he pushed the clock off the dresser."

Meow.

"Because, you nitwit, the clock broke when it hit the floor."

Meow.

"I have no idea how much it cost. My dad bought it for me ten years ago. It tells the temperature and the weather."

Meow.

"*Brookstone?* I don't know, maybe."

Meow.

"Yes, I will ask him."

Meow.

"I am not going to go find him and ask him right now." I close my eyes and wave my hand at him. "Listen, all I'm trying to say is that while you are sleeping, mini-dingbat over there is running amok. You need to discipline him."

I don't want to discipline him. I want to be cool Uncle Henry.

Lassie looks at Archie, then back to me.

Meow.

"Take away his PlayStation for a week? We don't even own a PlayStation."

Meow.

"You want to buy him a PlayStation so we can take it away from him?" I shake my head. "And this has nothing to do with the tantrum you threw on Christmas when Santa didn't bring you a PS4?"

Meow.

"No, you weren't good all year. Actually, you were awful."

Meow.

"Uh, for one, you brought like five bunnies into my house, and God only knows what you did to them. Not to mention, you terrorized that little shih tzu down the hall to the point they filed a restraining order against us."

Meow.

"Yes, I understand that when they named him Captain Pancake they were probably asking for it."

Meow.

"*What else?* You and Murdock and those stupid goats destroyed a man's house, and you knocked up his tabby cat."

He glares at Archie, then back at me. His whiskers twitch and I know what he's thinking.

I sigh. "Yeah, I know, if you didn't do all that stuff, then we wouldn't have Archie."

The thought is unbearable. The little kitten can break something every day for the rest of his life for all I care.

I sit down on the bed, and Lassie and I join Murdock, and the three of us fawn over our little Archie.

He bites at Murdock's ear, then bats it around.

It's hilarious.

A couple minutes later, I leave and head downstairs.

It's 3:08 a.m.

I have a lot to do in fifty-two minutes.

I'm getting married tomorrow.

...

I stop halfway down the stairs.

What had yesterday been my father's living room is now in the process of being transformed into a makeshift wedding chapel. All the furniture has been cleared out and a white arch is situated where a flat screen TV sat a day earlier. White wooden folding chairs are stacked and leaned against the walls.

I suppose I was naive to think planning a wedding that would only last an hour would be easy.

I could not have been *more* wrong.

Because we only have sixty minutes, everything has to go perfectly. If the nuptials run long, there might not be time for the father-daughter dance. If we take too long with photos, we might not have time to eat. If it takes longer than expected to cut the cake, there might not be time for the champagne toast.

I weighed in when necessary — these flowers or those flowers, this cake or that cake — but most of the heavy lifting was left to Ingrid and my father.

Anyhow, I continue down the stairs and make my way into the kitchen where my father is hovering over a skillet.

"Hey, Sonnyboy," he says with a wide smile.

He is wearing flannel pajamas and red slippers. His glasses have slid down to the tip of his nose.

"Hey, Pops," I say, then nod at the living room. "Looks like it's coming together nicely in there."

"Yeah," he says, giving one of the pancakes on the skillet a flip. "It's going to look great when it's all said and done."

"What time did Ingrid leave?"

"Around 8:30. She and her parents were here for about three hours helping set up." He pauses, then adds, "Her mother seems to be doing pretty well."

Ingrid's mother had a stroke last July. She was in a coma for a number of days, and when she did come around, she'd lost all ability to speak. She'd been going to speech therapy for the past eight months and had made a lot of progress.

I met Ingrid's parents for the first time three days earlier, when they flew into town from Atlanta.

Over some of Isabel's amazing enchiladas, Ingrid's mother had said, "It's been f-f-forty years since I was up this l-l-late."

That got a good laugh out of all of us.

Her father asked a couple questions regarding my odd circumstances — as a retired investment broker he was especially interested in how I'd managed to amass a small fortune trading stocks online — but for the most part, they left my *one-hour day* alone.

I knew Ingrid had briefed them on my situation and history, though I wasn't certain if this included *The Choice.*

It had come eight months earlier.

I could undergo electroshock therapy on my brain and wake up normal, stay awake as many hours as I wanted in a day. But with an asterisk. My memory would be wiped clean. Not too different than what happened to Ingrid's mother, but when I woke up, I wouldn't have the ability to speak, or walk, or remember a single thing from my past. Every memory I had — my father teaching me math, my father setting up a 3:00 a.m. prom for me, the day I found Lassie, the day I rushed Lassie to the ER because he got beat up by a raccoon, the first time I met Ingrid, the day I asked Ingrid to marry me — would be gone. It would be as if I were a newborn baby.

Or, I could stay the same.

Live the rest of my days with Henry Bins.

A one-hour existence.

If I lived to be eighty, it was the difference between being awake 15,000 hours or 250,000 hours.

I chose the 15,000.

And I didn't regret it for a single moment.

I didn't have *time*.

"Your last meal as a bachelor," my dad says, breaking me from my reverie. He ushers me to the kitchen table and sets a large stack of pancakes in front of me. He quickly adds a plate of scrambled eggs, some bacon, and a tall glass of orange juice.

My dad pours hot syrup over my hotcakes and says, "Oh, Ingrid told me that she didn't want you to call. She said she will see you tomorrow and that she loves you."

I swallow a large bite of pancakes. "She probably wants one last night of restful sleep."

"Probably right," he says.

I take another bite.

My dad claps me on the shoulder and says, "I can't believe my boy is getting married tomorrow."

I laugh and clap my hand over his.

Eight months earlier, I'd learned that the man standing over me, the man whose eyes are growing moist as he thinks about me getting married tomorrow, is *not* my biological father.

My real father is Sidney Ewen, a crazed scientist responsible for creating a CIA black ops program that experimented on thousands of unwitting American citizens. One of them being me. It might be Ewen's DNA I share, but it is the man behind me who *made* me. It is the man wiping his eyes with his flannel shirt who is *my father.*

"Yeah," I tell him. "I can't believe it myself."

"Well, you couldn't have found a better one. That Ingrid, I think the world of her."

"And she thinks the world of you."

I feel him smile behind me, then he says, "Oh, I emailed you the finalized schedule for tomorrow."

Ingrid had christened my father the Time Czar. He would be in charge of making sure we stayed on schedule.

I tell him that I'll look it over.

"And another thing," he says. "It's supposed to snow the next couple days."

"Really?"

"Yep, they're calling for three to five inches. Supposed to start around midnight tonight."

"Think that will be a problem?"

"Shouldn't be. Everyone who is flying in is already here, and the hotel they're staying at is only a few miles away. And Robert only lives a mile down the road."

Robert Yoully is an old acquaintance of my father's and also happens to be an ordained minister. He will officiate the wedding.

"What about Isabel?" I ask.

"Her husband has a big truck. They'll be fine."

We are serving Isabel's lasagna for dinner. This, of course, at Ingrid's request.

"Alright," my dad says, clapping me on the shoulder once again. "I'm gonna hit the hay. Big day tomorrow."

He gives the back of my head a kiss, then ambles up the stairs.

For the hundredth time in the last several months, I ponder calling him back and asking him about his past. Asking him why a couple of US Army investigators had shown up on Isabel's doorstep inquiring about a hair sample of my father's, which I had Isabel send to a DNA testing facility. I wanted to know why his DNA sample triggered a red flag with the Army when, to my knowledge, he'd never served.

Luckily, Isabel had been quick on her feet and told the investigators that the hair sample belonged to one of her uncles who had returned to Mexico. That being said, it wouldn't have been difficult for the investigators to prove Isabel was lying, then connect the dots from her to me, then ultimately, to Richard Bins.

When nothing happened for a month, then two, I forgot about it. Decided it must have been some sort of mix-up. Then the wedding planning started, and it slowly drifted from my consciousness, pushed out by color schemes, flowers, and wine selections.

Speaking of which, I open up my laptop and find the schedule my father had emailed me.

3:00 a.m. - 3:03 a.m. — Put on tux/brush teeth/comb hair

Three minutes?
What if I have to poop?

3:03 a.m. - 3:08 a.m. — Small talk with guests
3:08 a.m. - 3:17 a.m. — Ceremony
3:17 a.m. - 3:20 a.m. — Photos
3:20 a.m. - 3:23 a.m. — Champagne Toast
3:23 a.m. - 3:31 a.m. — Dinner
3:31 a.m. - 3:34 a.m. — Cake ceremony
3:34 a.m. - 3:39 a.m. — First Dance ("All of Me"/John Legend)
3:39 a.m. - 3:44 a.m. — Father/daughter dance ("Isn't She Lovely"/Stevie Wonder)
3:44 a.m. - 3:58 a.m. — Open Dancing (*See Ingrid's Playlist)
3:58 a.m. - 4:00 a.m. — Bride and Groom time

Bride and Groom time?
Two minutes?
I laugh.
I wonder if this is Ingrid's time frame or my father's.

Next, I check the webcam to make sure it's working, open the video recording program I'd downloaded, then set the laptop to sleep mode.

It is 3:42 a.m.

I hear a clambering from the stairs and turn.

It's LAM.

Lassie, Archie, and Murdock.

The three of them sidle up to the table and sit down on their haunches. Archie is still learning and he topples backward.

I laugh, then ask playfully, "What do you guys want?"

They all look up.

It's like they can quadruple the size of their eyes on command.

"Fine."

Half of my "last meal" remains, and I go grab bowls and divvy it up.

All three devour the food.

I notice Lassie has left half a piece of bacon in his bowl. He nudges Archie over and nods at the bacon. Archie gobbles it down and Lassie jumps up on my lap.

"That was nice of you."

Meow.

"You gave Archie your last piece of bacon."

Meow.

"Scrawny? He's a *kitten.* Kittens are supposed to be scrawny."

We both turn and watch Archie. Murdock is lying on his side, and Archie is playing with his tail. Shadowboxing with it.

"Did you figure out a punishment?" I ask Lassie. "For him breaking my clock?"

Meow.

"He can't listen to any Justin Timberlake for two days? That doesn't seem very harsh."

Meow.

"*That* is your worst nightmare? Worse than the nightmare you keep having about being stuck on a Carnival cruise ship with Nicholas Cage?"

Meow.

"I know, he's your Voldemort."

Meow.

"Sorry, your You-Know-Who."

A couple seconds pass, then he looks up.

He puts both his front paws on my chest and narrows

his yellow eyes over his nose. I've never seen him so serious.

Meow.

"You think I should call off the wedding?"

Meow.

"Yes, I do understand that I if marry Ingrid tomorrow, she will be the only woman I have sex with for the rest of my life."

Meow.

"That's because you've never been in love before."

Meow.

"Brenda?"

Meow.

"A *hedgehog?* What is that even?"

Meow.

"A small nocturnal mammal with a spiny coat and short legs, able to roll itself into a ball for defense?"

Meow.

"The spinier the better?"

Meow.

"The one who got away?" I say with a laugh. "Well, maybe someday you'll find Brenda and then you'll understand."

My cell phone alarm goes off.

3:50 a.m.

"We'll have to finish this discussion later, buddy."

I set him on the ground, then head upstairs and spend the next five minutes showering and shaving.

I open the closet and make sure my tux is ready.

At 3:58, I lie down in bed.

Archie and Lassie both jump up on the bed and curl up on my chest.

They know tonight is a special night.

My last night as a bachelor.

:02

For the first time in a long time, I wake up a minute early.

2:59 a.m.

I take this as a good sign.

I push myself up and peek out the window. There are a couple inches of snow and more is streaming from the sky at a steep angle. There are five or six cars parked in front of my father's house, including a large Ford truck, which I'm pretty sure belongs to Isabel's husband.

I smile.

It takes me three minutes to put on my tux, shoes, and black bow tie.

I run into the bathroom and brush my teeth — Ingrid might call off the wedding if I show up with *twenty-three hour* morning breath — then walk out of the bedroom.

I reach the top landing of the stairs and peer down.

The living room has been fully transformed. An amazing array of lights has been strung, softly illuminating bouquets of Ingrid's flowers of choice, Gerbera daisies. There are two high-top tables; one is covered in hors d'oeuvres, the other a two-tier wedding cake. An aisle of burgundy carpet splits twelve white chairs, running from the bottom stair to the arch, now decorated with tendrils of green ivy. A keyboard is situated in the back corner as well as a tripod and a video camera.

I take in the handful of people — most holding a glass of wine in their hand — and start down the stairs. All heads swivel in my direction as I reach the bottom step.

A couple people clap.

My dad, looking as dapper as one can in a twenty-year-old tuxedo, rushes toward me and says, "Five minutes of small talk. Go!"

"Alright," I say with a laugh. "Where is Ingrid?"

"She's in my bedroom."

"Right, I'm not supposed to see her."

My dad nods then pushes me in the direction of Ingrid's parents and sister.

Her father has a linebacker's build, only one that has gone to fat in the last three decades. Unlike my father, he has a whole head of hair, light brown, though I guess he dyes it. He reaches out his hand and says, "You ready for this?"

I shrug and say, "Not really, but everyone is here in the middle of the night, so we might as well do it."

Thankfully, he finds this funny.

He then introduces me to Ingrid's older sister. She is a half-sister from Don's first marriage and is twelve years Ingrid's senior. She gives me a hug and tells me how much she's heard about me. I tell her the same, though Ingrid had only mentioned her once before. If I had more time at my disposal, I'm guessing I would have heard more about her, but Ingrid was pretty good about what she called "triaging my time."

I hug her mother, tell her how beautiful she looks in her splendid lavender dress, then continue my rounds.

Isabel is next.

She is petite, still a head shorter than me even with two-inch heels on, and clad in a light brown dress. I lean down and give my *maid/cook/executive assistant/time-saving fairy godmother* a kiss and thank her for bringing her lasagna. She tells me she brought four trays, which was enough to feed thirty people, then introduces me to the mustachioed man next to her.

Jorge.

He pulls me in for a long hug, then thanks me profusely for the Christmas gift I gave them: a trip for their entire small family — they have two niños — to Disney World.

"*Donde Archie?*" Isabel interrupts.

With my one hour and Ingrid's crazy schedule as a homicide detective, Isabel spent more time with Archie than anyone else and she is absolutely smitten with him.

I gaze around for Team Rampage, but don't see them. I'm guessing they are keeping Ingrid company in my father's bedroom.

She waves me away with a "*Vámonos*," and I move to the next group.

An older couple is seated in the back row of seats. They are both in their seventies, and they could easily pass for a married couple, but they have come separately. The gentleman is Robert Yoully, an old friend of my father's, whom I've never met. He is white-haired and looks every part the minister in a long-sleeved black clergy shirt. A tattered bible is on his lap on which he is resting a glass of red wine. The woman, Bonnie, lives in the house directly across the street from my father. She is pleasantly plump and has squished into a floral dress two sizes too small. When I was younger, the few times my father went out of town, Bonnie would stay over and watch me. She always had something planned for my one hour, whether it was playing board games or making cookies, and we'd kept in touch by email for the past decade.

I spend a quick minute chatting up the two, then head toward a group of three young women, all blonde and all clad in emerald green dresses — Ingrid's bridesmaids: Charlotte (her Maid of Honor), Rebecca, and Megan. All were best friends from high school.

I quickly tell them how much it means to Ingrid that they came all this way, and at this "godforsaken" hour.

Next up, two gentlemen, both from the Alexandria Police Department.

The younger of the two is Billy Torelli, a second-year detective and Ingrid's newest partner. He is dressed in jeans and a purple polo shirt and is holding a beer in each hand.

I'd met him a dozen times in the past year and a half and liked him tremendously.

"Thanks for dressing up," I say.

"What?" he says, grinning. "This is the best stuff in my closet."

"I don't doubt that," I say, ribbing him.

We both laugh.

I turn to the older gentleman.

He is dressed immaculately in a navy suit.

"I've heard so much about you, Captain Marshall," I say, shaking his outstretched hand.

"Likewise," he says.

"Thanks for coming."

"I wouldn't have missed it for the world."

I know how close Ingrid and James Marshall are, him being her first partner when she joined the Alexandria Police Department nearly a decade earlier.

"Sorry your wife couldn't make it."

"Yeah, Linda was pretty bummed that Roger — he's our youngest — that his recruiting trip happened to coincide." He points to his iPhone and adds, "She gave me a twenty minute tutorial on how to shoot video on this thing, and if I somehow screw it up, I might be looking at some divorce papers."

I chuckle and we chat for a quick minute about Roger, a star linebacker at one of the nearby high schools. He is being courted by many of the top schools, but has his eyes set on playing somewhere out west.

There is a knock at the front door and everyone turns.

I didn't think we were expecting anyone else, and I watch curiously as my dad pulls the door open.

A rush of freezing air spills into the living room as two men step inside.

The living room goes silent.

It isn't every day you see the President of the United States.

...

There are murmurs from behind me.

Is that the President?

He's so good looking in person.

Look how tall he is.

How does he know Henry and Ingrid?

Who is that other guy?

I thought he was campaigning down in Florida.

Connor Sullivan and Red — the head of the President's Secret Service detail — are covered in a light dusting of snow.

At six feet five inches tall, Sullivan is the second tallest president in history. Red is five inches shorter, but thicker, and even wearing a dark navy suit instead of the typical black, he still looks like the prototypical body guard.

My father takes both gentlemen's top coats, then ushers them forward.

Though my father has met Sullivan a couple times previously, it is entirely different to have the most powerful man in the world in your home, and I can't help but notice my dad is grinning from ear to ear.

I'm shocked as well.

Ingrid and I sent Sullivan an invitation addressed to the White House, but we never thought for a second he would actually attend. He was in the middle of his reelection campaign. This was crunch time.

Yet, here he is.

Apparently, running the most powerful country in the world can cause insomnia and Sullivan would call me from time to time to chat. The last time we talked was three weeks earlier, a couple days before the Super Bowl. He wanted to bet on the game. He took the Panthers; I took the Broncos. (I have limited football knowledge, but even I know about Peyton Manning.)

We bet a bottle of good tequila.

I won.

Two days later, a package showed up.

It was one of the most hard to come by tequilas in the world, gifted to Sullivan by the President of Mexico himself.

But the President and I hadn't always been so friendly.

We'd first crossed paths a couple years earlier when Sullivan was arrested for the murder of the woman who lived across the street from me. I found myself knee-deep in the investigation, and that was actually when I first met Ingrid, who was one of the homicide detectives investigating the case. In the end, I was able to prove Sullivan was innocent, and the President, feeling indebted to me, gave me his direct contact number.

We were headed for fast friendship, and he and Red actually came to my condo once to join me and my father in our weekly poker game. But not long after this, the President used both me and Ingrid as pawns in an attempt to locate a secret CIA black site operating on US soil. Playing pawn, I was waterboarded, chained up, and beaten, and it's safe to say that Sullivan had lost my vote. He made up for it in a big way, handing over my mother's top secret CIA file. This, of course, would send me down a rabbit hole of experimentation, lies, deceit, and even murder. (Turns out my mother had an affair with Sullivan's father, David, and at one point I was even convinced that the President and I were brothers.) Anyhow, it would take me nearly two months to claw my way out of the abyss, ultimately ending with *The Choice*.

But even now, it is impossible to see Sullivan and not think of my mother, Sally Bins, aka Elena Janev. The woman who walked out on my father and me when I was six years old. For all I knew about her, she was still shrouded in mystery. A novel with the last hundred pages torn out. It had been nearly eight months since I learned that she had experimented on herself when she was pregnant with me. That *she* was the reason I was having an hour-long wedding at 3:00 *a.m.*, instead of an all-day affair at 3:00 *p.m.*

Even harder than that had been stomaching that my mother was a murderer. That she'd killed a sixteen-year-old girl.

It takes me two long breaths for the mirage of my mother to fade. I decide she's already stolen so much from me, I'm not going to let her steal one more nanosecond of my wedding day.

I make my way toward the two men and say, "Look what the cat dragged in."

Red sticks his hand out and says, "Good to see you."

Red and the President have known each other since college. Red is quiet, reserved, yet was known to pull out a hilarious one-liner every now and again. I have a special affection for him, as he had saved my life a couple years earlier.

"I didn't think you were going to be able to make it."

Sullivan waves me off and says, "I needed a break from campaigning."

"Sick of kissing babies?"

"More like sick of kissing ass."

"I bet," I say, then ask, "You guys didn't have any problem getting out?"

Both Red and Sullivan smirk. Though they never give me any specifics, I know a hidden elevator and a secret tunnel are involved.

"Where does the First Lady think you are?"

"Kim sleeps like a stone. I'll be back under the covers before she even knows I'm gone."

We all laugh.

"How are things looking?" I ask, meaning of course the 2016 election.

Sullivan shakes his head. "Not so good."

I knew he was down in the polls, that the unemployment rate and tax hikes had affected his popularity, but I was under the impression as incumbent, he would win re-election easily.

"Well, you got my vote," I tell him with a smile.

"Thanks," he says, giving me a hard pat on the shoulder, then adds, "Have you got any of that tequila I sent you leftover? I could really use one right now."

"Haven't even touched it." I point to a table near the back where the bottle he sent me is chilling on ice. "I was saving it for a special occasion."

The three of us walk over to the small bar and I pour three drinks.

"None for me," Red says. "The roads are going to be hell going back."

"Relax," Sullivan says, handing him the glass. "That's why we brought the Range Rover."

Red takes the glass.

"To Henry and Ingrid," Sullivan says.

We clink and sip.

The tequila is incredible.

A moment later, my dad shouts, "All right, let's get this show on the road!"

The bridesmaids and Ingrid's father disappear upstairs; everyone else finds a chair. My dad motions for me to take my place next to Minister Robert, which I do, and then he signals for Bonnie — who has offered up her musical talents — to begin playing the processional.

From my vantage point under the arch, I can see down the aisle and up the stairs.

I'd never been to a wedding before, but I watched *Wed-*

ding Crashers and *27 Dresses* over the last couple months, so I know what to expect.

At least, I thought I did.

Rebecca and Billy appear at the top of the stairs. All the guests turn in their seats and watch as the two descend arm-in-arm. They continue down the aisle, then separate, Billy finding his way to my side.

He smiles and says, "They needed an extra grooms-man."

I laugh and say, "Glad to have you aboard."

Next are Megan and another of my groomsmen.

Murdock.

He is dressed in a tuxedo.

I glance at my father in the front row. He smiles and nods at Bonnie behind the keyboard who, I know, is also quite the seamstress.

Everyone laughs.

Murdock clomps down the aisle next to Megan, looking quite comfortable in his new duds.

Megan joins Rebecca and Murdock sidles up to Billy.

"Looking good, Big Guy," I tell him.

He licks himself.

Next, you guessed it, are Charlotte and Lassie.

Unlike Murdock, Lassie does not look pleased to have been crammed into a tuxedo.

My father will pay for this at some point in the not-too-distant future.

When Lassie reaches me, I lean down and adjust his little bowtie. "Dude, how could you let this happen?"

Meow.

"Ten Slim Jims? I think you should have held out for more."

He agrees.

There is a collective *awwww* and I stand back up.

Slowly making his way down each stair, in the tiniest little tux ever made, is Archie.

There is a little pillow tied to his back with two pieces of jewelry.

He's the ring bearer.

"Aww," I say, unable to help myself.

He stops on the bottom stair, his green eyes huge, and sits down.

He's trembling.

It's too big a stage for him.

After twenty seconds of coaxing, and the little kitten not moving, Isabel gets up and goes and picks him up. She retakes her seat in the front row with the kitten on her lap, ready to untie the rings from the little pillow on his back when the time comes.

A moment later, the *dum, dum, dee, dum* begins.

I take a deep breath.

I am relaxed, ready for the moment.

That is, until I see Ingrid standing next to her father at the top of the stairs.

A bit of a tomboy and forced to downplay her looks daily as a homicide detective, Ingrid rarely puts much effort into her appearance. Not that she needs to; she is as naturally beautiful as they come. But today, she is angelic. Her chestnut brown hair is up and braided with a couple of perfectly placed daisies. The wedding dress rides low, showing off her perfectly toned shoulders and the neckline of a goddess. Against the white of the dress, her hazel eyes shimmer a bright gold.

"Holy shit," I mutter.

She slowly makes her way down the stairs, her small arm intertwined with her father's.

Her dad's eyes are glassy, and I know my eyes have taken on a similar sheen.

Her beauty is simply unfathomable.

My life is measured in seconds, and I try to make the next twenty last forever. I soak up each graceful step, each quick glance in my direction, as she moves down the aisle.

She smiles meekly as she approaches, and I know she is almost embarrassed by her exquisiteness.

Her father gives her a kiss, wipes his eyes, and then takes his seat next to his wife.

"Oh, hey," Ingrid says with a smile.

I laugh.

"You look amazing," I say.

"I know," she says.

This gets a good laugh.

Minister Robert clears his throat and it reminds me we have a schedule to keep.

I hold out my hands and take Ingrid's in mine.

It is the best moment of my life.

"We are gathered here today," Minister Robert begins.

Seven minutes later, we are pronounced husband and wife.

...

I blink my eyes open.

I turn over and say to Ingrid, "Good morning, *Mrs. Bins*."

Only, she isn't there.

She was scheduled to have the next two days off, but as a homicide detective, sometimes those things are out of her control.

I check my phone, but don't have any text messages from her.

I walk to the window and pull down the blinds with my finger.

My eyebrows jump.

I've never seen so much snow.

Three, maybe even four feet, with drifts on the sides of houses six feet or more. And the snow is still coming. Lined up on the street in front of my dad's house are a series of enormous lumps. The cars from the guests.

Is everyone still here?

That would explain Ingrid's absence.

Maybe she is asleep on the couch.

Maybe everyone had gotten into a *Fargo* marathon and they *are all* asleep in a big pile on the couch?

I make my way into the bathroom and glance in the mirror. Even after twenty-three hours of sleep, I have bags under my eyes.

The wedding reception was forty minutes long and in that short amount of time I had two glasses of champagne, a glass of red wine, and I think I even shotgunned a beer with Billy.

Then the dancing.

Granted it was only for twelve minutes — Ingrid had put together a play list of small bursts of popular wedding songs as well as many of her favorites — but the muscles in my back and legs throbbed; muscles I didn't even know I had.

Maybe it was that one minute of doing the Twist.

Or the Chicken Dance.

I certainly wasn't sore from any Bride and Groom time.

As it never occurred.

In fact, I barely made it to my bed in time, Ingrid dragging me up the stairs while still dancing to *Billy Jean*.

I quickly brush my teeth, not wanting to give Ingrid any reason to annul our one-day-old marriage, pull on some sweats and a tee, then make my way out of the bedroom.

I head to my father's bedroom and stop.

The room is empty.

No humans.

No dogs.

No cats.

Strange.

I start down the stairs.

The living room looks the same as I last saw it. Ivy-covered arch, chairs moved out of the way for dancing, flowers, half-eaten cake in the corner.

I thought my father would have cleaned everything up by now.

And where is everyone?

It must have something to do with the crazy blizzard.

Maybe they are all across the street at Bonnie's.

I continue down the stairs, then stop.

"What the—" I mutter.

There are two bodies on the floor.

Captain James Marshall and Red.

Both are covered in blood and clearly dead.

...

I run through the house.

"INGRID?"

"DAD?"

"LASSIE?"

"MURDOCK?"

They are all gone.

What is going on?

I run back upstairs and grab my cell phone. I call Ingrid. No answer. I call my father. No answer. I call Billy. No answer.

I open the front door.

The snow is packed up against the door waist-high. There are no footprints leading away from the house. I consider running across the street to Bonnie's to check if anyone is there, but it will take me five minutes to plow through the waist deep snow.

I try Ingrid's cell again.

Voicemail.

"Ingrid, what the hell is going on? Your captain and Red are dead and everyone is gone. Call me, plea—" I suddenly realize how ridiculous leaving her a message is and hang up.

She would have called me if she could.

That's when I hear it.

A low whining.

I run to the laundry room and look around.

A head pops up from the laundry hamper.

Archie.

I pick him up.

He is still in his tiny little tuxedo.

He's shaking.

"It's okay," I tell him.

He whines, and I realize he wants me to set him down. I do.

He scampers forward and then begins clawing at a door. The basement door.

I didn't even think to look down there because, with all my dad's crap, there simply wasn't any room for anything or anyone.

I pull the door open and flip the lights, illuminating a sea of my father's failed tinkerings.

I hear loud murmuring.

The boiler room.

Of course.

I wind my way through the small cleared path to the far back of the basement and pull open the door to the boiler room.

A wave of musty air rushes over me.

My eyes grow wide.

Crammed into the forty-square-foot space, piled one on top of the other, is everyone from the wedding — including

Murdock and Lassie. I scan the faces, searching for Ingrid. She is near the front, lying on top of Isabel and Minister Robert, still clad in her wedding dress. Like all the others, her hands have been zip-tied behind her back, her ankles zip-tied together, and her mouth covered in duct tape.

I scramble to my *wife* and pull the tape off her mouth.

She takes a long breath, coughs, then says, "They took him."

"Who?" I say, then realize I already know.

The President.

:03

It takes me thirty seconds to find something to cut the zip ties with. I return with a box cutter, cut the ties around Ingrid's ankles and wrists, then help her to her feet.

She groans, the muscles in her legs too stiff to stand, and she leans against the wall. She murmurs, "They took Billy too."

"Shit."

I want to ask who took him, but don't. There will be plenty of time for that later.

"Give me your phone," she says, still grimacing from the pain of the blood finding its way back into her extremities.

I hand my phone to her, then move to the next closest person.

Isabel.

I pull the tape from her mouth and she says, "*Gracias a Dios!*"

I cut her restraints, then attempt to pull her to her feet. Like Ingrid, her limbs don't respond, and I surmise that even though the eleven captives attempted to keep the blood flowing, there simply wasn't enough space to do so.

Next, I free Minister Robert, then one of the bridesmaids — Megan, I think — then I come to my father.

My dad has terrible sinuses — his snoring sounds like a truck downshifting on the highway — and sucking air through just his nose for the past twenty-odd hours must have been like trying to breathe through a straw. I pull the duct tape off his mouth and watch as he pulls in a few long satisfying breaths.

I push his glasses up onto his nose, magnifying his watery eyes.

He forces his mouth into a crooked smile, too emotional to speak.

"I'm okay," I assure him, then clip his restraints.

I hand him the box cutter and tell him to get started on the others while I look for something else to use.

"There are scissors in the junk drawer," he says.

I run upstairs and grab the scissors. I am set to head back down when I return to the kitchen and open the fridge. Twenty-four hours without water wasn't life or death, but it was highly unpleasant — shallow breathing, unfocused eyes, slurred speech — and I grab as many bottled waters as I can hold.

Ingrid is still on the phone when I return, and I hand her a bottled water. She sucks down all twenty ounces while she listens to whomever is on the other end. She tosses the bottle on the ground then hikes her wedding dress up and says, "I gotta get out of this thing."

She leans in and gives me a long hug, then disappears up the stairs, her gait still a bit wobbly.

My dad has freed both of Ingrid's parents and is working on Bonnie. I hand bottles of water to both of them, then fall to my knees and begin helping my dad. I clip the restraints on Rebecca and can't help but notice her dress is damp.

My nose twitches.

Urine.

She senses my gaze and her face flushes.

I consider telling her that people weren't designed to go twenty hours without urinating but decide this will only embarrass her further.

My father is now helping people to their feet, leaving me to free the remaining three captives.

Jorge, Murdock, and Lassie.

I pull the tape off Jorge's mouth.

He says, "Free them first."

"Okay," I say, genuinely moved by this small act of humanity.

I survey Murdock and Lassie.

The duct tape has been wrapped around Murdock's large snout multiple times, then both pairs of his legs have been zip-tied together. As for Lassie, the attackers apparently didn't see him as much of a threat and their answer was simply to zip-tie him to Murdock. The zip-tie went around his neck, then around the zip-tie securing Murdock's back legs. They were *literally* attached near the hip.

I snip the zip-tie from around Lassie's neck and pick him up.

Meow.

"He's okay. He was hiding in the hamper."

He gives my nose a quick lick, then I set him down and he scurries off to find Archie.

Next, I gingerly unwrap the tape around Murdock's snout, knowing the last layer is going to hurt no matter what I do.

"I'm gonna do this like a Band-Aid. Okay, buddy?"

I pull off the tape with an audible tearing and Murdock whines. He recovers quickly and attacks my face with his tongue. I clip the zip ties securing his front and back legs, and to my dismay, he finds his feet.

Lastly, I free Jorge.

It is 3:14 a.m.

...

As I carry Bonnie upstairs — not the easiest of tasks — I hear Ingrid shout, "This is a crime scene! Don't touch anything and be careful where you step."

"There's four feet of snow out there. How am I gonna get home?" asks a voice I'm pretty sure belongs to Minister Robert.

"The authorities should be here soon," comes Ingrid again.

"Not without a snowplow they won't be," my father interjects. "I haven't seen this much snow in thirty years."

"Where are we supposed to go?" asks Ingrid's father.

Bonnie and I reach the top of the stairs and she leans into me and whispers, "Everyone can go to my house." She pauses, then adds, "I have Cranium."

Part of me wants to laugh, but under the circumstances, I can't find the energy. I gingerly set Bonnie down in one of the white folding chairs and gaze around.

Everyone is spread out, holding a bottled water in one hand and an energy bar in the other. You can already see the water and the calories taking effect. Pale, listless faces have regained a bit of their color.

I cough a couple times.

Everyone's eyes find me and I say, "Like Ingrid said, this is a crime scene, so we can't stay here, and because of the blizzard, we can't go far." I cock my head toward Bonnie in the chair next to me, and add, "Miss Bonnie has been kind enough to offer up her house as a haven until we can figure things out."

I look at Ingrid.

She nods.

I turn toward my dad and say, "Load up all the leftover lasagna, plus whatever food you can find and pack it up. Who knows how long we're going to have to ride this out over there."

My dad gives me a thumbs up.

I turn to everyone else and say, "Bonnie's house is directly across the street. Jorge, Don, and I will go first and try to clear a path."

"Oh, and another thing," I say. "Bonnie says she has Cranium."

...

By 3:26 a.m., everyone is settled in at Bonnie's.

I trudge back through the snow, which is still coming down hard, and back to my father's house.

"Ingrid!" I shout.

"I'm right here," she says, coming down the stairs. She has swapped out the wedding dress for jeans and a Washington Redskins sweatshirt. She lets out a long sigh and says, "That was the greatest pee of my life."

"I bet," I say, pulling her to me.

We hold each other for a long moment, then I say, "I thought you were dead."

I feel her dissolve in my arms.

She would have been the strong one, the one who, from behind the duct tape, was murmuring to others that everything was going to be okay. But now, the tears run freely.

"It was impossible to tell time down there," she says with a loud sniff. "I was sure 3:00 a.m. passed hours earlier and that maybe you were—"

She stops, wipes her eyes, then finishes, "Then we heard the footsteps."

We hold each for a couple minutes, then she wipes her eyes with her sweatshirt. Her gaze moves over my shoulder to where Marshall's body lay on the floor.

"Poor Linda," she says. "I have to call her. And Billy's mother. Oh, God."

She pulls out her cell phone, then realizes that it's mine. That their numbers aren't programmed.

I gaze at Red.

I'm not sure if he had any family.

My eyes begin to mist over and I wipe them. I let out a long exhale and ask, "What happened?"

Ingrid takes a deep breath and says, "After I got you upstairs, I came back down. With the snow, no one really wanted to leave and we kept dancing."

"Even Sullivan? I thought he would have left right at 4:00 a.m."

"Yeah, me too, but he seemed to be having just as much fun as everyone else. He and Marshall were chatting in the corner for quite a while, but he made it onto the dance floor for a couple songs."

"I'm surprised Red didn't make him leave, with the snow and all."

"I don't think they were too concerned. They were in a friggin' Range Rover. Plus, Red kept looking out the window to make sure it wasn't getting too bad."

Was one of those lumps of snow out front the President's Range Rover? Did it have tracking? Of course not. They wouldn't use a car from the presidential motor pool. Not if they were going to sneak out.

Ingrid takes another deep breath, then continues, "At around 4:30 a.m., Megan put on this old song and we start doing this dance we used to do in seventh grade. Everyone is laughing, having a great time, then the front door bursts open and three men barge in and start screaming in Arabic."

"Terrorists?"

"Yeah, they were dressed like those ISIS guys: fatigues, long black shirts, and black hoods. The only thing you could see were their eyes. One had a long black beard."

With only an hour a day, I didn't keep up much on current events, and I knew almost nothing with respect to ISIS, but even I'd heard about the attacks in Paris.

"The one with the beard started yelling in Arabic and pointing to the ground," Ingrid continues. "Red and Marshall wouldn't go down. Marshall made a go for one of the terrorists. Red tried to stop him, but it was too late. They shot Marshall twice in the chest, then turned the gun on Red and shot him too. They had silencers, no way any of the neighbors could have heard. Then they zip-tied and duct-taped everyone, confiscated all cell phones, watches, jewelry — they even took the video camera — then they forced us downstairs and put us in the boiler room."

I look down at her hand. The four-carat diamond ring I bought her, the one I slipped on her finger twenty-four hours earlier after saying "I do," is gone.

I shake away the thought, then say, "And Billy and Sullivan never made it down?"

"Nope."

Billy and Ingrid had grown very close since she was paired with the rookie detective a year and a half earlier. He was the little brother she never had. At least once a week, she would update me on whatever woman Billy was dating — he was something of a playboy and had slowly worked his way through the Alexandria Police Department — and she would do it with a smile threatening to leap off her face. It was Billy, not Sullivan, who would keep Ingrid sharp, who would keep her from letting her emotions get the better of her.

I let out a long exhale, then add, "And nobody was looking for any of you because of the blizzard."

She nodded. "Isabel and Jorge had a babysitter, but the sitter probably just figured that they got caught in the storm. And if friends or family were trying to contact any of the others, they would have figured the same. No one would have suspected foul play, and I doubt anyone was declared missing."

"Except for Sullivan."

He never made it back into bed next to the First Lady. So when she woke up and no one could find him, shit hit the fan.

"Right," Ingrid said. "Except for Sullivan."

Ingrid pulls my Samsung Galaxy out of her pocket and shows me the top news story.

President Sullivan Missing!

Underneath the main headline is the second lead story: *Snowpocalypse hits DC!*

I shake my head in awe, then say, "And when this gets out, tomorrow's headline is going to read '*President Sullivan Kidnapped by Terrorists.*'"

"Can you imagine?"

It would, undoubtedly, be one of the biggest stories in the history of the world.

"How long until the cavalry shows up?" I ask.

It's closing in on 3:40 a.m.

"I called my contact at the FBI and he's rounding up the troops."

She explains how tricky the situation will be, at least from a jurisdictional standpoint. Technically, my dad's house is in Annandale, which is within the Fairfax County Police Department's jurisdiction. Technically, they should have been informed and would likely have jurisdiction as far as the double homicide went. But as a kidnapping was involved — and not just any kidnapping, but the kidnapping of the most powerful man on planet Earth — the FBI would take the lead. Then with ISIS in the mix, you had the Department of Homeland Security, the DOD, even the CIA. And with Red being Secret Service, who knew what their involvement would be.

"I can't believe they aren't here yet," she mutters. "Friggin' blizzard."

...

I return to Bonnie's at 3:50 a.m.

A snowplow, actually five snowplows, have made their way onto my father's street and are clearing the snow away for what I guess will be absolute chaos in the coming hours.

I expect Bonnie's to be a frenzy, everyone buzzing about

what has happened, but mostly everyone is exhausted — not to mention traumatized — and many have found their way to a bed.

No one is playing Cranium.

Ingrid's father is sitting in a chair in the living room, sipping a glass of brown liquor. His wife is asleep on the couch. Don asks how Ingrid is doing and I tell him she is doing well, that she is getting her game face on, and I suspect she won't get much sleep for the next forty-eight hours.

He nods solemnly.

He, like everyone else, appears emotionally spent. Hollowed out by the preceding twenty-four hours.

Isabel and Bonnie are in the kitchen, cleaning dishes. I give them both hugs and ask them how they're doing. Isabel was able to get in touch with her sister who was watching their children, so she is relatively calm. Bonnie also seems remarkably okay. Maybe she is still in shock. Maybe in three weeks she will wake up with night terrors, then spend the next two years in therapy combating PTSD. But for now, she seems fine. She tells me to take a seat and that she'll get me some food.

I join my father, Minister Robert, and Jorge at the kitchen table. There are clean plates in front of all three, each marked by residual tomato sauce.

"How are you guys doing?" I ask.

"I still can't believe it," says Minister Robert, rubbing his wrists which are red and raw from the zip ties.

"Sort of hard to wrap your head around," my dad says. "Terrorists crashing your son's wedding and kidnapping the President of the United States."

"*Loco*," quips Jorge.

Bonnie and Isabel descend on me with all manner of food and drink: two slices of lasagna, a big glass of milk, some Oreos, an apple, and some sort of pink juice.

I take a bite of lasagna, wash it down with a swig of milk and ask, "Where are the dingbats?"

My dad says, "They're downstairs, playing with Chester and Gretchen."

Chester?

Gretchen?

"You remember Chester and Gretchen," my dad says. "Bonnie's dogs."

My jaw drops.

"Chester and Gretchen are still alive?"

Chester and Gretchen are two little Yorkies. Sometimes Bonnie would bring them over when she would watch me. I'd always try to play fetch with Chester, but he never seemed interested. He just wanted to hump your leg. And Gretchen would just follow one step behind Bonnie at all times. She never so much as licked my hand.

"They cannot still be alive."

"Sure are," my dad says nodding. "Chester is sixteen and Gretchen is going on nineteen."

Nineteen!

What was that in dog years?

I do the calculation.

Gretchen was one hundred and thirty-three years old!

"How is that even possible?" I ask.

My dad shrugs.

"Can they, like, function?"

"Eeh," my dad says, his face grimacing.

"What's that mean?"

He tells me that I'll have to see for myself, then readjusts himself in his chair.

I notice him wince.

I didn't even think about my dad's back. He slipped a couple discs a few years earlier dragging me up three flights of stairs, and his back was never the same.

Sitting in the boiler room with his arms wrenched behind his back and his legs shackled together — it's a miracle he can even walk.

"I should have grabbed your pills," I tell him.

"I'll sneak over and grab them in a bit."

"You should go soon. There are going to be fifty guys in FBI windbreakers there pretty soon and they're not gonna want you taking anything."

He nods, but I know he won't go for another six minutes, not until I fall asleep.

Jorge says he will go and my dad tells him where to find the pills in his bathroom.

I ask, "What are you going to do about the house?"

"I haven't given it much thought."

"Do you think you could sleep there knowing two men

were shot dead in the living room?"

"Probably make the property value skyrocket," chimes Minister Robert.

"I don't think that's how it works," I say. "Not a whole lot of people in the market for a house with a double homicide."

"Of course not," Robert says. "But the house where the President was kidnapped by terrorists? I mean, come on, people are going to pay top dollar for that."

I nod.

He's probably right.

I spend the next couple minutes eating everything in front of me, then say, "Well, I better find a place to crash."

"Bonnie made up the couch for you in the basement."

"Thanks, Bonnie," I say.

She blows me a kiss.

I stand up, as does my dad, and I pull him into a hug. "I never got to thank you for putting on the wedding."

"Went off without a hitch," he says. "Well, *almost.*"

...

Unlike my father's, Bonnie's basement is finished. Her late husband was a contractor and he put in the carpet and drywall himself. There is a small bar, a pool table, and a large sectional sofa surrounding a TV. The couch is covered in blankets and graced with a plump pillow.

Murdock, Lassie, and Archie are all circled around the pool table, gazing beneath it. At some point the three of them had shed their tuxedos.

I lean down on my haunches and peer under the table at what appears to be a large rodent. It takes me a moment to realize the rodent is, in fact, a dog.

Poor Chester; half his fur has fallen off, his eyes are soft blue orbs, one of his ears is gone — just gone — his tongue droops out of the left side of his mouth, and his little red wee-wee hangs limply from its sheath.

I watch as he walks forward, hits one of the leg posts of the pool table, turns around, and walks directly into another one of the leg posts.

I cringe.

"Why are you guys just staring at him?" I ask.

Meow.

"You guys are playing a game? What game *exactly* are you playing?"

Meow.

"You're playing *tag*?"

Meow.

"Chester is *It*?"

Meow.

"He's not very good? Well, I wonder why. Maybe it's because he can't see and he can't hear." And he probably wishes he'd died three years ago.

Meow.

"It was *not* his idea."

I gaze down at him and say, "Just promise me you'll be nice to him while we're here. Remember we are guests."

Murdock barks.

"I know, buddy. You're nice to everyone."

I give his big ears a rub and notice for the first time that his snout is red and raw where the duct tape had been pulled off. "Sorry about your nose, Big Guy," I say, giving his big black nose a kiss.

He smiles and wags his tail.

"Okay, now where is Gretchen?" I ask.

Lassie leads me over to the back corner, where there are two dog beds. Gretchen is lying in one of them, asleep. She more or less looks the same as Chester, and I suppose when it gets to that point, it can't get much worse. The only difference, she is wearing a small little diaper.

Meow.

"No, you cannot start wearing one."

Meow.

"She can't control her bowels. *You* are just too lazy to walk to your litter box."

Meow.

"What's a GILF? Nevermind, I don't want to know."

I tell him that I don't want him within twenty feet of her.

I make him pinky promise.

He does.

:04

"What was the President doing here?" asked the Deputy Director of the FBI. "That's what I want to know."

It was nearing 9:00 in the morning. Ingrid hadn't slept in more than forty hours, but her mind was alert. She'd spent the last few hours at Bonnie's consoling her sister and Charlotte. Both had been traumatized by the event and Ingrid attempted to prep them for what was to come: that they were witnesses to a horrible crime and they would be interviewed soon by the Feds. She'd also spent twenty minutes on the phone with Billy's mother, breaking the news and assuring her she would do everything in her power to make sure Billy came back safe. Then she made the call that she'd dreaded, to Linda, her captain's wife, and told her that James had been shot. Killed. Ingrid was barely able to get the words out.

Linda had been inconsolable. She said she would get the first flight back, but Ingrid told her it would be days until any of the airports reopened.

Now, Ingrid appraised the second-highest-ranking official in the FBI, a man two inches shorter and a hundred pounds heavier than herself, and said, "My husband had become friends with Sullivan over the past year."

The word *husband* felt odd on her tongue. It was the first time she'd said the word. After it came out, she decided she quite liked how it tasted.

"Friends?" the deputy barked, his fleshy face flushing. "I'm friends with the President too, but he didn't come to my kid's bar mitzvah."

Ingrid highly doubted FBI Deputy Director Jonathan

Beech and President Connor Sullivan were friends. Unless Sullivan was lying when he compared the man to having a splinter in your ass you just couldn't get out.

"It was a surprise to us when Sullivan and Red showed up," Ingrid said.

"I bet," huffed Beech.

Presently, Ingrid and Beech were in one of the FBI's mobile command centers. It had taken the large customized cargo van four hours to travel the twelve miles from DC to Annandale, shuffling along behind the three snowplows carving out the road.

In front of her father-in-law's house, snowplows had been running full force since 3:45 a.m. and Ingrid thought it safe to assume that the cul-de-sac where the command center was now parked was the only serviceable street within a fifty-mile radius of DC.

The snow had finally let up an hour earlier, ending its thirty-hour onslaught. The storm, which meteorologists predicted would drop a few *inches*, punished the mid-Atlantic with upward of three feet. A state of emergency had been declared in DC, as well as multiple counties in Virginia, Maryland, Delaware, and North Carolina.

According to the mayor of DC, it could be as long as a week until the city dug itself out.

"And how exactly did the President get out of the White House without anyone knowing?" Beech asked.

"I have no idea," Ingrid said, shrugging. "But it wasn't the first time they did it." She explained how on at least three other occasions she knew of, Red and Sullivan had snuck from the White House undetected. "Why don't you ask the Secret Service about that?"

Beech sneered at her. "Yeah, that never crossed our mind." He took a deep breath and said, "We've been working with the Secret Service looking for Sullivan since 9:00 a.m. yesterday morning when he missed a briefing with his Chief of Staff."

And they didn't have a single lead on his disappearance until nearly twenty hours later when Ingrid called her contact at the FBI and reported the President's kidnapping.

"Can you bring me up to speed on what the FBI has done so far?"

Reluctantly, Beech spent the next ten minutes detailing the actions the FBI had taken since the President was declared missing. Nearly every FBI agent in the United States was working the case, as well as over twenty thousand other law enforcement officers. The interstate and all airports within a one-hundred-mile radius were shut down. Every airport in the US was on Severe Alert and passengers were being advised to arrive five hours before their flights to make sure they made it through the increased security. All private and chartered flights were on a seventy-two-hour flight restriction. Every interstate and highway in America was covered in checkpoints. The borders, both north and south, were closed. All ports, closed. It was an unprecedented, near nationwide shutdown of travel and commerce.

It was one thing to kidnap the President; it was another thing to get him out of the country.

And as of 6:00 a.m., an APB for three Arab men went out. Already five hundred men had been detained for questioning.

The door to the van opened and a gentleman and a woman entered. The man was dressed impeccably in a dark suit and an even darker coat; the woman was clad in jeans, a red parka, and a matching beanie.

"About time," spat Beech.

"Yeah," said the woman. Ingrid guessed her to be in her late thirties. Her skin was caramel brown, and she reminded Ingrid of the character Olivia Pope from her favorite TV show. "I'm second-guessing buying that Prius now."

The woman introduced herself.

Tasha Reeves.

The man was Greg Cooper.

Though Ingrid had never seen either of them, she knew them by reputation. Cooper was the SAC, Special Agent in Charge, of the FBI Field Office in DC, and Tasha worked out of the Baltimore field office, heading up the FBI's Violent Crime Unit.

"Has anyone been over the crime scene yet?" Cooper asked, rubbing his fingers through a well-kept goatee that was a couple shades darker than his wavy brown hair.

The goatee reminded Ingrid of Cal, her partner before Billy. Cal was no longer alive, having eaten a bullet at the hands of Red over a year and a half earlier.

She thought about Red.

Lying on the ground, two bullet holes in his chest.

Then she thought about Billy.

Where was he?

Was he still alive?

"No one has been inside yet," Beech said. "We get one shot at this and we don't need a bunch of idiots mucking up the scene. Bad enough there was a wedding there last night."

"Yeah, sorry about that," Ingrid said sarcastically.

Reeves' face brightened and she said, "Congratulations."

Womanly instinct cast her gaze down to Ingrid's left hand.

Ingrid brought her hand up and said, "They took the ring."

"Assholes," Reeves said, shaking her head from side to side.

"If you two gals are done," Beech said, "I was hoping maybe we could solve a double murder and find the President."

Ingrid nodded. "And Billy."

"Billy?"

"Billy Torelli, my partner at Alexandria Homicide."

Beech scoffed as if Billy were as germane to the situation as the last time Ingrid flossed her teeth.

Ingrid was tempted to kick him in the shin.

She didn't.

"Anything being done to clear these streets?" asked Cooper.

Beech shook his head. "The whole mid-Atlantic got crushed. Every snowplow in a two-hundred-mile-radius is already working. We've hired every private plow from Kentucky to Indiana to come help, but it's going to take time."

"Media?" asked Tasha.

"Nothing yet," Beech said. "But I'm going to have a press conference here in about an hour. We're going to need the public's help with this. We can't let these guys get Sullivan out of the country."

"They could be already," said Cooper, who Ingrid assumed had been working the President's disappearance since early yesterday. "It's been nearly thirty hours since they took him. They could already have him back in the Middle East by now."

"What about ISIS?" Ingrid asked. "Have they taken responsibility for the kidnapping?"

"There are a lot of terrorist groups out there," said Cooper. "Let's not jump to any conclusions."

Ingrid supposed she was profiling. From the very second they barged through her father-in-law's door, she'd decided the terrorists were ISIS.

"Nothing yet," Beech said. "But we're monitoring every terrorist website we know of."

"NSA have anything?" asked Cooper.

"They have half their techs reviewing the past seventy-two hours, but last I heard, they hadn't picked up any chatter."

"So we have no idea who these guys are or how they got into the country?" asked Reeves.

Beech shook his head, but said they were exploring every avenue.

There were a couple moments of stilted silence, then Beech nodded at Ingrid and said, "Why don't you give them your firsthand account?"

Ingrid spent the next twenty minutes detailing the wedding, the attack, the gunning down of Red and Captain Marshall, her subsequent captivity, Billy and the President never making it to the boiler room, Henry discovering them, and their release. She broke the time frame down to the best of her ability, to the minute when she could. She described the terrorists, though with their hoods, she could only tell so much. Unlike most witnesses, Cooper, Reeves, and Beech never had to interject, never had to prod her for details. She was painstakingly methodical. From the angle the bullets hit Red and Marshall, to the manner in which the three terrorists walked, to the tightness of the zip ties.

"Did you try tracking the cell phones?" asked Cooper.

Ingrid had given Beech the names and cell phone numbers of everyone at the wedding.

Beech nodded and said, "We tried tracking all of them. Only one had a signal. It was coming from one of the cars out front."

Minister Robert's car.

He was the only one who hadn't brought a cell phone inside. The only one who hadn't cared about taking pictures.

"They must have destroyed the others or taken the batteries out."

Cooper exhaled, then said, "Well, let's have a look inside the house, shall we?"

Tasha and Cooper started for the door of the van and Ingrid made to follow.

"Wait," Beech said, grabbing Ingrid by the sweatshirt. "Where do you think you're going?"

Ingrid glared down at his hand on her prized Redskins sweatshirt. Wisely, he released her.

"I'm a homicide detective," Ingrid said curtly. "And I was there. And they have my partner. I'm going in."

"No," Beech said, with a smile. "You did your job. Now, why don't you go take your honeymoon?"

The urge to kick him in the shins returned, though this time Ingrid wasn't positive she'd be able to fight it down.

"She's right," said Cooper, his body halfway out the van. "We need her to be part of this."

Beech's brow furrowed. Though it was urban legend the FBI didn't play well with others, especially local law enforcement, from Ingrid's experience, the legend was more true than false.

Ingrid locked eyes with him.

Two seconds.

Three.

"Okay," he finally shrugged. "But you leak anything to the local PD and your ass is grass."

...

Twelve hours later, Ingrid was sitting at a conference table at FBI Headquarters, just a mile from the White House. They hadn't seen a single other car on the partially cleared roads, which, because of the snowplows, were shielded by ten-foot high walls of snow.

"This is the best I could do," a young FBI staffer said, setting a bunch of croissants, muffins, bananas, and the like in the center of the table.

Ingrid and the other members of the task force looked at the spread questioningly.

"What is this crap?" asked Tim Welds — a beefy guy with close-cropped blond hair — from the Department of Homeland Security.

"Nothing is open," the young woman said. "Not a single grocery store, supermarket, restaurant. Only five percent of the streets are plowed. No one can get out of their house."

"I'm sure they aren't eating this crap over at the White House," Welds said, picking up a stale muffin, sniffing it, then putting it back down on the plate. "Why don't you swing over there and get us some *real* food?"

Welds was alluding to the White House Situation Room, which more than likely was filled with the Vice President, Defense Secretary, the National Security Advisor, the Director for Counterterrorism, the Director of National Intelligence, the Directors of the FBI, CIA, and DHS, a couple people from the DOD, plus a few high-ranking military officials. FBI Deputy Director Beech was rumored to be there as well.

Ingrid was thankful she would no longer have to deal with Beech. In the last twelve hours, she'd stomached all she could of the pretentious, little, fat man.

"You guys have the helicopter you flew me in on," continued Welds. "Use that and go get us some real food. Something that used to be alive."

"Uh," the staffer stammered. "I don't think— "

"You tell Beech we can't work if we don't eat. Half of us haven't eaten a lick all day."

Welds peered around the table for confirmation.

Besides Ingrid, Cooper, Reeves, and Welds, there were three others:

Natalie Cambridge, a forensics expert with the FBI.

Donald Rutledge, with Chesapeake Port Authority.

And Susan Wilhelm, a liaison with the Secret Service.

Three men, *four* women.

It wasn't lost on Ingrid that twenty years ago it would have been seven men in the room. Heck, ten years ago, they would have been lucky to have one woman in the mix.

None of the others felt as strongly as Welds on the food issue and many began diving into the platter.

Ingrid, who'd only eaten an energy bar in the last thirty-six hours, grabbed a muffin and a banana and began eating.

"What I want to know," Cooper said, all eyes turning in his direction, "is how these guys knew the President was going to be there?" He turned to Ingrid and said, "I mean, you guys didn't even know he was going to be there, right?"

Ingrid swallowed down a bite of muffin, then said, "We sent Sullivan an invitation a couple months earlier, but he never responded. I doubt it even made its way to his desk."

"But you also said that your husband speaks with him on the phone every once in a while."

"He does. In fact, they talked just a couple nights before the Super Bowl, but Henry said the wedding never came up."

"And no one else, no other guests, knew he was coming? Or posted about it on Facebook or Twitter while it was happening?"

Cooper and Reeves had spent a good portion of the afternoon at Bonnie's interviewing everyone who attended the wedding. Ingrid knew everyone's social media outlets had already been checked and there were no postings about the President, let alone the wedding itself. Still, Ingrid couldn't help but notice the air of uncertainty in Cooper's voice.

She shook her head.

"You never mentioned to your parents or friends that you knew the President?" Cooper asked.

Ingrid blushed. She *had* told her parents. Told her mom that Henry had the President's private cell phone number. Her mother had found this terribly amusing.

"Sure, I mentioned it to my parents, but nobody else."

"What about your husband, how many people do you think he told?"

Ingrid had briefly explained Henry's condition to the group, but she didn't go into much depth. She said, "Well, with being awake only an hour a day, he doesn't have much contact with the outside world. If he told anyone, it would have been Isabel, who is basically his executive assistant, or his—" she stopped herself, biting her tongue.

"Or his what?" demanded Cooper.

"Or his cat." She fought down a smile. "He talks to his cat."

Natalie, the forensic expert, laughed from across the table and said, "Oh, I do that too."

Ingrid shook her head. "Not like this. He has, like, full on conversations with him." She found herself smiling just thinking about the two idiots. *Her* two idiots. No, she forgot about Archie. Her *three* idiots.

"Do you have the statements from everyone at the wedding?" asked Welds.

Cooper slid a folder across the table and said, "These are all the witness statements, plus all the statements from every house on the block."

Ingrid had spent most of the afternoon trudging through the snow, going door-to-door. There were about twenty houses on her father-in-law's street and cul-de-sac.

"Anybody at any of the houses see anything?" Welds said, opening the folder.

Cooper shook his head. "A woman in the house next door said she heard music coming from the house around the time of the wedding, but that's about it." He added, "There were four or five houses on the block where no one came to the door."

"They probably all got snowed in somewhere," said Natalie Forensics.

Cooper nodded and said, "Anyhow, copies are being made for everyone right now. Unfortunately, we are working with a skeleton crew. It's only Jessica, the woman who brought the food, and an intern named Jake or Jack, who were able to dig their cars out."

"You need to get some more staff here and fast," quipped Donald Port Authority, the first words Ingrid had heard him utter.

"I think that's what Beech is trying to accomplish right now," Cooper said. "Sending snowplows and SUVs to pick people up from their homes. And he's trying to get his hands on all those Hummers that no one wants to buy these days."

Ingrid tried to think of the last time she saw a Hummer on the road.

It must have been six months.

"But they can't get us any pizza," Welds said, shaking his head.

"There probably isn't a pizza place open in the sur-rounding hundred miles," retorted Tasha. "Now quit being such a pussy and eat a fucking muffin."

Ingrid bit the inside of her cheek to keep herself from laughing.

She would have to get a couple glasses of wine in Tasha when this was all said and done.

She'd be a hoot.

"Okay," Cooper said, the team leader, a role he wore well. "Let's go around the room real fast and update what we know." He pointed to Donald Port Authority and said, "Why don't you start us off?"

Donald worked for the Chesapeake Port Authority which oversaw all the seaports and harbors throughout Delaware, Maryland, and Virginia. He spent the next five minutes tell-ing them what he could have summed up in three words: "Everything is shut down."

Next was Natalie Forensics.

She spent twenty minutes telling them what they found.

They'd pulled twelve fingerprints from the crime scene, and all but one matched the elimination prints they'd taken from the witnesses at Bonnie's. The one unmatched finger-print was on a piece of duct tape, which could have come from one of the terrorists prior to them putting gloves on. They ran the print through AFIS, but it didn't match any known persons or terrorists. The bullets that killed both Red and Captain Marshall were consistent with Kalashnikovs, and the perforations indicated silencers were attached. Bal-listics was running more tests, trying to match the bullets to any other crimes, but it was doubtful they would get any hits. They had found the President's Range Rover parked on the street. They ran the plates and the car had come back registered to John Legend, Sullivan's favorite musician.

"Well, that fingerprint on the duct tape is at least something," Susan Secret Service said.

Natalie shrugged. "It could have come from one of the terrorists, but it also could have come from the guy at the hardware store who stocked the tape, or the checker, or a hundred other people."

Cooper nodded, then said, "How about you, Susan? Anything to report?"

"Yeah, like how did the Secret Service lose the President?" Welds spat.

"Cool it, Tim," Cooper said. "It's not like Susan lost the President. And the President knew what he was doing. No one forced him to sneak out of the White House; it was his decision."

"You guys figure out how they got out undetected?" asked Donald Port Authority.

Susan shook her head. "We haven't. We know there has to be some secret exit somewhere in the private residence, but apart from ripping the place, well, apart, we won't know."

"So rip the place apart," Welds said, shrugging.

"You just want us to start smacking walls down with a sledgehammer?" Susan asked. "This isn't a frat house, Tim. This is the White House."

Ingrid smiled at the exchange. Susan and Tim obviously knew one another. Ingrid wondered if they knew each other more than just professionally. Something told her they did.

"Any video surveillance?" asked Tasha.

"There isn't any in the private residence. Sullivan's orders. There are agents stationed outside the only ingress twenty-four/seven, but no cameras."

Donald said, "So there is, what, some secret elevator shaft behind a wall somewhere that leads to the underground tunnels—"

"It doesn't matter," Ingrid said, breaking her silence. "Who cares how he got out? He did."

"The hell it doesn't matter," Welds muttered. "The Secret Service let the President slip out of the most protected house in the known universe."

Susan stammered, "We didn't—"

"Ingrid's right," Cooper said. "It doesn't matter how he got out. All that matters is that he was taken by terrorists."

He nodded to Welds, "You're up."

If Welds was a giant ass, and Ingrid was absolutely certain he was, his knowledge was equally giant when it came to the chess match that was the Middle East and overall terrorism directed at the United States. He listed off a number of different terrorist groups, but he, like everyone else at the table, felt strongly this was the work of ISIS.

He said, "We have to hope and pray these assholes don't get Sullivan back to Sandland because if they do, there isn't a chance in hell we're ever gonna see him again."

"It isn't just the President," Ingrid said. "They have my partner."

"Right," Welds said. "Sorry."

The door opened and the female staffer who dropped off the food earlier, Jessica, walked through. She was a holding a large stack of pizza boxes.

Welds whooped.

For the next hour they ate.

At around 1:00 a.m., like Tasha and a couple others, Ingrid found a slice of the floor and fell asleep.

:05

To most people, February 29th, *leap day*, is just another day. But for me, it feels like Christmas.

An extra sixty minutes in my year.

Yahoo.

Well, fifty-eight, on account I wake up at 3:02 a.m.

I push myself up.

I'm alone in the basement.

At least, that's what I think at first.

Lassie has made his way under the blankets, and I can feel him between my legs, which he is prone to do when he feels a little chilly.

I lift the blanket.

Er.

It isn't Lassie.

It's Chester.

I watch the tiny Yorkie, who can't weigh more than five or six pounds, to see if his chest is moving.

One second.

Two.

Three.

Four.

His chest moves.

He is alive.

For now.

I stand up, then bunch the blanket up, and set him in the middle. I head upstairs and find my dad asleep on the living room sofa. Murdock is snuggled up against the side of the couch, my father's hand resting on his back.

I wonder where Archie and Lassie are.

I head down the hallway and poke my head into the first bedroom. Ingrid's parents and sister are sharing the bed.

In the master bedroom I find Bonnie, Isabel, and Jorge. Bonnie's pleasantly plump frame is taking up half the mattress, with Isabel and Jorge squished into the other half.

I also find Archie.

He is snuggled up in Isabel's arms.

I watch him sleep, savoring each rise and fall of his tiny little chest. After a long minute, I gingerly extract him, careful not to wake Isabel.

"Hi, little guy," I whisper.

He paws at me, his little whiskers firing like the wings of a hummingbird. I rub his belly with my fingers, and his mouth opens and his eyes close.

Happy kitten.

"Let's go find your dad," I say, walking back into the hallway.

I dip my head into the third bedroom.

I should have guessed.

The three bridesmaids, Charlotte, Megan, and Rebecca, are sharing the bed. Lying across both Megan and Rebecca's breasts, like a small feline bridge, is Lassie.

"Your dad is a total perv," I whisper to Archie, closing the door and heading back toward the living room.

The only person unaccounted for is Minister Robert. He only lives a mile away, so he probably just walked home.

I carry Archie to the front window and peek out.

The street has been plowed, but in their haste, the plows pushed all the snow to the sides, entombing the cars parked there in an extra thousand pounds of snow.

No wonder everyone is still here.

Behind the giant mounds of white, crime scene tape crisscrosses the front door of my boyhood home. There are several Fairfax County Police cruisers parked on the excavated area of the street, though I have difficulty believing the FCP was given much authority as far as the case goes. My guess is that the FBI offered them guard duty, and they decided this was better than nothing.

I'm interested in how the case is progressing and decide to call Ingrid for an update.

I check my sweatpants pockets for my cell phone, then remember Ingrid has it.

It takes me a moment to locate Bonnie's landline phone, then I dial my phone number. It goes to my voicemail, and I leave a short message that I hope everything is going well and that I love her.

She has no way to contact me, other than email, and I think about my laptop. In my rush to get out of the house yesterday, I didn't think to grab it. I contemplate sneaking over to my dad's house to get it, then think better of it.

Maybe tomorrow.

Plus, Bonnie should have a computer.

But first, I need to clean up and get some food.

I step into the hall bathroom, relieve myself, then run water over my hands. I notice black smudges on the fingertips of my left hand and pause.

I was fingerprinted.

In my sleep.

Of course, they would need to take elimination prints from everyone, but the idea this was done to me while comatose is eerie. Then I see it, on the palm of my opposite hand.

A small heart.

It was from Ingrid. Her way of telling me that if any funny business had been done to me while I was asleep, she was the one to do it.

God, how I love that woman.

I rub the black from my fingers, splash water on my face, and give myself a quick rubdown with a hand towel. Then I sneak into Bonnie's master bath and find some mouthwash to rinse with. Feeling somewhat human again, I make my way to the kitchen and open the refrigerator.

There is a Tupperware container with a pink post-it note on it: *For Henry, Don't Touch.*

Bonnie, with the help of Isabel I presume, had whipped up a big pot of chili.

I toss the Tupperware in the microwave, eat a banana, and gulp down a couple glasses of water while I wait, then take the chili to a small office where I assume Bonnie keeps her computer.

It is 3:09 a.m.

In the middle of a small desk is a laptop.

I check my email but there is nothing from Ingrid. Then I check the news. It is absolute madness.

The only other thing I can compare the media blitz to is 9/11.

President Sullivan Abducted!

Nationwide Manhunt for Terrorists!

Will President Sullivan be Executed?

Does ISIS Have the President?

Arabs Detained All Across the Country.

The details concerning the President's abduction are vague — there is no mention of Red, Marshall, or Billy, nor my father's house, the wedding, or the attack — and I think back to my fingerprints.

I highly suspect I was the only one at Bonnie's who didn't undergo intense interviewing and scrutiny by the FBI the previous day. During their witness interviews, the FBI most likely used power phrases like *national security*, *best interest of the nation*, *need-to-know basis*, and possibly even threatened incarceration if anyone leaked information about the attack to friends, family, or most paramount, to the press.

Anyhow, I read a quick story detailing Snowpocalypse, which is officially the biggest storm to ever hit DC and the second biggest storm to ever hit the mid-Atlantic. Three feet of snow fell in downtown DC, Annandale got forty inches, and Manassas, twenty minutes southwest, got forty-nine. It would have been one thing if meteorologists had correctly forecasted the storm — they only predicted three to five inches — and people could have prepared for it. But it snuck up on everyone. It came in like a lamb at just after midnight on Saturday, dropping light feathery snow for a few hours. But then around 6:00 a.m., the storm began to surge, dropping two and half inches *per* hour. By noon, over a foot and a half had already fallen, and without a Hummer the roads were impassable. If you hadn't stocked up on food and water by then, you were SOL.

The snow continued to fall for another twenty hours packing the city in more snow than it had ever seen.

Forty percent of the affected blizzard area was without power, the heavy snow toppling power lines, and Pepco, the electric company, wasn't making any promises the power would be restored within the week. Also, many of the cell phone towers, most with back-up generators only equipped to last twelve hours, had begun to fail.

Thank God we didn't lose power.

At least, not yet.

I take a big spoonful of hot chili and think about how much worse things could have been. Then I find myself speculating on the timeline of events from my wedding night.

I wake up at 2:59 a.m.

There are two or three inches of snow at this point.

Tux/I do/Lasagna/Cake/Dancing/Bedtime.

At around 4:30 a.m., the ISIS bastards crash through the door of my father's house. According to Ingrid, it takes the terrorists fifteen minutes to tie them all up and transport them to the basement boiler room.

They leave, at the earliest, at 4:50 a.m.

By this point there are five, maybe six inches of snow.

Depending on what car the terrorists are driving — there's a big difference between a Honda Civic and a Ford Explorer in a half foot of snow — they might not have made it very far.

Of course, theoretically, they could have driven directly to a private airstrip and hopped on a plane, but this would be easy enough to track. Plus the snow was already beginning to surge. Flying might not have even been possible by this point.

No, whether or not they wanted to, they would need to get out of town by car. Which is easier said than done in a blizzard.

Snowpocalypse was blanketing the entire east coast, from Delaware down to North Carolina, so it would have been difficult to go north or south. And east was the Atlantic. The only option was to head west where, even going at a crawl, eventually the terrorists would have pushed through the storm and into West Virginia.

And from there, they could have gone anywhere.

Either way, by 9:00 a.m., Sullivan had missed a meeting with his Chief of Staff and been declared missing. The entire nation would be on an unparalleled level of alertness and lockdown. There would have been roadblocks and check-points set up on every highway and interstate in America. Possibly every street.

The terrorists would have had to hole up somewhere.

"Where are you guys?" I say.

Then I realize I don't even know *who* they are.

I don't even know what *ISIS* stands for.

I do a Google search.

It is 3:17 a.m.

...

The Islamic State of Iraq and Syria.

That's what ISIS stands for.

I read for twenty minutes, and basically this is what I come away with:

- ISIS is a terrorist group that follows an Islam-ic ultra-fundamentalist ideology and controls a vast region across Iraq and Syria.
- They consider themselves at war with all na-tions and with all people who do not meet their standards for "true" Muslims.
- ISIS's first obsession is the apocalypse. They believe their mission is to bring on the apoca-lypse as foretold in scripture.
- Their leader is a little-known and deeply pious Iraqi named Abu Bakr al-Baghdadi.
- For the past two years, they'd been wreaking havoc. They were responsible for sixty attacks in over twenty different countries, most nota-bly, killing one hundred and thirty people in Paris this past November.
- They'd kidnapped the President of the United States and Billy Torelli, and they were doing God knows what to them right now.

I look at a bunch of photographs of the men, dressed in military garb or all black, guns slung over their shoulders, and black hoods with only their eyes visible. Many have beards poking from beneath their hoods. In every picture the landscape is beige, either from the sand or the buildings.

Had a group of these jihadists really snuck into the United States, then barged through the door of my father's house, and kidnapped the President?

I wonder how I would have reacted when the men came in with their guns drawn. Would I have stepped in front of Ingrid, like Red and Marshall had shielded the President?

I like to think I would have, but you never know.

What I'm really curious about is how these pricks knew Sullivan was going to be at my wedding when *I* didn't even know he was going to be there.

Who did Sullivan tell?

And who did *they* tell?

Somehow this information made its way into some very bad people's hands.

And not just the day of.

This thing took some planning.

My brain starts to ache and I flip off the computer.

It is 3:34 a.m.

...

The white snow glows gold under the full moon. Someone, probably Jorge, has shoveled a path to the street, and Murdock takes three gallops onto the concrete, then dives into the snow piled in Bonnie's front yard.

Archie pitter-patters a couple feet onto the concrete, then stops and paws at the tall wall of white.

I laugh.

It must look like The Wall from *Game of Thrones* to him.

I pick him up and softly set him down atop the waist-high snow. He is light enough that he doesn't break through the frozen top crust. He takes a small step then looks back over his little shoulder at me. His orange fur is even more pronounced against the whiteness of the snow, his green eyes full of wonder and a bit of doubt.

He takes another step, then a little jump.

He disappears into the snow.

Murdock starts whimpering, then goes into rescue mode, digging frantically for Archie. A moment later, Uncle

Murdock lifts him out by the scruff of his neck.

Archie is completely white.

But smiling.

Murdock totes him off to where the snow isn't quite so deep, and I look down at Lassie and say, "He seems to like the snow."

Meow.

"Snow is stupid?"

Lassie has his back turned, facing the front door.

He's sulking

"Dude, are you still mad?"

He ignores me.

"Come on, it couldn't have been that great."

He turns around.

Meow.

"The best sleep of your entire life? But, you sleep on Ingrid's boobs all the time."

Meow.

"That is very true. She does not have *four*."

Meow.

"I have to make it up to you?"

Meow.

"A thousand jingle balls? You have like fifteen already."

Meow.

"They have not all run out of jingles."

I make a tiny little snowball and I throw it at him.

It hits him with a puff.

His eyes open wide, unbelieving.

Meow.

"Because you are acting like a little baby." I point to Archie and Murdock. "Look how much fun they are having. Now go play."

He cuts his eyes at me.

"Go play in the snow with your kid."

He takes a deep breath, then he jumps into the snow and joins Archie and Murdock. The three of them dive, roll around, and wrestle.

A minute later, I join them.

Once we are wrestled out, we make our way down to the street and to the end of the cul-de-sac.

"Do you guys hear that?" I say, stopping.

It's a cracking sound.

Murdock's giant head swivels toward one of three houses rounding out the cul-de-sac.

I follow his gaze to the roof, where bits of snow are raining down.

There is a massive shelf of snow on the angled roof. The cracking sound is the weight of the snow and ice calving away. The entire shelf of snow is getting ready to fall.

It takes another minute of cracking, rumbling, tiny sections falling away.

Then it happens.

A thousand pounds of snow and ice breaks away, sliding off and crashing down.

It's awesome.

Murdock barks, scared by the piercing noise.

"It's okay," I tell him. "It's just snow."

He calms down and we head back to Bonnie's.

As I'm going to bed, Lassie tells me that he will accept *fifty* jingle balls and that after more research, snow isn't that bad.

:06

"Up and at 'em."

Ingrid opened her eyes and looked up.

Tasha Reeves was standing over her, holding a steaming mug of coffee. Ingrid pushed herself to her feet and reached for the cup.

"Thanks," she said,

Reeves pulled the cup back. "Girl, this isn't for you."

Ingrid grinned sheepishly and Reeves pointed to a coffee machine someone, probably staffer Jessica, had brought into the room.

Tasha continued going around the room, waking the others.

As Ingrid made her way over to the coffee machine, she could hear Welds groan as Tasha prodded him with her foot to wake up.

Ingrid pulled her cell phone — well, Henry's cell phone — out of her pocket and checked the time.

4:58 a.m.

She noted the one missed call and guessed it was Henry calling from Bonnie's landline. She listened to his voicemail with a smile, then let out a sigh. She wished she could call him back, but he'd been asleep for almost an hour.

Not for the first time, she thought about the one-hour constraint with her husband. But as always, the thought was fleeting. She wouldn't trade twenty-four hours in a day with George Clooney for the one hour she got to spend with Henry.

The others slowly began to wake and made their way over to Ingrid.

Donald Port Authority rubbed his eyes and grumbled, "I slept in my contacts."

Susan Secret Service, who had just poured herself a mug of coffee, set her mug down and found her purse on one of the chairs. She dug her hand around, then fished out a bottle of eye drops. She handed them to Donald and said, "These should help."

"Oh, thank the Lord," he said, then dropped multiple drops into each eye. "Ahhhh, that feels better."

The six of them — Cooper was absent — made small talk and sipped coffee. Ingrid was the first to make her way over to the pizza boxes, find a cold slice, and dig in.

Everyone else soon followed.

"Takes me back to college," quipped Natalie Forensics.

Ingrid nodded. "Cold pizza cram session."

"More like cold pizza hangover cure," quipped Tasha.

Everyone laughed.

This led to a quick discussion on where everyone attended college.

Natalie went to Michigan.

Susan went to Georgetown.

Tasha, Florida State.

Ingrid went to Maryland.

Welds went to Penn State on a football scholarship.

And Donald attended Virginia Commonwealth.

"How about Cooper?" asked Susan. "Anyone know where he went?"

"Temple," Cooper boomed, walking into the room. It was obvious that unlike the rest of them, he hadn't slept a wink, though you would never have guessed it by looking at him. His hair was perfectly parted, his eyes clear, his voice strong. "I played three seasons for Cheney."

"No kidding," Welds said, looking impressed.

Cooper grabbed a slice of pizza, told a quick story of missing a crucial free throw that would have won them the Big East Championship, then immediately switched gears. He said, "Jessica was able to get some extra toiletries from a nearby hotel and they're in the bathrooms. Wash up and be back here in five minutes."

They broke huddle.

Ingrid brushed her teeth with a small brush and small

tube of toothpaste, splashed water on her face, then used the restroom.

She checked the time on the phone.

Five minutes had already passed.

She thought about Henry.

This was his life.

Again, she cursed herself for missing his call.

...

Cooper had spent the past few hours in the White House Situation Room. He briefed them on all he'd learned.

Reports had come back from FBI agents all over the US who were investigating the more than sixty thousand leads that had come in, most having to do with the Middle Eastern family down the block. So far, nothing had panned out.

Ingrid felt a twinge of guilt.

All those poor innocent Arabs profiled, detained and questioned just because of a couple freak jihadists. And all because of the descriptions she'd given.

The NSA had yet to pick up any definitive terrorist chatter in their logs that may have hinted at the attack, nor had they found any leads from the more than 250,000 surveillance cameras they were hacked into.

A $5,000,000 reward was being offered for any information that led to the location of the terrorists.

TSA, with the help of several different agencies, was searching travel manifests going back three months. They were corroborating with agencies from both Mexico and Canada.

The CIA was shaking down every informant they had in the Middle East.

The First Lady was planning a joint press conference with the Vice President who, under the terms of the twenty-fifth amendment, was now Acting President.

"Sullivan's only been missing forty-eight hours," Susan said, shaking her head, "and now Cortney has the reins."

"Well, if you guys hadn't lost him," Welds said, picking up right where he had left off.

Vice President Ted Cortney wasn't Ingrid's first choice as Commander-in-Chief. When he ran against Sullivan in the previous election, he was eighth in the polls when he finally pulled out after the Iowa caucuses. After winning the primary, Sullivan had added him to the ticket. Ingrid had always found him a bit pompous and melodramatic. More suited to host a daytime talk show than be the second most powerful man in the country.

"We can't not have a president," Donald Port Authority spat. "What if we have to nuke somebody? Gotta have somebody to push the button."

Ingrid pushed that thought away and asked, "Have we heard anything from any terrorist group yet?"

"Not yet," Cooper said.

A moment later, his phone buzzed and he excused himself to take the call.

He returned a moment later and said, "Looks like I spoke too soon."

...

Cooper pulled up the video on his laptop and said, "This was posted twenty minutes ago on an ISIS website."

They *were* ISIS.

Ingrid felt a quick stab of vindication, but it was short-lived.

Cooper pushed play.

The screen filled with a black flag clinging to a concrete wall. White Arabic lettering filled the black flag.

Welds, who was fluent in several Middle Eastern languages, pointed to the flag and said, "The writing translates to 'There is no god but Allah. Muhammad is the messenger of Allah.'"

On-screen, four men stepped into frame: two terrorists — clad in all black, hoods over their heads — plus Billy and Sullivan. Both Billy and Sullivan had gags in their mouths.

Ingrid took a deep inhale.

"Dammit," Tasha said. "They got them back to the Middle East."

The two terrorists forced Billy and Sullivan to their knees, then rested long knives against both men's throats.

Ingrid gritted her teeth.

Please, no.

A third terrorist, ostensibly the camera man, entered the frame. He was the one with the beard. He too was fully covered in black from head to toe.

He began spouting in Arabic.

Welds translated.

"This is a message to America. In the name of Allah and Muhammad, we have captured your President. We warned you that if you insisted on fighting the Islamic State you would have blood on your hands. And soon that blood will be spread. We are here because of your President's arrogant foreign policy toward the Islamic State and the continuing bombings in Muhassan, Al-buomar, and the Mosul Dam despite our serious warnings. We take this opportunity to warn those governments who have entered this evil alliance with America against the Islamic State to back off and leave our people alone."

The terrorist paused and glanced over his shoulder at both Billy and Sullivan.

Ingrid could feel both men's unease. They knew the clock on their lives was ticking down.

There was a soft crashing noise and the three terrorists stiffened and looked around at one another.

"Just another day in Sandland," Welds said in reference to the bomb or missile strike.

The terrorist recovered, turned back toward the camera, and said, *"To save your President and this other man, America has until noon two days from now, Iraqi time, to pull all soldiers from Iraq. If you comply, we will return your President unharmed. If you do not, we will send him back in pieces."*

The video cut out.

...

"Noon, two days from now, Iraqi time?" asked Natalie. "What does that translate to here in Washington?"

"Sandland is eight hours ahead," Welds replied.

"So that would be 4:00 a.m. two days from now," quipped Natalie. "4:00 a.m on Wednesday."

Ingrid checked her phone.

5:56 a.m.

She said, "That gives us forty-six hours."

"To what?" Welds asked incredulously. "To pull four

thousand troops out of Iraq. Logistically, that would be close to impossible, not to mention that we don't negotiate with terrorists."

"I meant—" Ingrid said, "—that we have forty-six hours to *find* them."

...

Billy pulled in a long breath through his nose. It was hard to breath with the gag in his mouth. But at least he was alive, a fate he hadn't been certain about a couple hours earlier. When he felt the terrorist rest the knife — a long Bedouin dagger — against his throat, he was sure he was headed to meet his maker.

In that moment, he found himself silently muttering *Our Father*, a prayer beaten into him when he was a little boy attending Catholic school.

Billy gazed at the President across the room, or cave, or wherever it was they were being held.

After the men burst through the front door at Henry's father's, then gunned Red and his captain down, Billy expected to take a bullet himself.

But he hadn't.

But not for lack of trying. When they attempted to zip-tie him, he made a go for one of the terrorist's guns. He got his hand around the barrel, but wasn't able to do anything before he took a hard kick to the gut.

Again, he expected a bullet.

Again, it hadn't come.

Then Ingrid, her parents, and all the others were marched to the basement. Billy assumed he would join them, but instead of being ushered downstairs, one of the terrorists put a rag over his nose and mouth.

Chloroform, he guessed.

He came to a couple times, a hood over his eyes. Once he thought he was in a car, another time, an airplane. But each time he twitched awake, within seconds the rag would find its way under his hood and three breaths later, the darkness would close in.

He'd finally woken up here.

It was a small room, hardly tall enough to stand in, full of concrete and dirt.

The faintest of lights trickled from beneath a door and Billy gazed at the President next to him.

"You okay?" he asked, though it must have sounded like mumbled gibberish through the gag in his mouth.

The President mumbled back.

Billy flexed against the zip ties holding his hands behind his back. He'd tried repeatedly to slip his arms down over his butt, but his wrists were fastened too tightly.

He wanted more than anything to get the gag out of his mouth. It kept bringing him back to a horrible experience with a young woman. She seemed shy the first two or three dates, but the moment they made it to the bedroom, she was anything but.

"Just try it," she prodded, handing him the ball gag.

He shrugged. Why not?

YOLO and all that.

Big mistake.

Now he was back in that room.

With *Angela*.

Though he would give anything to be back there right now. He didn't care what Angela made him put in his mouth, or anywhere else for that matter. Anything was better than being kidnapped by ISIS.

He'd seen the videos.

The executions.

Billy couldn't understand a lick of Arabic, but he knew what the terrorist had said in the video they filmed. They had demands.

What they were, Billy had not the faintest idea. But their demands were the only reason Billy and the President were still alive. Though he wasn't so naive as to think they would be released. No, this was a death sentence.

He had to find a way out.

The door opened and one of the terrorists walked in. Billy tried to see past him, but it was too dark to make anything out. The terrorist kicked the President, hefted him to his feet, then dragged him toward the door. Sullivan gazed over his shoulder, his navy eyes pleading with Billy for help.

But there was nothing Billy could do.

:07

The video on YouTube has over two hundred million views.

Five of them are mine.

I watch it a sixth time. Each time I watch I concentrate on something different: Billy's face, Sullivan's, the background, the terrorist's eyes. This time I concentrate on the transcribed words at the bottom.

We have your President...

My dad is gazing over my shoulder. I wonder how many times he's seen the video. No doubt the video has been playing on a loop on nearly half the television channels.

...evil alliance with America against the Islamic State to back off and leave our people alone.

I note the crashing sound in the background and how little it startles the terrorists.

Just part of life in Iraq or Syria.

...if you comply, we will return your President unharmed. If you do not, we will send him back in pieces.

I scoff.

He was coming back in pieces no matter what.

"How many troops do we have in Iraq?" I ask my father, who I'm sure has absorbed every facet throughout the day.

"Some reports say thirty-five hundred, others say four thousand."

"Could we do it?" I ask. "Pull four thousand troops out of Iraq in time?"

"We won't."

"I know. But is it even feasible?"

"Maybe," he says, thinking. "But they won't."

I exhale as I consider the timeline.

Iraq is eight hours ahead. Noon tomorrow in Iraq is 4:00 a.m. here. The irony that I will be falling asleep at the same time Billy and Sullivan are having their throats cut isn't lost on me.

"Are there cops still parked outside?" I ask.

"No, they left late last night."

"Have you been back over?"

"Just for a couple minutes to grab a clean set of clothes. There's still blood everywhere."

It would be awhile until a carpet cleaner could get over there, though I guessed my dad would want to rip the carpet out and put in new stuff.

I ask him about this.

"Yeah, but it will be a few more days until any of the hardware stores are open."

"I'm sure Jorge would help you, at least rip out the old stuff."

Jorge still wasn't able to get his truck out of the snow, though it was half uncovered.

"That's a good idea," my dad says. "I'll ask him."

I tell him that I'm going to head over to the house.

It is 3:13 a.m.

...

Murdock, Lassie, and Archie join me.

Holding Archie in my left arm, I push the front door open.

I set him down and flick on the lights.

The first thing I see are the two blood stains on the carpet.

"Don't go near those," I tell the three monsters, but they have already disappeared up the stairs.

I survey my father's living room. It looks the same as when I last saw it. The FBI crime scene techs didn't move anything, or if they did, they returned it to its exact same position.

I look at the arch.

Three days earlier, I stood under it and took Ingrid to be my wife.

It feels like it was months ago.

My dad doesn't have a landline, and I curse myself for not calling Ingrid from Bonnie's before I left.

I decide to send her an email.

It takes me a couple seconds to locate my laptop.

It's on the kitchen counter. The screen is black and I tap a couple keys. Of course it's dead. Laptop batteries don't last four days.

I run up the stairs into my bedroom and find the power cord. I poke my head in my father's room. Archie and Lassie are both under the bed and Murdock is trying to get at them with his enormous paws.

I watch for a long minute as Lassie and Archie dart under, over, and around the bed, while Murdock chases one, then the other.

I don't think I've ever seen anyone have so much fun.

Morons.

I make my way back downstairs and plug my laptop in.

Though Bonnie had a grilled cheese sandwich waiting for me in the fridge when I woke up, I'm still hungry. I grab two energy bars from the cupboard and a Gatorade from the fridge.

I lean against the counter and check my email. Still nothing from Ingrid.

I'm set to write her a quick hello when I freeze.

How could I be so stupid?

My heart races as I pull up my video recordings.

The reason my laptop is on the kitchen counter is because it was pointed at the living room to record the ceremony.

I downloaded a program where you could set up the video to start and stop. Kind of like a nanny cam. I set the laptop to start recording at 2:45 a.m. and to go until 4:00 a.m., but then at the last second, I decided to extend the time to 5:00 a.m., knowing the party wouldn't end just because I went to sleep.

I click on the last recording.

It is two hours and fifteen minutes long.

I could very well have recorded the entire attack.

I fast-forward until 4:30 a.m., then hit play.

Everyone is on the dance floor.

In different circumstances, I would smile and laugh as I watch Ingrid and her childhood friends go through a choreographed dance from two decades earlier. Everyone else is circled around watching and clapping. Thirty seconds later, I hear what I am waiting for. Under the music, the sound of the door opening is hardly audible, but then Ingrid and friends stop dancing. All heads turn in the direction of the front door.

The terrorists are out of frame, shouting Arabic from the foyer. I guess they are telling everyone to get down on their knees because everyone in camera shot does. Ingrid and Billy eye each other and whisper something. They are calm. Everyone else is shaking with fright. Rebecca openly sobs.

Red and Marshall are off camera, shielding Sullivan.

I'm not sure what happens, but a moment later there are two soft clicks, followed quickly by another two.

"Dammit," I say.

Why did you guys go after them?

Why not just do what they asked?

But I know why.

It was their only chance of saving the President's life. They knew why these men were there, and the second the two of them were restrained, Sullivan was a dead man walking.

At the back of the screen, Ingrid's hands cover her face at the sight of her ex-partner and mentor gunned down right in front of her.

The terrorists enter the screen. As Ingrid described, they are dressed from head to toe in black. They are masked, with holes cut out for their eyes. One of the terrorists has a long black beard poking from beneath his hood. Two of the terrorists point their guns at the group while Beard moves through the bodies, checking each person for cell phones, removing watches and jewelry, zip-tying hands behind backs, and duct-taping mouths.

They start with Sullivan.

The terrorist lifts his chin.

Sullivan says something, but the music is still blaring and I can't make it out. When they are finished restraining Sullivan, they move to Ingrid's father. Then mother. Then

Minister Robert. Then Isabel. They continue down the row. They come to Ingrid.

Don't you fucking touch her.

The terrorist frisks her, running his hands down her wedding dress.

I feel my hands ball into fists.

"Where is she gonna keep a phone, you dipshit?" I shout at the screen.

Then he grabs her hand and pulls off the ring I slipped on her finger an hour and a half earlier. Ingrid's teeth are gritted and I can tell she's imagining cutting the terrorist's balls off. He tosses it in a bag with the other loot, then zip-ties her hands behind her back.

Next, the terrorist moves to Billy.

Billy lunges for the man's gun, getting his hand around the barrel and yanking at it. It starts coming off the terror-ist's shoulder, but not before another one of the men runs in and kicks Billy violently in the stomach.

Billy crumbles, the terrorist yanking his arms behind his back and zip-tying them together.

Once everyone is patted down and restrained, the ter-rorists begin marching them one by one down to the base-ment, where purportedly they are forced into the boiler room and their ankles are zip-tied together.

When it is only Billy and Sullivan remaining, the terror-ists place rags over both men's mouths. Five seconds later, both Billy and Sullivan are lying on the ground unconscious.

Then two of the terrorists disappear.

I know where they are going.

Upstairs.

To check to make sure no one is hiding.

They must have stumbled across me asleep. Maybe they tried to wake me but couldn't. Or maybe they knew about my disorder. Either way, they left me alone and continued on to my father's bedroom where they would find two fu-gitives.

Murdock enters the screen first. He appears to march to the basement and down the stairs willingly.

"Come on, Dude," I say.

Lassie puts up a fight, clawing at one of the terrorist's hooded face.

"Thatta boy."

I check the time left on the video.

Three minutes remaining.

I let out a sigh, knowing there is nothing earth-shattering on the video. Basically, all it did is confirm what Ingrid and the others already told the authorities.

Then it happens.

One of the terrorists walks toward the table at the back.

Where the cake is.

He grabs a handful of cake with one hand, then lifts his hood with the other.

I let out an audible gasp.

The man isn't Arab.

He's white.

And judging by the tattoo on his neck, I would guess he's Russian.

...

A couple years back, I bought a bunch of Russian Rubles thinking it would be a good investment. I did my fair share of research beforehand — twenty minutes, which for me was a prolonged amount of time — and I stumbled across quite a bit of Russian text. The Russian alphabet is unmistakable, especially their letter 'b,' which looks like this: Б.

A minute later I have translated the Russian script tattooed on the terrorist's neck.

I live in sin, I die laughing.

Wow, dark.

From my research on ISIS, I know the group isn't confined to only Arabs, that they are open to any Muslim. But at least from the man's tattoo, he didn't appear to be a Muslim.

So maybe the Russians want us to *think* ISIS had kidnapped Sullivan.

I run upstairs and say to Team Rampage, "Come on, we have to get back to Bonnie's."

We trudge back across the street, my laptop tucked under my arm.

"What's gotten into you?" my dad asks as I storm past him into the kitchen.

I set the laptop on the counter and flip it open. "I didn't tell anyone, but I had my laptop set up to record the wedding."

"But I told you Bonnie was going to do that."

"I know," I say, waving him off. "But I wanted it on my laptop as well. I wanted to make something silly with it for Ingrid someday. But that's not the point. I got the attack on video."

My dad's jaw drops.

"And not only that. One of the terrorists lifted his hood to eat some cake. You can see his neck and the bottom half of his face. I think he was Russian."

"Russian?"

I tell him about the tattoo.

"You have to get the video to Ingrid."

"I already emailed it to her," I say, then pick up the phone.

I dial my cell.

No answer.

I dial again.

No answer.

Again.

Finally, Ingrid answers groggily.

I tell her about the video.

"Oh my God," is all she can say.

:08

"Oh my God," Ingrid said into the phone, still trying to wrap her head around what Henry just told her.

She wanted so badly to talk to him for the next five minutes, until he had to go to sleep, but she couldn't.

She had to move.

"I love you," she said. "I can't wait to get back home."

"I love you too," Henry said. "Now, go find Billy."

"And the President."

"Yeah, him too."

She hung up the phone and pushed herself up and off the floor. In the soft light of the conference room, she could see the six others, even Cooper, fast asleep. Most had found their way to the floor, though Cooper was asleep in his chair.

It had been a long, grueling day.

The manhunt for the terrorists was now global and the task force had spent the entire day reading memos from different agencies throughout the world. The Brits, the French, the Saudis, they were all following their own leads, filing reports, and she and the others had to disseminate what was credible and what was cockamamie bullshit. (Ingrid was used to being hands-on, getting dirty at the crime scene, not looking at memos.) There had been raids on several known ISIS compounds, possibly even some enhanced interrogation — code speak for torture — but so far, they had nothing to show for it.

Ingrid knew they weren't the only FBI task force. She knew there were many others, perhaps thousands of little task forces across the United States, all poring over the same data they were receiving, but it felt like it was up to her, up to the seven of them, to save Billy's and Sullivan's lives. Maybe it was because they were at the epicenter, in DC, or that she herself was part of it, or that Cooper, perhaps the number one SAC in all of the FBI, was leading the charge.

But they hadn't come up with one tangible lead in two days.

Now, finally, here was something.

Ingrid found her way to one of the laptops and pulled up her email. She downloaded the video. She fast forwarded to her and her bridesmaids on the dancefloor, then hit play. She watched in rapt horror as the events of that night unfolded before her a second time. Finally, near the end of the video, just as Henry described, one of the terrorists partially lifted his hood to cram a handful of wedding cake into his mouth.

Her wedding cake.

"Asshole," she said.

Ingrid stuck two fingers in her mouth and whistled loud enough it could be heard two floors above.

"What in the—" Welds cried.

"Everybody get up!" Ingrid shouted.

Once all eyes were on her, she told them.

:::::

"What do the Russians have to gain by kidnapping the President?" Susan Secret Service asked.

They had just watched the video three times.

"They hate us," Welds said. "And Putin especially hates Sullivan."

Ingrid knew this was a two-way street. Sullivan and Putin couldn't have been more different. Putin was a bear. Sullivan was a fox.

With the approaching US Presidential Election, Putin had started promoting anti-Sullivan propaganda, and one of his top officials in a tweet — though rumored to have been written by Putin himself — called Sullivan a *tuzik*, Russian slang for a pathetic small dog.

"We're on the brink of another Cold War," Welds said.

"In the last couple years Putin has gone from a strategic defense to a strategic offense. Ukraine, Crimea, Syria, Moldova, threatening Poland, threatening the Baltic. Russia is trying to expand."

"Like the Soviet Union 2.0?" asked Donald Port Authority.

Welds nodded, "More or less."

"Okay," Cooper said. "But what would the Russians gain by us thinking ISIS kidnapped the President?"

"They want Iraq," Welds said.

Everyone looked at him.

"Russia already has a big presence in Syria," Welds stated. "Backing up Assad and fighting off rebel troops there. Hell, they built an airport, an entire flipping Russian airbase in Syria. But Syria is small potatoes. It's a chess game. Russia put a pawn in Syria, but they want to put a rook in Iraq."

"And we're standing in their way?" asked Tasha.

"The United States and ISIS," quipped Welds.

Natalie Forensics said, "Explain."

"The Russians kidnap the President under the guise it was ISIS and demand the United States pull all their troops out of Iraq. If we do, then there are four thousand less US troops in Iraq for the Russians to worry about. But, of course, we don't negotiate with terrorists so this is never gonna happen. When we don't pull them out, the Russians kill Sullivan and the US wages full-scale war against ISIS."

Tasha said, "But then we would send a hundred thousand troops into Iraq and Syria and we wouldn't stop until we'd wiped them out. It would be the same thing as when we went after Al-Qaeda and Bin Laden."

"Yes and no," Welds said. "We would declare war on ISIS, but we wouldn't necessarily send in more troops. The Iraqis are still recovering from when we declared war on Al-Qaeda; they're not just gonna let us waltz in there again without some pushback. That being said, Russia has a much better relationship with Iraq than we do, at least on the surface. Plus, they are already engaging ISIS in Syria and are looking for a reason to ramp up their fight. ISIS killing the President of the United States is the perfect cover for sending in their cavalry. They get points from America, all of

Sandland — basically the whole world — and before you know it they have expanded into Iran, Turkey, even Saudi Arabia."

Donald said, "If it goes public that Russia is behind Sullivan's kidnapping, we might be headed toward World War III."

"Nuclear holocaust," chimed Natalie.

Everyone took a moment to silently absorb this.

"I think it will be best if we just keep this video between us," said Cooper.

Ingrid cut her eyes at him. "How is that going to help us locate Billy and Sullivan? We need everyone working the Russia angle."

She again thought about all those Arab men who were still being detained and questioned.

"Just because one of these guys is Russian doesn't mean a whole lot," Welds said. "These assholes come from all over the place to join ISIS."

Tasha said, "And we don't even know if he's really Russian. He could be a light-skinned Arab. I mean, they were speaking *Arabic*."

"Only one of them was," Ingrid pointed out. "The only one to ever talk was the one with the beard, the same one who is talking on the video."

"Maybe the Russians hired an Arab to help," said Tasha.

Welds said, "Or maybe one of them learned Arabic. You know, like me."

"Maybe," said Natalie. "But his tattoo doesn't exactly jibe with the Muslim faith."

Donald laughed. "That doesn't mean anything. I got a Nike symbol on my thigh when I was eighteen. Now it doesn't mean shit to me."

"Yeah," Ingrid said, "But if you got that Nike symbol on your neck, I bet you would have had it removed."

Donald thought about this for a moment, then nodded, "Yeah, probably."

"What about the website the first video was posted on?" Susan said. "It was an ISIS website."

"It's easy enough to hack into those sites," remarked Natalie. "I could probably post a video on the same website if I really wanted to."

"What's the play here, Greg?" Tasha asked.

Everyone looked at Cooper.

"It's one thing to declare war on a group of terrorists," he said. "It's a totally different ballgame when we are dealing with a superpower and an ally."

"Not to mention one that has more than eight thousand nuclear warheads," Welds said.

"Did you say 'eight thousand?'" asked Natalie.

"Yep, even more than the US of A."

Ingrid knew Cooper and Welds were right.

She knew what would happen if it leaked that Russia was involved in the President's kidnapping.

Bedlam.

Panic.

Possible war.

They had to be certain before making any accusations.

"If Russia *were* involved," Tasha said. "What are the chances this was done without Putin's knowledge?"

Welds grimaced. "I'd say very slim."

"Putin had a press conference yesterday," Cooper chimed in. "And he said he was employing all of Russia's resources to help find the President."

"See?" said Welds. "He already has a reason to send a shitload of troops into Iraq."

It was quiet for a long second.

Finally, Cooper turned to Ingrid and asked, "Who else did Henry send that video to?"

Ingrid said, "As far as I know, just me."

"Okay, so the seven of us in this room are the only people that have seen it," Cooper said, seemingly more to himself than the other six.

He looked at Ingrid then said, "I'm not dismissing that this could be the work of the Russians. I'm just saying we need to handle this very diplomatically."

Ingrid nodded, "I get that."

"I have a friend at the CIA," Cooper continued. "I'm going to send him the picture of this guy's tattoo and have him quietly poke around. If this guy has a record or is a known terrorist, he'll find out and hopefully not trigger any red flags. And if he comes back with something, I promise we'll move on this."

Ingrid didn't think she could expect more than that.
"Okay."

...

The bottled water they gave him had writing on it. Writing he couldn't read. It was slightly bitter and he wondered if they filled the bottles up directly from a stream. Or lake. No reverse osmosis here. Now, as far as the bologna sandwich they gave him was concerned, it tasted about the same.

Good old Oscar Mayer.

One of the terrorists had stood over him while he ate, a gun pointed at his chest. When Billy finished, the guard had motioned him over to a bucket in the corner. Once Billy relieved himself he was once again restrained, the gag replaced in his mouth.

That had been six hours ago. Or what felt like six hours to Billy. It could have been two hours. Or eight.

He'd been by himself in the small dank room since the President had been dragged out the day before.

Or had that been two days ago?

He supposed it didn't really matter.

He flexed his wrists back and forth.

His wrists were raw.

He could feel the blood oozing from beneath the tape.

The terrorists had run out of zip ties and now they were using duct tape. Billy had worked his wrists back and forth in the tape, creating a bit of wiggle room. Once he'd worked his wrists flat, he found a small groove in the concrete wall and began grinding the tape against it. Leaning against the wall, squatting up and down wasn't too taxing at first. But after three hours, his quads, his butt, and every muscle in his legs ached. The first cramp had started twenty minutes earlier. It was in his left calf. The muscle balled up into a tight fist.

He grimaced and pushed up against the wall.

Up and down.

Up and down.

He had to free himself.

It was his only hope.

It was *their* only hope.

...

Cooper received the call back from his CIA contact at 11:00 a.m. Ingrid overheard his side of the conversation and knew it wasn't good news.

He hung up and said, "My contact ran the picture of the tattoo through every database in Russia and about six other databases the FBI doesn't have access to. No hits."

They all sat there silent for a long moment.

Finally Tasha said, "Where does this leave us now? The deadline is in seventeen hours and we are no closer to finding them."

Ingrid glanced at Tasha and gave her a smile.

Not him.

Them.

Ingrid thought for a long moment.

There was only one way they were going to find them.

She took a deep breath, and said, "Whether they're in Russia, Iraq, or friggin' Antarctica, there's only one way we're going to find them. We have to find out who knew Sullivan was going to be at my wedding."

"And who leaked it to the Russians," spat Welds.

Ingrid nodded. "And then we need to make them talk."

...

It was closing in on 9:00 p.m.

Seven hours until the deadline.

Only half the roads had been plowed — most of these relegated to half a lane due to the vast amount of snow pushed to the sides — but the United States government, the White House, Congress, and the Senate were all scheduled to return to work the following day.

Business as usual.

Except Vice President Cortney would be running the show.

Because President Sullivan would be dead.

And so would Billy.

"Anybody have anything to report?" asked Cooper.

The seven of them had spent the last ten hours interviewing people. Make that re-interviewing people. Everyone

Ingrid sat down with had been interviewed at least twice prior. Ingrid interviewed more than sixty Secret Service agents, White House interns, senators, and White House kitchen staff, many of whom still were unable to get out of their homes and had to be picked up by one of the now seventy-five Hummers the FBI had acquired.

"The congressman from Tennessee, Graftry or something, admitted he embezzled a thousand dollars from his last campaign fund," Tasha said. "But other than that, nobody I interviewed could have been the leak."

"Me neither," Natalie said.

Ingrid shook her head and said, "No one I talked to seemed even remotely suspicious."

"I don't think the President was stupid enough to tell anyone he was sneaking out," Welds said. "I mean, that's Sneaking Out 101."

Ingrid nodded.

Welds was right, Sullivan wouldn't have told anyone.

Except.

"What are you thinking?" Cooper asked.

Ingrid gazed around, felt the six sets of eyes on her face. She had been replaying the night over in her head. She must have gone into a daze.

"Um," she muttered.

"Just spill it," Welds said.

She took a deep breath, then said, "At the wedding, I thought he kept looking out the window because of the snow."

"Who?" Tasha chimed from across the table.

Ingrid gulped.

"Red."

...

Susan Secret Service walked into the room. She had a dour look on her face. She put her phone back in her pocket and said, "They just ran Red's — real name Terry Freille — financials. Nothing interesting on his bank statements or credit card statements, but there was something of note on both of his mortgages. Both were upside down and threatening foreclosure. Both were paid off entirely in the last month."

"How much money in total?" asked Tasha.

"One point six million."

"Where are the houses?" asked Cooper.

"One here in Adams Morgan, and another in Brighton Beach."

"Brighton Beach?" shouted Welds incredulously.

Ingrid's face dropped.

So did everyone else's.

Brighton Beach.

New York.

The Russian District.

...

It took twenty minutes to get to Red's house in Adams Morgan. His street had been plowed, almost immaculately, which happened when you lived in an upscale, gated neighborhood.

"Why would he need a house this size?" Natalie asked. "Guy was single, living in DC. Why not get a decent apartment or a condo downtown?"

"Maybe he wanted a family," Ingrid said. "Planning for his future."

She couldn't help but give a quick thought about Henry's condo. Would he still want to live there when they started their family? She knew he wanted children, but was he ready now? They hadn't really discussed a timetable, though she was thirty-two.

Was she even ready?

"All clear," Cooper said, opening the front door. Tasha and he had hit the house first, on the off chance there were any threats inside.

As for the other members of the task force, Welds was tapping all his Russian contacts at DHS and reaching out to a couple close friends at the CIA, looking for any connections to Red. Donald was targeting a myriad of different ports known for Russian smuggling. And Susan was searching Red's White House locker.

As for Brighton Beach, a team from the New York FBI field office was preparing to hit the property within the hour.

Natalie and Ingrid stepped inside and, along with Tasha and Cooper, spent the next hour combing over the house.

Ingrid went through every drawer in his bedroom, searched his closet high and low. She didn't find anything incriminating and still held out hope that Red wasn't the leak. The paid-off mortgages, the house in Brighton Beach, there could easily be explanations for both. Maybe he came into some family money. Maybe he'd purchased the Brighton Beach property simply as an investment.

Ingrid didn't want Red to be the leak. He seemed like such a nice guy. And he'd known Sullivan for thirty years. They were like brothers. Would he really betray him?

And if he was the leak, why had he been killed?

"Take a look at this!" Natalie shouted from the living room.

Ingrid exited the bedroom and found Natalie sitting on the couch, a laptop computer on her lap. Cooper and Tasha were already sidled up behind the couch, peering over her shoulder.

"Looks like Red was a big Fantasy Football fan," Natalie said. "He spent over sixty thousand dollars on one of those websites this season."

"Sixty thousand?" Cooper asked.

She nodded. "Then another twenty playing online poker."

"Why wasn't that in his financials?" asked Tasha.

Natalie clicked on his account and saw the last four digits of the card on file. "This card didn't come up on the report that Susan ran."

"Can you get someone to run the card?" Cooper asked. "See what other charges are on there?"

"I'll try." She took out her phone and made a call.

Cooper's phone rang nearly simultaneously and he stepped away to answer.

Ingrid pulled out her cell phone.

Almost midnight.

Cooper returned and said, "That was the New York SAC. They hit the house in Brighton Beach, but no one was there. They are searching it now, but it doesn't look promising."

Ingrid nodded and said, "It was a long shot."

"Yeah, but it was our *only* shot."

"Maybe Welds will hear something," said Tasha. "Get us a location in Russia."

"Don't count on it," Cooper said, then returned to his search.

:09

Everyone is gone.

Jorge was finally able to dig his car out and he spent the entire day chauffeuring everyone else around. He took Ingrid's parents, sister, and friends all to their hotel to get their stuff, then dropped them at the airport which was set to open midday tomorrow.

With checkpoints and roadblocks on half the streets still in effect, not to mention the roads still slippery with ice, it took him over four hours to make the twenty-mile round-trip.

He even stopped by one of the few grocery stores open and returned to Bonnie's with groceries. And this was all after he helped my father rip up the carpet in the living room.

"Jorge said the snow in the Safeway parking lot was piled thirty feet high in the back half," my father says.

"Thirty feet?"

"Yeah, it's where the plows dump all their snow. They take it to different parking lots. You should see what the parking lot at FedExField looks like."

FedExField is where the Washington Redskins play, which oddly enough is located in Maryland.

"What are they reporting on the news?" I ask. "Did the Russian angle leak yet?"

My dad shakes his head.

I'm not surprised.

You don't accuse the third most powerful county in the world of kidnapping your president based solely on a tattoo.

My dad says, "The First Lady and the Vice President did have a press conference."

"How is the First Lady doing?"

I'd never met Kim Sullivan, but I knew quite a bit about her from when I had been trying to prove the President innocent of murder. She'd met Sullivan in college in Ohio, then followed him to his home state of Virginia, where he would climb the political ladder to governor, then ten years later to President of the United States.

She wasn't quite as beloved as Michelle Obama, but then again, few are.

"She tried to keep composed, but she choked up a couple times. She kept it short, asked for prayers for her husband, to bring him back safely."

"What about the VP? What'd he have to say?"

My dad recounts what Vice President Cortney had said. That if it were up to him, he would pull the troops out of Iraq in a heartbeat, but that the United States doesn't negotiate with terrorists, not even for the President of the United States. "He said they were closing in on those who were responsible, and whether or not the President was harmed in the coming hours, he was declaring war on ISIS and their leader, Abu something."

"Abu Bakr al-Baghdadi," I say.

"Right, him."

"But what if they weren't behind it?"

"Well, Abu Baker Baghdad or whatever took credit for everything in a video that was posted."

My dad ushers me to Bonnie's office and pulls up the video.

Abu Bakr al-Baghdadi, with his long black beard spends five minutes at a microphone taking credit for the most historic kidnapping in the modern era. He is so animated that for a brief moment I find myself thinking maybe ISIS really *was* responsible. Maybe that Russian guy was a Muslim. Or maybe ISIS had paid him, like a mercenary. Maybe the other two guys were as Arab as the day is long and they just needed a third guy to help.

Still, I'm not convinced.

Of course Baghdadi is going to *say* ISIS was behind it. It would have been foolish for him not to take credit for it.

After the video finishes, my dad leaves, saying he will return with some food. While Jorge was busy running my wedding guests all over town, Isabel had cooked up some spaghetti.

I look at the clock on the computer.

3:11 a.m.

Forty-nine minutes.

I'm not counting down for me.

I'm counting down for Billy and Sullivan.

...

I hear a pitter-patter and turn.

Lassie walks into the room and jumps up on the computer table, then finds his way to my lap.

"Hey, dork," I say, scratching him behind the ears.

Meow.

"What have you guys been up to?"

Meow.

"Just hanging out? Does that include terrorizing Chester?"

Meow.

"Yes, the zombie-dog."

Meow.

"And what about Gretchen? Have you been keeping clear of her like you promised?"

Meow.

"Hmm, that's interesting, because according to the note that Bonnie left for me this morning," I show him the little blue sticky note, "you *haven't* been."

Lassie tries to jump off my lap, but I hold him down. I clear my throat and begin reading, *"Dear Henry, please keep your awful little cat away from my Gretchen. I caught him, well, doing things to her that I'd rather not say. Thanks, Bonnie."*

"My awful little cat? Things she'd rather not say?" I swat him on the head. "Dude, you pinky promised." I swat him again. "She's a hundred and thirty-three years old."

If a cat can turn green, he does.

Meow.

"Yes, one hundred and thirty-three!"

Meow.

"No, you are not going to turn into a zombie-dog."

Luckily, my dad returns with a plate of spaghetti. I feed Lassie a couple noodles as an apology for smacking him, then I decide to pull up the first video and watch it again. Actually, I'm really interested in how many views the video has now.

Over nine hundred million views.

I wonder if this makes it the most-watched video of all time and Google this.

It makes it the twenty-fifth, a couple million shy of the over two *billion* views a video titled "Gangnam Style" has racked up.

I'm curious and click on it.

It's awesome.

Even Lassie can't tear his eyes away from it.

Meow.

"Yes, an Asian Timberlake."

After wasting five minutes and two seconds of my day, I return to the demand video and re-watch it.

When the crashing in the background occurs, Lassie's ears perk up.

Meow.

I rewind it ten seconds.

Hit play.

His ears are straight up.

Meow.

I rewind it again.

Hit play.

"Dude, what?"

Meow.

"What are you talking about?"

Meow.

I turn up the volume and put my ear right next to the speaker.

My eyebrows jump.

"You're right," I tell him.

Right after the crashing sound in the background, just faintly, you can hear a dog bark.

But according to Lassie, it wasn't any dog.

It was Murdock.

...

I listen to it three more times before I'm sure.

The crash in the background wasn't a far-off bomb or missile strike. It was a huge avalanche of snow and ice falling to the ground.

The demand video wasn't shot in the Middle East or Russia.

It was shot ten houses down from my father's.

...

"Wait," my dad says. "Explain this to me again."

I take a deep breath. "Three nights ago, I went outside with the dingbats to play in the snow. We walked down to the end of the cul-de-sac and we saw this huge shelf of ice fall off one of the house's roofs. It crashed down onto all the other snow, but it was still pretty loud. It scared Murdock and he barked a couple times. You can hear both the crash and Murdock barking on the video that the terrorists posted."

"Wait," my dad says, pushing his glasses up on his nose. "You think Sullivan and Billy are being held in a house down the street?"

I nod.

"This thing would have taken a lot of planning," I say. "This wasn't something that came together overnight. Somehow the Russians learn that Sullivan is going to be at the wedding. I'm not sure who, or how, but we did send an invitation to the White House, so it could be any number of people. Anyhow, they find a house close by, a rental or one of those Airbnb's. They find one nearby and lay low. The night of the wedding, they hit the house, take Billy and Sullivan. They probably plan on getting out of town, but because of the storm they can't, so they turn back."

"That's pretty hard to believe outright, but what makes you think they would still be there? After the streets get plowed, why not leave?"

"No way. I bet the Feds were checking every car going in and going out. Then the Fairfax PD was camped out the next two days. Their only chance would have been yesterday, but there are still checkpoints and roadblocks on every street."

"But the Feds would have gone to every house on the cul-de-sac. Knocked on every door. And if someone were Airbnb-ing, they would have been doubly suspicious."

"Not if no one answered. They would just have assumed they got snowed in somewhere."

"Maybe," my dad says.

I describe the house. "Do you know which one I'm talking about?"

"I think so."

"Do you know who lives there?"

"I knew the family who used to live there, but they moved late last year. I'm not sure of the new owners. There's so much turnover in this neighborhood, it's hard to keep up."

Not to mention that my dad is a hermit, preferring his ever-changing projects and Murdock to actual human contact.

I look at the clock.

3:31 a.m.

I have to tell Ingrid.

They have to check this out. Even if it is a wild goose chase.

I run to Bonnie's landline.

There's no dial tone.

I run back to the office and say, "The phones are out."

My dad grimaces and says, "Oh, right, I forgot. The weight of the snow took out a bunch of power and phone lines. We didn't have power for half the day yesterday."

"Does anyone have a cell?"

My dad thinks, then shakes his head. "The only person's cell the terrorists didn't take was Minister Robert's. It was in his car. But half the cell towers are down because of the power outages, and last I heard his wasn't working."

"Okay, then we'll have to drive to the police station."

"We don't have time. It will take us ten minutes to get there, and that's if we don't drive off the road. Then another ten minutes for the police to get here. By that time, the deadline will be just about up."

"What are you saying?"

He lets out a long exhale and says, "We're going to have to go ourselves."

...

We send emails to both Ingrid and to the Fairfax Police Department. I try to make a call using Google phone, but you need a cell phone to set up an account. I'm sure there is another way to make a call using the internet, but by the time I figure it out, both Billy and Sullivan will be dead.

It is 3:38 a.m. when we enter my father's basement.

"I thought you had a gun," I say.

"I do," my father says, holding a gun-like thing out in front of me.

"That's a nail gun."

"Still a gun."

"No, no it's not," I say with an audible sigh.

Meow.

I turn around.

Lassie, Murdock, and Archie are all standing on the stairs. They refuse to be left out of the fun.

Lassie meows again.

"Does it look like there are any swords down here?"

Meow.

"Yes, I agree, a sword would be great right now."

Meow.

"Yes, or the flamethrower from Contra."

All I can find is a box cutter, the same one I used to slice through some of the captives' restraints, and a big wrench.

I tell my dad to bring the nail gun.

It's better than nothing.

:10

"I found something," Natalie said.

It took a couple hours to obtain the statement from the credit card Red used for gambling. Natalie had been poring over the transactions for the last twenty minutes.

Ingrid rushed over, once again joining Cooper and Tasha behind her.

"See these charges here?" Natalie said. "They are to Airbnb."

Cooper looked confused and Ingrid explained, "Stands for Air Bed and Breakfast or something. Basically, people rent out their homes to strangers."

He nodded.

Natalie said, "Payment on February 17th for seventy-five hundred dollars."

"That's a lot of money," said Cooper.

"Can you find out where the place is?" asked Tasha.

Ingrid knew a little about Airbnb. When she and Henry were planning their trip to Fairbanks, Alaska, Henry sent her numerous links to different properties. Unfortunately, Airbnb wasn't confined to the US. It was global. Red could have paid for a place anywhere in the world.

Natalie pointed to her cell phone on the desk and said, "You hear that music…"

Ingrid could hear faint music playing from the phone's speaker.

Natalie explained that the person she spoke to at Airbnb refused to give her any details as to the property. She put her on hold and went to talk to her supervisor. That was ten minutes ago.

Ingrid checked the time.

3:27 a.m.

Thirty-three minutes until the deadline.

"Did you tell them what this was concerning?" asked Cooper.

"Sure did. Even used the words 'national security.'"

Tasha asked, "Did you check his search history?"

Natalie rolled her eyes and said, "Of course. Airbnb didn't come up."

"Yes, but he still might be logged into his account. Did you try the website on his computer?"

Natalie shook her head and Ingrid could see her cheeks flush. To her credit, she swallowed her pride and logged onto Airbnb.com on Red's laptop.

Red's username was there, but they were asking for a password.

Damn.

Cooper picked up Natalie's phone and dialed the same number. He left the room to try his hand at securing an address.

Ingrid looked at the password box. She'd only chatted with Red a few times, but it was always about their beloved Redskins. In fact, that was the reason behind his nickname.

Every single one of her passwords was Redskins something or other.

Could Red be the same?

"Try Redskins," Ingrid said.

Natalie and Tasha both eyed her curiously. Natalie typed in the word. She didn't hit enter. Instead she opened a second Airbnb.com tab and began setting up her own account. Ingrid wasn't sure what she was getting at until she said, "Password needs at least one number."

From behind her, in the kitchen, Ingrid could hear Cooper shouting into the phone, "This is the President of the United States we're talking about!" He was probably talking to someone in Indonesia, and Ingrid didn't give him much hope.

Ingrid took a deep breath.

One number.

"Try Redskins, seven," Ingrid said, then added, "Joe Theismann,"

Natalie nodded, though the name didn't appear to mean anything to her. She typed, then shook her head. "Nope."

"Do not put me on hold!" Cooper screamed.

Ingrid took a deep breath.

Looked at the clock.

3:31 a.m.

Twenty-nine minutes.

She tried to think back to the conversation she and Red had. He mentioned Joe Theismann was his favorite player, a childhood idol.

What else had he said?

Then it came to her.

In the last couple years, there had been a huge controversy regarding the Redskins name. "Redskins" was considered a derogatory slur toward Native Americans. There had been a huge pushback from fans, sportscasters, columnists, and the like to refer to the team as "The Washington Football Team" instead of the Redskins. When she and Red chatted, he always referred to them as "Washington," which she found odd at the time.

Ingrid leaned over Natalie and said, "Try Washington, seven."

She watched to make sure Natalie typed it in correctly.

Natalie glanced up at her.

Ingrid nodded.

"It worked!" Natalie shouted.

"That's my girl," Tasha said, squeezing her arm.

Natalie quickly navigated to Red's account and clicked on his bookings.

The page refreshed.

Ingrid glanced at the address and her jaw nearly dislocated.

"Cooper!" Tasha belted. "Get in here."

Cooper ran into the room.

"We found the property," Ingrid said.

It was on the same street as her father-in-law's.

...

Billy glanced at the video camera the terrorist with the beard was setting up. This video would be far different from the first video. This time, the dagger wouldn't just rest against his throat; it would cut into it. His execution would be broadcast to millions. Maybe even billions.

The President was sitting against the wall across from him. Floodlights from behind the camera illuminated a man who had aged twenty years in the last three days.

Sullivan's face was a pulpy mess. His right eye was swollen shut. His white shirt was covered in blood. His one good eye was trained on Billy.

Billy tried to give him the slightest of nods. A signal that he was going to make a move. He tried to telepathically send the President a message.

After eight hours, I was able to get the tape removed from my wrists. Then I found the roll of duct tape on the floor and re-taped my hands behind my back. But quite loosely. I can pull my hands out at any second. I'm just waiting for an opportunity.

The President lolled his head up and down.

Did he understand?

No, of course not.

He was half dead.

Billy moved his gaze to the terrorist sitting in the chair near the door, the gun on his lap. He was twelve feet away. There was no way Billy could rush him before the man got the gun up and shot him. As for the terrorist behind the camera, Billy could easily tackle him this very second. He didn't have a gun, at least, not one that Billy could see. Could he save himself and Sullivan without getting his hands on one of the terrorists' guns?

He doubted it.

Still, Billy pondered rushing the terrorist.

Then the door opened and the third terrorist entered.

Now it was too late.

...

"We checked this house out, didn't we?" Cooper said.

"Yeah," Tasha said. "But no one came to the door."

"Why didn't we look into it further? Ask the neighbors when the last time they saw them was, or try and track down a cell phone number and call them?"

"Because we weren't thinking about them being held

hostage in one of the houses. We were just trying to see if anyone saw anything suspicious. And they weren't the only house where no one came to the door. Five of the twenty houses were empty. We just figured it was because of the blizzard."

"We could have checked back the next day, or two days later. We should have been more thorough."

"Hindsight's twenty-twenty," quipped Natalie.

Natalie was right, thought Ingrid. It hadn't crossed any of their minds that the terrorists could have been holed up on the very street of the attack. It certainly hadn't crossed hers.

But it should have.

"How much farther?" asked Cooper.

"Twelve minutes," Tasha replied from the passenger seat.

Natalie was in the back seat, next to Ingrid.

Ingrid checked her cell phone.

3:41 a.m.

"You need to step on it," she said.

Cooper hit the gas, the Ford Explorer zipping forward between the seven-foot piles of brown snow.

"We're no good to them if we're dead," Natalie said, then added, "Why not just call the Fairfax PD?"

Cooper shook his head. "Then we would never be able to keep the Russian angle quiet. It would be front page news tomorrow."

"So what?" Ingrid shouted. "Better to let Billy and Sullivan die?"

"If that saves us from World War III, then yes."

"That's bullshit."

"Say what you will, but this is in the best interest of the United States. What are the chances they are there anyway? Five percent? Ten? They probably rented the place to stake out your father-in-law's house, but have since left. Plus, if they are there, we have a better chance of rescuing the President than the local police. They'll send a fricking SWAT team, and Billy and the President will just get caught in the crossfire."

Ingrid supposed Cooper was right in this regard.

Still, it made her furious.

Cooper's phone rang and he tossed it to Tasha.

"Answer that," he said, eyes glued to the icy road he was barreling down.

Tasha answered it.

She listened for a couple seconds, then hung up. "Live video feed just went up," she said. She told Natalie the website address, and a moment later, Natalie brought it up on a tablet she pulled from her briefcase.

Ingrid peered at the screen. She could see Billy and Sullivan sitting back against the wall. Billy, though ragged, didn't look too bad, but Sullivan looked like he'd been hit by a bus.

Ingrid checked her watch.

3:44 a.m.

"How much farther?" asked Cooper.

"Eight minutes," Tasha said, then she added, "Shit."

"What?"

"I just lost cell phone service."

Ingrid checked her phone.

No service.

"The power outages took out a bunch of the cell towers," Natalie said.

Ingrid glanced back to the laptop and asked, "Why is the video still playing?"

Natalie looked at her, then said, "The car has its own Wi-Fi."

Cooper took a left and Ingrid turned her head to look out the window.

She knew they were going too fast.

The car started into a slide.

"Hold on!" Cooper yelled.

The car continued to slide, then it smashed into a large snow pile.

Then it flipped on its side.

It was 3:48 a.m.

:11

My father and I slink down the street.
The house is visible, a hundred yards away.
"What time is it?" I ask my dad.
He stops, checks his watch.
3:49 a.m.
Eleven minutes.
Thirty seconds later we reach the house.
"How are we going to get inside?" my dad asks.
I check the front door, just in case, but it's locked.
"Let's go around back," I whisper.
We trudge through the snow, then jump over the fence.
By the time we make it to the back sliding glass door, two minutes have passed.
My dad tries the door.
It slides open.
My dad enters first, the nail gun held up with two hands, ready to fire. I am behind him, the wrench held high in my right hand.
We look more like two frightened construction workers than American heroes.
My dad's foot hits a chair in the dining room, sending it clattering to the ground.
I flex every muscle in my body.
I wait for a door to the basement to open and three guns to step out.
They don't.
The gun comes from the stairs leading to the second floor.

"Down on the ground!" someone yells.

I squint my eyes at the man.

White.

Fifty-ish.

A tank top and briefs.

A pistol in his hands.

My father and I look at each other.

"Get on the ground!" the guy barks.

I hear clattering upstairs.

A woman asks, "What's going on, John?"

My dad lowers the nail gun and squints. "John? John Irwin?"

The man's gaze narrows at my dad.

"Richard?" he asks.

John lowers the gun.

"I thought you guys moved," my dad says. "Late last year."

"We couldn't get the damn place to sell, then my promotion fell throu—" He shakes his head. "Wait, what the hell are you doing breaking into my house?"

My dad gives him the Cliff Notes.

"You thought the President was being held hostage in my house?" he asks.

I tell him about the avalanche of snow falling off his roof, Murdock barking, and the sound on the video.

"I remember the sound you're talking about. Three nights ago. Scared the shit out of my wife and kids. I told her it was just a snowbank falling off the roof."

"You didn't hear the barking?"

"I just figured it was one of the neighbor's dogs barking."

My eyebrows jump.

Neighbors.

The avalanche fell off John's roof, but it landed between his house and his neighbor's. The two houses were only separated by twenty feet and the sound would have been equally as loud at the house next door.

"Your neighbors," I say, pointing to the east. "When is the last time you saw them?"

"Before the New Year. They spend their winters in Florida."

"Have you seen anyone there?"

"They Airbnb the place. A family was there a couple weeks in January. A couple guys a few weeks back."

"You think that's where they are?" John asks.

I nod.

Then I ask him for his gun.

...

John has a spare key to the house next door.

To the Henderson's.

Before we leave, I ask if he has a phone that works. He shakes his head, then says that his son knows how to make calls over the internet.

I tell him to call 911.

My father and I trudge through the snow of the Henderson's drive, then make our way to the front door.

It is 3:56 a.m.

Four minutes.

To save Billy and Sullivan's lives.

And for me to find a place to sleep.

This is not going to end well.

I slip the key in the front door and turn the knob.

It opens.

...

The SUV righted itself, but it was stuck in four feet of snow. There was no chance of getting out. But not for lack of trying.

Cooper had spent the last five minutes revving the engine. Natalie had even taken the wheel while Ingrid, Tasha, and Cooper pushed. But the SUV hadn't budged a single inch.

They were stuck.

Destined to watch Billy and the President executed on a tablet.

On-screen, Billy and Sullivan wore on their knees, knives once again held to their throats.

The terrorist with the beard began speaking in Arabic.

Welds wasn't there to translate, but they didn't need a

translation to know what was being said.

Your time is up.

...

Ingrid had shown me how to hold a gun, and though I'd never fired one, it doesn't feel alien in my hands. I check to make sure the safety is off, then push through the front door.

The layout isn't much different than my father's, and I see light cascading from the bottom of what I assume is the door that leads to the basement.

I look back over my shoulder at my dad.

He nods.

I slowly turn the handle on the door to the basement and pull it open.

...

Billy could feel the cold steel of the dagger against his neck.

The terrorist was behind him and a second terrorist was directly behind the President. The terrorist with the beard was behind them all, barking Arabic into the camera.

It was now or never.

Billy lunged backward as hard as he could, knocking the terrorist behind him backward and into the man speaking.

He rolled over, ripped his hands from behind his back, and tackled the wide-eyed terrorist standing behind the President.

...

The basement is softly lit.

It is all concrete, though unlike my father's, it is nearly empty.

It isn't until we are halfway down the stairs, not until I hear the Arabic being spoken from somewhere, that I'm sure Billy and Sullivan are here. From the video, I guess there must be some sort of crawl space, or storage, or bunker where they are being held.

When we reach the bottom of the stairs, the Arabic stops abruptly, replaced by the sound of toppling bodies.

I hold the gun with two hands and dart across the cold concrete.

In the far back, there is a door.

"Stay out here," I whisper to my dad.

I whip the door open, take two steps inside, and I fire.

...

"Henry!" Ingrid screamed, her voice echoing through the SUV.

She was shocked when Billy lunged backward, even more shocked when he jumped to his feet, freeing his hands from behind his back, but now...

Her Henry had just barged into the room holding a gun, and from what it looked like, he'd just shot one of the terrorists.

...

Billy heard the gunshot. Knew it had to have hit him somewhere. Only he couldn't feel it. He'd heard it before, stories on the force or in war, how in the heat of battle people didn't even know they'd been shot, only to find out later they had a gaping wound in their leg or their side.

He continued to pry the knife from the terrorist's hands. To his right, he could see the President on his side, his hands still taped behind his back, the gag still stuffed in his mouth.

Billy kneed the terrorist in the balls, the knife falling to the ground. Then he picked it up and slammed it into the man's heart.

...

Out of the corner of my eye, I watch as Billy slams a knife down into one of the terrorist's chests.

My bullet had struck another of the terrorists in the throat, and he is on the ground, his hands wrapped around his neck, gurgling to death.

I hold my gun pointed at the third terrorist.

Beard.

He doesn't have a weapon.

He is the speaker.

"Take off your hood!" I shout.

I want everyone to see these guys for who they really were.

Billy turns around. He still has the gag in his mouth. He pulls it out, his head shaking from side to side.

I can't blame him. He probably had thought he was somewhere in the Middle East. He would have no reason to suspect he was being held just ten houses down from my dad's.

Sullivan has a similar expression on his face.

"Henry?" Billy asks.

"Hey, fellas."

I return my eyes to the lone living terrorist.

"Take off your hood," I repeat.

He doesn't.

I send a bullet over his shoulder and into the flag on the wall.

"Take off your *fucking* hood."

He slips it off.

Even with the beard it is easy to see the man isn't Arab.

In fact, he looks like an Ivan.

"These assholes aren't ISIS," I tell Billy. "They're Russian."

I see the surprise on Billy's face, but it is a far cry from the look of incredulity that has formed on Sullivan's face on the ground.

"Get the gag out of his mouth," I tell Billy.

I feel, more than see, Ivan move his hand behind his back. I see his hand snake out from behind him. See the glint of the metal.

Then I feel the blackness close in.

It's 4:00 a.m.

I'm out of time.

...

Ingrid watched Henry's knees buckled. Watched as he fell over, crumpling to the ground, the gun clattering from his open hand.

"Oh my God!" Natalie screamed.

"What happened?" Tasha asked. "Did he get shot?"

No.

He was out of time.

"Stop!" the terrorist screamed, pointing the gun he'd procured from behind his back at Billy.

Billy stopped for a moment. He glanced at Henry, then back to the terrorist. Ingrid knew what Billy was thinking. It was the same thing she was thinking: if only Henry had pulled the trigger one second sooner.

"You're Russian?" Billy asked on-screen.

The terrorist with the beard smiled.

"Fuck you and fuck Putin."

It took Ingrid a moment to realize Billy hadn't said the words.

Sullivan had.

Billy had gotten the gag half pulled out of the President's mouth, and Sullivan had managed to wiggle it down near his chin.

From the front seat, Cooper let out the longest sigh Ingrid had ever heard, and said, "Well, say hello to World War III."

He was right. Probably a hundred million people were watching this right now. And half the globe would watch it over the next couple days.

Fuck you and fuck Putin.

The five words that reignited the Cold War.

The Russian terrorist narrowed his eyes at Sullivan, then he pulled the trigger.

The bullet caught Sullivan in the chest, his body lurching.

"Oh, God!" Natalie screamed.

...

A shadow moved into the screen.

"Who is that?" Tasha asked.

Ingrid fought down a smile.

It was Richard.

Her father-in-law.

He was holding something in his hands.

A huge gun.

"Is that a nail gun?" asked Cooper.

It was.

He had it pointed at the terrorist.

"Drop the gun!" her father-in-law yelled.

The terrorist smiled.

Laughed.

He must have known it wasn't a real gun.

"I mean it!" her father-in-law shouted.

And he did.

The terrorist slapped his hand to his face and began screaming.

A nail was sticking out of his eye.

Another nail hit him.

Then another.

Billy scrambled to the gun near Henry. He picked it up, then he shot the terrorist in the forehead.

:12

"One more time," I say to Ingrid.

She rewinds back two minutes.

The video has over three billion views.

Take that, Gangnam Style.

Ingrid hits play.

I watch as my legs buckle, as I fall to the ground.

Forty-eight hours later and my left shoulder is still sore.

Still, I didn't let that stop me from finally consummating my marriage.

Twice actually.

Ingrid and I are still naked, intertwined like a buttery pretzel. The laptop is on my stomach. On-screen I watch as Ivan points the gun at Billy and Sullivan, then listen as Sullivan shouts the five words that turned the nation, the *world*, upside down.

On that note, Putin denied all involvement in Sullivan's kidnapping. The powers that be were still trying to link the three dead Russians to Putin, but it didn't matter. Sullivan's words ignited a flame and a brushfire was under way. World War III wasn't imminent, but it was out there, faint against the horizon.

On-screen Sullivan's body shudders from the gunshot.

It hit him in the chest.

His right lung.

Luckily, John Irwin called the cops — actually, his son did — and they showed up ten minutes later. Sullivan was rushed to the hospital and underwent emergency surgery. He is still in critical condition.

If he does pull through, he will have no problem winning reelection come November. His kidnapping, his outburst, and his near death had caused his numbers to skyrocket. Overnight he jumped forty-two points in the polls.

My dad enters the screen and I can't help but smile.

"Look at him holding that ridiculous thing," Ingrid says, shaking her head.

My dad is holding the nail gun with both hands. Arms straight forward. Shoulders back.

"What? That's not how they teach it at the Academy?"

Ingrid laughs.

On-screen, the terrorist slaps at his face.

"Right in the eye," I say.

My dad shoots three more times.

That's when Billy makes his move.

Two seconds later, it's over.

"Again?" Ingrid asks.

I gaze over at the clock on the bedside table.

It's 3:23 a.m.

I shake my head and Ingrid closes the laptop.

This was our first night back at the condo. Ingrid and I had stayed at Bonnie's the previous night. Ingrid was only awake for a couple minutes during my hour and even then, she was hard-pressed to keep her eyes open. Four days of little sleep had taken its toll on her.

She did quickly narrate how they discovered Red was the leak, hacked into his Airbnb account, were en route when their car got stuck in the snow. Then watching the execution on the tablet and absolutely freaking out when I entered the room.

And, of course, you know the rest.

I found it hard to believe that Red was the leak.

Then again, who else would have known they were coming to the wedding?

This also explained why the terrorists hadn't hurt me. Red must have told them about my condition, and they decided I wasn't a threat. But they had double-crossed Red, so I still counted myself exceptionally lucky.

"Who lugged me back up to the condo?" I ask Ingrid.

"Billy."

I nod. "How was he?"

"He was pretty shaken, but after going home, getting a shower, and seeing his mom and brothers, he actually came back to the crime scene and helped walk us through it."

"What a trooper."

"Yeah, he's a tough kid. He wanted me to thank you for saving his life."

I scoff. "Tell him to thank my dad."

Captain Nail Gun.

"Oh, he plans on it. He's actually going to help your dad install new carpet in a couple days."

"That's nice of him."

Ingrid rolls herself out of the pretzel and pushes herself off the bed.

I soak up her delicious backside.

She quickly pulls on a robe and I make a frowny face.

"What haven't we done yet?" she asks.

Eaten. Gone to the bathroom. Brushed our teeth. Drank water. Had sex a third time.

"I don't know."

"Opened our wedding presents!" she shouts, clapping her hands and pulling open the door to the bedroom.

I shake my head and smile.

"Oh, hi guys," I hear her say in her squeaky, talking-to-animals voice. "Sorry we had to kick you out. We had to have some mommy and daddy time."

"Don't call it that," I say, laughing.

A moment later, Lassie springs onto the bed.

Right behind him, Archie.

They both dart to my chest.

"Hi, guys!"

Archie attacks me with kisses.

"Oh, wow, oh, yes, yes, yes, I missed you too."

Lassie sits next to my face.

Meow.

"Watch?"

Meow.

"No, next time you cannot watch."

I cover his head with my hand, which he does not like one bit.

He claws at me, bites my hand gently.

Archie wants in and attacks my hand as well.

We wrestle like this for a few minutes until Ingrid returns. She has a big bag full of gifts in one hand, and a big plate of gooey nachos in the other.

"Nachos?" I say.

"Hey, it's slim pickings out there." She smiles and adds, "Maybe you should try grocery shopping sometime."

"My wife does the grocery shopping."

"Well, your wife tried to go to two grocery stores yesterday, and they still weren't open, and the third one was so packed she thought she would probably pull out her gun and start shooting people."

It has been six days since the blizzard, and the city is just now beginning to get a semblance of order back.

"Isabel emailed me that she'll be back tomorrow," I say.

"Thank God," Ingrid sighs, setting the bag down and feeding me a nacho. I gaze down at her hand, the large ring on her finger.

They found the bag of lifted watches and jewelry that the terrorists had taken in the house. They also found a bucket of salt water with twelve cell phones in it.

She squeezes back into bed, Lassie quickly curling up on her lap.

"He asked if he could watch next time," I tell her.

Her mouth opens and she points her finger at Lassie's face.

"You," she says, laughing.

Lassie licks the tip of her finger.

The four of us spend the next five minutes eating.

Archie is puzzled by the nacho I give him. He looks at it suspiciously. Licks it. Takes the tiniest of bites. After the first one, he can't get enough.

"Alright, let's see how we made out," Ingrid says, dumping the presents out on the bed.

There are four actual gifts and the rest are envelopes.

She tackles an envelope.

"Look at this," she says, showing me a gift card. "From Bonnie. Two hundred bucks to Kohl's."

"Nice."

"Maybe I'll get some pots and pans."

I nod at the empty plate of nachos. "You don't cook."

"I can learn," she says, slapping me on the legs. "Then you can get rid of Isabel."

We both laugh.

Ingrid relies on Isabel as much, if not more, than I do. To the point where I'd raised Isabel's salary forty percent.

"What did they get us?" I ask.

"Isabel?" she says, searching around. "Oh, this is from them. Oh, it's heavy."

I take the box from her.

It is heavy, maybe ten pounds.

I rip off the wrapping paper.

Archie attacks the paper, clawing and biting at it.

He is *ferocious.*

"Wow," I say, gazing at what's inside.

"What is it?"

"I don't know. A stone bowl and a mallet."

"A *molcajete!*" she shrieks. "For making guacamole." She picks up the stone bowl and says, "This is nice. I bet this was super expensive."

I shake my head at her.

"What?" she asks.

"Nothing. Sometimes, I forget how girly you can be."

She slaps me on the shoulder. "I'm plenty girly."

"Sure you are," I say, rubbing my shoulder.

"Oh, God. Was that the shoulder you fell on?"

I nod.

She kisses my shoulder.

Licks it.

I glance at Lassie.

His head is perked, his eyes wide.

"Look away," I say.

He shakes his head no.

Ingrid gives my shoulder one last kiss, then gets back to the presents.

Her parents gave us cash.

Her sister got us a toaster.

Seriously, a toaster.

Her bridesmaids all went in together and got us embroidered *his* and *hers* bathrobes.

I've never worn a robe before and slip mine on.

"I may never take this off," I say.

Billy got us some weird sausage and cheeses.

Ingrid picks up a card and lets out a deep sigh.

I didn't need to see it to know it was from her captain.

"His funeral is in two days," she says, wiping her eyes.

"Tell his wife how sorry I am."

She nods, then looks at the clock.

It is 3:43 a.m.

I know what she's thinking. That there would be plenty of time to mourn on her own time. This was our time.

"It's okay," I say.

Her face brightens and she moves on to the last gift.

"This one is only addressed to you," she says.

I take it from her.

It's small.

Rectangular.

The kind of box a nice fountain pen might come in.

On a small card is my name.

"Who is this from?" I ask.

She shrugs.

I rip off the wrapping paper and set it aside.

Archie doesn't notice it. He is too busy exploring the empty box the *molcajete* came in.

His new fort.

I lift the lid on the small white box.

I glare down at the contents for a couple seconds.

My eyes open wide and I turn to Ingrid.

She nods.

Inside the box is a pregnancy test.

"We're gonna have a baby," she says.

...

Murdock sprinted toward the door and began barking.

Richard Bins said, "Be quiet, it's just the doorbell."

He looked down at his watch.

10:45 a.m.

He wasn't expecting Billy until around noon. Maybe he'd decided to come early.

Richard pulled the door open.

A man and woman stood on his front steps.

For the past two days the street had been overflowing with news vans. Every affiliate in America wanting to get a glimpse of the house where the President was held hostage.

"If you are looking for an interview," Richard said, "I'm sorry, but I'm not your guy."

The woman shook her head. "We aren't reporters," she said.

She pulled out a badge.

Richard read it.

The United States Army Criminal Investigation Command.

Richard forced a smile and said, "I didn't know you guys had an interest in the President's kidnapping."

"We don't," the man said.

Richard should have noticed it right away.

The way the man stood.

The short cropped hair.

"You know what this is about," the woman said.

He did.

He'd been dreading this day for the past forty years.

He sighed and said, "How did you find me?"

The man and woman looked at one another.

"That's not important," the man said.

But Richard knew. It was the fingerprints. The *elimination prints* he'd been forced to give.

"You have to come with us," the woman said.

"Okay."

He turned around.

Murdock was sitting behind him.

His big eyes drooped.

He knew something was wrong.

"It will be okay, Big Guy. Bonnie will take care of you and then you can stay with Lassie and Archie."

His tail wagged for a brief moment, then stopped.

Richard turned back around and asked, "What am I being charged with?"

"Treason," the man said stoically. "And murder."

Author's Note

Dear Reader,

There are millions of books out there and I just want to thank you for choosing one of mine.

When I first wrote *3 a.m.*, I knew the premise was cool, that Henry was a great character, that Lassie was unlike anything I'd read before, and that the storyline was pretty catchy. Beyond that, I had no idea where the story would go, or if it would continue at all. I didn't know if the one-hour time constraint could even lend itself to another installment. Surely, the magic couldn't be the same as the first book.

But now, here we are...

I have two more books planned for the series: *3:53 a.m.* and *4:00 a.m.*

Look for those soon. :)

If you would like to see some ridiculous pictures of me and my pups, go to www.nickthriller.com.

Lastly (but firstly), I would like to thank God for this incredible gift. I am so blessed and so thankful each day for His love, guidance, and grace.

God is love.

Nick

.

Printed in Great Britain
by Amazon